D1287490

A GHOST OF CARIBOU

Also by Alice Henderson

A Solitude of Wolverines

A Blizzard of Polar Bears

A GHOST OF CARIBOU

A NOVEL OF SUSPENSE

ALICE HENDERSON

wm

WILLIAM MORROW

An Imprint of HarperCollinsPublishers

A GHOST OF CARIBOU. Copyright © 2022 by Alice Henderson. All rights reserved. Printed in Canada. No part of this book may be used or reproduced in any manner whatsoever without written permission except in the case of brief quotations embodied in critical articles and reviews. For information, address HarperCollins Publishers, 195 Broadway, New York, NY 10007.

HarperCollins books may be purchased for educational, business, or sales promotional use. For information, please email the Special Markets Department at SPsales@harpercollins.com.

FIRST EDITION

Designed by Nancy Singer
Caribou art © @jenesesimre/stock.adobe.com
Map by Jason C. Patnode

Library of Congress Cataloging-in-Publication Data has been applied for.

ISBN 978-0-06-322300-4

22 23 24 25 26   FRI   10 9 8 7 6 5 4 3 2 1

For my parents, who encouraged my love of wildlife and writing

For Jason, fellow adventurer and amazing wildlife photographer

And for all the researchers and activists out there who are
working to preserve caribou and their habitats

South Selkirk Mountain Caribou Range

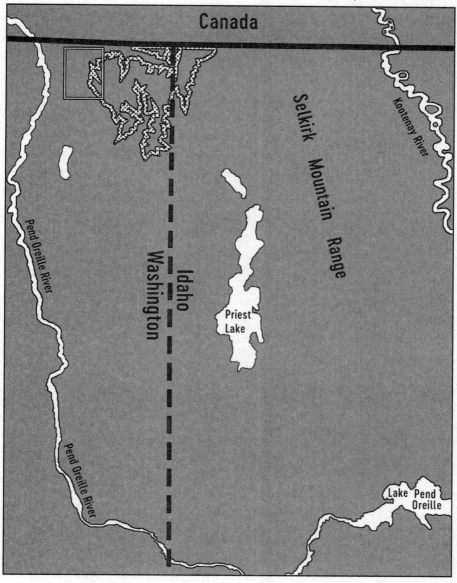

U.S. / Canada Border

Canada

Selkirk Mountain Range

Kootenay River

Pend Oreille River

Idaho
Washington

Priest Lake

Pend Oreille River

Lake Pend Oreille

☐ Location of Selkirk Wildlife Sanctuary
▬ Designated Mountain Caribou Critical Habitat

PROLOGUE

Colville National Forest, Washington
Fourteen months ago

Amelia Fairweather had just entered her tent to sleep when a strange hum sounded from outside. She crouched there in the dark, listening. She had backpacked miles away from any town, any source of man-made noise. The hum grew louder and she pivoted back toward the tent door, kneeling there, alert. Darkness pressed in close around her, so she grabbed her flashlight from the tent pocket.

The peculiar hum grew in intensity. She gripped the flashlight to her chest, wondering if she should peer outside. And then a glaring light erupted over her, illuminating the tent like a glowing yellow beacon. She gasped.

Unzipping the door, she crawled out. She had pitched her tent in a small open meadow with a creek running through it, trees gathered on all sides. The forest glowed around her, lit up in a dazzling white light. Shielding her eyes with her hand, she stared upward, but could see nothing through the blinding brilliance.

The light lowered in the sky. Panic took hold. She shoved the flashlight into her pocket and raced for the cover of the trees.

The hum grew in intensity, the brilliance following her, spotlighting her, as she hit the tree line.

She moved between trunks, leaping over logs, weaving between strewn boulders. The thing kept above the trees, its blazing light following her every move. She had to find better cover. Or get help. But the nearest town was more than twenty miles away. She'd hiked out here on one of her regular backcountry treks, a chance to get away from the bustle of the city and be alone with her thoughts.

At seventy-two, she was in great shape from backpacking. But as she tore through the trees, with no plan other than to get away, panic swept over her. Her feet splashed through a creek and she stumbled over a log on the far bank. She went down hard on one knee, then scrambled to her feet again and kept running.

A sudden deafening blast of noise erupted from the thing, so low in pitch that the sound vibrated through her chest. It blared out two more times, pulsing, like some kind of warning klaxon. She stumbled again, but caught herself. The thing followed relentlessly, a piercing, radiant light that lit up everything around her. There was no way she'd be able to hide from it. And it was so fast that it streaked along above the trees, matching her pace. She had the feeling it could go even faster if it wanted to. Her heart pounded in her chest, and she struggled to still her mind, to think of a plan. What the hell was it? What did it want?

She ran into a dense patch of old-growth forest, with Douglas fir trees that stretched up hundreds of feet into the air. She knew that even at the height of day, only dim sunlight reached the forest floor here. The strange craft soared above the trees, its light struggling to penetrate the canopy.

Now was her chance. She had to break away, get ahead of it. She kept to the dense cover, leaping over logs and mossy rocks. She didn't dare turn on her flashlight, even though the terrain around her was now harder to make out.

Her heart thudded with relief as the thing veered off in the wrong direction, searching for her. She sped on, her lungs burning in her chest, a stitch developing in her side. She crossed another creek, diving back into another section of old growth. She wove between massive trunks, her panicked brain rejoicing as the thing continued in the wrong direction, its piercing beam lighting up a different section of forest.

In the ensuing darkness, with only the moonlight to guide her, she ran until she thought her lungs would burst, down a steep incline beside a cliff, still surrounded by towering trees. She could barely hear the thrum of the thing now, far off in the distance. She heard one more blast of cacophonous noise from it, and then its light switched off abruptly.

She'd lost it.

She paused, catching her breath, leaning over with her hands on her knees. Terror still buzzed in her mind, clouding her thoughts. She didn't have her map or her compass, and now she had no idea exactly where she was. Blood thrummed in her ears.

Then the hum returned, growing louder. She jerked her head in its direction. No light splayed from the thing, but it was definitely drawing closer. She stared around in the dark, then spotted a long hollow log on the ground. She raced to it and lay down on her stomach. Then she crawled forward on her elbows, shimmying her way inside the hollow until it swallowed her head, torso, legs, and finally her feet. She flipped over, face just inches from the inside of the log. She waited, breathing in the scent of earth and moss.

The thing flew closer, and she could sense it was directly overhead. It drew lower, lower, and she started to panic in the tight confines of the log. It knew where she was. The light wasn't on, but somehow it still knew where she was. That long, low booming noise erupted from it and she jumped. She struggled, torn between hiding and scrambling out to flee again. Then it was almost on top of her. There was no doubt it had found her.

She shimmied out of the log and took off across the forest floor. The blinding light switched on, pinpointing her location, mere feet away, and then something bit into her neck, a stinging sensation.

She kept running, weaving between tree trunks, but suddenly she felt dizzy and couldn't keep her balance. She stumbled and fell, struggled to stand up again, and a wave of nausea spread over her.

She pitched forward, her face pressing into a bed of pine needles, and darkness swam up into her world.

ONE

Town of Bellamy Falls, Washington
Current day

Alex Carter approached the coffeehouse, instantly spotting Ben Hathaway waiting just outside. He looked the same as he had when they'd first met at the Snowline Resort in Montana last year, when she'd started her wolverine study there. His tousled sandy-brown hair hung almost to his shoulders now; his tall, athletic frame dressed in a worn blue flannel shirt, faded jeans, and hiking boots.

He turned, eyes falling on her, and grinned. "Alex Carter!" he called.

"Ben Hathaway!"

He held his arms open, and his familiar scent washed over her, a little spicy, like cinnamon, as he drew her close.

He pulled away, grinning. "It's great to see you."

"You too."

He gestured around them, to the small town at the foot of the towering snowy Selkirk Mountains. "How about this place? So great to be out here, away from my desk in D.C." Ben was a co-ordinator for the Land Trust for Wildlife Conservation. He oversaw projects all over the country and even the globe, traveling as needed. He hooked his thumb at the coffee shop. "You want something to drink?"

She smiled. "Sounds great."

He held the door open, and the rush of warm, coffee-scented air embraced her. Local art hung on the walls, and the vibe was welcoming, laid-back, and artistic. People around them read books, sketched, and worked on laptops.

They ordered a mocha and a latte, then took a table by the window.

As they sat down, Alex couldn't help but grin at the sight of Ben. She'd met him just as everything had fallen apart for her when she lived in Boston, and he'd been a wonderful kindred spirit at a time when she felt like few people understood her call to the wild.

She took a sip of her latte, and they caught up with each other's lives. Ben told her about a new anti-poaching program he was running at an LTWC preserve in South Africa. Alex related her adventures in the Canadian Arctic studying polar bears. She listened with interest as he described a new six-thousand-acre parcel of land the LTWC might acquire in Alaska, where salmon swam upstream and huge brown bears caught them as the fish leapt up waterfalls.

Alex drank more of her latte. "How much time do you have here?"

He frowned, glancing down at his watch. "Not nearly as much as I'd like. I have to catch a flight back to D.C. tonight. I guess we should get down to business."

Alex fought the small pang of disappointment that he had to leave so soon. "So what have you got?" When he called her up for this assignment, he'd been vague, asking her only to meet him in the quaint town of Bellamy Falls, Washington, and to bring her back-country gear. That was easy: ever since she'd closed up her apartment in Boston, she'd been on the move, first in Montana and then in Manitoba. So everything she needed, she carried with her.

He pulled a laptop out of his satchel and powered it up. "Two weeks ago, one of our volunteers was out on the Selkirk Wildlife Sanctuary and downloaded this." He clicked on a photo and turned the screen so she could see it. The image showed a towering old-growth forest in the background and the furry side of an out-of-focus dark brown animal close to the camera. It was so blurry she couldn't make out what it was.

"What am I looking at?"

Ben grinned, leaning forward. "This volunteer goes out a few times a year to the various remote cameras we have placed around the sanctuary. She collects the memory cards and replaces the batteries. So she was out there two weeks ago and saw what at first she thought was an elk in the trees. But then it drew closer, and she got a better look at its head. She thinks it was a mountain caribou, but it ran off before she could be sure. When she checked the nearest remote camera, she found this image on the memory card."

Alex's mouth fell open. "A mountain caribou? Is she sure?" Alex knew that at one time, the U.S. had been host to herds of mountain caribou, but none were left now in the lower forty-eight.

Different from the barren-ground caribou that roamed the vast expanses of Alaska, the Northwest Territories, and the Yukon, southern mountain caribou were a thing all their own. They were so elusive that people referred to them as the "gray ghosts of the forest." Instead of traversing the open tundra, they lived in small herds in dense old-growth forests. Their big shovellike feet allowed them to navigate in extremely high-altitude snowy locations during the winter, where they survived off lichen. But due to logging and other factors, eventually their numbers dropped to a single tiny herd surviving in Idaho and Washington, known as the South Selkirk population. As a last-ditch effort to save them, Canada took the final two members of the herd, both females, and moved them north to join that country's own dwindling mountain caribou population in British Columbia.

Now mountain caribou were extinct in the lower forty-eight. To think that one had wandered down from Canada, into the state of Washington, was huge. After a lot of back-and-forth and numerous lawsuits by conservation organizations, the U.S. Fish and Wildlife Service had finally designated critical habitat for the species. This caribou had a chance. If indeed it was here at all.

Alex looked down at the blurry photo from the remote camera. "The fur does look quite dark brown. Too bad we can't see if it has any white patches." Most mountain caribou sported dark brown coats with some white on the sides and a white shoulder and neck patch. They had white bands or socks just above their hooves. And unlike other deer species, both sexes could grow antlers, though they were less common in females. She squinted at the photo. "It's so out of focus."

He nodded. "It obviously passed quickly in front of the camera, and too close."

She leaned back in her chair. "So you think there's a mountain caribou on the preserve?"

He exhaled, that charming smile returning. "There just might be."

"And you want me to find out for sure?"

"You got it."

Alex stared down at the picture again.

"There's an old ranch house on the preserve," he continued. "It belonged to the previous owner of the land. It's nothing like the grandeur of the Snowline, but it's got heat and running water. Indoor plumbing."

"I think you mean the *spookiness* of the Snowline." She laughed, thinking of where she'd been stationed in Montana, how the wind howled through the broken windows, and how the stories of the horrors that had transpired in the place before it became a wildlife sanctuary were local lore.

Ben laughed, too. "This place has no ghosts." He paused, taking a sip of his mocha. "At least I don't think it does. And there's another plus, too."

"What's that?"

He leaned forward. "Later this week, Kathleen Macklay is going to be out in this area."

Alex broke into a smile. "You're kidding." Kathleen had been the police dispatcher in the town of Bitterroot, Montana. She'd met the woman during her first job with the LTWC. Alex and Kathleen had instantly hit it off, and she'd looked forward to seeing her again.

He nodded. "Yep. She comes out here every summer to be a fire lookout. She's actually the person who tipped us off that this piece of land here was for sale. Her lookout lies in the adjacent national forest." He sipped his mocha. "So are you intrigued?"

"I am."

"Then let's go out to the preserve. I can show you the house, and we can walk around the place, give you a sense of it."

"When do we leave?"

"Whenever you're ready."

They finished their coffee, then headed out. Ben had rented a Toyota Prius and offered to drive. Alex left her own rental car, a four-wheel-drive Jeep, on the street. They took the main road out of the charming turn-of-the-last-century town, passing art galleries, a general store, a movie theater with a 1930s marquee, and two saloons. The whole area had a bohemian feel to it, with a new age crystal shop, a public art studio, a small community theater, and two live-music venues.

Outside town, Ben turned off onto a smaller road, paved but full of potholes. Ten miles in, he veered onto a dirt road. At the intersection stood a collection of metal U.S. Postal Service boxes.

"This is where your mail will come once you forward it. I'll give you the key."

He took the dirt road up a steep series of inclines into the mountains. Alex rolled down the window, smelling sun-warmed pine on the wind, comfortable with Ben. He looked over at her and smiled, clearly enjoying the wild spaces around them as well.

He turned off onto a final road and bumped along its rutted dirt surface to a small two-story house made of clapboard.

"It was built in 1936," Ben told her, parking in front. "A family moved out here to raise horses." Alex glanced around, seeing the decaying remains of old fence posts and corrals. The fencing wire had been removed at some point.

They stepped out of the car and Ben fished a set of keys from his pocket. They climbed three stairs to the front door and he unlocked it. The door opened to a comfortable living room with a couch, a coffee table, and a bookshelf full of volumes.

He took her on a tour through the place, which held two bedrooms, an old-fashioned kitchen with a gas range, and a bathroom with 1930s-style fixtures.

"There's no cell signal up here, but the house has two landlines—one in the kitchen and one upstairs in the main bedroom." He wrote down the number for her. "It even has satellite internet. It's slow, but it works."

They returned to the living room, and Alex examined the books on the shelf more closely. She was delighted to find volumes on painting and bird identification, and books on tracks and scat. She pulled down a guide to wildflowers and turned to him. "This is a treat. I'm getting spoiled lately. I'm used to sleeping in a tiny backcountry tent. My last few gigs have had hot water and everything."

Ben laughed. "Glad you like it. C'mon. I'll show you the rest of the preserve."

They grabbed their daypacks out of Ben's car and set off on a trail that crossed a glorious wildflower-strewn meadow. Alex thrilled to the sight of yellow glacier lily, brilliant orange Columbia lily, scarlet paintbrush, and the delicate purple petals of alpine lewisia. They hiked up steep terrain and over a saddle in the nearest mountain. Snowfields covered talus slopes. Curious hoary marmots, their golden coats shining in the sunlight, emerged from rock piles to watch them. She even heard the telltale "Eep!" of an American pika, a small vocal relative of the rabbit that lived in high-elevation sites. Above them, a golden eagle wheeled in the sky, crying out.

She already knew she was going to love this gig.

They passed a sapphire-blue glacial lake. A family of mergansers paddled on its surface, diving down and emerging back up, buoyant as corks.

Alex and Ben wound along the shore of the lake, climbing higher again toward another saddle. Her legs burned from moving over the steep terrain. She was used to being out on the flat ice of Hudson Bay.

When they neared the top of the slope, above them stretched dense old-growth forest. They stepped into the cool, shadowed heart of it. Enormous trees rose hundreds of feet into the air. The wind smelled sweet and fragrant.

"Oh, wow," she breathed, Ben pausing beside her.

"It's really something, isn't it?"

"I'll say."

He pointed to one of the nearer trees. "This is where the volunteer saw the caribou."

Alex spotted the remote camera strapped to the trunk of the tree. They both paused, standing in silence, staring around them. Alex half expected a caribou to come striding out of the forest right then.

He gestured for her to follow. "C'mon. I've got to show you the not-so-glorious part."

They began to ascend again, following an old game trail, winding through the forest. Sunlight streamed through the branches, illuminating parts of the forest floor in gold, where delicate ferns and moss as green as emeralds clung to the logs and tree trunks.

They crested a rise and Ben made a left turn onto another game trail that climbed steeply up above the tree line onto a gray talus slope. Brilliant orange and gold lichen clung to rocks here, snow still surviving in shadowy patches.

Down below, the old-growth forest extended for hundreds of feet until it abruptly stopped. Alex gasped. A swath of destruction cut through it, a strip completely denuded of trees. Stumps covered the area.

"Clear-cutting?" she asked.

"That's where the sanctuary ends. Beyond that is private land. The owner decided to clear-cut it to sell the timber."

Beyond the decimated area grew more old growth, part of it cut down, as well. Amid the stumps stood logging equipment: skidders, log loaders, de-limbers.

Ben pointed. "See that part where all the equipment is?"

Alex nodded.

"That's where the national forest boundary starts. There was a moratorium on clear-cutting old growth there, but a congressman getting kickbacks from the lumber industry attached a rider onto a recent bill that exploited a loophole. So they started cutting."

Alex could see strange patches of color, like cloth, draped over some of the equipment. "What is that?" Fishing her binoculars out of her backpack, she rotated the focus wheel to zero in on them.

Yellow, white, and green banners came into view. STOP THE DESTRUCTION! one of them read. TREES NOT GREED, read another.

She could see people milling about now, moving among the banners. Some sat on top of the equipment. Others had pitched tents in front of the yellow machines.

"Protesters," Ben said. "They've been camped out there for days. Several conservation nonprofits sued about the clear-cutting, so right now there's a temporary halt while a federal judge weighs the case."

Alex gazed to the north, toward the border with Canada, which lay some fifteen miles distant, as the crow flies. If these tracts of old growth continued to be destroyed, the mountain caribou would have no path to reach this area. "So you think if we can show that a mountain caribou has moved here, we can apply extra pressure to halt the clear-cutting?"

"Exactly. Not just with the national forest, but with this private landowner, too. He has other stands of old growth on his property that he hasn't touched yet. The land trust has made overtures to him about putting a conservation easement on his land. And if he's not open to that, we've been trying to get some donors to come up with enough money that it will be worth his while to sell, saving the trees."

"What did he say?"

"He's thinking about it. We're still negotiating."

Alex knew how little old growth was left in the U.S. and hoped the negotiations would be successful.

"So what do you think?" he asked, turning to her.

"I'm in."

Ben smiled. For a second she thought he was going to hug her, but he seemed to decide against it. He looked at his watch and frowned. "Why does time have to pass so quickly out here? I better get back to town and start my drive to the airport."

Once again Alex felt that pang, knowing she would miss Ben's genial nature and camaraderie.

They hiked back as the afternoon sunlight wore on, slanting through the forest, painting the tree trunks gold. Thick gray clouds gathered in the west, and Alex looked forward to some rain. She loved cloudy days and the scent of a forest after a downpour.

Back at the house, Ben retrieved a huge box from his car and placed it on the dining room table. "This is all the equipment you'll need: GPS unit, topo maps, additional remote cameras, batteries, memory cards, collar cameras in case you find the caribou." Alex noticed that the collars would also record the animal's temperature and if it passes away. He gestured toward a black metal case standing against the wall. "There's the tranquilizer gun." He patted the box he'd brought in. "And there are extra darts and sedative in here, along with supplemental oxygen to administer if you sedate one. It would be amazing if you could tranq the caribou and attach a collar camera to it. We've already secured a permit with the Washington Department of Fish and Wildlife to do so."

Alex had seen incredible footage from collar cameras attached to all kinds of wildlife. Coupled with GPS, it allowed researchers not only to track the movements of animals, but to see what kind of habitat they were using, and what food sources they took advantage of.

"I'll do my best."

He smiled. "Well, I guess you're set. Shall we head back?"

Alex nodded, still feeling a little sad at his leaving.

They drove back to town, and Ben pulled over behind Alex's Jeep. "I'd love to stay here for a few days, hike around the preserve with you. But I have to get back for a budget meeting. The fun never stops."

Alex smiled, feeling bittersweet. "It's a shame you can't stay, at least for a little while."

"I know. This is déjà vu—my meeting you quickly, setting you up, and having to take off." He unbuckled his seat belt. "Let's get out and let me take one long last look at these amazing mountains."

They climbed out and stood for a few moments on the sidewalk.

Then he hugged her, and she rested her chin on his shoulder for a moment. He stepped back and looked at her. "Good luck out there. Keep me posted. Enjoy the wilderness for me."

"Thanks again for the opportunity."

He smiled wistfully. "You take care of yourself. And say hi to Kathleen for me." Then he climbed back into his Prius and pulled away.

Alex watched him go, waited until the car turned off toward the highway that would take him to the Spokane airport.

She took a deep breath, staring up at the snowy mountains, glad to be in this place. Deciding to head to the grocery store to stock up for a few days, she climbed into her Jeep and headed into the main part of the town.

But as she neared the grocery store, she slowed. A huge group of people had moved into the street by the city park. So many people clustered together that she couldn't move forward, so she parked and climbed out.

"What's going on?" she asked a young woman wearing an apron from the local grocery store and bakery.

She turned to Alex, eyes haunted. "They found something. Over there by the playground." She pointed into the distance, where a tangle of people gathered. "It's a dead body."

TWO

The sheriff arrived and pushed through the crowd. Alex guessed that more than forty people had emerged from their businesses and errands to gather in the park.

One woman rushed away, toward the street, clutching her hand to her mouth. Her pale skin had taken on a greenish hue. Murmurs stirred through the throng, and Alex listened in.

"It's Irma. It's got to be."

"Did you see her face? Jesus."

"All cut up."

"Who's Irma?" Alex asked the person standing next to her, an elderly woman with snowy-white hair and a wrinkled-peach face.

"Irma Jackson," the woman whispered. "She vanished seven months ago. Worked for the Forest Service. Went out on backcountry patrol one day and didn't come back. Search parties looked for weeks but came up empty. Everybody thought she must have gotten lost or fallen or something. No one expected this."

The sheriff, a short woman with long gray hair in a braid down her back, bellowed to the crowd, "Everybody just back away. You don't want to trample any evidence."

People did as she instructed, moving away en masse. Alex could tell from their faces who had drawn close enough to see the corpse. Their haunted eyes, expressions of shock, were all too familiar to her. She'd seen enough of her own horrors.

The crowd parted, and suddenly Alex got a clear look at the body. This was no natural death. She stared aghast at the scene before her. The woman had been strung up on the parallel bars in the playground. Even from where Alex stood some distance away, she could see vicious cuts marking the body in several places. She also couldn't help but notice that the woman had been dead for some time. She looked positively mummified.

"I've seen this happen with animals in the desert," one man declared. "She's been dead a long time. Months, I'd say. Look at the state of her."

The crowd weighed in.

"If she's that far gone, you can't be sure it's Irma."

"She's wearing a Forest Service uniform. Or what's left of one," he insisted. "Looks like she'd been crawling in it. It's filthy. Knees are all torn out."

Others chimed in.

"No utility belt. No radio."

"No gun."

"Where's she been?" asked the woman in the baker's apron. "Why hang her body up like this now?"

Suddenly an older man in front, with long, stringy white hair and a full beard, raised his hand accusingly toward the sheriff. "I told you this would happen!" he shouted. "But you didn't want to listen."

"Now, Bill," the sheriff said, holding up a placating hand. "This isn't the time to start all that nonsense again."

"Nonsense!" the man yelled. "*Nonsense!* Goddamnit, Maggie, I've been telling you for months that they're out there."

"Not this again," one woman groaned, waving a dismissive hand at Bill.

"I've seen 'em!" Bill shouted, staring around at the crowd. "Don't pretend you haven't. Those bright lights in the forest."

People shrugged and shook their heads.

"You think I'm *kidding*?" he thundered. "Look at those wounds on her! It's cattle mutilation all over again. You remember what happened to Carl's herd?"

The sheriff put a hand on her utility belt. "That wasn't mutilation, Bill. Those lesions were caused by ringworm."

"You don't think I know cattle mutilation when I see it?" Bill rushed over to the sheriff, grabbing her arm. "Just look at her, Maggie! What do you think did that to her?"

"It's not freakin' aliens," one man shouted back at Bill. "For god's sake, let the sheriff do her job."

Alex decided to give the sheriff room to work and walked back toward her car. Her appetite had completely deserted her, but she knew she'd need food in the coming days.

As she walked toward the grocery store, she cast a glance back at the throng of onlookers in the park. The townsfolk looked rattled, one of their own meeting a violent end. She wondered what had happened to the woman, and if whoever did it was one of the very people with whom she'd just stood shoulder to shoulder.

Down the street, Alex entered the grocery store, a small wooden structure with hand-painted windows that advertised natural foods, fresh produce, and fresh baked goods.

HEIRLOOM TOMATOES ONLY 52¢ EACH!

BANANAS ON SALE!

READY-MADE APPLE AND BLACKBERRY PIES!

The door slid open and instantly the smell of fresh baked breads and cakes greeted her. She picked up a small handbasket, realizing quickly that she was the only customer in the store.

A lone cashier stood at the register, staring out the window, a spooked expression on her face. "Did you just come from the town park?" she asked Alex.

Alex nodded.

"What's going on there? Who is it?" The cashier was young, maybe only sixteen or so, with a pierced nose and a long stripe of blue in her black hair. Her name tag read *Sophie*.

"I heard people say that it's someone named Irma Jackson."

The cashier's mouth fell open. "Jesus. And they think she was murdered?"

"Yes. The sheriff is there now."

Her eyes grew big, and she shook her head. "I can't believe it."

"Did you know her well?"

Sophie nodded. "She taught me how to read tracks. She had this great orienteering program for kids."

"I'm so sorry."

The cashier looked down, staring past the register, her pale face a mask of shock.

"Can I get anyone for you?" Alex offered.

She looked up and sniffed. "No. I'm okay. I'm just waiting for Carol to come back." She hooked a thumb at the baked goods counter in the back of the store. "She's our baker."

"I think I saw her over there. People are starting to come back. The sheriff was telling them to go home."

The cashier sighed. "Oh good." She looked around. "Never felt spooked in here before, but now I am. It's a ghost town. And whoever did that to Irma could be . . ." Her voice trailed off. She managed a smile. "Sorry. Go ahead and get what you need."

Alex gave her a reassuring smile. "I'll just be a minute."

"Take all the time you need. Seriously. I'm creeped out here alone."

Alex moved through the aisles, choosing food that was quick and easy to prepare. Pasta, cans of nuts, vegetarian Beyond Meat sausages, oat milk, makings for brown rice and avocado burritos, kale to sauté with red pepper and olive oil. She wasn't much of a cook, and viewed food only as a necessity, so that was about as fancy as she got.

When she returned to the checkout, she found the girl standing at the window, staring out. Other residents shuffled down the street, heads together, talking.

"Everyone's coming back," Sophie breathed with relief. She returned to the register and started scanning Alex's items. "You visiting family here?" she asked.

"No, I'm a wildlife biologist. I'll be posted up at the Selkirk Wildlife Sanctuary for a while."

"Oh, that's great. That must be a cool job."

Alex smiled. "It is pretty cool."

She finished tallying up the purchases. Alex paid, then turned to leave. "I'm sorry about your friend."

Sophie bit her lip. "Thank you."

As she left the store, Alex passed the baker on her way back in. The cashier hurried over to her. "What happened? What are they saying?" she heard Sophie ask in a rush.

Alex walked to her car and stowed the groceries. The post office stood across the street, so she ducked inside and filled out a mail forwarding card, changing her address from Churchill, Manitoba, to here. A lone clerk stood at the counter, staring out the window as people filed past outside.

He broke out of his reverie when Alex approached and glanced down at the address she'd written on the card. "You staying up at the Selkirk Wildlife Sanctuary?"

"Yes. I'm a wildlife biologist; I've been posted there."

"Beautiful place. You'll love it up there."

He took the card and then resumed staring out the window.

Not wanting to intrude further on the townspeople's grief, she returned to her car and took the main road out of town, glancing again at the old movie theater and art galleries. A few stragglers still lingered in the town park. A deputy waved at them to go home while the sheriff moved around the body, taking notes.

She turned off onto the smaller road toward the sanctuary, bouncing along past the many potholes. She rolled the window down, enjoying the hint of coming rain in the air.

When she reached the dirt road, she climbed up the steep route, taking the hairpin turns cautiously. On her right the road fell away sharply, and she wondered how many people had taken it too fast and careened down the mountain. The hairpins were so tight that she couldn't see if anyone was coming from the other direction. A concave mirror stood at only one of the turns, and she wondered if a collision had occurred at that spot in the past, prompting the mirror's installation.

Finally she turned onto the road to the sanctuary, jostling along the pitted route to the ranch house.

As she climbed out of the car, she took a moment just to stare at the mountains in wonder. The air carried with it an even stronger scent of ozone now. She couldn't wait for the rain. Few things soothed her like the sound of rain pattering on her parka hood.

In the kitchen, she put away the groceries. After everything had been placed in cabinets or the fridge, she took a seat at the dining room table and opened up the box Ben had left.

Inside lay replacement batteries and memory cards for the numerous remote cameras placed around the preserve. Unlike at her job in Montana tracking wolverines, this preserve already had a network of remote cameras. Still, Ben had included five more that Alex could place in likely spots of caribou habitat.

She also pulled out the tranquilizer darts and vials of sedative, along with the reversal drugs she'd need to counteract the sedation when she was done attaching the camera. Next she unfolded the topographical map of the preserve. Ben had marked where the existing remote cameras were. She pored over it, comparing the locations to satellite images on her computer. She needed to find areas of old growth.

Mountain caribou relied on old growth because in the winter they fed on tree-growing lichen that took sixty to a hundred years to grow on mature trees. These lichen hung high in the branches. But when the deep snows arrived in winter, caribou could use the snowpack as a platform to reach those high limbs and pull down the lichen. No other member of the deer family could survive on lichen, which was poor in nutrients. Caribou were unique.

But as old growth was clear-cut, young seral forests took over. These attracted deer, moose, and elk, which normally didn't share this habitat with caribou. And with these grazers came the wolves, who used logging roads and snowmobile trails to access the high country. They fed off the caribou, which they usually wouldn't have access to.

And so, through unprecedented predation, reduction of snow-pack due to climate change, and the destruction of their habitat, the last caribou in the lower forty-eight, from the South Selkirk herd, vanished.

At the bottom of the box, Alex also found four collar cameras equipped with GPS. They were experimental cameras that she couldn't wait to try out. Typically, researchers employed collar cameras that were designed to fall off an animal at the end of a season. Researchers then had to seek out the cameras on the forest floor to retrieve the footage.

But the LTWC had hired a team to design these new models. They sent out videos via satellite that she would be able to download with a Wi-Fi connection. So instead of waiting months to view footage, she could immediately see the caribou's current behavior, along with the GPS coordinates of where the videos were recorded.

Maybe, she hoped, if she found the caribou and managed to affix a collar, she'd discover that it had been joined by other caribou. Ben's inclusion of four cameras made her smile. He was obviously optimistic that she'd find more than one. She pursed her lips. Or maybe he was pessimistic, thinking a camera might fail and she'd have to replace it.

She'd seen collars like this at work with barren-ground caribou and with white-tailed- and mule-deer studies. She loved seeing the creatures meandering through their habitats, interacting with each other, and at this time of year, grooming their young.

With any luck, she'd get the chance to use at least one of these cameras.

She opened the tranquilizer gun case and checked it over. It was a black Pneu-Dart G2 X-Caliber with a thirty-nine-inch stainless steel barrel that used a CO_2 cylinder to launch tranquilizer darts.

The first thing she'd do, she decided, would be to return to where the volunteer had spotted the caribou and start walking transects looking for tracks and scat. She glanced at her watch. It was almost six P.M. Too late to set out today.

Instead she made an early dinner and ate it on the porch while gazing at the stunning scenery.

When she finished, she glanced at her watch. For a change, she was in the same time zone as her dad, so she picked up the landline and dialed his number.

Her father, a renowned landscape painter, lived in Berkeley, California. He answered on the second ring. "Hello?"

"Dad, it's Alex."

"Hi, pumpkin! I didn't recognize the number."

"It's the landline for the house I'm staying in. I took another gig with the land trust."

"That's great! What species is it this time?"

"Mountain caribou."

He gave a low whistle. "Well, that's a bit of all right. But didn't you tell me they're gone from the U.S.? Are you in Canada?"

"No, I'm in Washington State. A volunteer on the preserve here thinks she saw one."

"Wow! That would be something."

"I'm hoping to confirm it," Alex told him. "How are things with you?"

"Doing okay." She heard him shift in his chair. "Kind of on pins and needles, actually."

"Why? What's going on?"

"I applied to be an artist in residence for the plein air festival at the Grand Canyon this year. There was a last-minute cancellation, and I'm waiting to see if they pick me to fill it."

"That's great!" Every year, her father applied to be a guest artist at a different national park. The competition was tough, and he'd been disappointed before. But he'd also been accepted multiple times before, and had painted in some incredible places. *Plein air* meant the artists would be painting outside, capturing landscapes daily as clouds shifted and weather changed the lighting and mood. He'd wanted to get into the Grand Canyon festival for years. "I've got my fingers crossed for you."

"Thanks! So what are your digs like there?"

"Great! An old ranch house from the 1930s."

"That sounds pretty posh. A far cry from living out of your back-country tent like in your grad school days. Let me know how it goes. This is the number to reach you on?" he asked.

"Yeah, there's no cell reception here."

"Okay, pumpkin. Stay in touch. Oh, and email me your address. I've got some mail to forward to you."

"Thanks! Let me know if you get into the Grand Canyon!"

"Will do. Love you!"

"Love you."

As rain began to patter on the roof, they hung up and she returned to the dining room table, where she decided to dig into the latest mountain caribou research. Alex had a jump start on the subject. She'd worked on a barren-ground caribou project one summer while earning her PhD, and at the time had become fascinated with mountain caribou, which were so different from their Arctic tundra counterparts.

Caribou were the most widely distributed ungulate on the planet and had evolved to survive in a wide range of habitats. Some roamed the vast flat, open tundra of the Arctic, while others occupied the taiga, the coniferous forest that grew just south of the Arctic Circle in North America, Scandinavia, and Russia.

All caribou on the planet belonged to a single species, *Rangifer tarandus*. But these varied habitats had allowed the caribou to evolve into numerous subspecies, each taking advantage of a particular niche.

Many people Alex had talked to didn't even realize that America had had caribou in the lower forty-eight at one time. This subspecies, mountain caribou, or *Rangifer tarandus caribou*, were the southernmost-ranging caribou in North America, but had now lost more than 60 percent of their historical habitat. They used to live across the northern United States, including Wisconsin, Maine, Michigan, Idaho, Washington, Montana, Minnesota, New Hampshire, and Vermont.

The southern mountain caribou were also unique in their behavior. Unlike their northerly neighbors, these animals did not migrate long distances. Instead, they moved up and down steep, mountainous terrain several times a year, shifting between valley ecosystems and high alpine locales depending on the season.

These southern mountain caribou were separated geographically and genetically from other mountain caribou herds. They roamed the inland temperate rainforests, where western red cedar and western hemlock grew to gigantic proportions. Life abounded from the forest floor to the top of the tree canopy. They occupied this unique terrain in British Columbia and, prior to their extirpation in 2019, in areas where the inland temperate rainforest extended down into the Selkirk Mountains of Washington and Idaho.

She couldn't wait to see if one had returned to Washington. On the topo map in front of her, Alex plotted out the route she'd take tomorrow. Feeling her eyes start to droop, she folded up the map and climbed the stairs to the bedroom.

She emptied out her backcountry pack on the bed, then folded up her clothes and stowed them in an antique dresser with an art deco waterfall pattern. The wood smell that emanated from the drawers inside reminded her of her grandmother's house, and for a moment she had a sharp pang of missing her.

Her paternal grandmother had been from the South, and everyone called her Miss Lacey. She'd taught Alex how to read and do math before preschool, so Alex had leapt ahead in her studies when she started school. This was an advantage, since Alex had moved around a lot as a kid, a side effect of growing up in a military family. Her mother had been a fighter pilot for the U.S. Air Force, and Alex and her father had lived all over the world with her.

During the summers, Alex got to stay with her grandmother for long stints of time, and Alex relished it. Playful and loving, her grandmother told Alex ghost stories that thrilled her. She even had an old rocking chair in her house that was known to rock on its own.

Alex inhaled the scent from the old wooden drawers, and with a sad smile slid them shut.

She unpacked the rest of her belongings: rain gear, extra boots, her Canon DSLR, a GPS unit, and a mystery novel that she placed on the bedside table. Then she hung the pack in a closet.

Finally, back aching from being up so long, she changed into her pj's and lay down on the antique bed. She thought of reading the novel, but instead stared up at the ceiling, letting her thoughts drift. What would she find out there in the old growth? She smiled to herself, excited. Then slowly her eyes closed, and she faded off to sleep.

ALEX STARTED AWAKE, THE GLOW of the moon streaming through the bedroom window. She sat up, her throat dry. Taking a sip from the glass of water on her bedside table, she gazed out the window at the silvery landscape beyond. Pine tree limbs stood silver against the black silhouette of the mountains.

A dazzling display of stars beckoned, and she climbed out of bed, moving to the window. She'd left it open, and the delicious scent of pine carried through. She breathed it in deeply, gazing out at the path of the Milky Way, sweeping in an arc across the summer sky. Sagittarius hung low on the horizon, the center of the galaxy sweeping up from it like steam from a teakettle. She could see the Lagoon Nebula with her naked eye and couldn't help but grin.

She closed her eyes, savoring the moment, the darkness, the scent of the forest.

When she opened them again, a small, strange light pulled her attention to the right. It zipped away, out of sight in the distance. She craned her neck to catch another glimpse of it, but the window screen prevented her from leaning out.

Then she saw it again, in the far distance, probably miles away, a quickly moving orb of light dancing just above the trees. At first she wondered if it might be a drone, but it looked too large. It dipped down, illuminating the tips of the forest canopy, then shot up again, skimming along above the trees.

Alex furrowed her brow, puzzled. She'd seen footage of the Marfa Lights in Texas, those strange balls of light that danced above the desert floor and had never been explained.

Could it be something like that? Or swamp gas? Or some weird refraction of light in the moist air? Or . . .

Her mind flashed back to the old man who had confronted the sheriff in the park. *I've seen 'em!* he had shouted. *Don't pretend you haven't. Those bright lights in the forest.*

She stared out, transfixed. And just like that, the light was gone.

She stood there for a long time, wondering if it would come back, but it didn't. Finally, feeling her eyes burn with lack of sleep, she drew the curtains and climbed back into bed.

She lay awake, imagining the orb coming closer to the house. Sometimes having an overactive imagination while out in the middle of nowhere did not do her any favors. She listened to the wind sighing in the pines outside the window. A great horned owl called out.

Finally she closed her eyes, but the memory of the strange orb of light made it difficult to fall asleep.

THREE

The next day, Alex ate a quick breakfast and sipped her coffee out on the porch. Then she retrieved her backcountry pack from the closet and began sorting out what she'd need for her first round on the preserve to check all the remote cameras. She loaded it with supplies for only a single day out: a compass, a sandwich and energy bars, a map, a water bottle and filter, rain gear, her GPS unit, and an additional remote camera. She was just stuffing her small first aid kit into the pack when she heard a car turn onto the long drive to the house.

The house was so far out of the way, she couldn't imagine who would drive up here.

She moved to the window, peering out, and watched as a police SUV pulled up. The sheriff climbed out, tucking her shirt into her belt and pulling on her hat. She leaned into the SUV and pulled something off the passenger seat. Moments later, she rapped on the front door.

Wondering what she could want, Alex descended the stairs. The screen door creaked as she opened it.

The sheriff removed her sunglasses, tucking them into the collar of her shirt. "Dr. Carter?"

She nodded. "Can I help you?"

The sheriff extended a hand and Alex shook it, finding it dry and calloused. "I'm Sheriff Maggie Taggert. May I come in?"

"Sure." Alex stepped back, gesturing for her to enter.

Taggert glanced around the place, eyes roaming over the furniture and bookshelves. "Been a while since I've been in here. Used to know the family who owned it. Nice bunch of folks." She spotted the couch with the long coffee table before it. "Can we sit?"

"Sure. Do you want coffee? I just made some."

Taggert smiled. "That'd be real nice."

Alex moved to the kitchen and poured them each a cup. She retrieved the oat milk from the fridge and placed it on a tray with some sugar and two mugs.

Back in the living room, Taggert slumped down on the couch, adjusting her utility belt. She mixed some sugar and oat milk into her cup and took an appreciative sip.

Alex wondered if her visit had something to do with the body in the park. Taggert pulled out a manila folder from under her arm and spread out a series of photographs on the table. Remnants of black grease clung to her fingernails, like she'd been tinkering under the hood of a car.

"Take a look at these."

Alex sat down beside her and stared at the photos. They depicted the same smiling woman, eyes crinkled at the edges, short gray hair styled in a no-fuss way. Alex guessed she was in her early seventies. All the pictures had been taken in the outdoors. Alex recognized Yosemite, Yellowstone, and Glacier National Park. In all of the photos, the woman wore a thick purple fleece jacket covered with patches from various national parks. She also wore a distinctive necklace: a silver bear paw set with a purple drusy stone, its fine coating of crystals sparkling in the photographs.

The sheriff laid a slender finger on the Yosemite photo. "This is Amelia Fairweather. She was an enthusiastic backcountry camper and trekked all over the U.S. and Canada. She disappeared in this area over a year ago. It's a case that's really stuck with me."

Alex studied the woman's kind eyes in the photographs. Her

joie de vivre was obvious, even from a photograph. "She was never found?"

The sheriff shook her head. "Some people think that maybe she absconded to Mexico with some illicit lover. She wasn't poor by any stretch of the imagination, and she had been dating a younger man. Some speculate that she ran off with this guy to the Caribbean or South America or some other tropical paradise.

"But her daughters are firmly convinced that something happened to her. They say there's no way she'd go this long without reaching out to them. Plus she had a thriving plant nursery business in Seattle. It was her life's dream. She'd been a corporate lawyer for years. She and a partner had their own law firm and everything. Then one day she just quit and opened up a plant nursery with her savings. Of course, some people pointed to that, saying she could obviously make major life changes at the drop of a hat. The law partner she left wasn't too happy when she suddenly quit. He's one of the people who's convinced she's lounging on a beach somewhere in Acapulco or Rio."

The sheriff stared up at the wall, her gaze distant. "I got the feeling there were some sour grapes there, though. Like maybe he'd been interested in her and she'd rebuffed him. You know, jealous that she took off with some younger guy."

"What do you think happened to her, Sheriff?"

She cleared her throat and stared down sadly at the picture. "I'm inclined to agree with the two daughters. From everything I've learned about her, she was a devoted mother. I don't think she would have just abandoned her family like that." She looked up at Alex, her face grim, and gestured out the window. "I think something happened to her out there. Maybe she got lost, or broke her leg, or got hypothermia or something, and just didn't make it back."

Taggert shifted uncomfortably on the couch. "Anyway, I know this is pretty morbid, but if you could keep an eye out when you're hiking around out there, I'd really appreciate it. Rangers found her abandoned tent and gear not far from the preserve's boundary." She sifted through the contents of the folder and brought out a well-worn topo map. She unfolded it. A bright dot made in red Sharpie stood out against the greens, grays, and blues of the map. Taggert jabbed a finger at it. "This is where they found her tent."

Alex leaned over to study the location. "That *is* right on the preserve's boundary."

Taggert sifted through the folder again and came up with a printed list. "Here are some items that her daughters swear she'd never part with. So if you see any of these things out there, I'd sure appreciate a heads-up. Or if, you know . . . you come across . . ."

"Human remains?" Alex asked.

Taggert pursed her lips. "Exactly."

Alex took the list from her and read it over:

CASIO G-SHOCK WRISTWATCH WITH ALTIMETER AND THERMOMETER
ENGINEER'S LENSATIC COMPASS ENGRAVED WITH THE INITIALS AF
SILVER BEAR PAW NECKLACE WITH PURPLE DRUSY STONE
PURPLE FLEECE JACKET WITH NATIONAL PARK PATCHES

The sheriff pointed at two close-up photographs. "You can see the necklace and jacket here. The necklace had been her mother's. Apparently she never took it off. And she'd been collecting patches on the jacket for every national and state park she visited."

"I'll certainly keep an eye out."

Taggert gathered up the photographs into a neat stack, leaving one out. "You keep that one." The rest she tucked away. Then she leaned forward, drinking more of her coffee. "I'd like to think she's on a beach somewhere, having the time of her life."

Alex gazed down at the smiling woman, her eyes vibrant, her face lit up and full of life. "Me too."

The sheriff finished the last swig and stood up with a groan. Alex noticed that instead of wearing the typical boots a sheriff might wear, Taggert sported a pair of worn Birkenstock sandals over rainbow-colored socks. "Well, I've taken up enough of your time. I appreciate it."

"No problem. And it's good to meet you."

She walked her to the door and they said their goodbyes.

As Taggert climbed into her car, Alex looked down at the photograph, wondering what had happened to the woman.

She checked her watch and considered calling her friend Zoe Lindquist before she set out. Alex would be unreachable on her cell with no signal, and she hadn't yet told Zoe about her new gig. They'd met in college when Alex played oboe in the pit orchestra for a musical that Zoe acted in. Zoe had gone on to become a very successful actor in Hollywood and was in such demand, traveling around and shooting on location, that Alex hadn't seen her in person in a couple years.

She moved into the kitchen and dialed Zoe's mobile on the landline. Zoe never picked up an unknown number and even had a fake voicemail message in case a stalker or tabloid got ahold of her personal number.

Alex smiled as she listened to Zoe's outgoing message. She always chose a weird name that sounded like some officious member of a neighborhood gardening club. "Hello. You've reached Eugenia Puddlejump. Please leave a message."

"Hey, Zoe. It's Alex. I'm out of cell reception and will be for the foreseeable future. This is the number to call me back on."

She hung up. Moments later, the phone rang.

"Hello?"

"Alex!" came her friend's familiar voice. "Good to hear from you!"

"You too! How are things?"

"Good! So I take it you're somewhere remote again. Antarctica? Greenland?"

"Washington State."

"Hey, that's not so bad! Did you fly in to Seattle? It's such a cool town."

"I actually flew in to Spokane, then rented a car."

"And let me guess. You totally passed up any time in that city in order to drive to some middle-of-nowhere place where you could make friends with stoats or something."

"I don't think we have stoats in America. That's a British thing. And as a matter of fact, I spent the night in a hotel in Spokane, and even went out to eat at a rather posh little microbrewery."

"And you didn't invite me?"

"Well, you are in the middle of filming." Zoe was currently on set in Studio City, California, filming scenes for an epic big-budget sci-fi film. "How's it going there?"

"Crazy, Alex. In fact . . . hold on a sec." She could hear Zoe moving, and suddenly the background noises got a lot quieter. "Okay. I'm back. I'm hiding in a closet."

"What?"

"I think someone is trying to sabotage the movie."

"For real?"

"Totally."

"What's been going on?" Alex asked.

"Well, the first weird thing was that someone hired what we thought was a special chef to make canapés for the craft services table. Everyone was really excited at first. You know, normally we just have bowls of fruit and stale bagels and things like that. But suddenly, here was this chef with a little portable oven and everything, and he was making the most delicious little toasted brioche sandwiches and canapés and crepes. We all hovered around him between shots. The food was divine. Or so we thought."

"What happened?"

"Well, first the key grip complains that he doesn't feel so good. He starts sweating and looking green. Then *boom*—same thing happens to one of the gaffers. He starts looking like any second he's going to toss his cookies. Then the second AD *does* start throwing up. She's clutching her stomach and barely makes it to one of the trash cans on set, and she just starts tossing *her* cookies right into this waste bin like she's trying to eject her own stomach.

"Then that seems to set everyone else off. People start running for any available receptacle. I'm telling you, Alex, it was the grossest thing you've ever seen. And of course, I'm starting to feel sick, and trying to hold it in, and I'm sweating through all my makeup, and the director, who didn't eat anything from the craft services table, starts yelling at everyone to take their places because he doesn't realize that half the crew is currently expelling their own guts, and it's just chaos.

"By the time we're all done and don't have anything left to throw up, we notice the chef is gone. Come to find out that no one hired this guy. Just *poof*. Took the little oven and everything. Vanished. The director didn't hire him, and neither did the production team. No one's even heard of the guy."

"That's awful. You think he poisoned the crew? Or that it was just unintentional food poisoning?"

"I don't know. Either way, it effectively shut us down for filming the rest of the day. People moaned and headed off to their trailers and hotel rooms. I've never felt so sick in all my life."

"How are you now?"

"Better, but that was just the first weird thing that happened."

"What else?"

"It's this sci-fi epic, right? The executive producer is pals with the head of a special effects studio and wanted to go practical for the alien instead of CG. So we have this massive animatronic alien with a complicated control panel that fourteen puppeteers have to manipulate. I mean, this thing is twenty feet tall with a lashing tail and working jaws, and this huge cranium with piercing eyes that can narrow and blink and fix on you. It's creepy enough just sitting there. But when those puppeteers go to work, this thing moves unbelievably fluidly. So I'm in my trailer one night, relaxing after dinner, and this thing is supposed to be locked up in the warehouse overnight. Only, I happen to glance outside just before I pull my shades to turn in, and the thing is standing just outside the warehouse docking doors."

"What?"

"Yeah. Just standing there. Staring at me. Not a puppeteer in sight. It's all done with radio controls, right? So I'm thinking maybe they're all still in the warehouse, having a good laugh. I don't want to fall for it, so I just pretend I'm going to bed and I switch out the light. That way I can see out, but they can't see in. Only, when I move back to the window, the thing is halfway across the parking lot, nearer to my trailer. It's still standing stock-still. I didn't see it move. Just suddenly there it is, twenty feet closer. At this point, I'm feeling a little nervous, even though I still think it's all a joke."

"I can see why! What did you do?"

"I grabbed my phone and flipped through the set's contacts until I found the lead special effects guy to tell him that someone's tampering with the alien. He picks up, and I hear this Irish music playing in the background. It's super loud, like he's in a bar. He sounds surprised to hear from me, and tells me to hang on, that he and his crew are all out celebrating one of their birthdays. They're nowhere near the warehouse, let alone controlling this thing. Then I look back outside the window, and it's right up against the glass, staring in with one of those baleful eyes. I shriek and tell the guy that his puppet is malfunctioning or shorting out or possessed or whatever, and he comes racing back to the set with some of his pals. They open up the warehouse door, only to find the controls exactly as they'd left them, shut off with no power. But by now this thing is pressed against the side of my trailer, staring in like it's King Kong and I'm Fay Wray."

"What did they do?"

"They powered it up and walked it back into the warehouse.

Said it must have been some kind of joke, though they couldn't figure out how someone could have gotten into the warehouse, let alone gotten the thing to walk over without a crew of operators. Even he and the four guys he brought with him had a hell of a time getting it back into the warehouse. I don't know. It was creepy."

"I'll say," Alex commiserated.

"And if that thing had gotten damaged, it would have set us back some serious time. So, between that and the food poisoning, I'm thinking sabotage."

"Could it have been a coincidence?" Alex ventured.

"Maybe. But I have a weird feeling about it." She exhaled. "So anyway, tell me about you! What's it like there?"

Alex started by describing how gorgeous it was, and then, with some reluctance, told Zoe about the body found in the park and the missing hiker.

"Are you kidding me? That's terrible."

"The sheriff asked me to keep a look out for the missing hiker. Apparently she wasn't far from the preserve's boundary when she disappeared."

"Are you scared? What if she got eaten by a bear or a wolf or something?"

Alex chuckled. "Contrary to popular belief, attacks like that are exceedingly rare. No, I think it's more likely she got lost. Or maybe got hypothermia and wandered off."

"Or whoever killed that ranger got to her, too," Zoe added.

"Yes. I've been thinking the same thing," Alex admitted.

"And you're just alone out there?"

"I've got bear spray. And a tranquilizer gun."

"That's not very reassuring."

"I'll be careful. Keep my eyes peeled."

"You better," Zoe commanded.

"And keep me posted on things there."

"I will."

They hung up, and Alex smiled. It always felt good to talk to Zoe. She'd been a close friend all through their undergrad and grad years, and supportive when Alex had moved to Boston and things hadn't worked out with her boyfriend there. She was lucky to have Zoe.

She finished the last cup of coffee in the pot, then gathered up her gear and set off to do her first batch of rounds on the preserve.

She hiked for much of the morning, stopping at remote cameras to swap out their batteries and memory cards. Each padlocked camera hung on a tree, mounted with a strap, and used infrared beams. If an animal crossed the beam, it triggered a photo and a video. A small screen inside the camera allowed her to preview the photos on the memory cards, but she decided to swap them out so she could review the images on the bigger screen of her laptop.

She hoped to see a mountain caribou on one of the images. They were so rare, she'd never seen one in the wild, but they fascinated her. They survived severe winter temperatures because of special adaptations in their coats, which contained semi-hollow hairs that insulated them. But because of this same feature and their dark fur, they could also overheat during the summer.

And all caribou subspecies, mountain included, sported large rounded hooves that allowed them to stay on top of the snowpack, much like snowshoes. Barren-ground caribou could travel at least a hundred miles a day, and run up to ten miles an hour. Their wide feet also allowed them to swim, using the massive hooves as paddles. They could swim for miles, as fast as five miles per hour.

As the day wore on, she munched on a sandwich as she hiked and finished the last of her water. She began casting around for a water source to refill it and came upon a tumbling stream cascading down from the steep peaks around her.

Alex followed the bank for a few feet until she found a place where a rock sloped gently down into the tumbling water. She took off her pack and pulled out her filter. She draped the long hose into the water and then placed the pump handle onto the opening of her water bottle. Relishing the thought of drinking the cold glacial water, she pumped it through the filtration system in the handle, watching the roaring whitewater go by.

When she finished, she took a long drink, then topped her bottle off again. As she knelt, cold water splashed up on her knee. The roar of the water was so loud she couldn't hear anything else. It was the kind of tumbling whitewater where she'd paused to fill up her water bottle once in Yosemite, then looked up, startled, to see a black bear on the other side of the river, also drinking. The bear was startled, too, the water roaring so loudly that neither had heard the other's approach. The bear had watched her with curiosity, then turned around and disappeared into the forest.

Here, towering western red cedar and western hemlock trees grew to immense proportions, lichen hanging off their branches. The soil smelled damp and earthy, and she lingered, reveling in being out here in the mountains, the crisp air on her face.

She stood up and pulled out the topo map. She oriented herself with her compass, seeing that she had another half mile to go in order to reach the next camera, over a ridge to the north.

This camera lay almost at the border of the national forest, just a few hundred feet inside the sanctuary's boundary.

She was just about to rise when a soft patch of mud at the river's edge caught her attention. There, perfectly preserved in the soft soil, was a hoofprint. She leaned toward it, hand on the soft mossy bank. She could see the hoof, even the two small imprints in the back where the dewclaws, special claws that protruded just above the hoof, had pressed into the soil. These specialized claws provided traction when walking on ice. So it wasn't from a mule deer or a moose. Alex stared, amazed.

It was from a caribou.

Quickly she dug out her camera, as if the print might somehow magically disappear, and snapped photos of it. Then she pulled out her multitool for scale; she couldn't help but smile every time she used it. Her father had given it to her when she graduated from high school. He'd had it engraved with *Alex Carter—Adventure Awaits*. She placed it next to the track for size reference and took a few more photos.

The track looked fresh. She gazed around her, watching for any hint of movement.

She quickly stowed her filter and put her multitool back in her pocket. Walking parallel to the bank, she searched for more tracks, mouth agape when she found them. The caribou had followed the stream for a good fifty feet before turning back into the forest. Here the soil was drier, and she struggled to find its tracks. She came across a kinnikinnick bush and bent down beside it. Several branches had been clipped off and eaten. She photographed these, too, and kept going.

A soft bed of moss and lichen stood a few feet away, and bare patches of earth peeked through where the caribou had eaten great tufts of the soft vegetation. Here Alex found two additional tracks on a patch of bare soil amid the moss.

She paused, listening intently, hoping to hear the caribou's footfalls as it broke twigs beneath its hooves. But the nearby river drowned out most of the forest sounds.

She pulled out her multitool and photographed the additional prints, and then came across a small mound of caribou droppings. Kneeling down, she crushed one with a stick to see how fresh it was, finding the insides moist and green. So the caribou was nearby.

Alex grinned, pumping a fist in the air. She took photographs of the scat and then bagged it, stowing it away in her pack and laughing to herself as she did so. Ah, the glamorous life of a wildlife biologist. She could send the fecal matter away to a lab to determine what the caribou had been eating.

She continued on, staring down. She found a few more places where the caribou had browsed on some shrubby cinquefoil bushes, and one more print. But as the animal had climbed the ridge, the soil became drier, and she found it harder and harder to follow its path.

Then she lost the track completely. She peered around, then pulled out her binoculars, scanning for any sign of the animal, with no luck. She drew out the topo map, seeing where the closest cameras were. The nearest was by the boundary to which she had been heading. Another lay to the west, possibly in the direction the caribou might be moving along the ridge.

She turned back toward the riverbank where she'd first spotted the hoofprint. Pulling the new remote camera out of her pack, she glanced around for a suitable tree. A perfect one stood about twenty feet from the print. She added fresh batteries and a memory card, then retrieved the camera's strap from her pack and secured it to the slender tree trunk.

She powered the camera on and tested it, happy to see it had captured three images of her walking near the bank. She closed the camera housing, padlocked it, and took a minute to study her surroundings, hoping the caribou would come back. But she suspected it wouldn't return right then.

But now she knew that one definitely lived on the preserve, and that it had been in this very spot.

Donning her pack, she headed up the ridge again, toward the other camera. Her mood light, she barely felt the weight of her pack all the way up. Already her mind thought about ways to improve and restore habitat for the caribou, and she wondered if it had come down alone, and if it was a bull or a cow.

She was so happily consumed by these thoughts that she didn't see the man with the rifle until she had started down the other side of the ridge.

FOUR

Alex froze. Down below, the strange man crouched inside the national forest, just past the preserve's border. She could see the red painted metal stakes that denoted the boundary. He hadn't seen her, and she backed up, then lay down at the top of the ridge.

He dug around in the ground with a small folding camper's shovel. His hair hung in long, dirty strands past his shoulders. His pale face, smeared with mud, examined the ground. Wanting to see what he was up to, Alex pulled out her binoculars. A frayed poncho hung off his lithe shoulders, his pants a patchwork of different materials, all held together with rough stitches. His boots were more duct tape than boots, toes covered in newer, shinier tape and the rest in old, weathered strips. On his back, the barrel of his rifle gleamed in a ray of sunlight. Beside him lay a small daypack.

As the man dug, he paused, suddenly looking up around him. Alex ducked out of sight. A few minutes later, she peeked out again. He was standing now, staring down at the ground, and had turned so that she could see his face. His beige features were leathery and freckled from years of sun damage, and she could see a few raw, red wounds on his skin from exposure to the elements. His greasy hair looked like it hadn't been washed in weeks. Stealthily she switched out her binoculars for her camera, adjusted it to its full 40× optical zoom, and took a photo of him.

He looked like he'd been living out here for some time.

He squatted and pulled out a small notebook from a hip pocket. Writing furiously, he seemed to take notes, then grabbed his folding shovel and daypack and stalked off into the national forest. Alex lay still for several long minutes, making sure he didn't double back.

When she was certain he had gone, she stood up, climbed over the rise, and headed toward the nearby camera. Maybe it had taken photos of him. She reached it, following her GPS unit's compass, nervously checking for movement among the trees. Her high spirits had been dampened, and she worried about the man crossing onto the preserve with his gun, or the caribou crossing over into the national forest, where it would be vulnerable.

She opened the camera's housing and clicked through the photos of the last hour. The man appeared in none of the pictures. But he might have done so on another day. She exchanged the memory card and batteries and hurried away, heading back up over the ridge, deeper into the preserve.

IT HAD BEEN TOO LATE to call Ben when she returned to the ranch house. He was three hours ahead of her in Washington, D.C. So she'd paced excitedly around the living room, sipping tea, thinking over her day. She flipped through the photos she'd taken of the tracks, and at the sight of her multitool she'd used for scale, she was suddenly hit with the sinking sensation that she hadn't seen it when she got home and emptied her pockets onto the kitchen table.

She went through them again, then took everything out of her pack. It was gone. *Damn.* She must have dropped it in the excitement, not stowed it properly in her pocket. She frowned. At least she'd lost it out on the preserve. It wasn't like a busy city street where anyone could pick it up. Tomorrow she'd retrace her steps and look for it.

Finally she sat down to pore over photographs from the memory cards she'd collected. She knew that most of the current cameras set out on the preserve hadn't been placed in areas that caribou would frequent, because no one had realized one could be here.

She knew she should place cameras in old-growth locations with lots of tree lichen. Alex had always been fascinated with lichen and all the different forms it took. She'd first seen a *Cladonia* species as a kid and thought the delicate green, cuplike forms were fairy goblets. She'd gone home and read all she could find on them in her father's field guides, learning that lichen were symbiotic—algal cells living with fungus. The algal component gleaned nutrients from sunlight, and the fungus fed off it. She delighted in lichen's dazzling array of shapes, appearing as leaflike, crust-like, as long draping hair, and then the weird and enchanting shapes like the *Cladonia* fairy cups.

While mountain caribou ate all kinds of vegetation, including grasses, the leaves of deciduous trees and shrubs, the tips of plants like willow and birch, lichen, and moss, their survival depended particularly on the availability of lichen that grew in trees, as this food source allowed them to survive the long winters when other vegetation was buried beneath snow.

Alex knew that mountain caribou especially relied upon two kinds of tree-growing, or arboreal, lichens: *Bryoria* species and *Alectoria sarmentosa*. The *Bryoria* species of lichen was often called horsehair lichen, and hung from trees in brown, hairlike clumps. *Alectoria sarmentosa,* on the other hand, grew pale green in long, intricate branches, and was known as common witch's hair.

Unfortunately, both of these lichens grew incredibly slowly, and lived mainly in old-growth forests that had been around for more than 250 years. So as areas were clear-cut, this vital food source grew rarer and rarer.

She had the highest hopes for the camera that had been nearest the caribou prints, so she started with that one. She also wondered if she'd find images of the strange man.

As she flipped through photograph after photograph, she saw a plethora of wildlife. The camera had been well placed by a creek, and many creatures came to the streambed to drink: a black bear, two mule deer, a cougar, a family of raccoons, a pair of wood ducks, and a red fox. It had also captured images of more birds in a tree opposite, including an Oregon vesper sparrow, which itself was endangered and made her grin to see. She made a note of which images contained wildlife so she could share them with the LTWC.

When she reached the last photo, she felt the rise of disappointment. There'd been no photos of the caribou. And there'd also been none of the man. Maybe that meant he wasn't trespassing on the preserve. But the camera had been angled slightly so that some of the national forest land was captured in its frames.

As she noted the image number of a pine marten climbing the tree, she paused. The image numbers were not consecutive. They should all have been in sequential order, yet some numbers were missing. The pine marten photo was number 1225, and the next photo 1233. Seven images were gone. She scanned back through the rest of the files in the folder, finding five images deleted between 427 and 433, and twelve missing between 241 and 254. She double-checked that they hadn't been labeled differently for some reason, but they were definitely gone.

And the only way they could go missing like that would be if someone had opened the camera and deliberately deleted the photos manually. But the cameras all had padlocks on them. She leaned back in her chair, frowning. Someone could have had an extra key, she supposed, or even picked the locks. Instantly she thought of the armed man. He could be on the run out there, hiding, and realized his photo had been taken. He might want to stay anonymous.

She thought of the missing hiker, Amelia Fairweather, and wondered if the man was dangerous. He might just be a squatter, she reasoned, or he might be something a lot worse.

THE NEXT DAY, ALEX PERCHED on a tall stool by the landline in the kitchen. She called Ben Hathaway in Washington, D.C.

His cheerful voice instantly lifted her spirits. "Alex! How's it going out there?"

"Very promising!" she told him. "I found tracks and scat."

"You're kidding me."

"Nope. I set up a new camera along a creek bed where a caribou had stopped to drink."

"I can't believe it. I mean, I hoped, but this is great news!"

She grinned. "I agree!" She thought then of the other events since his departure and fell quiet.

"I get the sense something else is going on."

"There's been a lot of disturbance in town. A forest ranger was murdered."

"What? That's awful!"

"And did you know that a backcountry hiker went missing in this area?"

"I did know about that," he told her. "A little over a year ago, right? And they never found her?"

"That's right. The sheriff asked me to keep an eye out for any signs of her because she vanished not far from the preserve's boundary. And I did see this guy when I was out there . . ."

"Where?"

"On the north side of the preserve, near where I saw the caribou tracks. He was on the national forest side, with a rifle strapped to his back. He didn't see me. And it was kind of weird. He was digging around in the dirt there with a little folding shovel. But he might have just been a hunter or squatter. He was really dirty. His clothes were all ragged."

"That's weird."

"I looked for him on images from the remote camera nearest there and found that several photos had been deleted."

"You think he's poaching? Maybe removed some evidence of his movements?"

Alex frowned. "Maybe."

"The thought of him killing that caribou makes me sick."

"Me too. I'll let the sheriff know. With one woman murdered and another missing, it could be important."

"You being careful out there?" Ben asked.

"Always. I'm going out today with the tranq gun in the hopes of finding the caribou and putting a collar camera on it. I'll email you the coordinates of where I found those tracks."

"It's great news about the caribou in the midst of all the bad stuff."

"Definitely. How are things there?"

"Good. We're negotiating to have a conservation easement put on this huge six-thousand-acre property in New Mexico. It's right on the border, and we're hoping that jaguars and Mexican gray wolves might be using the area."

"That's exciting!"

"The owner is really keen on wildlife conservation. His entire spread out there is off the grid. All solar and wind power."

Alex could picture it already, the sweeping mountains and dark skies. "Good luck with the talks."

"Thanks. Oh, and I have Kathleen's number for you. She's going to be in the area later today and wants to meet up with you at some point."

Alex smiled and wrote down the number as he read it off. "I look forward to seeing her."

"You take care."

"I will. I'll call you soon with an update."

"Okay."

They hung up and Alex prepared to venture out in the hopes of finding the caribou.

FIVE

A half hour later, Alex set out, the tranq gun strapped to her pack. She carried another two trail cameras for when she found good places to hang them, as well as the supplemental oxygen and all four collar cameras, just in case something went wrong with one of them. She would hate to tranq the caribou only to discover the camera was faulty. She had tested them out at the ranch house, and all four were in good working order, but better safe than sorry.

Working with technology in the field always had its share of problems. Once she'd hiked out to a remote area to download data from several temperature sensors she'd stashed where American pikas lived. Small relatives of the rabbit, pikas lived in high-altitude rock piles. They spent the short alpine summers gathering grasses, which they cured in the sun. Then during the long, cold winters, they ate this store of food and kept warm beneath the insulating snows.

She'd been monitoring populations in the Sierra Nevada and the Great Basin for years and was worried about their decline. So she'd hiked out with her laptop one afternoon, intending to download the data and then leave the sensors where they were to collect more readings. Only, when she got there, she discovered that the battery in her laptop was faulty. She'd been unable to boot it up, and had to hike all the way back out, wait for another laptop battery to be delivered, and then venture out again. Ever since then, she'd been all too aware that technology can fail, and tried to use redundant systems whenever she could.

Another time, she'd used a new type of temperature logger, and it had quit working five hours after she'd left it in the field. She'd returned weeks later only to discover the temperatures at the site hadn't been recorded on it at all. Thankfully, that time, she'd also deployed a redundant source, a data logger brand she'd used many times in the field, and therefore had a backup.

So carrying all four collar cameras added weight to her pack, but it was worth it.

As she set out, a light rain fell, and she pulled out her rain gear and cover for her backpack. A mist crept through the forest, lending an aura of mystery to the place. Droplets cascaded off the hanging horsehair lichen, and the rich scent of the earth, ferns, and fallen logs filled the air.

She reached the stream where she'd found the caribou track, noticing that the recent rain had caused the mud to shift in that area. The track was now a distorted depression. She searched up and down the bank but saw no recent sign of the caribou. She flipped through the few photos the new camera had taken, but they were of a moose, a black bear, and a raven.

She continued on in the direction the caribou likely took before, eyes glued to the ground for any hint of scat or tracks. But she didn't see anything. She kept a constant eye out for her multitool, too, and was disappointed not to see it. She'd now retraced much of her previous route and frowned at the thought of having lost it.

She checked the next nearby camera, but found no hint of the caribou, the armed man, or any missing photos this time.

Checking her map, she decided to move on to two other cameras she hadn't checked yet. Frequently she paused to listen, but all she could hear were birds singing happily in the rain and the cascade of water from the upper canopy pattering down on the soft bed of pine needles, moss, and ferns.

She reached the next camera as the rain fell more heavily, so she stopped beneath a thick patch of tree cover to eat her lunch. She'd made a brown rice and black bean burrito with avocado, and munched it happily while listening to the wind sigh above her. A Swainson's thrush sang its bright cascade of notes. She smiled; she'd always loved the cheerful sound of thrushes.

To wait out the heavier part of the rain, she sat down on a log, her Marmot rain pants and parka keeping her completely dry. *This is the life,* she thought, *out here, in this magical place, listening to the patter of rain and birdsong.* She was just another animal in the forest, and she felt completely content and at home.

Her burrito finished, she rose and resumed her trek to the next camera as the rain lessened. She spotted the camera strapped to a tree, and her heart lifted at the thought that it might hold photos of the caribou. She unlocked and opened its housing, leaning over it to shield it from the light drizzle with her parka hood.

Hundreds of images had been recorded, so she swapped out its memory card for a blank one. She'd have to go through them back at the ranch house.

She shut the housing and was just turning away when something caught her eye, lying in the pine needles a dozen feet away. She moved to it, bending down to examine it. Before her lay an olive-green compass, its case dotted with raindrops. She picked it up, turning it over gently in her hands. Then she pressed the button on the top of it and the case flipped open.

It was a Sportneer Military Lensatic Compass. She stared at its white dial and green fluorescent arrow. Its plastic sides sported rulers, and these were scuffed and banged up, as if it had seen a lot of use. A spiral design, drawn in permanent marker, graced one corner.

Instantly she thought of the printed list Sheriff Taggert had given her, the one with Amelia Fairweather's belongings. One item had been a compass. But she was sure the compass listed there had been engraved with Amelia's initials. She turned it over in her hands, finding no such marking.

She got out her map and estimated her distance to the national forest. She was only about two hundred yards from the border. Someone could easily have accidentally crossed onto the preserve and dropped it while hiking. She thought of the armed man she'd seen. The compass didn't look like it had been dropped all that long ago. Then again, with the activists and loggers in the area, there could be all kinds of people cutting through this part of the preserve.

She slipped the compass into her pocket and examined the map for the next camera location. It, too, lay on the outskirts of the preserve near the national forest boundary, and she walked along the border. Here trees rose up into the sky, massive trunks covered with moss and lichen.

So far, she hadn't seen any more tracks or scat and was beginning to feel a little discouraged.

She'd just decided to head back to the ranch house before dark when sudden, angry shouting stopped her abruptly.

Alex moved through a dense cluster of old growth, trying to determine the location of the shouting. The boundary between the national forest and the preserve cut through the grove. She paused, listening, the rain sprinkling on her parka hood. She lowered it, listening more intently. A man's angry voice shot through the trees, and a chain saw erupted into a racket. Its motor revved as the man cursed. She couldn't make out what he was saying, only that he was shouting in anger.

She hurried down the ridge, unsure if the chain saw was coming from her side of the boundary or not.

She stopped again just as the chain saw cut its engine, and the trailing sounds of a woman's voice carried faintly through the air. Alex could make out her words, and realized she was closer to the woman than to the man with the chain saw.

"... here to hurt anyone ..." The woman's words died on the

wind. Rain pattered the ground around Alex, but the dense canopy kept most of the drops off.

The chain saw revved again, and now she could see the man, about a hundred yards ahead, a puff of blue exhaust pluming above him. An ATV waited nearby. He shouted again in anger, and ran toward the woman's voice, revving the chain saw's motor. He was on the national forest side. Alex ducked behind a massive trunk. The man paused at the base of a tremendous red cedar. Alex guessed that six people with their arms outstretched would not be able to encircle it. He revved the chain saw again. "I'm gonna cut you down right outta that tree!"

"There's an official moratorium on logging here," the woman called back faintly. Alex realized her voice was coming from far up in the canopy. She craned her neck, staring up into the massive cedar, where she spotted a series of makeshift platforms. Branches and the crowns of other trees obscured her view, but she was sure the woman was up there, at least two hundred feet in the air.

"I can climb a neighboring tree, you know, cross over onto your platform and cut you right down!" the man shouted, his voice full of vitriol.

"I'm not hurting anyone. I just don't want to see this grove demolished," the woman called down.

"You *are* hurting people. You're hurting jobs. You and your tree-huggers caused this halt."

"This is one of the few remaining old-growth forests in the country," she called down, her voice level and patient.

The man kicked the trunk and revved his chain saw again.

A sudden hand fell on Alex's shoulder and she whirled around, her heart hammering. She hadn't heard anyone approach.

A gawky teenager crouched behind her. "Hey," he said. He wore a rainbow-colored knit cap over an unruly mess of red hair, his thin frame clad in a hemp shirt and baggy canvas pants. "Pretty crazy, huh?" he said, pointing at the man with the chain saw.

"Who are you?" she asked, noting that he seemed completely unsurprised at the angry confrontation unfolding before them.

"Dennis Copperfield. You the wildlife biologist? We heard one was coming."

"Yes."

He pointed up at the massive branches. "Agatha's been up in that tree for seven months, if you can believe it. She climbed up there in the middle of the night about three months before the moratorium started. They can't cut it down with her in it. It's the biggest one in the grove. We call it Gaia."

Alex noticed that he held a basket full of bottles of water, food, and fresh batteries. "I need to get this basket up to her. She's got a pulley system she can lower. But I can't get by that guy." His mouth cracked into a crooked grin. "You wanna create a diversion?"

Alex stared at the guy, aghast. "What?"

"Seriously. She hasn't had water in two days, and the batteries in her walkie are almost dead. Can you help us out?"

"What do you want me to do?"

The kid shrugged. "I dunno. Start a conversation with the dude?"

Alex rocked back on her heels. "With the angry chain-saw-wielding dude?"

That grin again. "Exactly."

She looked down at the basket, thought of the dedication of the woman up in the tree. Even though she was clearly holding her own, the guy was still threatening her, and the woman was right. She wasn't hurting anyone, and there was a moratorium on logging in the area, anyway.

Alex stood up. "Okay. I'll see what I can do."

Dennis produced a walkie-talkie and spoke into it. "Okay, I'm coming. Get ready to lower the rope."

Alex walked about twenty feet down the property line and called out to the man. "Hey!"

He continued to rev the chain saw. She didn't think he'd heard her over the din.

She crossed over into the national forest. "Hey, excuse me."

He turned, wheeling angrily, then paused when he saw her.

"Hey," Alex said again. "Sorry to bother you. I'm new here. I've been stationed at the preserve next door. Alex Carter." With him wielding the chain saw, she decided not to extend her hand in greeting.

The man just frowned, looking at her as if she were a piece of trash he'd stepped in on the street. At least he'd stopped gunning the motor. "And?"

Alex plowed on. "I just wondered what all the hubbub is about. Everything okay?"

He hooked his thumb at the massive conifer. "Damn girl's been up in that tree for months. We need her to come down. You got any influence with the Forest Service?"

"I might," Alex lied. Behind him, she saw Dennis run to the base of the cedar, attach the handle of the basket to a hook at the end of a rope, and dash back to the cover of the huge trunks. The basket quickly shot up into the canopy and out of sight.

The chain saw still idled in the man's hands. "Maybe you can talk to them about getting this logging project going again. My crew's being reassigned to other areas, and I've been left here to keep an eye on all that expensive equipment just gathering rust up the way." He pointed in the direction where she'd seen the logging camp on her first day out with Ben.

"I'll see what I can do," Alex told him. She didn't want to help this anger-filled guy, but she did want to know if there was any news about the logging project. Confirming that Dennis was safely out of sight, she said, "You take care now."

She started to walk away, but he said, "Hey, wait a minute. You said you were from the land trust?"

She turned back. "That's right."

"Then you're the one trying to find that damned caribou?"

Alex's face went stony.

"If it's even out there, then there's only one," he said angrily. "Not enough to justify shutting down a whole logging operation."

She pursed her lips. "But if we preserve this old growth, then more could return to the area."

His eyes flashed with anger. "And what good is that gonna do?"

Alex knew that there was no point in engaging with the man further. "I need to get back to work." She turned and started hiking away.

"If I were you," he called, "and I found that damn animal, I'd keep it to myself."

She ignored him and kept walking. The man shut off the chain saw and stomped back toward his waiting ATV. When he roared off in the direction of the logging camp, Dennis emerged.

"Hey, thanks. That was brave."

"No problem."

"You really going to talk to the Forest Service about the logging?"

"I can try to find out what the current status is with the judge considering the case."

He stared up at the towering old growth. "I hope the moratorium becomes permanent." He looked back at her. "Hey, thanks again."

"Sure thing."

"And if you feel like reporting that guy, his name is Clyde Fergus. We've complained about him to no avail."

"I'll see what I can do," Alex told him. Then, waving goodbye, she turned and crossed back onto the preserve, feeling sick at the thought of losing those trees. The old growth was invaluable to caribou and so many other species, like grizzly bears, great gray and flammulated owls, Vaux's swifts, the threatened Canada lynx, and many more. If it was clear-cut up to the border of the preserve, it would be a huge, irreplaceable loss.

These lichen-bearing trees, mainly subalpine fir, Engelmann spruce, western hemlock, and western red cedar, took a long time to reach old-growth maturity and would take many years to grow back, if they were even allowed to. And with climate change causing a reduction in snowpack each winter, the pack was not always high enough for caribou to reach the lichen that did still exist. And so the devastation of old growth and rising temperatures meant that this necessary food source was vanishing.

She walked back to the house in a somber mood. The rain picked up, and she raised her parka hood again. Mist descended, enshrouding the peaks around her. The forest smelled amazing, of wet pine, moss, and earth. She breathed it in, savoring being there. Witch's hair lichen hung from tree limbs, rain dripping off the sea-green strands. And everywhere she looked, brilliantly green wolf lichen clung to the red and brown bark of the trunks, an excellent indicator that the air here was particularly clean and fresh.

She hoped that tomorrow she'd have more luck spotting the caribou.

BACK AT THE RANCH HOUSE, Alex made rotini pasta in marinara sauce and ate at the dining room table while poring over images from the remote cameras.

So much wildlife used the preserve that it made Alex smile as she scrolled through the photos. A black bear, a browsing moose, a prowling mountain lion, and a coyote had all been captured on the cameras.

But still she found no images of the caribou and exhaled with deep disappointment. If only she had a better idea of where it roamed on the preserve. Then a sick feeling hit her—what if it had wandered back north, across the national forest, and she'd never find it?

Alex knew that the last known caribou crossing from Canada into Washington had happened back in 2014, when a radio-collared male had spent ten days in the state. But he had then returned to Canada.

She had looked into the history of government action for the South Selkirk herd. Southern mountain caribou in general had been listed as endangered under the Endangered Species Act in 1984. But the U.S. Fish and Wildlife Service delayed designating critical habitat for the Selkirk herd until 2011, after they were hit with numerous lawsuits by conservation organizations. While USFWS originally proposed designating 375,562 acres, in the end it was only 30,010 acres.

Since that initial listing of southern mountain caribou in 1984, special interest groups had repeatedly sought to delist the species, and this happened again after the critical habitat was designated. In the meantime, South Selkirk caribou numbers dwindled to dangerously low levels. The two surviving members of the herd, who were both female and therefore unable to reproduce, were translocated to Canada in 2019.

Finally, the same year, the USFWS decided not to delist the mountain caribou, but reaffirmed their endangered status and specifically defined their subpopulations, including the South Selkirk herd.

On her laptop, Alex pulled up satellite images of the preserve and scanned them for pockets of old growth she hadn't yet explored. She marked the locations on a topo map. Tomorrow she'd try these.

Starting to feel blue, Alex got up, taking a break. She glanced at her watch. She could call Kathleen, make plans for a coffee date. It would be good to catch up with her. Alex moved to the kitchen and dialed her number on the landline.

As the phone rang, Alex smiled at the thought of seeing Kathleen. She'd been welcome company when Alex had spent a few months at the Snowline Resort Wildlife Sanctuary outside the tiny town of Bitterroot, Montana. Kathleen had been the first person in the town to really warm up to Alex. It would be fun to see her again.

Her friend answered on the third ring. "Hello?"

"Kathleen, this is Alex Carter."

"Alex! Ben told me you'd call."

"How are you?"

"Good, good. Almost in Bellamy Falls. Then I'm going to stock up on groceries and make my way out to the fire tower. My official shift starts in four days."

"You want to get coffee beforehand?"

"I'd love to!"

They made plans to meet up at the same little café where Alex and Ben had met.

"Looking forward to it!" Alex told her.

"Same here!"

She hung up and switched off her laptop, the day's hike finally catching up to her. She climbed up to the bedroom, changed into her pj's, and stood for a moment, looking out the window at the forest.

And then she froze.

The strange light was back.

SIX

Alex watched the light dancing above the trees, lowering into the canopy and then skimming along above the forest. She guessed it was miles away, but it was difficult to determine the exact distance or how big the thing was. Then it shot out of sight to her right.

She couldn't lean out the window to get a better view because the screen blocked her. So she slipped on her boots and hurried downstairs.

Throwing open the back door, she stepped out onto the rear porch. Now she could clearly see the thing, moving erratically and quickly above the trees to the north, dropping down into them occasionally only to shoot back upward.

She could hear no sound from it whatsoever, which she chalked up to her distance from it. But it had to be big if she could see it from where she stood, much bigger than a civilian drone. She felt a primal fear of the unknown wash over her.

It dipped again into an opening in the dense tree cover, vanishing from view. She watched, waiting tensely for it to return. And then it shot straight upward, speeding away into the distance and winking out.

Brow furrowed, she continued to stare for a long time. What the hell was it?

Finally, when darkness had held the forest for ten solid minutes, she ducked back inside and locked the door, still puzzling over the strange craft.

She climbed the stairs and crawled under the covers, feeling a sudden shiver. Whatever it was, it was disconcerting.

THE NEXT MORNING, AS ALEX'S tea finished steeping, the kitchen phone rang. She moved to answer it.

"Hello?"

"Alex, it's Ben."

Alex grinned, feeling a flush at his voice. "Hi, Ben. How are things in D.C.?"

"Busy. The final papers for that huge preserve in New Mexico hit at the same time as some extra funding to hire rangers to patrol for poachers on one of our preserves in Kenya."

"Not a bad reason to be busy."

"Right? Listen, are you doing anything specific today?"

"No, I just had plans to make some rounds, put out more cameras."

"I've got a lead I want you to check out, if you're up for it."

"What is it?"

"There's a nonprofit a couple hours away from you that had been gathering supplemental feed for the South Selkirk herd when they were still in the U.S. The group used to gather lichen from areas where caribou had been extirpated and transport it out to where the herd was still surviving. But when Canada took the last two, they had all this lichen that was just going to go to waste. We could use it for our caribou when winter comes. Do you think you could drive out there and pick it up?"

The thought of a drive to see even more of this gorgeous area of Washington State appealed to Alex. "I'd be happy to. What's the name of the organization?"

"Conservation Washington. I'll email you directions. They're a nice bunch of folks. I've dealt with their director before. His name is Clay Halvorson. Among other things, he takes volunteers out in the winter to track wildlife. They've got a trailer and everything, which should be simple enough to hook up to your Jeep."

"Sure thing. I'll go out there today."

"Fantastic. Really appreciate it. Thank you. How is everything else going?" he asked.

Alex thought with misgivings over her recent experiences. "You know that section of old growth that's in dispute? I met an angry logger who's harassing a woman sitting in the top of a tree there."

"That doesn't sound pleasant."

"He was anything but. And I set out with my tranq gun yesterday, but no luck yet."

"I'm keeping my fingers crossed."

When they hung up, Alex sat at the kitchen table drinking tea. Ben's email came through, and she saved the address. Then she read online about Conservation Washington. The organization intrigued her. They funded caribou, wolverine, and wolf research, and as Ben had mentioned, sponsored community wildlife-tracking projects.

She loaded up her daypack with water and a couple energy bars and filled her insulated cup with tea. Then she headed out, deciding to stop by the mailbox to see if there was anything new. At the main intersection, she pulled over at the large collection of silver USPS boxes. She unlocked the small door and pulled out a stack of mail.

Thumbing through it, she saw that most of it was addressed to "Box Holder": a grocery store mailer and a collection of coupons. At the bottom was a large envelope from her dad containing her forwarded mail. Inside she found donation requests from several nonprofits and from her alma mater, the University of California, along with a brief note from her dad and several articles he'd clipped out from the *New York Times*. And then she froze, her mouth suddenly going dry.

There was a postcard. And it was from *him*.

She'd half expected to get a postcard before finishing her polar bear study in Churchill, Manitoba, but none had arrived. She lifted it tentatively, her mind suddenly gone numb, a pounding rush of blood making her heart skip a beat.

Returning to the Jeep, she placed the rest of the mail down on the passenger seat and held only the card. The front depicted Auckland, New Zealand. She flipped it over. In that familiar block handwriting, it read: ALEX. SORRY I'VE BEEN SILENT. I'M NOT SURE WHAT TO SAY. BUT KNOW THAT I'M THINKING ABOUT YOU AND WANT NOTHING BUT THE BEST FOR YOU.

She'd been receiving these unsigned cards since she first took the gig in Montana to study wolverines. For a long time, she had no idea who was sending them. The cards always depicted locations she'd spent time in, as if the sender had been following in her footsteps, exploring the places she'd been. They'd given her a chill. And she'd only just discovered the identity of the sender a few months ago but hadn't heard from him since. He was in the wind.

She stared down at the card. So he was still out there, thinking of her. But unlike all the previous postcards she'd received, this one wasn't from any place she'd ever been. He was no longer following her.

She wondered what he was doing in New Zealand. Mixed emotions flooded her. Would she ever see him again? Did she *want* to see him again?

Her blood thrumming in her ears, she placed the card with the rest of the mail, and started up the Jeep.

As she drove on to Conservation Washington, she forced herself to think about the caribou study and retrieving the lichens. She didn't want to dwell on the card. Every time she thought of him, her heart started to beat too fast. Soon the stunning scenery shifted her mood. She started to enjoy the drive, sipping hot tea and staring out at the towering peaks around her. She'd never been to this section of Washington State before and found it breathtaking.

As she came around a bend, she slowed to let a mother deer and two speckled fawns cross the road. Moving cautiously with pricked-up ears and nervous gaits, they crossed and stepped safely into the woods on the other side of the road. Seeing the fawns made Alex wonder if the caribou on the preserve was a female. If so, this was the time of year when it could have a young calf.

Unlike other species of deer, which often gave birth to two offspring, caribou had a single calf in a season. After mating in early winter, caribou mothers gestated for seven to eight months. Female caribou shed their antlers in late spring, much later than their male counterparts, who lost them in early winter. This allowed the cows extra time to use those antlers to excavate for more food beneath the snow and bulk up during pregnancy. When born, caribou calves were precocious; within one hour of birth they took their first steps, and within just a few more hours, they could run for several miles.

In the weeks after their birth, calves stuck close to their mothers, who could be fiercely protective, charging at threats, even perceived threats from other caribou. Cows talked to their babies using grunts and provided them with some of the richest milk in the animal kingdom, comprised of a whopping 20 percent fat, compared to just 5 percent that dairy cows produced in their milk.

After only one month, calves were weaned, and as the summer wore on, calves ventured farther afield in a herd, mixing with other members.

Alex drove on, finding herself ruminating again on the postcard. She passed through a huge burn scar, and estimated that the wildfire had happened late in the previous year. The area stood completely black, not a living tree or bush in sight. Burn crews had cut down all the dead, blackened trees and stacked their trunks in piles perpendicular to the road.

The route here took a series of steep switchbacks winding down, and it looked like an area ripe for a landslide, with no surviving vegetation to hold the soil in place.

She took the hairpin turns slowly, frowning. Fires like these, severe fires that reached the canopy of trees and left nothing alive, were consuming the West, brought on by climate change, drought, and years of ill-considered fire suppression. Human fire suppression had allowed the understory of forests to build up dangerous levels of material. Normally this material would be cleared out by smaller, naturally occurring fires that burned along the forest floor, but with these fires stamped out by humans in the past, undergrowth amassed. Couple that extra material with devastating drought brought on by global warming, and fires were now taking on epic proportions, wiping out vast swaths of forest. Many trees that were adapted to withstand milder fires that burned on the forest floor could not survive these disastrous ones, which reached the canopy.

At the bottom of the steep section, she continued on, feeling a little blue. She passed numerous road signs that had been shot at, locals doing target practice and leaving bullet holes in speed-limit and yellow curve-ahead signs.

Then she turned off the main road onto a smaller dirt one and followed it two miles to a low white building with a flat roof. Painted on the side was the name Conservation Washington and its logo: stylized silhouettes of a caribou, a wolverine, and a fisher beneath a pine tree.

As soon as she pulled up, a man emerged from the front door and waved at her. She parked and climbed out.

"Dr. Carter?" he asked.

She smiled, extending her hand. "Clay Halvorson?"

"That's me." They shook. He was a tall man, his long, sun-bleached blond hair pulled back in a ponytail. Years of working outside had damaged his beige skin, and laugh lines gave his face a friendly look. His green eyes twinkled. "We're so glad you can make use of the lichen we collected. We didn't want it to go to waste."

"It's my pleasure. I know the land trust really appreciates it. If the caribou decides to stay down here in the States over winter, I'm sure this supplemental feed will really help."

"Ben told me you've definitely confirmed its presence on the preserve."

She nodded. "I have. I'm planning to fit it with a collar camera if I get the chance," she told him.

"That would be amazing. I wonder if it's alone."

"Exactly what I'm hoping to find out."

"That's not unusual, right? For one to wander down, a male looking for new territory?"

"They've been known to do that, yes." She pointed to the logo. "I was reading about your organization before I came up," she told him. "I really admire the work you're doing."

He smiled. "Yeah, since caribou became extirpated here, we've shifted our focus to wolverines and fishers. Hoping to get them stronger protections."

"Wolverines are fascinating," she said, sliding her hands into her jeans pockets. "I did a wolverine study last year."

He arched his eyebrows. "Is that so? Whereabouts?"

"Montana. Have you seen them here?"

"There are a few in our research area. We've got bait stations and cameras stashed all over the state. Hoping to get a handle on their population density."

"Learned much yet?" she asked.

"We've recorded three individuals in the Cascades."

"That's amazing."

He grinned. "Now if we could just get the federal government to list them under the Endangered Species Act."

Alex bit her lip. "That would be great." She knew, though, that the U.S. Fish and Wildlife Service had been refusing to extend protections to wolverines for decades, despite the fact that they were declining. They had once roamed as far east as the Great Lakes region and as far south as New Mexico, but now they survived in only a couple pockets in the Rockies and the Cascades, and numbered fewer than three hundred in the lower forty-eight.

"C'mon," he said. "Let me show you the lichen we have." He started walking toward a storage shed about a hundred yards from the office, and she fell in beside him. "We took the liberty of loading it all up onto a trailer. Feel free to return it to us when you get the chance. We won't be needing it anytime soon."

They reached the storage shed and he slid aside its large aluminum door. Inside, metal racks held various tools: rakes, shovels, a couple chain saws, trowels, bolt cutters. Cans of gasoline stood in one corner beside toolboxes, cinder blocks, old galoshes, and several pairs of cross-country skis. In the center of the room waited the trailer with a tarp cinched down over its contents.

Clay detached one of the bungee cords holding down the tarp. He lifted the blue plastic covering. Inside lay dozens of clear bags full of horsehair and witch's hair lichen.

"This is great," she told him, stooping down to get a better look.

"Glad it's going to a worthy cause. After Canada took the remaining caribou, we weren't sure what we were going to do with it."

"I'll put it to good use."

Clay replaced the tarp and reattached the bungee cord. "Help me push it out of the shed and we can hook it up to your Jeep."

In a few minutes, they'd shoved the trailer out into the daylight and spun it around so Alex could back the Jeep up to it.

Alex climbed into the driver's seat and Clay directed her as she lined up the tow bar with the trailer. In moments they'd hooked it up and she was ready to go.

"Hey," he said, hooking his thumb toward the office. "We've got some sandwiches in there, and coffee cake, too, if you want to stay for a bit before you take off."

She smiled. "Thanks. That would be nice."

Alex followed him inside, finding a comfortable room with a battered wooden desk, a corkboard plastered with flyers and maps, and a small kitchen with a table and plastic chairs. Classic rock played softly from a radio in the corner.

Alex noticed they were alone. "We had a birthday party earlier for one of our volunteers," Clay told her. "Everyone's gone off to grab a beer at a local pub. I'll join them when we're done here." He moved to the fridge and pulled out a large party tray of sandwiches. Most of them were already gone.

She selected a seven-layer veggie sandwich. "Thanks."

"It's from our local deli," he told her.

They sat at the table and she bit into it. "It's good."

They spoke comfortably, comparing travel and adventures and sharing their favorite wildlife experiences. She downed a cup of coffee.

After a while, Alex glanced at her watch. The sun would set in half an hour, and she still had a long drive back to the ranch house. "I'd better go."

When they emerged from the office, she spotted dark clouds building on the western horizon. The air smelled of ozone.

"It's going to rain," Clay said.

"Yep."

"Hey," he said, pulling a card out of his wallet, "I'd love to hear what happens with this caribou. Would you mind shooting me an email?"

She took the proffered card. "Not at all. It'd be my pleasure."

They said their goodbyes, and she climbed into her Jeep and headed back down the dirt road, the trailer bumping along behind her. She was grateful when she hit the paved road and the ride smoothed out considerably. Raindrops began pattering down, splashing on the windshield and drumming on the roof of the car. The sky darkened further, and as the sun set, the rain picked up in intensity, the wind sweeping it across the road in gray sheets.

Alex switched the windshield wipers on high, listening to their rhythmic beat. She turned on her headlights, creating tunnels of light that pierced the heavy downpour. A car passed her going the other way, the driver not bothering to switch off his brights. Alex squinted as he passed her, sending up a wave of water that slapped loudly against the driver's side of her Jeep.

The rain grew even heavier, and she slowed, the downpour increasing to what her mother would have called a "frog strangler." Alex could barely see. She envied the superpower vision of caribou just then. They could see in far fainter light than humans, way down into the dim ultraviolet range. This allowed them to navigate during the long, dark winter nights above the Arctic Circle when the sun never peeked above the horizon. And that wasn't the only cool thing about caribou eyes, Alex thought, smiling. They also changed colors depending on the season. In winter, they turned blue, the dark color allowing them to drink up even more light. Then in summer, their eyes turned a beautiful golden color, able to reflect back more of the intense summer sunlight.

Up ahead, Alex spotted a wide pull-off coming up on the right and eased into it, slowing to a stop. Rain pummeled the roof of the car and then became a sharp racket. Hail rained down, bouncing off the windshield and collecting in the little gutter below the wipers.

As she waited for the downpour to subside, movement on her left drew her attention. A black wolf appeared, moving cautiously out of the tree line to stand on the edge of the road. She hoped it wouldn't cross in front of a car, so she searched the road ahead nervously for signs of oncoming traffic. But only darkness lay there, and relief spread through her as the handsome wolf loped across the road and disappeared into the trees on the other side.

She thought of the deer family she'd seen earlier that day and wondered what this wolf fed on predominantly, and if it had run across the caribou.

As she waited for the rain to subside, her mind turned to the conflict that had sprung up lately around wolves and caribou conservation. Wolves had followed their usual prey—deer, moose, and elk—into new areas where old growth had been clear-cut and younger forests had taken over. And wolves had an especially easy time doing this because reduced snowpack caused by climate change, as well as logging roads and snowmobile paths, allowed them to access caribou-populated terrain, which they normally wouldn't be able to reach in winter.

And so wolves began to predate on mountain caribou, but they did not share a predator-prey relationship with caribou. Normally as a predator fed on a prey population, that species would decline. This in turn made the predator population go down, and the prey species would rebound. And the cycle would start all over again. But because caribou weren't the normal prey of wolves, as caribou populations dwindled due to wolf predation, this did not in turn make the wolf population go down, because wolf numbers were dictated by the abundance of deer, moose, and elk.

Unfortunately, government reaction in both the U.S. and Canada to this unprecedented wolf predation of caribou wasn't to halt the clear-cutting of old-growth forests, leaving the mountain caribou in the safety of their natural habitat. Nor was it to enact powerful climate change legislation to counter the reduction of snowpack. The reaction was instead to hunt wolves. Alex knew that more than a thousand wolves had been killed by government-sponsored hunters to reduce predation of caribou.

Feeling sick at the thought, she stared into the dark trees where the wolf had vanished. Just then a semi passed her, the wave of concussive air buffeting the Jeep as he sped by.

Hail pinged off the windows and metal of the Jeep, collecting on the ground and giving the illusion of a thin blanket of snow in the dark.

No other cars came from the opposite direction, but another semi came into view behind her. She squinted in the glare of its lights reflecting in her mirrors. It braked as it passed her, slowing, piled high with immense strapped-down logs, then fell out of sight over a rise.

Soon the hail became smaller and then stopped altogether. But the rain continued, walls of gray drifting across the road and gushing in torrents in the gutters. When visibility returned, Alex pulled back onto the road. Now it became a lonely, dark drive. No other cars emerged from the opposite direction, and she didn't see any headlights behind her.

She topped a rise and spotted the logging truck that had passed her idling in another wide pull-off area, a place where motorists could attach chains to their tires during a snowstorm. She passed it and continued toward Bellamy Falls. She'd been driving for about twenty minutes, not seeing anyone else on the road, singing along with an oldies station she'd found on the radio, when the headlights appeared behind her.

They grew closer and closer until they blinded her. She flipped the little tab on the rearview mirror to deflect the glare. The other driver drew dangerously close. If she had to slam on her brakes for a deer, the guy would definitely rear-end her.

She studied the road ahead, a long stretch with no turns, and a dotted yellow line that indicated he could pass if he wanted to. But he didn't. He just barreled down behind her. She could tell it was a truck, and a big one. A semi. She leaned awkwardly in her seat, trying to move out of the glare streaming in from the driver's-side mirror.

She glanced at her speedometer. It wasn't like she was going under the speed limit.

The road continued straight for almost a mile before it started to ascend again. A pull-out appeared for slow-moving vehicles, and Alex eased into it.

The truck raced by, and she saw it was the logging truck that had passed her previously.

With blessed darkness replacing the truck's dazzling head-lights, she pulled back onto the road. Towing the trailer, the Jeep was slow to build up speed again on the steep incline, but eventually she crested the hill and gained momentum on the other side.

With her headlights piercing the rainstorm ahead of her, she saw that she was in the burn scar again. Her beams flashed over the giant piles of blackened logs stacked up on both sides of the road. It grew steep here, a series of switchbacks up the mountain. She reached the bottom switchback, her Jeep slowing under the weight of the trailer. She remembered that at least five switchbacks lay above her, and settled in for a laborious trek up the steepest part of the drive.

She'd just rounded the first hairpin turn when the rain picked up again, thundering down on the roof of her car and streaming in rivulets across the asphalt. She slowed. The road here was narrow, no pull-outs, so she just continued to power forward.

Then movement caught her eye on the steep mountainside to her left. She stared up to see gigantic logs tumbling down the mountain there, crashing onto the road above and then spinning off onto the other side, careening down the rest of the way, aiming directly toward her.

Alex slammed on the brakes, her Jeep hydroplaning to the side, and for a heart-stopping moment she thought the weight of the trailer was going to swing off the road and pull her down the mountain along with the tumbling logs. She stared up the slope and slammed the Jeep into reverse when she saw logs bearing down on her. The trailer almost jackknifed in her haste to back up, and she swerved, trying to angle the Jeep in the right direction even as the first of the logs reached her section of road. It barely missed her, the trunk bouncing on the asphalt and then spinning away into the darkness.

She kept backing up, but wasn't so lucky with the next log. It struck her front fender, the force of the blow rocking Alex in her seat. Then it tumbled away out of sight. She kept backing up as one log after another crashed down the slope above her, narrowly missing her car. She didn't know what she was going to do when she reached the hairpin she'd taken earlier. No way could she back up at any kind of speed, not with the trailer attached.

But then the last of the logs rolled by. Alex waited, heart jackhammering. But no others came into sight.

She gripped the wheel, amazed and relieved she'd managed to evade most of the giant logs.

She peered up in the darkness, but couldn't see much of the mountain in the gloom. Fishing around in her daypack, she pulled out her headlamp and shone it upward. The mountain had been almost completely denuded of trees, just as she had remembered from this stretch in the daylight. She thought of those piles of blackened trees that had been cut down and stacked in neat piles. One of the piles must have come loose in the downpour, which had probably destabilized the bare soil beneath it.

But those logs had been stacked perpendicular to the road. Still, it was possible they'd come loose and somehow shifted to roll parallel down the mountain.

Leaning over the passenger seat, she shone her headlamp down that side of the car. The log that had struck her Jeep, slowed by the impact, had come to rest just below the road on a sawed-off tree stump. Alex directed the beam along its length and frowned. It wasn't blackened. The tree had never burned. Its bark was still brown, lichen clinging to it in some places.

She slid all the way into the passenger seat and pulled a giant Maglite out from the back seat. Its strong beam pierced the darkness all the way to the switchback below her, where a tangle of logs had come to rest at the bottom of the incline. None of them had burned, the beam of light revealing only healthy brown bark. She replaced the Maglite and shifted back to the driver's side. So if the logs weren't one of the piles the burn crews had made, then where had they come from?

Once again she peered up the mountain toward the other switchbacks, seeing nothing but the blackened mountainside.

She put her Jeep into drive and continued up the slope, taking the next hairpin turn, constantly on alert for more tumbling logs.

The rain thundered on the Jeep roof. With no trees or vegetation to hold the soil in place, mud slid down onto the road, moving in brown rivulets against the black of the slick asphalt. Alex started to worry about a landslide and wanted to get off this steep section as soon as possible. She reached the next hairpin turn, taking it slowly, checking on the trailer in the rearview mirror. She had only two more switchbacks to go, and she'd be up. Water streamed across the road, carrying with it rocks and mud. She briefly thought of waiting for the rain to ease, but if a landslide was going to happen, hanging out there in the middle of the road was the worst place to be. She kept climbing.

A solid ooze of mud flashed onto the road and Alex had to slow as she drove over it. Suddenly her steering became sluggish and pulled to one side, and for a second she thought the muddy sludge had snagged her back wheels or the trailer and was pulling her down. She fought with the steering, the wheel heavy in her hands. When she reached the next turn in the road, she found the car so unresponsive she knew something was wrong.

Coming to a stop and putting on the emergency brake, she stared at the winding road above her. Just one more switchback to go. She grabbed her rain gear out of her pack and donned the jacket. Flipping up the parka hood, she stepped outside.

Gazing down at the car, she immediately saw the problem. One of her tires had gone flat. She frowned, debating whether she should just keep driving, get past this inundated, wet soil that was slowly slithering down off the mountain. If the rain got any heavier, it would definitely turn into a landslide, blocking off the road and possibly taking her with it. She knelt down by the tire, wondering if she'd driven over something. And then the beam of her headlamp fell on a small, dark hole in the wall of the tire. She knelt down for a closer look.

It was no nail she'd driven over. Her tire had been shot out.

She rocked back on her heels. She hadn't heard a shot; the thundering of rain on her car roof must have drowned it out. Earlier she'd passed those road signs that someone had shot up. Maybe someone had been out, aiming for the sign, but accidentally got her instead, and it had just taken a few minutes for the tire to go completely flat. If they'd fired from some distance, the shot would have been even harder to hear over the car engine and rainstorm. It had probably happened a while ago. But even as she thought that, an eerie feeling crept up her back. She glanced around, suddenly nervous.

She could feel someone's eyes on her, watching her.

Then she heard it. Above the din of the pattering rain and the hiss of rivulets of water and mud sliding down the mountain. An engine. Revving. She followed the noise to the very top switchback and saw lights flick on, red taillights and white headlights belonging to the logging truck. It had been idling there in the dark, all its lights off, the engine noise drowned out by the rain, but now that it was pulling away, she could see and hear it.

Only now she could see that the truck held no logs. Was it a different truck? Or had its logs spilled down the mountain, almost taking her out? And when that hadn't worked, had the driver stopped? Taken a shot at her car, hoping she'd career off the side of the mountain?

Fear crept into Alex's gut. Quickly she rushed back to the driver's door and climbed in. As she watched the truck pull away, continuing down the road and out of sight, she had a decision to make. Should she struggle to change the tire here on an incline, out in the open, where anyone could take another shot at her? Or should she continue to drive up to the top of the road, to change the tire on level ground, above the burn scar, where trees could offer some shelter?

She pulled her phone out of her pack. No signal. She wasn't surprised. She hadn't had one for much of the drive out to Conservation Washington. So much for calling AAA or Sheriff Taggert.

Finally, she decided to keep going up the hill. It would be tough to maneuver, but better than getting shot out in the open or waiting for a landslide to bring the whole mountain down on top of her. She eased the Jeep around the penultimate hairpin turn and up the last switchback. Then she was taking the acute turn at the top, the sluggish Jeep and trailer fighting her the whole way. But she made it onto level ground. Here the road stretched out before her in a straight line. Trees towered above her on both sides. She reached the pull-out where the truck had been idling. She stopped and switched off her lights. Waited. Listened. She didn't hear another engine or see any lights in the distance. Of course, the guy could be waiting in the dark. Alex had to make this quick.

She donned her headlamp again and jumped out, not switching it on yet. In the back, she could barely open the rear door with the trailer attached, so she had to squeeze in and feel around in the dark Jeep for the compartment that held the jack and tire iron. She found them and quietly pressed the back door closed.

Moving quickly to the tire in question, she slipped the tire iron over the first lug nut and stood on it, loosening it. She did this for all four lug nuts, then slid the jack under the car. It was hard work in the dark, and her hands and strands of her hair quickly got soaked as she worked. She could feel the cold rain seeping in through her socks, soaking the insides of her boots. With the car raised, she removed the lug nuts. Quickly she returned to the rear of the car where the spare hung, feeling exposed. She unzipped the wheel cover and used the tire iron to detach the spare.

Rolling the tire to the front of the car, she put on the spare, which thankfully was a full-sized wheel and not a small doughnut spare. When she'd attached it, she lowered the jack, then used her weight on the tire iron again to cinch the lug nuts down tight.

All the while she listened to the roar and hiss of the rain, tried to hear above the drumming on the car's hood and roof.

She was almost done when she heard the unmistakable sound of a shot pinging off metal. She hit the ground and rolled under the car, the scent of wet asphalt strong as she pressed her face against the road. Another shot rang off metal. Then she heard it again, the faintest sound of a truck accelerating some distance away. She peered out from under the Jeep, not seeing any head- or taillights. She sniffed the air for a hint of exhaust, but smelled only wet soil and ozone.

Her heart hammered. She longed to shimmy out, jump in the driver's seat, and get the hell out of there. But she didn't want to leave the old tire. The bullet was probably still inside it, and she wanted to know who the hell was shooting at her, if it was just some local kids trying to scare her, or something more calculated.

She thought of the angry logger, Clyde Fergus. Had he or one of his buddies been driving the truck? They might have picked up some work transporting logs while waiting for the moratorium to end. She knew Fergus was no fan of the land trust, and that the land trust's influence could sway a judge to rule in favor of ending the logging permanently.

Alex stayed pressed to the road, underneath the car, the cold rain soaking through her jeans. At least she had her rain parka on and her upper body was dry. She didn't want to wait too long, though, in case whoever was out there was aiming for a better angle on her. When she'd waited a couple more minutes without the sound of a shot, she scrambled out, grabbed the damaged tire, wrenched open the driver's door, and threw the tire into the passenger footwell. Then she hopped inside and started up the engine, roaring out of the pull-out.

She didn't hear any more shots, and hoped that whoever it was wouldn't shoot out another tire. She sped up, taking the road as fast as she safely could in the downpour. The last thing she wanted to do was hydroplane out of control and end up in a ditch.

As she gained some distance, she kept expecting to catch up with the taillights of the truck, but she didn't.

When she reached Bellamy Falls, she stopped at the sheriff's station. Taggert was just leaving for the night, making her way through the parking lot.

Alex pulled up beside her. "Sheriff Taggert?"

"Hi, Dr. Carter."

"I just had quite the experience. Can you take a look at something for me?"

Taggert put her hands on her hips. "Sure."

Alex shut off the engine and hopped out, coming around to the passenger side. "Someone just took some shots at me out on that steep switchback section of road."

"Seriously?"

"Yeah. At first I thought it might have been kids, shooting at signs and accidentally hitting my tire. But then someone fired at me on purpose. And that's not all." She told her about the logging truck she'd seen and the unburned logs tumbling down the mountain and striking the car. "Maybe the logs were an accident. I don't know. But I saw a truck without logs on the mountain above me."

Alex hefted the old tire out of the Jeep and stood it up next to Taggert. "There might be a bullet inside this. Can you see what you can find out?"

Taggert placed her hand on the tire, rolling it closer. "Unbelievable. Of course. In the meantime, come inside and make a statement."

Alex followed the sheriff into the station, and at the front desk filled out a form describing what had happened to her. When she left, Taggert walked her to the door. "I'll get a tech to remove the bullet. See if we get any leads."

"Thanks, Sheriff." Alex liked Taggert, found her kind and helpful. "You have a good night." She exited and returned to her Jeep, heading back for the ranch house.

Rain still poured down when she got home, so Alex left the trailer with its tarp attached, deciding to unload the lichen in the morning if it had stopped raining.

She slept fitfully, her mind tossing between the postcard she'd received and visions of logs pummeling down toward her.

ALEX WOKE FEELING A LITTLE tired. It had stopped raining, so after she dressed, she unloaded the bags of lichen from the trailer, storing them in the house's pantry for now.

She made tea and grabbed a quick energy bar for breakfast, pocketing a couple more for later in the day. Then she packed up supplies for another day out on the preserve. She wanted to check out those areas of old growth she'd spotted on the satellite images.

Before she set out, she decided to call her dad. He answered on the third ring.

"Pumpkin! How are you?"

"I'm good, Dad." Wanting to respect her privacy, he probably hadn't read the postcard. She decided not to mention it or her experience on the road. She didn't want to worry him. "About to head out to try and put a collar camera on the caribou. It's definitely here somewhere. I've seen its tracks."

"That's great, honey! Good luck! I've got some good news, too."

"Oh, yes?"

"I got accepted into the Grand Canyon plein air festival! I just arrived."

Alex knew it was quite a feather in his cap to be accepted. "That's great, Dad! Congratulations!"

"Thanks, pumpkin."

"So what all does being a guest entail?"

"I'll hike around to different vistas along the rim with my field box and paint landscapes. I'm on the South Rim right now, but next week I'll be on the North Rim. I just get to sit, watch the light creep over the canyon, drink in all the colors of gold, red, and orange."

"Your job is such a difficult ordeal, Dad."

He laughed. "I don't know how I'll survive. Then a couple times a week, I'll do demonstration paintings for the public. They come along and stand behind me while I paint, staring at the easel, asking questions. It's a little intimidating."

"But you're such a great painter. I bet they'll be blown away."

"Some of them can be sharp as tacks. Painters themselves. I remember one fellow in Zion a couple years ago who was a bit of a nitpicker. But mostly observers pick up on little tips and tricks I show them. Then at the end of the festival in a couple weeks, we'll have an art show where people can bid on the paintings."

"That's fabulous, Dad. I'd love to be there."

"Guess we both get to look at some gorgeous scenery right now."

"Definitely." She went quiet for a moment.

"Is everything okay?"

Her mind churned. *Postcard. Missing hiker. Angry logger. Strange light in the sky.* She snapped herself out of her apprehensive feeling. She had a caribou to find. "Yes. Absolutely."

"Let me know how it goes out there."

"Will do. And enjoy being at the canyon."

"Thanks, honey."

They hung up and Alex returned to her pack, where she'd left it by the back door. She made sure the tranquilizer gun was affixed firmly to the side of it. Then she slung on the pack, secured the chest and hip straps, and locked the door behind her.

As the morning sun streamed through the trees, she set off in search of the elusive caribou. Soon she was ascending and descending the steep terrain of the preserve, breathing in the fresh air. The recent rain had left the ground spongy, reflective droplets of water collecting on the delicate fronds of emerald-green ferns.

She kept a special eye out for lichen species. She loved all the creative names and shapes for lichen in the area, like deep-purple peppered moon lichen and the intricate chambers of netted speckle-belly lichen, and wrinkled gray cryptic paw lichen.

She smiled as she hiked, feeling the sun on her face as she crossed a meadow. The forest felt teeming with life. Birds sang, grasshoppers buzzed, bees pollinated the vibrant wildflowers. Right about now, female caribou would be raising their young calves. Females gave birth in late spring and early summer, choosing high-elevation locations near ridges with old-growth forests, and high-altitude mountain basins. This enabled them to evade predators, though at the risk of having less nutritious food. During this time, the females returned to tree-growing lichen as they had during the winter. Other caribou during these warmer months also shifted back upslope, feeding in high-elevation forests.

As she hiked, she thought about this lone caribou, wondering if it had a calf.

Before the South Selkirk population had vanished, their range was estimated at being just over 19,000 acres. But their current range was vastly diminished from historical records.

Originally, the southern mountain caribou population roamed in connected habitats where, prior to the 1900s, observers wrote that so many of the mountain caribou existed, they blackened the mountainsides. However, due to habitat fragmentation, the population became isolated and broke off into fifteen groups, some of which then died out. Alex had read recent research that estimated thirteen of these original fifteen groups would be extinct in the next fifty years.

She stepped over massive fallen logs covered in moss, small trees growing from their bones. Nurse logs, botanists called them. Lush plants covered the forest floor, and she delighted in the delicate fronds of brilliantly green *Dryopteris filix-mas*. It was weirdly called "the male fern," as for years it was mistakenly thought to be the male version of the common lady fern, or *Athyrium filix-femina*.

Mist soon descended to the forest floor, and she found herself in a gray, dreamy landscape, feeling like something magical could happen at any moment. A dragon could swirl out of the mists. *Or even,* she thought, *I could meet the elusive gray ghost of the forest.*

She continued on, smiling to herself.

And then the mists did part, and in front of her, not fifty feet away, stood the caribou.

Alex stopped in her tracks, her eyes wide, a thrill moving through her very core. The caribou watched her with its soft golden eyes, then bent to strip some leaves off a creeping snowberry bush.

He was a bull with a gorgeous set of antlers, and he returned his wary eye to her as she held her breath, not daring to move. After deciding she wasn't a threat, he bent his graceful head and stripped more leaves off the shrub. He chewed and walked away from her, tearing off more leaves and nibbling at the bed of moss and lichen on the forest floor. Alex saw that he was a large caribou, standing a little over four feet at the shoulder. She estimated his weight at four hundred pounds.

The mists shifted, fog swirling magically, hiding him.

Alex moved forward quietly, the soft bed beneath her feet muffling her steps. She could hear the bull chewing and pulling vegetation off the forest floor in front of her but couldn't see him. She could hear him stomp his hooves as he shifted his weight.

She filled a tranquilizer dart with the correct dosage for his estimated weight and then quietly, slowly swung the tranq gun out in front of her. The mists parted and she saw the caribou again. She hated to do this, hated to scare him, but if attaching a collar camera could help his survival, she had to. Carefully she took aim at his rump and fired. The dart hit home and the caribou startled and began running through the forest.

Alex took off in pursuit.

SEVEN

Not wanting to add to the caribou's fright, Alex hung back as the tranquilizer took effect. She knew it would take about three to five minutes. The caribou slowed, then stopped, standing groggily, eyes blinking. Then his front legs folded and his body lowered to the ground. He slumped completely, eyes closing.

Only then did Alex approach him. Normally she would have a team to handle such a large animal, but she didn't have that luxury. She slung off her pack and set it down next to the caribou's head.

Rummaging through the pack, she pulled out a soft eye mask and slipped it over the caribou's face. She attached the supplemental oxygen. Then she took quick measurements of his length and width in order to more accurately judge his weight. She glanced at his teeth, finding them healthy.

Then she pulled out one of the collar cameras and switched it on, programming it to take ten seconds of footage every two hours. Such short bursts of video would lengthen the life of the battery. Gently she attached the collar so that it hung loosely on the caribou's neck and wouldn't restrict his movements.

She sat next to him then, feeling his warm breath snorting out of his nostrils. She examined his eyes for the presence of parasites like *Besnoitia* and inspected him for signs of botfly infestation but found none. Then she swabbed inside the nostrils to check for *Mycoplasma ovipneumoniae*, or *M. ovi*, as researchers called it, a bacterium that could lead to respiratory disease. She stowed the swabs in a specialized container, then took a clipping of the caribou's fur, gathered a fecal sample, and took a vial of his blood. A lab could run tests on these samples to glean all kinds of information: levels of the stress hormone cortisol, presence of toxins, disease, diet, and more.

She monitored his heart rate, blood oxygen level, and soft breathing, ensuring he wasn't suffering any ill effects from the tranquilizer. She took in his velvety antlers. The caribou really was a beautiful animal.

Mountain caribou were polygynous, or in other words, bulls competed to breed with multiple cows in the fall. These handsome antlers would serve him well if he found a mate.

Caribou typically lived for about eight to ten years, and because females gave birth to only a single calf each year, and didn't start until they were three years old, the reproductive rate was not as high as for other deer species. Add to that that the chance of survival for baby caribou was a mere 30 to 50 percent, and it was easy for Alex to see how perilous their situation was, with added factors such as climate change, deforestation, and unprecedented predation. Lack of food during a cow's pregnancy meant that calves were often born weak and susceptible to disease.

Alex hoped that this bull would find a mate come fall.

Finished with taking samples, she administered the reversal agents to counteract the sedation. He began to stir, trying to lift his groggy head, and Alex removed the eye mask and supplemental oxygen. Then she grabbed her pack and stepped away. Taking up a position behind a massive western hemlock, she kept watch on him. She definitely didn't want wolves or mountain lions finding the caribou in his dazed state.

He got to his feet and shook his head, then stood for a few minutes, blinking. Finally the caribou moved off into the misty forest and Alex tracked him for some time, just to be sure he had no ill effects from the drug. But soon he was browsing on shrubs normally and pulling down low-hanging lichen from the trees.

She smiled and breathed a sigh of relief. Now she'd be able to determine his movements. Maybe even see if he wasn't alone. She grinned. The caribou was here. The gray ghost of the forest. And she knew she would fight with everything in her to see he was protected.

ON HER WAY BACK TO the ranch house, Alex swung by one of the cameras. She detached its padlock and flipped open the housing.

Suddenly a chill crept up her back, a feeling that she was being watched.

She paused beside the camera, sensing eyes boring into her back. She spun but saw only the forest behind her: mossy logs, huge trees, ferns dappled in sunlight. Hesitantly, she turned back and powered up the camera's screen. Checking the battery life and memory card space, she found both in good shape. She stood there, flipping through the recent photos. Several showed white-tailed deer passing by. A raven landed on a branch in the tree opposite. A fisher climbed that same tree a few minutes later. But no gray ghost.

She shut the camera and made a note in her field journal about the date and time she'd stopped by the camera and how full it was. Pulling out her GPS, she brought up the location of the next closest camera. She slung her backpack on and headed that way.

She hadn't gone more than a hundred feet when the feeling of being watched returned. This time she casually looked around instead of spinning, in the hopes of spotting whoever it was. She paused, pretending to look down at her GPS unit, then raised it and turned slowly, as if she were trying to acquire a signal. In her peripheral vision, she gazed around, not seeing anyone.

The uneasy feeling persisted, and her mind flashed to the murdered ranger found in the park. Alex's body gave an involuntary shudder. She reached down for her bear spray, unsnapping its holster. Somewhere out here, a killer could be stalking through the trees. She lowered her GPS unit, resting her right hand casually on the bear spray. She started walking again. The closer she got to the next camera, the more the sensation faded.

Somehow, she thought, she had walked out of the person's territory.

She picked up her pace, wanting to leave that feeling of being watched far behind her. But as she moved through another cluster of old growth, it returned once more. Was someone following her?

She employed the same trick again, lifting her GPS and moving in a slow circle as if she were trying to get a signal. A flicker of movement from behind a tree about twenty feet away caught her eye: a flash of clothing, before someone ducked back behind the massive trunk. Immediately Alex pulled out her bear spray. She paused, unsure of what to do. The person was trespassing on the preserve. They could be a poacher with a gun. She had only her bear spray and a currently unloaded tranq gun. Her heart thumped in her chest.

Part of her wanted to confront the person now, while she was aware of his location, instead of later, when he could sneak up on her again. She wanted to know what he was doing here, why he'd been watching her. She took a hesitant step toward the tree, bear spray out and ready. It had a range of thirty to sixty feet, and her finger rested on the trigger, ready to blast the guy with it.

She took another step. Suddenly the man stepped out from behind the tree. Their eyes met. He was the same man who'd had the rifle earlier and been digging around with the camp shovel. His hair hung in long, dirty strands past his shoulders. His pale face, smeared with mud, stared out at her. His cheekbones jutted out from a shrewd face, and he met her gaze unflinchingly. She could see the rifle's barrel right now, peeking out from behind one shoulder from where it was strapped to his back.

"Who are you?" she asked.

He stared at her for a few more moments before turning his back and walking away into the forest. She watched after him, filled with indecision. He went up to the top of the rise, onto national forest land, and disappeared on the other side.

Alex still held out the canister of bear spray. Finally she holstered it but continued to stare after him, waiting to see if he'd come back. The feeling of being watched had completely faded now. She took the opportunity to load another tranquilizer dart into the rifle.

Creeped out, she turned and resumed the long hike back to the ranch house, along a segment in which the national forest cut into preserve land. She could either stick to the preserve, going the long way around, or take the shortcut across federal land. She opted for the fast route, trying to fight off the bad feeling. The man was probably a squatter in the national forest. The fact that he was armed and crossing onto the preserve made her uncomfortable. But maybe he wasn't poaching. Maybe he was just someone who had parted with society and was trying to survive out here away from people. She'd definitely mention him to the sheriff now. Maybe Taggert was already aware of him.

Trying to lift her spirits, Alex thought back to the caribou. She couldn't wait to download the first batch of footage from the collar camera.

With only a couple hours of daylight left, she knew that the camera wouldn't have many images from this first day, but she hoped it was working properly. She didn't dare dream that more than one caribou might have ventured down here, but it was just possible.

A light mist began to fall, and droplets collected in strands of her hair. She lifted her face to the sky, the cool moisture welcome on her skin after a hot day of hiking. The precipitation cheered her. She'd always loved gray, rainy days.

She grew so happy and was walking so quickly, eager to get back to Wi-Fi so she could connect with the camera, that she almost tripped across a thin wire strung between two trees.

Alex drew up short, almost losing her balance, catching her boot just before it would have tripped the wire.

She looked to where the cable led to a bell hanging from a tree.

It was a booby trap alarm.

EIGHT

Gingerly Alex stepped over the wire, becoming hyperaware of other traps that could be in the area. She stepped carefully between the tree trunks, judging each patch of lichen and moss before she set her boot down.

Between other pairs of trees, she found additional wires connected to bells that hung from low branches.

She stopped to examine them, wondering who could have set them up. Then a dark hole beneath a moss-covered fallen tree caught her eye. At first she thought it might be a fox den, and crept closer. Branches lay over most of the entrance, revealing only a two-foot section of the opening. She lifted a few of the branches aside, finding a much bigger tunnel disappearing down beneath the huge fallen tree. Fresh dirt lay at the entrance, recently excavated. She searched for the customary tiny bones and other detritus left by foxes but saw none.

Moving aside two more branches, she discovered the tunnel was big enough for her to crawl into. Something about it felt unnatural, and not just because it was surrounded by booby traps.

For a long moment, she crouched and listened to the forest around her, eyes and ears alert for any hint of movement. Could this be the dwelling place of the squatter? Or was it just an animal den? She thought of the missing hiker, Amelia Fairweather. Maybe she'd decided to leave society, too? Live out here? Alex had been asked to keep an eye out for her or her belongings. She debated, staring at the dark hole. If no one was around, she could take a quick look.

A Steller's jay cawed from the trees, and a mountain chickadee whistled out a garbled series of notes. They didn't seem alarmed. Alex didn't sense other humans were around.

She shucked off her pack and pulled out her headlamp. After strapping it on, she got down on her hands and knees and shone the beam inside the hole. The light fell on a red flannel shirt lying neatly folded about six feet in. She pulled her head out and again listened intently to the forest around her. Several chickadees conversed. The light mist continued to fall. She didn't hear any movement.

Grabbing her tranquilizer gun, she held it in front of her. Then she stuck her head back into the tunnel and crawled a few feet inside. It veered away to the left, and she followed it, hands pressing into the soft, cool dirt.

This is crazy, she thought. *I should go back.*

And then the tunnel opened up into a large room. Branches shored up the walls. An old rug covered the dirt floor. An army cot stood in one corner with a makeshift table made of ammo boxes next to it. The table held two flashlights, batteries, and a Sterno stove, along with a Zippo lighter engraved with the same spiral design that was on the compass she'd found. The cot lay buried beneath dirty blankets and a filthy pillow. An old cardboard box crammed with worn paperback books took up another corner.

She didn't see any of Amelia's items the sheriff had described. Canned food stood stacked against one wall, along with a rusty can opener. And next to the can opener, Alex spotted her multitool.

She hurried to it and picked it up, seeing the familiar engraving: *Alex Carter—Adventure Awaits.*

A sudden overwhelming feeling of dread swept over her. This didn't feel like a place where an outdoor-loving plant nursery owner would hole up. It felt desperate and lonely, the refuge of someone who had left society behind out of some deep wound. She turned around and scrambled out of the tunnel into the daylight, sucking in the fresh air. She panted, catching her breath, and then held it and listened, scanning the forest for any hint of movement.

Then she ducked low against the massive fallen tree and scampered to her pack. Throwing it on and keeping the tranq gun handy, she moved away from the tunnel, watching for additional wires and traps. She almost triggered another bell alarm and stepped over it just in time. Before she left the area, she took a GPS reading and saved the recording.

Then she walked away hurriedly, constantly checking behind her.

As Alex hiked back, the light mist turned into a heavier rain. She pulled up her rain parka hood and listened to the droplets cascading onto the material, a sound that had always soothed her. But her mind kept churning back to the strange tunnel and the man with the rifle. The tunnel had been on national forest land, not on the preserve, but she'd tell the sheriff about it anyway.

The forest grew darker around her as the sun dipped behind the jagged peaks. Shadows crept over the forest floor. Alex loved this time of day, the gloaming, when day and night existed at the same time, a magical liminal period when anything felt possible. The rain stopped, clouds drifting away, and she perked up a little as an almost full moon rose over peaks to the east, casting a silvery glow on the treetops above her.

As it often did after long hikes, her mind turned to dinner. She wasn't a big eater, but being out in nature always perked up her appetite. When she'd lived in Boston, she'd eaten only once a day. She realized now she'd been heartsick there. Separated from nature, she'd felt the joy leach out of her life. But here, she felt whole again.

Just then she heard a lone wolf howl, its haunting notes fading away into the night. Moments later, another wolf answered, then both joined together for a duet. She broke into a grin, resisting the urge to belt out her own howl. The long notes trailed off. She worried about them, too. Wolves certainly had their share of hardship.

At last the ranch house came into view, and Alex let herself in. She slid off her heavy pack near the back door, suddenly feeling so light she could float up to the ceiling. She stretched, her aching shoulder and back muscles stiff, and rubbed them.

Then she called the sheriff.

"Taggert," the woman said after the second ring.

"Hi, Sheriff. It's Alex Carter, up at the Selkirk Wildlife Sanctuary."

"Oh, hello, Alex."

"Listen, I don't know if this has anything to do with the missing hiker or the ranger, but I ran across someone out there. He's a bit worse for the wear. Maybe a squatter. Found a tunnel he might be living in. I didn't see any signs of Amelia's things there, but I thought maybe you'd want to know. I've got the coordinates, if you like."

"Read them off to me."

Alex grabbed her GPS unit and related the lat/long.

"That on national forest land or the preserve?"

"National forest."

"I'll ask a law enforcement ranger to check them out, then."

"Okay. I've got a photo of him, too. I can email it to you."

"Can you do that now?"

"Sure." Alex moved to her laptop and pulled the image off her camera's memory card. Then she sent it off.

She heard the sheriff's email ping on the other side. "Just a sec." A minute later she came back. "I don't recognize him. But I'll stay on it. Thanks for letting me know."

"Sorry it's not more helpful."

"Hey, we got the result on that ammo pulled out of your tire. It was a .308, probably from a hunting rifle. But the ballistics didn't match any cases we've got on file. You had anyone take another shot at you?"

"No, thankfully."

"Okay. I'll keep you posted if I learn anything else."

"Thanks, Sheriff."

They hung up and Alex fixed a cup of hot tea. Eager to check the collar camera footage that had been uploaded so far, she stood at the counter and wolfed down a hastily made black bean burrito.

Then she moved to her laptop, booted it up, and connected to the server that held the footage. To save on batteries, the camera was programmed to upload only once a day, at ten P.M. Alex checked her laptop's clock. Ten minutes ago. She logged on and grinned to find several files waiting. She clicked on each one, thrilled to see that the camera was working perfectly.

Each video ran only ten seconds long. By watching them, she experienced a slice of the caribou's day. The camera hung so that she could see out from beneath his chin. The first video featured him lying down and resting. He had tucked his head along the side of his body so that she could see one hoof nestled amid a bed of moss and lichen. She clicked on the next file. Now the caribou meandered across the forest floor, nibbling on shrubs and lichen as he went. She could see his chin moving with the motion of chewing.

When she'd gone through the available files and written down the GPS coordinates of various spots the caribou had visited, Alex leaned back and grinned. Now she would get a good idea of how the caribou spent his days, where he foraged, and what he dined on. She could also learn what predators might be present, and how much time he spent locomoting versus other activities such as napping or expending energy to avoid insects. She'd hoped to possibly see him in the company of other caribou, but so far, he seemed to be the only one.

She glanced at her watch. It was too late to call Ben on the East Coast, but not too late to reach Zoe, who was a night owl.

After powering down her laptop, she moved to the kitchen and sat down by the landline. She called her friend, smiling when Zoe picked up. "Hey, Zoe!"

"Alex! How are things?"

"Pretty good! I found the caribou today! Even managed to fit it with a collar camera."

"So now it can take selfies?"

Alex laughed. "Yep. And send them straight to me."

"Easy-peasy. What else? Any news on the missing hiker or the body in the park?"

"No, nothing yet. But I did run across something weird today."

"You? Run across something weird?" Zoe laughed.

"There's this guy I've seen a couple of times now. I think he's a squatter. He's a little creepy. Found this tunnel where he might be living."

"What? Like out in the woods?"

"Yeah. It had a bed and books, a camp stove. And he'd taken my multitool."

"What?"

"I dropped it somewhere. He must have found it."

"Or he picked your pocket," Zoe said, alarmed.

"I don't think he got that close. At least I hope not!"

"Do you think he's dangerous?"

"I don't know," Alex said, biting her lip. "I told the sheriff about the tunnel in case she wanted to check it out in connection with the murder and the missing hiker."

"I'd be out of there so fast!"

"It's definitely eerie, but I want to see this caribou thing through. So how about you?" Alex asked, wanting to change the subject. She didn't want to needlessly worry her friend. "Any more incidents of sabotage?"

"Totally. Conditions on the set are seriously wonky. I'm beginning to think this shoot is cursed."

"What's been happening?"

"For one thing, the heating and cooling system keeps going on the fritz. The AC will kick on full blast, but only in certain spots. So you're sitting there, going over your lines, comfortable as a bug in a rug, and suddenly this blast of cold air hits you and you're shivering so much your lips are turning blue. It's been happening all over the set."

"Weird!"

"And then there's the smell."

"The smell?"

"Yeah. We're on set yesterday, and suddenly this stench starts wafting across the place, like some kind of silent but deadly reek creeping up from the sewers. I could see it hitting the crew like an invisible wave. First the gaffers start gagging, then the puppeteers start pulling their shirts up over their noses, then this guy in a motion capture suit punches a key grip in the arm, thinking the poor guy just let one loose or something. Then it hits me and the director, sitting in our chairs behind the camera. And I mean this is a *stench*. I immediately start gagging. A PA threw up into an empty coffee cup she was carrying, only it wasn't big enough, and this reek continues to roll through the set until it's pervaded the whole place and we have to roll up the big docking doors and run for our lives, eyes streaming. It even got into my trailer."

"Eww. What was it?"

"No one knows. A stink bomb? C.H.U.D.?"

"C.H.U.D.?"

"You know, cannibalistic humanoid underground dwellers? We couldn't resume filming that day. The fire department had to come down and make sure it wasn't a gas leak or something. They couldn't find anything, but I noticed one fireman take off his face mask and immediately slap it back on. I thought he was going to throw up inside that thing."

"That's awful!"

"It was. I have no idea what's going on with this movie. Between all these things going wrong, we're already five days behind schedule, and we only have a thirty-six-day shooting schedule for principal photography as it is."

"Sorry things are going so rough there!"

"Thanks. The life of an actor. You have no idea of the stress." Zoe laughed, self-conscious.

"So what's next?" Alex asked.

"Wire work. I get to be suspended in front of this gigantic green screen tomorrow, facing off against the alien puppet."

"Sounds exciting."

"I'm kind of looking forward to it." Alex heard someone knock on Zoe's trailer door. "Oh, shoot. Miranda's here. She's the script supervisor. She wants to go over the shot list for tomorrow."

"I'll let you go. Break a leg!"

"You too. Oh, wait—no! Don't break a leg out there. Please don't do that."

Alex smiled. "I'll try to avoid it."

"Call soon. I worry about you. And I have no way to reach you except some old-fashioned landline that doesn't even have an answering machine or voicemail."

"It's like it's the twentieth century over here. I don't know how I'll survive in such rugged conditions."

"Take care!"

"You too."

Alex returned to her laptop, recording the coordinates from the collar camera into her GPS unit. Tomorrow she'd hike out to those spots and look for signs of other caribou. She could also make note of what vegetation the caribou browsed most heavily, see what the land trust could do to improve habitat for him, and if any invasive vegetation was crowding out the preferred food.

She climbed the stairs to the bedroom and stood for a long moment staring out, wondering if she'd see the strange light again. But tonight the trees stood in darkness, the stars above them sweeping and vivid.

Finally she changed into her pj's and lay down to read, excited for her foray tomorrow and a better glimpse into the life of this lone, brave caribou.

THE NEXT DAY, FRESHLY SHOWERED and backpack restocked with food and water, Alex set out, her spirit light. She hiked out to the first place where the collar camera had sent back coordinates.

Her boots slid in the soil as she climbed a steep mountain slope. Witch's hair lichen hung from ancient trees, the forest floor shaded and inviting. Above her, the sun streamed down, shedding golden light on ferns and tree trunks, setting the forest aglow. But in the west, gray clouds churned, and Alex knew that it would likely rain in the next hour.

She climbed higher and higher, breathing in the crisp mountain air. Though the temperature dropped, her thermal shirt trapped in heat, keeping her warm. At last she reached the location of the first video. She spotted the place where the caribou had lain down and rested, the vegetation still flattened there. She cast around for tracks, finding two in a patch of damp soil. But most of the forest floor here was covered with a soft bed of moss and pine needles, making it difficult to spot other prints.

As she bent over, peering closely at the ground, the first patter of rain began to fall. She pulled out her rain parka and donned it, lifting the hood. She found several places where the leaves of bushes had been snipped off and recorded each plant species in a small notebook she kept in her jacket pocket.

She saw only one depression where the caribou had rested. After she'd gleaned all she could from the area, she set off for the next one, the place where the caribou had been browsing in the video.

She hiked a considerable distance, back toward the boundary of the national forest, and soon walked parallel to it. Her GPS beeped as she neared the second caribou site. She moved quietly, hoping to spot him again, but today the caribou was apparently using a different part of the property.

She snapped some photos of browsed vegetation, once again recording the species in her notebook. Scanning for tracks, she moved along the area, staring closely at the ground. This time she found only one print.

Then the sudden crunching of pine needles drew her attention to just inside the national forest, where the tree sitter was camped out.

A man stood there, staring at her.

NINE

The man wasn't the same person she'd seen before helping the activist. He was dressed in bright, colorful clothes that looked to be made of hemp. A woven beanie covered his head, long blond dreadlocks sticking out of it, framing a pale face. For a few moments he stared at her with a fearful look, then turned and took off through the trees, disappearing over a rise.

"Hey!" cried the tree sitter's voice from above her. "Hey! Come back! You pulled the rope down! Don't leave! Damn it!"

Alex heard the squawking of a radio high in the tree. "Is anyone there? Trevor panicked and ran off. He pulled the rope down. All my food is just sitting on the forest floor." The tree sitter went quiet, listening for a response. None came. "Hello?"

Alex walked around the side of the tree and found a large basket stocked with cans of nuts, bread, protein bars, fruit, some carrots, batteries, and bottles of water. A thick rope lay sprawled next to it.

"Do you need help?" Alex called up.

"Who's that?" came the reply.

"I'm a biologist from the preserve next door."

"You're a lifesaver! If I lower a rope, can you attach it to the basket?"

"Sure."

Moments later, a rope descended from the tree. Alex affixed it to the basket, and the woman—her name was Agatha, Alex recalled—lifted both back up into the tree.

"That guy is always panicking," Agatha called down. "I don't know why they keep sending him. There aren't even any loggers around right now."

"Yeah, I was here before when that angry one was threatening you."

"Oh, you're the one who created the diversion?"

"Yep."

"Thanks for that. Luckily that logger hasn't been around today. I'm so relieved. He's got it in for me."

"The other guy, Dennis, said you'd been up there for seven months. That's impressive." She thought of Julia Butterfly Hill, who spent a little over two years in the top of a California redwood named Luna, protecting it from being cut down.

"Thanks. It's been both amazing and terrifying."

"You're all part of the activist group that stalled out the logging?"

"That's right. And damn, have they been unhappy. But we just can't let them destroy this old growth. There's hardly any left in the U.S."

Alex could imagine that tempers flared among both communities, loggers and activists. "I admire your conviction."

"Thank you!" she called down. "Hey, what's your name?"

"Alex."

"I'm Agatha."

"Nice to meet you."

"You too!"

Alex turned to leave. "You take care up there."

"I will."

As she crossed back onto the preserve, Alex thought about the remaining old growth in this area, and how the lone caribou depended upon it. She hoped the trees would stay standing, and made a silent wish for the preservation of the giant tree Dennis had called Gaia, after the Greek goddess of the earth. A fitting name.

Deciding to check on the camera she'd installed where she first spotted the caribou tracks, Alex left the area and hiked along the perimeter of the preserve. Suddenly she heard a man shouting through the trees.

"Goddamnit!" he cussed. "Goddamn tree-huggers!"

She stopped, listening, trying to pinpoint his location. Voices, especially shouts, carried so far in the wilderness that it took a minute to narrow in on his location.

"Is anybody out there?" he shouted.

Alex faced the national forest. His voice was definitely coming from in there. She took a few tentative steps over the boundary, listening.

"Hey! Goddamnit! Anyone there? If you're out there right now, laughing about this, I swear to god I'm going to kill you!" the man shouted. She recognized his voice. It was the logger who had been threatening Agatha.

She followed the sound of his cursing until she came to a circle of trees. Pine needles sifted down into a small clearing. She didn't immediately see him. "Hey! You! Are you with those goddamn activists?" he shouted.

Alex realized his voice came from high up and craned her neck to see the man dangling from a net. It spun wildly.

"I'm getting sick up here. Cut me down! Then get ready to die for this!"

Alex stared up at him, at his beet-red face and bushy black beard. The guy obviously didn't know when to shut up for his own good.

"I didn't put the trap up," Alex told him.

"The hell you didn't! Then why are you here?"

"Because everyone can hear you shouting a mile away."

"Then some goddamn tree-huggers put the trap here. I'll kill 'em! You know how long I've been stuck up here?"

Alex thought of the tunnel she'd found and the booby trap alarms. And this wasn't too far from where she'd first seen the man with the rifle. She remembered him digging around in the dirt with the shovel near here. He could have been in the last stages of covering up this very trap. Alex wondered if other tunnels snaked through the forest, and how many traps he'd set up and why. She'd have to be careful.

"I've been hanging here for more than an hour! And I dropped my goddamn knife."

Alex looked down among the pine needles and spotted a folding knife, its carbon-fiber blade silver against the brown soil. She picked it up. Then moving around the clearing, she spotted the trip wire the man had triggered. Her gaze followed it up to the tree where the net hung.

She had half a mind to just cut the rope and let him drop straight to the ground. Maybe the painful thump would teach him a lesson. But if he broke something, she didn't want to have to help him out of the forest. And besides, even though this guy was pure venom, she herself was often too kindhearted for her own good.

"I'm not sure I should help you. You know anything about an unleashed load of logs?" she asked him.

He struggled inside the net, his jaw set in a stubborn expression. "I got no idea what you're talking about."

"Or someone shooting at me?"

He did a full spin, his fingers laced in the net. "What the hell are you talking about? You gonna get me down or what?"

She stared up at him, tempted to just leave him up there. But she didn't *know* he was the one who'd shot at her. Sometimes she regretted her better nature. "Okay," she called up to him. "I'm going to cut you down and try to slow your descent."

"You? You ain't got the weight to do that. Go and get help!"

She shrugged. "Suit yourself, if you want to keep spinning up there until you throw up. Might take me a while to find someone."

"Okay, fine!" he spat. "Just get me the hell down!"

The rope hung over a thick tree branch, and she traced it back to its other end, which was tied around a tree trunk. She tugged on it with all her strength to get a little slack, then wrapped it around her back. With his knife, she sawed through the thick rope. As soon as his full weight hit her, she slid in the pine needles, using her weight to slow his descent all the way to the ground.

He smacked down. Instantly he pulled at the net, struggling to stand. She helped him loosen it, and he stepped out, angrily brushing himself off. He grabbed his knife out of her hand. "When I catch the little shits who did this . . ." he started again.

She stared at the trap. "I don't think it was the activists."

"Who, then? You?" he snapped, glaring at her.

"Why the hell would I do it?"

"Who knows why the hell anybody does anything anymore! Whole world's gone crazy. People care more for some damn fool tree than a man's livelihood."

He stomped off in the direction of the logging camp without even glancing over his shoulder at her, let alone saying thanks or even goodbye.

"You're welcome!" she called at his back.

He waved a dismissive hand in the air without turning and continued to storm away.

Ego got a little hurt there, huh? she silently asked his retreating form, chuckling to herself.

She glanced around at the forest floor, wondering again if other traps lay in wait. She checked her GPS unit. She was only a quarter mile or so from her newly installed camera.

She headed out that way and found another flattened area of vegetation where the caribou had perhaps lain, as well as several areas that had been pawed up, and two more hoofprints.

Eagerly she reached the camera by the creek, hoping that it had captured an image of the caribou and any companions he might have. She unlocked it and opened the housing, scanning through the pictures. She grinned and punched a victorious fist in the air when one of the photos clearly depicted the caribou drinking from the stream. Around his neck hung the collar camera. She didn't see any other animals in the images. But she couldn't wait to send the pic to Ben.

She switched out the memory card, putting in a fresh one, then locked up the camera again.

Excited to download the latest footage and email Ben the photo, Alex hiked quickly back to the house. She didn't know what would come of this revelation. She hoped that the government would step up its efforts to protect the caribou. Or maybe the caribou would be relocated farther north into British Columbia, or other caribou moved down here to join it.

But these translocation efforts were a mixed bag. In the 1980s and '90s, several attempts were made to move caribou from Canada to supplement the South Selkirk herd. But this augmentation didn't take, and by 2018, very few of the animals had survived. So when Canada took the two remaining U.S. mountain caribou in 2019, they released them into a protected pen in British Columbia and provided them with food. They hoped that this would allow the animals to acclimate to their new environment. They then released the animals with GPS tracking collars, integrating them into the Columbia North herd in the Shuswap-Revelstoke area of British Columbia. These caribou were accompanied by four individuals translocated from the South Purcell herd, as well. But presently, the Columbia North herd was still declining.

So the struggle to conserve them continued, and Canadian First Nations, including the West Moberly, Saulteau, Athabasca Chipewyan, and Mikisew Cree First Nations, were also making concerted efforts to preserve caribou.

Alex returned to the ranch house and made a quick dinner. She sat down at her laptop, excited to download the latest footage. This time seven videos awaited her, ten seconds recorded every two hours.

She clicked through them, watching a range of behavior with delight.

In the first video the caribou stood still, ruminating. Like many other animals—including other deer, hippos, cows, and pigs—caribou were ruminants and belonged to the class Artiodactyla, or even-toed ungulates. They possessed a four-chambered stomach that allowed them to process vegetation low in nutrition. When initially eaten, food passed through into their rumen, or first stomach. They then brought this food back up and chewed on it with their back teeth. Interestingly, caribou had no front incisors on the top, but instead used an extra-thick layer of skin on the roof of their mouth to grind food against with their bottom teeth. When a caribou ruminated, it usually meant it felt safe.

Beyond the caribou's moving chin she saw the forest, patches of sunlight shining through to the forest floor. In the second video he craned his neck around to scratch his side, and in the third he ran quickly across an open meadow. He ran at full speed, bounding over logs and weaving between trees. The camera bounced haphazardly. She wondered if something had spooked him or was chasing him.

In the rest of the videos, the caribou slept, ruminated, and ate while walking. In none of the clips did she see other caribou. But that didn't necessarily mean they weren't there. She'd watched footage from collar cameras attached to the Porcupine herd that roamed in Yukon and Alaska, and though that herd of barren-ground caribou was big—thousands of members—clips often didn't show any other caribou in the same frame.

So she could still hope that more had wandered down from Canada with this individual.

Unlike their barren-ground brethren, mountain caribou did not gather in big numbers. Instead, they kept their herds small. A typical one might number only fifty or so members. And with all the challenges to their survival, herds often dwindled to far smaller numbers than that. This meant that a single incident like an avalanche could wipe out an entire herd in one go.

The sudden ringing of the phone snapped her out of her dark thoughts. She moved to the kitchen and picked up the receiver, perking up when she heard Zoe's voice on the other end.

"How are you doing?" Zoe asked her.

She took a seat at the kitchen table. "I'm doing okay." She filled Zoe in on the latest weirdness with the logger caught in the booby trap.

"Yikes! Who is this guy and his booby traps?"

"Don't quite know yet. So what's the latest with your cursed set?"

"Oh, Alex. You just wouldn't believe all the craziness here. I had to do all this wire work for a bunch of scenes today. The film is sort of like a dragon story in space. A group of colonists wake something in the ground, and they have to fight it. The director wants me to fly around for these battle scenes. I've got this fake jet pack strapped to my back, and I'm suspended by wire twenty feet in the air against this giant green screen, and the alien is supposed to swoop in to fight me.

"So they set me up for the first take. Now I don't know if a solar flare hit the earth right then or what, but suddenly everything electronic just started going crazy. The set klaxon went off, lights flickered, the wind machine cranked up to full blast, so I'm flopping around up there like a flying monkey from *The Wizard of Oz,* and then the controls for my wire rig go haywire. I'm zipping around up there and suddenly these sparks just start flying out of the monster, and it's like it *comes to life,* Alex.

"It starts writhing around and a couple of the puppeteers scream and leap back as their control board bursts into flame. They go running off, never mind me whipping around up there twenty feet in the air, and suddenly I'm doing battle with this alien thing for real. Its tail is thrashing like a stinger, and it starts swinging around on its gimbal like something alive on a spit.

"And all I've got is this prop gun that they're going to add laser effects to in post. The monster lunges straight at me, and I'm bonking this thing on the nose with my fake gun while trying to keep myself straight and not spin around like a top. Then the lights stop flickering and go out for good, and the whole set plunges into darkness. But I can hear this thing moving around me. I'm trying to get my bearings and next thing I know I'm crashing into the green screen with that thing fast on my heels, and I know this time it's truly come alive in the dark. Then it's like a switch goes on, and suddenly the lights are back, my rig stops moving, and the monster is just hanging there limply, all innocent like it didn't just try to murder me."

Alex couldn't stop chuckling. "I'm sorry I'm laughing, Zoe. It's just the way you're describing it."

"Oh, sure. Maybe it's a little funny now, but it wasn't then. And besides, I'm really starting to think someone *is* trying to sabotage this movie. They don't want it to go on. But I'm not sure who could be behind it."

"Jinkies."

"Don't quote Velma to me. I may not have the Mystery Machine gang here with me, but I'm going to get to the bottom of it."

"I bet it was Old Farmer Joe who doesn't want you to film on his property because he has a hidden gold mine there."

"I'm serious!"

Alex reined in her mirth. "Okay. I'm sorry."

"That's more like it. So do you want to hear my list of suspects, or what?"

"Definitely."

"Okay. Well, first off is Old Farmer Joe, who doesn't want us filming on his farm because—"

"Oh, stop it!"

"Okay. Seriously. The first suspect is our executive producer's son. He's something of an aspiring writer/director, and I think he wants all this money to go to *his* movie, not ours. So he's aiming to shut us down before we've spent a lot on it."

"Sounds like a viable suspect."

"Totally. He's been skulking around the set on the premise that he's learning from the director. A couple of times I've caught the son messing around by the alien's controls. And another time I saw him sneaking bagels off the craft services table. Not eating them, mind you, just stashing them away, like he's going to poison them and put them back on the table later. Maybe with some tainted cream cheese."

"I see. And who else is on your list?"

"There's this janitor. Only, I don't think he's a real janitor."

"Ah, the old fake janitor ruse, eh?"

"Exactly. I never see him cleaning anything. And he keeps leaving books around the set about mechanical engineering and cooking."

"What? That's weird."

"Right? He might even have arranged for that fake chef who made us all sick. I mean, who lugs around a cookbook to read in their spare time? And with his knowledge of engineering, he could have sabotaged the puppet."

"Good point."

"I keep finding him in places where he shouldn't be."

"Maybe he's just starstruck and enchanted by the magic of moviemaking."

"Maybe." Zoe sounded doubtful.

"Anyone else?"

"Yes. Jack Farthington."

"He's an up-and-coming actor, isn't he?"

"Exactly. And he's got a smaller, supporting role in this film. They've only shot one of his scenes so far, so I think he might be angling to replace one of the bigger actors if they get hurt by this lumbering alien or some other set mishap. Jack almost got pinned beneath the monster during that fritz-out on stage. He rolled away before it could crush him."

"That was lucky. But if he was the one who almost got stomped on, would he have been responsible for setting up the disaster in the first place?"

"But that could be his plan, see? He almost gets hurt a bunch of times, and then he could demand that he'll walk unless he gets a bigger role to make all these risks worth it."

"This is interesting. You've got a good array of suspects, and it does sound like you might be right. Someone is trying to sabotage the movie."

"And I'm going to find out who."

"Be careful."

"I will."

They talked a little longer about the mountains, and then Zoe's latest beau, a thirty-five-year-old CrossFit instructor whom she'd been dating for three weeks. Zoe's romantic interests usually didn't last more than a few months. A lot of men were intimidated by her fame and soon tried to undermine her. At that point, she always dumped them on the spot. So she wasn't that lucky in love. Neither was Alex, she had to admit to herself. She'd ended her last serious relationship the year before, when the man had wanted her to stop going out into the field and to settle for a job at a Boston zoo.

They hung up, with Alex promising to be careful and Zoe agreeing to keep Alex updated on the sabotage investigation.

Alex clicked through the footage one more time, then got ready for bed. But once she lay down and switched off the light, images of the squatter flashed through her mind. She imagined him stealthily, silently, walking up to the house . . .

No, she told herself. *I won't get spooked.*

Even still, she got up, pulled the bear spray out of its holster, and brought it back to bed with her.

THE NEXT DAY, ALEX DRESSED excitedly, looking forward to seeing Kathleen. They hadn't really talked since Alex had left for her last gig in Canada, and she wanted to hear what her friend had been up to.

The drive into town offered up gorgeous views of the surrounding mountains as Alex jostled along the dirt roads. Along the way, she stopped to pick up her mail. She paused as she moved to unlock the box, wondering if another postcard awaited her.

One did, this time sent directly to her address here. In the familiar block handwriting, it read: ALEX, I'VE BEEN TRAVELING, WANDERING, BUT MY THOUGHTS KEEP RETURNING TO YOU. IT'S BEAUTIFUL HERE. The front depicted the emerald-green ferns and forests of Whanganui National Park, New Zealand.

A flyer for an art show in town, addressed to "Current Resident," was the only other piece of mail. Alex read the postcard again. Her thoughts often strayed to him, too. Slowly she moved back to the car, imagining him hiking in that green paradise.

In town, she easily found a parking space, something that still surprised her after years of living in the San Francisco Bay Area while earning her doctorate. There, you had to make a prayer to the goddess of parking to find a spot within a mile of your destination.

But here, she pulled up right in front of the café.

Inside, she picked the same table where she'd sat with Ben because she loved the painting above it, an abstract representation of musical notes and treble and bass clef symbols worked into it, like a visual depiction of big band music. She sipped her tea and glanced around appreciatively at the other art on the walls. All by the same artist, the paintings stood out in vivid colors, some with swirling starscapes and bright, delicate nebulae.

The door opened and Alex turned, grinning when she saw Kathleen standing there, her long silver hair pulled back in a braid.

"Kathleen!" she called, standing.

Her friend spotted her and walked over. They hugged.

"It's so good to see you," Alex told her.

"And you, too! How about this? I didn't think I'd see you again, and now we're just a few miles apart."

Kathleen ordered a cup of coffee at the counter and returned to the table.

"So how have you been?" she asked Alex.

"Really good. I just spent a few months in the Canadian Arctic studying polar bears."

"Wow! That sounds fascinating!"

"It really was." She told Kathleen a little more about her adventures up there.

Alex spotted a book peeking out of Kathleen's purse. "What are you reading?" Kathleen followed her gaze to the book and smiled. "It's not reading." She pulled it out. "It's KenKen. Like Sudoku but it incorporates math. Mathdoku. You have to fill in different numbers for each square, but they also have to multiply, divide, add, or subtract with each other to make those numbers."

Alex raised her eyebrows. "Sounds fun."

"It is!" Kathleen laughed. "I'm a firm believer in always keeping the mind sharp. Using different parts of the brain. For instance, I'm also learning Polish."

"Do you have Polish family?"

"No. I just love the sound of the language. It's really beautiful. And in a few weeks, I'm taking an online course in oceanography."

"How cool! I love the idea of always learning new things." She took a sip of her tea. "How are things in Bitterroot?"

"It's been pretty quiet since all of that craziness last year when you were at the Snowline. But I've been taking advantage of the peace and gotten in some great hikes."

"And how is Frank?" Kathleen, at seventy-two, had started dating a fellow book lover and BBC mystery enthusiast while Alex was still stationed in Montana.

Kathleen blushed a little. "Good."

"You're blushing!"

"Oh, shut up," she said with a shy smile, then sipped her coffee. "So how about you? Any promising romance on the wind?"

Alex shook her head. She thought of Ben and then Casey, whom she'd been with during her harrowing experience out on the ice of Hudson Bay. At the thought of Casey, her heart suddenly started jackhammering and she put her fork down.

"You okay?"

Alex cleared her throat. "Yes. Yes, I'm fine." She sipped her tea, the heat from it soothing. "No, I don't have any romantic prospects. But I'm okay with that."

Kathleen scrutinized her, as if trying to determine if she really *was* okay with that. "All right. I hear you. So tell me what this assignment is about."

"Mountain caribou."

Kathleen sat back, astonished. "You're kidding. I thought they were all gone from the lower forty-eight."

"They were. But at least one of them has come down from British Columbia. I just put a collar camera on it."

"That's amazing!"

Alex smiled. "It really is. And so cool to see it browsing and exploring on the video footage." She thought of the strange booby traps and the conflict between the logger and the activists. "So that's been fascinating. But there's been a lot of tension in town and out in the forest. An old-growth logging project has been halted, and a camp of activists are near the boundary of the preserve. There's even a woman who's been sitting in the top of a tree for seven months."

Kathleen gave a long, low whistle. "Now *that's* dedication."

"One logger is not happy about it." Alex sipped her tea, then lowered her voice, not wanting to be insensitive to anyone around them who might have known Irma Jackson. "Have you heard, too, that a ranger was murdered?"

Kathleen's eyes went wide. "What?"

"She was on a backcountry patrol and disappeared. They found her body in the town square, murdered."

"That's awful."

"And a hiker has gone missing. They're not sure yet if she got lost or ran away somewhere, or if it's something worse. But she's been missing for more than a year."

"I think I remember hearing about this last year. Where exactly did she disappear from?" Kathleen asked.

Alex brought out her phone and pulled up a topo map. She'd been marking locations of interest on it: her remote cameras, places that might be particularly inviting to mountain caribou. Now she pulled up the coordinates of where the woman's tent had been found. "Here."

Kathleen took the phone. "That's about twelve miles from my tower. Creepy. And they have no idea what happened to her?"

"None. They found her tent and camping equipment, but never any sign of her."

Alex brought up the woman's photo on her phone. She'd snapped a pic of the one the sheriff left with her. "This is what she looks like."

Kathleen studied her face. "I wonder what happened to her. Do the police think it's connected with the murdered ranger?"

"They don't know."

Kathleen stared out the window as a car pulled up. A couple stepped out and ducked into the hardware store. "Creepy to think that the murderer might live right here, in this town."

Alex nodded. "It is."

A beat-up pickup pulled in across the street and an older man stepped out. He met their gaze through the window before stepping into the grocery store. A burly, bearded man with red hair followed him inside.

"It could be anyone." Kathleen gave a shiver and finished her coffee. "Anyway!" she said resolutely, bringing up a smile. "You want to go check out that Thai place down the street? I'm starving."

Alex grinned. "I'd love to."

They moved down the street to the Thai restaurant, choosing another seat by a window. As the server brought them menus, Alex gazed out at the majestic tree-covered peaks. A storm had moved in to the west, the mountains there veiled in thin wisps of mist.

"So what's it like up on the preserve? Is it as remote as the Snowline?" Kathleen asked, referring to the abandoned ski lodge where Alex had lived when she first met Kathleen while studying wolverines in Montana.

Alex laughed. "Not nearly as creepy! It's a rather charming ranch house built in the 1930s. And the preserve itself is a little busier than in Montana."

"You mean in addition to the logger and the activists?"

The server stopped at their table and took their order. Alex got pad see ew jay, sweet noodles with veggies, and Kathleen opted for pad thai. Both of them ordered Thai iced tea.   ·

Alex nodded. "For one thing, there seems to be a squatter moving between the preserve and the national forest. From the looks of him, he's been living out there for a while. His clothes are ragged. And there was this tunnel."

"Tunnel?"

The server brought them tall glasses of cold tea and they both stirred the concoction. "Yes. I think this guy might have dug it out. I found it on the national forest side. It had a cot and stove and a bunch of books. He'd set up booby traps around it, too. Some are just simple alarms, like bells dangling from trees, triggered by wires. But the weird thing is that I dropped this multitool my dad had given me, and I found it later in the tunnel. I guess he picked it up."

"Eerie."

"I've seen the guy a couple times, and I keep getting the feeling I'm being watched. And then there's the super-angry logger. He's been threatening the woman who's tree sitting. She's got a network of helpers, from what I can tell, who bring her food and supplies."

She told Kathleen about getting shot at on the road, and her narrow escape from the logs.

"It does sound busy out there."

"To say the least." Alex suppressed a small shudder at remembering how she felt, exposed on the road while trying to change the tire in the downpour. She longed to change the subject. "So what's your fire tower like?"

"Pretty isolated. It's my third season out there. I love it. There's a little house at the base of the tower that I live in. Every morning I get up before dawn, just as the birds are beginning to sing. There's no running water in the tower, and it's not potable in the house. So I have to boil all the water I'm going to use for the day and then lug it up all the stairs to the tower lookout. It's good exercise."

"Sounds like it!"

Kathleen lifted her arm and flexed her bicep. "You should see these babies at the end of the summer."

Alex laughed. "Get fit and protect the forest."

"Exactly." Kathleen took a bite of her food. "Then I sit up there in the tower, gazing out at all that gorgeous greenery. Got binoculars and a spotting scope in case I see smoke, and a radio to stay in contact." She smiled. "I get a lot of reading done. And KenKen."

"And Polish."

"That's right." Her eyes twinkled. "You want to come up tomorrow, check the place out?"

"I'd love to."

They finished their lunches and paid the bill. Alex walked Kathleen to her Forest Service truck and the two said goodbye, making plans to meet up tomorrow.

Then Alex made the long drive back to the ranch house. She spent the rest of the day hiking to the remote cameras, switching out memory cards, and looking for tracks and scat. A light rain fell as she headed back toward the ranch house in the early evening. The day had been restful—seeing Kathleen, hiking on the vast preserve.

No squatter, no angry logger, just Alex and the peace of the forest. As she hiked back, she looked forward to reviewing more footage from the collar camera and checking on her dad to see how he was doing at the Grand Canyon.

Back at the house, she made a quick dinner and sat down by the landline.

Her dad picked up on the second ring. "Hey, pumpkin!"

"Hi, Dad. How's it going out there? Have you got any new comrades yet? Fellow painters?"

"It's been really fun. Yeah, I met this one fellow George. He mainly paints in acrylics, so it's interesting to watch." Alex's dad painted solely in oils or watercolors. "He's really good. We got to chatting the first day and have been bumming around a bit together. He's something of a daredevil, though. Always getting a little too close to the edge for my taste, trying to find unusual angles and less visited places. You know people fall off the edge here all the time? It happens to a lot of them when they're having their photos taken, and their friends or family will say, 'Back up a little. A little more,' and the next thing they know, their loved one is plummeting over the edge."

"I've read about those incidents. Wasn't there a kid who was riding his bike along the edge and shot right off the rim, falling something like a hundred feet onto a ledge?"

"Yes! I remember that. And all he did was break his arm. Amazing. Other people aren't so lucky. Every day my heart's in my mouth as I watch people get so close to the edge for one more photo, or even climb over the guardrails to be daredevils to their friends. Seeing my friend George do that, stumbling around with an easel and paint box, is just too much for me. But it's amazing being here. Gorgeous! And the ravens here are so beautiful and charismatic, Alex. You'd love them. They're so smart. They have so many different vocalizations. I'd sure like to speak raven and know what they're saying."

"Me too, Dad. Why doesn't Rosetta Stone get on that?"

He chuckled. "Beats me, honey."

"So where are you staying there?"

"They've put the guest artists up in these great old stone cabins built by the Civilian Conservation Corps in the 1930s. I think mine has bats living in the attic. I can hear them moving around after it gets dark, and I saw one last night emerge from the eaves."

"That's so cool!"

"Cute little guys."

"So what's on the agenda tomorrow?" she asked him.

"I'm still on the South Rim, so I want to travel out to Hopi Point. Want to paint it at sunset."

"That sounds beautiful! Send me pics! I've got internet here."

"I will! So how are things going for you?"

Alex debated telling her dad about the man she'd seen. She didn't want to worry him, and the sheriff knew about him. She decided instead to focus on the good. "Great! I spotted the caribou today and managed to attach a collar camera to it. You should see the footage!"

"That's great, honey! Can you see if it's alone or with others?"

"I haven't seen any other caribou with it. But I only have a few videos so far. Tomorrow I'll have a lot more to go through."

"Good luck with everything!"

"Thanks, Dad."

They talked a little longer about the books they were reading and some good dining spots he'd discovered around the Grand Canyon. Then they hung up.

Alex reviewed the collar footage from that day, watching with a smile as the caribou foraged and strolled, napped and ruminated.

Then, tired from her day of hiking, she climbed up the stairs to bed.

THE NEXT MORNING, ALEX WOKE up, excited to see Kathleen's fire tower and enjoy some more social time. Spending time with others was a rare luxury in her line of work, and she seized it when she could.

She showered and dressed, ate a quick breakfast, and headed out the door to her Jeep.

As she drove, she kept the window down, letting the fresh air lift her spirits, and tried to focus on the good things—like this visit with Kathleen.

The first stretch of the drive passed pleasantly as Alex stared out at the wild scenery. She stopped to pick up her mail along the way. Bracing herself this time, she opened the mailbox, realizing she was holding her breath. A grocery store mailer lay on top. She didn't know if she wanted another postcard or not. She felt so conflicted. But underneath the mailer indeed lay another card, this one depicting the deep green waters and inviting beach of Abel Tasman National Park in New Zealand.

It read, IT'S SO PEACEFUL HERE. I'VE BEEN KAYAKING AND SNORKELING. I DON'T KNOW IF YOU WANT ME TO KEEP WRITING. BUT YOU ARE ALWAYS IN MY THOUGHTS.

She stared down at the writing. He never included a return address even if she *did* want to write him back, but she wasn't sure if she did. Her hand trembled slightly as she held the card, her mouth suddenly gone dry. Part of her *did* want to reach out to him, to talk about everything they'd gone through, what motivated him, what his past was like.

But how could she get in touch with him? She set the mail down on the passenger seat and continued on, stopping at the grocery store in Bellamy Falls to pick up a little welcome basket of goodies for Kathleen.

She continued the drive and soon reached the turnoff for the fire tower. Next to it stood a Forest Service sign with hours that the public could visit the tower. She turned up the road. At its beginning elevation, massive ponderosa pines with their alligator bark stood on either side, the forest floor beneath them speckled with sunlight and littered with gigantic pine cones. As she gained altitude, the trees transitioned to western hemlock and red cedar trees.

Her heart felt light.

Alex didn't have a lot of friends, though the two she did have were lifelong and she could count on them. One was Zoe, and the other her father. She was lucky enough to call him a friend. The fact that her family had moved around so much when she was a kid had made it difficult for her to form lasting friendships. Each time they left a base, friends would promise to write, and maybe she would get a couple letters here and there, but eventually her letters went unanswered.

This trend had continued into her adult life. As she moved from one wildlife assignment to the next, she'd tried to develop friendships with different researchers, and then stay in contact with them after she left.

But they'd email for a couple months, and then the time between her initial messages and their responses would grow longer and longer until they didn't answer at all.

Finally Alex realized, with no little degree of embarrassment, that she was putting in 99 percent of the effort trying to sustain the relationships. Sometimes she wondered if it was something about her in particular that made people not want to stay in touch. Was she too intense? Too focused on her mission to help wildlife? It did creep into conversation at times, but since she was talking to other biologists and conservationists, she doubted it was that, as they talked about the subject, too.

Other times she wondered if it had to do with the way communication had changed. People loved their smartphones and social media, and often spent more time keeping up with the anonymous masses than they did with people they actually knew in real life.

And other times Alex wondered if it was just part of her wiring to crave a deeper connection when others just wanted casual, surface interactions that required little to no effort.

Maybe moving around, finding and losing friends over and over again, had made her yearn for connection in this way. Or maybe it was losing her mom when she was twelve. That had been a devastating blow, to lose someone she loved, counted on, relied on. She didn't think such a thing was possible before that catastrophic day.

Airmen had shown up at her house, informing her and her dad that her mom had gone down in hostile territory, but that she'd given her life to protecting others. Her body, burned in the crash, was returned to them unrecognizable, and the air force couldn't even say where she'd died, because it had been classified.

Until that moment, Alex had thought her parents were immortal, infallible. They didn't *leave* you. They didn't *die*. And so she had lost one of her closest friends in her mother, one who had been a constant during all the moves. Her mother had played survival games with Alex as a kid, teaching her how to persevere in desperate situations, how to use whatever resources she had on hand, and how to handle firearms. But suddenly it was just Alex and her dad, struggling on, trying to survive the loss.

Until she had met Zoe in college. Wanting to balance out her heavily science-oriented education, Alex had learned the oboe and played in pit orchestras for musicals given at the University of California in Berkeley. Zoe, then an aspiring actor and talented singer, had been in a production of *The Man of La Mancha* with Alex, and they'd started hanging out at cast parties and instantly hit it off.

Over the years, Alex had worried that her friendship with Zoe, like so many others, would fade away, but so far, it was still going strong, and Alex felt blessed.

Now, as she drove up the road to see Kathleen, she hoped that this might be another friendship that would develop and strengthen. Part of her cursed the fact that she even felt the drive to make deep connections. But it was there nonetheless, and Alex couldn't help but hope.

She made the final hairpin turn in the road, and the fire tower came into view, a soaring frame of metalwork with a small structure on top. At its base stood a USFS house where Kathleen had said she'd live for the summer.

She counted four landings up to the top of the fire tower, stairs going up and up and up. At the top, a wraparound deck would allow Kathleen to make a circuit outside the structure and gaze in all directions.

As she pulled into the parking lot, she spotted the pale green USFS truck that was on loan to Kathleen while she was here.

She cut the engine and Kathleen appeared in the doorway to the house. "Alex!"

Alex climbed out. "Hey, Kathleen. I've brought you a little housewarming present." From the passenger seat, she pulled out the basket with fruit, tea, and coffee that she'd picked up at the grocery store.

She handed it to Kathleen, who looked over its contents with delight. "Thank you! Come on in."

They stepped into the shadowy cool of the house, and Kathleen gave her a brief tour. It was small and utilitarian: a bathroom, kitchen, bedroom, and living room with a couch that looked like it had been there since the early 1970s, when brown and orange plaid almost took over the world. The armrests were faded and frayed. A scarred coffee table stood in front of it with so many rings from carelessly laid coffee mugs that it almost looked like an intentional circular pattern in the wood.

"Home sweet home," Kathleen said, grinning. "You want to go up in the tower?"

"Definitely."

"Care to help me carry this water up?" She gestured toward the stove, where a large pot of water stood steaming. Alex remembered her saying that the water here wasn't potable.

"Sure thing."

Kathleen proceeded to pour the water into four gallon-sized jugs. Then she donned a small daypack full of snacks, a thermos, a deck of cards, and a notebook and pen.

Laden with water, they began the long climb up the tower. Alex admired the ease with which Kathleen moved and hoped to be in half as good shape when she reached seventy-two. They stopped periodically on the landings as they climbed, taking in the forest below, the trees growing smaller and smaller as they gazed down on them.

Then at last they reached the top. Kathleen opened the door of the small structure. Large glass windows graced all four walls, and Alex found herself gazing out at a stunning vista of the Selkirk Mountains. Snowy peaks towered in the distance, and beneath them, massive swaths of forest clustered on all sides.

The room contained a small couch and a cot, and Alex couldn't imagine the trouble someone had gone through to get the couch up all those stairs. A small table held a radio, a logbook, a cup full of pens, and several pairs of binoculars. A spotting scope stood by one of the windows, and next to it a small bookshelf with a number of field guides. Alex stooped and examined the well-perused titles: *Birds of the Pacific Northwest, Guide to Scat and Tracks, Trees of North America, Wildflowers of the Cascades and Selkirks.* She spotted one of her favorites: *All That the Rain Promises and More,* a book on mushrooms that incongruously featured on its cover a tuxedo-clad man with a trombone, holding a mass of chicken of the woods fungus. She'd used the guide many times in the field to identify mushrooms.

Alex straightened up. "This is a pretty sweet setup."

"Not too shabby, eh? And the views!"

Alex gazed out the window. "Yes, you certainly can't beat the views!"

Next to the radio sat a laptop, open and running. The screen showed a Rosetta Stone page with photos of people doing various activities with blank boxes beneath them. A series of bubbles above them held different choices of captions in Polish.

Kathleen noticed her interest. "I got the lifetime subscription to Rosetta Stone. Over twenty languages I can learn at my leisure."

Alex smiled. "I really admire your dedication to learning new things."

"I don't know how to be any other way. I have an incorrigibly curious mind."

Alex also noticed a planisphere beside the computer, a round star chart that one could adjust to the right season and time of night to know what stars shined overhead. Propped up beside it were three thick volumes titled *Burnham's Celestial Handbook.*

"Astronomy, too?" Alex asked.

"Can't help it. And Burnham's guide is so cool. It goes into all the stars, not just their spectral type, size, and temp and all that good stuff, but even the origin of their names and the mythology behind the constellations."

Alex picked up one of the volumes and flipped through it, seeing a comprehensive collection of star maps, photographs, and pages and pages of descriptions.

Kathleen gazed at the book admiringly. "My goal is to learn all the stars we've given proper names to. You know, like Aldebaran, Betelgeuse, Sirius, and then move on to the nitty-gritty of the ones that don't have names, like HR 2642."

Alex closed the book and regarded her friend. "You're pretty amazing. You know that?"

Kathleen blushed. "I'm just a nerd." She pulled a thermos out of her backpack. "You want some coffee?"

"I'd love some."

They sat down at the little table, and Kathleen poured the dark liquid into chipped USFS mugs that looked like they'd been there since the 1950s. Alex's sported Smokey Bear's smiling face.

"So tell me more about what you've been up to," Kathleen said. "How is your father?"

Alex filled her in on her father's latest paintings, where he'd traveled to paint them, and how he'd just gotten into the Grand Canyon plein air festival.

Kathleen told her the latest gossip from the town of Bitterroot, and how the Snowline Resort Wildlife Sanctuary was faring.

"Jolene's been checking on it regularly, and always updates me when she comes into town. There have been a couple other researchers after you. One fellow did a population study for bighorn sheep, and another did a butterfly study. Her work was really interesting. She was looking for an endangered butterfly there."

Alex lifted her eyebrows. "What species?"

"The Frigga fritillary. It's a little yellow-orange butterfly with a dusting of pinkish purple on its hind wing."

"That sounds like a really cool study."

"I'll say. Can you imagine lounging in mountain meadows all day, getting to look at wildflowers and butterflies?"

"Heaven."

Kathleen sipped her coffee. "Indeed. So what else? Meet anyone interesting in the Arctic?"

Alex's mind instantly flashed to Casey. But she wasn't ready to talk about him. "I met a really cool marine archaeologist named Sasha. She studied shipwrecks."

"That sounds fascinating."

"She and her partner had dived all over the world, and her partner was convinced that Vikings had reached as far west as Hudson Bay."

"Really?"

"Amazing theory, right? I have to say, after hearing that, I want to learn more about it."

They chatted for another couple hours, taking frequent breaks to gaze out over the forest with binoculars, searching for columns of smoke. Alex had fun joining in the search and could see why this life appealed so to Kathleen and why she did it every summer.

"It's really peaceful up here," Alex remarked.

"I love it."

They then played several hands of gin rummy. Alex couldn't remember the last time she'd played a card game, thinking it must have been as a kid, playing UNO with her mom and dad.

She enjoyed it immensely, even though she won only two out of five hands. Kathleen was a whiz.

The sun shifted from noon to afternoon, and reluctantly Alex stood up. "I guess I should be heading back."

Kathleen stood, too. "Keep me posted about the caribou. I get a day off in a few days. You want to have dinner in town?"

Alex smiled. "I'd love to."

"Great! I'll give you a call."

They hugged and Alex began the long descent back down to her car. She stopped at all the landings again, breathing in the fresh pine-scented air, and feeling the wind in her hair. The company had done her good. *This is a great life,* she thought. *Sure, I'm lonely at times, but then I meet people like Sasha and Kathleen, and it feels right. And then there's Casey,* she mused. *Casey.* She wondered if he was still in New Zealand.

At the small parking lot, she climbed into her Jeep. High above, she spotted Kathleen out on the wraparound deck, waving.

She waved back, and then turned around, heading out of the lot. It was back to the ranch house now, and another round of caribou footage.

SEATED AT THE RANCH HOUSE'S dining room table, Alex moved through the videos, jotting down notes as each one showed a window into the caribou's day. He stepped delicately over fallen trees and munched on green, leafy shrubs. He napped among bushes and stood ruminating while gazing out on the stunning mountainous landscape. He climbed into the high country, far above the tree line, and stepped over stones, feeding on moss and lichen where nothing taller than grass grew. He meandered over a few remaining snow-fields and pawed at the snow, exposing tender vegetation beneath to nibble on.

In one, the caribou shook his head vigorously as flies buzzed around it. Caribou had to contend with a variety of parasites, botflies being among the worst. Botflies could lay or spray their eggs into a caribou's mouth or nose, and the larvae then hatched inside, blocking the caribou's ability to breathe, crawling down even into its throat. And insidiously, the botflies didn't move on to their adult stage in life until the caribou had successfully snorted them out onto the ground, thus continuing the life cycle and the caribou's torment. Caribou had developed various insect-avoidance behaviors, including scratching, shaking their heads, and even one where they plunged their noses down into dirt or snow so the flies couldn't deposit eggs into them.

But unfortunately, due to global warming, these insects were present for longer each summer season. To avoid them, caribou often spent energy to move to higher ground earlier in the season, which meant relying on less nutritious foods like lichen for longer. This meant that female caribou had fewer fat stores for pregnancy, and nutrition for all caribou suffered.

She clicked through more videos. Still no sign of other caribou. She clicked on the last file, watching the caribou napping on a soft bed of moss in a dense grove of old growth. Movement on the forest floor caught her eye, and she watched as a raven bounced on a fallen log and landed in front of the caribou, who continued to sleep.

The raven had something shiny and long in its bill. It dropped the object onto the mossy floor and then pulled at it. Alex replayed the file again, then used the software to zoom in on that portion of the video. A couple frames caught a brilliant flash of purple in a patch of sun. The object was long and slinky, with a drusy stone set in a silver bear paw: a necklace. The raven then flew off.

Alex leaned forward, playing the video over and over again. She knew that piece of jewelry. She pulled out the photo of Amelia Fairweather that the sheriff had left with her. There was no mistake.

The raven had found the missing hiker's necklace.

TEN

Immediately Alex found the sheriff's number and called her. She knew it was late, but this was more important than polite considerations. Taggert answered on the third ring, sounding a little sleepy.

"Yes?"

"Sheriff Taggert?"

"Yes."

"This is Alex Carter."

Immediately she sounded alert. "Did someone take another shot at you?"

"No. I found the missing hiker's necklace."

"What?" The sheriff's voice went a little breathless. "Where?"

Alex checked the GPS info stored with the video file. "It's on the preserve, about three miles northwest of the ranch house."

"Did you see any sign of her?"

"No, I wasn't there in person. I was checking the footage from a collar camera I attached to a caribou. A raven in the video had the necklace. It dropped it and flew off."

"Hold on a sec. Let me bring up that area on a map." Alex could hear her shifting things around, a chair being pulled out. She grunted as she sat down. "Do you have the exact coordinates?"

"Sure thing." Alex read them off to her.

"Just a sec. I'm pulling them up now." The sheriff went silent for a few moments. Then: "Can you take us out to the site?"

"Yes."

"Great. I'm going to loop the FBI in on this."

"The FBI?"

"Yes. They're investigating in the area, and they've been assisting us. They're concerned that . . ." Her voice trailed off.

"Yes?"

"Well, there have been other murders in the area. Not just the ranger. They're on the case now. I'll let them explain. We'll be there at first light. Sound good?"

"I'll be here."

They hung up. Alex watched the video a few more times before retiring.

She slept fitfully that night, worrying about the missing hiker, wondering what had befallen her out there.

THE NEXT MORNING, AS SHE steeped tea in the kitchen, Alex heard the crunch of vehicles in the driveway. She moved to the front window. The sheriff's car pulled up, followed by a black SUV. The cars parked, and she watched a man climb out of the driver's seat of the SUV. He looked to be in his fifties, with a dour sepia face, a neatly trimmed black mustache, and dark sunglasses. His black hair, graying slightly at the temples, was neatly shorn close to his scalp. A gold badge hung from a chain around his neck. Two other people got out, and as they moved around the car, she saw the lettering on their jackets: *FBI*.

She opened the door as the SUV driver and the sheriff approached the house.

"Mornin', Alex," Taggert said warmly as she opened the door.

The FBI agent was all business, not even a smile. "Dr. Carter?" He held out his hand and she took it. His grip was warm and confident, web to web. "I'm Special Agent Harvey Fields. May we come in?"

"Good morning. Of course." She stood aside while he and Taggert entered. She noticed the two other agents stayed behind, milling around by their car.

"Show us this footage," Fields said.

She led them over to the dining room table and brought up the video file. Fields sat down in front of her laptop, playing the video a few times. "Well, there's no doubt about it," he said, addressing the sheriff. "That's her necklace." He turned to Alex. "Nice work. Where is this exactly?"

She pulled up the coordinates on a digital map.

"You familiar with the terrain out there?" he asked.

"I've been hiking all over that area."

Fields stared at the lines of the terrain, denoting steep inclines and valleys. "Can you take us out there?"

"Of course. May I ask, why is the FBI involved?"

Fields leaned back in his chair. "Another woman was abducted about forty miles away in another part of the Colville National Forest a couple years ago. Her body was found four months later, strung up in another town park, just like the body of Irma Jackson."

"Who was this other woman?" Alex asked.

"Another backcountry hiker like Amelia Fairweather. So we're concerned. We just want to follow up on all possible leads."

"I understand."

Fields stood up. "Great. Let me brief my team, and we'll be ready to leave in five."

"What about Search and Rescue?" Taggert asked. "Want me to loop them in?"

"Let's hike out first. See what we've got. We don't want a hundred volunteers trampling all over a possible crime scene. If it seems like a viable lead, we can get them out then. But let's call the head guy—what's his name?"

"Cody Wainwright."

"Yeah, him. He seems pretty competent. We can get his read on things."

"I'll call him." Pulling her cell out of her pocket, Taggert frowned when she saw she had no reception. She turned to Alex. "Can I use your landline?"

"Of course. It's in the kitchen."

She stepped away to make the call. A few minutes later, she returned and said, "Cody's on his way." Then Taggert sat down in the chair to watch the video a few more times herself. "You see anything else on these? Any sign of her?"

"Sorry, no. Just the necklace."

"Damn." Taggert put an elbow on the table and rested her head in her hand. "This is a tough one. And poor Irma."

A half hour later, bustling activity had taken over the ranch house. Alex had filled her daypack up with a water bottle, her rain gear, some energy bars, her GPS unit, and other necessities, then strapped bear spray to her belt.

The three FBI agents grabbed daypacks out of their car, and Cody Wainwright arrived. A fit man who looked to be in his late forties, he exuded confidence. His worn Asolo boots and his broken-in Patagonia jacket and hiking pants spoke of a life spent largely outdoors. He gripped Alex's hand in his own calloused one, blue eyes framed by sun-bleached blond hair that hung almost to his shoulders. "Cody," he said by way of greeting.

"Alex."

"You say you found Amelia's necklace?"

"Not exactly. A raven did."

"Excuse me?"

Taggert, overhearing their conversation, filled him in while the two agents who had been waiting outside came in to fill up water bottles at her sink. At her kitchen table, they changed out of their shiny black loafers and donned combat boots.

They turned to her, both pausing to greet her. "Special Agent Hernandez," said the first. He was young, in his early twenties, Alex guessed, probably fresh out of Quantico. He was burly and muscled, and she imagined he spent a lot of hours in the gym. CrossFit was probably his idea of exercise, not tromping around in nature. Perfectly coiffed and gelled hair framed his chiseled, terra-cotta face.

"Lipkin," said the other, offering his limp hand. He couldn't be more different from his colleague. Tall and lanky, he towered above them, with slightly greasy blond hair hanging above bushy eyebrows and narrowed green eyes set in a pink face. He looked slightly older than Hernandez, maybe late twenties. She didn't think he'd ever seen the inside of a gym.

"Nice to meet you both," she said.

As they all gathered on the porch, readying to leave, Taggert hooked her thumbs in her utility belt. "I think I might be more useful to you all back at the sheriff's station. You can radio if you need anything. If you find something, I can be in town to organize a bigger search party and arrange for any needed supplies."

Fields nodded. "Sounds good." He shook Taggert's hand. "Thanks for your help, Sheriff."

She grimaced. "I hope you find her out there."

"We'll do our best," Fields assured her. "Okay. Let's move out!"

Then, with Alex in the lead, they set off into the forest.

ELEVEN

As Alex led them into the backcountry, a light rain began to fall, then got heavier. She paused to pull on her rain gear. The FBI agents broke out clear ponchos and continued to trudge along. All of them soon had muddy, wet feet. Cody paused, his long hair dripping with rain, and pulled out a set of Columbia rain parka and pants.

Soon they fell into a rhythm, and at first no one said much as they hiked.

Then she heard Hernandez ask Lipkin, "Okay. So who would win in a fight: Muhammad Ali or Mike Tyson?"

Lipkin considered. "That's a tough one. But I'd say Tyson. He's got that raw power."

Hernandez shook his head. "No way. Ali's too fast. Too evasive. He'd definitely win."

Lipkin narrowed his eyes on Hernandez. "Okay, then. Who would win in a fight: Sherlock Holmes or Jessica Fletcher from *Murder, She Wrote*?"

Hernandez grinned. "Oh, that one's *easy*. Jessica Fletcher. In a heartbeat. I mean, she was like the angel of death. You know what the murder count must have been in Cabot Cove, Maine? Like, *way* more than even Detroit."

Fields whipped his head around with a glare that would have melted steel. "I swear, when I figure out who assigned you two knuckleheads."

Hernandez blinked. "You requested us."

Fields turned back around slowly. "Oh yeah. Remind me of why again?"

Lipkin spoke up. "'Cause we were the top of our class at Quantico and have an impeccable case clearance rate."

"Oh yeah. I nearly forgot." Fields rolled his eyes, his face inscrutable, unmoving. "These two," he said to Alex, shaking his head.

"So what did you study before mountain caribou?" Hernandez asked Alex.

"Before this it was polar bears, and before that wolverines."

"Oh, wow," Lipkin said, grinning. "So who would win in a fight: a wolverine or a polar bear?"

Fields glanced at her. "You don't have to answer that." Then he turned to them. "She doesn't have to answer that."

Alex thought a moment. "I think they'd brawl till they were both exhausted and then become friends."

Lipkin raised his hand in protest. "You can't do that! They can't become friends."

"Why not?" asked Hernandez.

"It's a cop-out!"

Fields set his mouth in a thin slash. "Who would win in a fight: my boot or your ass?"

"Point taken, chief," Hernandez said, then went quiet.

After another half hour of hiking in silence, Hernandez asked, "Is it much farther?" He paused in a vain attempt to shake some of the caked mud off the soles of his boots. Dirt flung off them and landed in a patch of moss.

Alex checked her GPS unit. "Only about half a mile," she assured him.

She could tell from his expression that it may as well have been ten miles. He frowned, gave one more defeated kick of his boots, tried to scrape the mud off on a rock, and continued on in silence.

Lipkin had lapsed into the hundred-yard stare, and he, too, walked on in silence.

Both Wainwright and Fields, though, were alert and chipper, stopping to study depressions in the ground, casting around for signs that humans had passed through. Wainwright found the spot where Alex had sat while eating lunch a few days before, and she was impressed. He must be a good search and rescue guy.

At last they reached the site where the raven had dropped the necklace. A large depressed place in the moss and lichen marked where the caribou had slept. Wainwright was quick to point out that it had also nipped off branches from a nearby cluster of willows. Fields asked Alex and Wainwright to stand to one side of the clearing while he and the other two agents went in and scoured the place. Fields supervised, pointing out places to pay careful attention to, organizing the search into a grid. He leaned down to ground level to look for depressions and tracks. Hernandez and Lipkin sprang into action, walking bent over, carefully covering the terrain.

Finally Hernandez spoke up. "I don't see the necklace."

"Or any footprints," Lipkin chimed in.

Fields stood up, hands on his hips. "I have to agree. The only thing I see here is that the caribou lay down for a while, then headed that way." He pointed north.

Hernandez shook his head. "The necklace could have been lying out here somewhere since her initial disappearance. Any sign of a human would be long gone by now. Who knows where the raven initially picked it up."

They searched for another few minutes, frowning, picking at a blade of grass here, a piece of moss there. Finally Fields straightened up, his mouth downturned in disappointment. "Even if it has been lying out here all this time, it's still a clue. Either she was near here or someone who took her necklace was. Or an animal moved it. But it's gone now." He turned to Alex. "So what does that mean?"

She found herself on the spot, all eyes on her. "At the start of the video, the raven already had the necklace, which means it was carried from somewhere else. The raven could have returned later and picked it up again." She thought about it a minute. "Or maybe a wood rat took it. They love anything that's shiny and add the objects to their nests."

Fields looked at her expectantly, waiting for her to continue.

"Wood rats create these big nests and stockpile all kinds of things. Their nests can be over sixty years old, passed down from generation to generation. They'll contain string, shiny gum wrappers, bottle caps, buttons. One researcher even found a tennis shoe in a wood rat nest." She smiled, then cleared her throat and got serious again.

"So which is it, the raven or the wood rat?" Fields asked, fixing her with a stern look.

"I'm not sure. We know from the video that the raven had the necklace at least for a while. We could search for wood rat nests, see if anything else turns up."

"And what, pray tell, does a nest *look* like?" Fields asked.

"Like a loose collection of branches and leaves, maybe some shredded bark."

Fields stared around, discouraged. "So they look like the forest floor?"

"Well, no. It'll be built up. It's pretty cool, actually—they have separate rooms for pooping, sleeping, raising young, and they decorate the rooms with all their absconded treasure, and—" Alex shut up abruptly as she took in Fields's disapproving face.

"Just find one," he ordered her.

Alex walked slowly around the perimeter of the search area, not wanting to evoke Fields's wrath by stepping into the imaginary cordoned-off parts. She made a circuit of the whole site, then moved out a little farther, circling again.

By her fourth circle, the FBI agents were all standing around impatiently, but Wainwright joined her. At last she came upon a tangle of branches of a wood rat nest. "Here!" she called.

The men hurried over to her.

"Search it," Fields told his two agents. They donned latex gloves and dug through the rooms of sticks and pine needles, finding gum wrappers, two bright blue climbing carabiners, the toggle closure from a jacket, two beer bottle caps, and a crushed Pepsi can.

Fields watched with interest as they pulled out object after object. "They really are collectors, aren't they?" He sounded interested now, despite himself.

"Their other name is pack rat," Alex told him, unable to contain her delight at the curious collection of goods the rat had amassed.

"What about this?" Lipkin said, pulling out a tattered piece of beige wool, probably from a hiking sock. "Could this be Fairweather's?"

With his gloved hand, Fields took the item and turned it over delicately. "It could be. I'm not sure. Lipkin, you got the list of her belongings that the family said she usually had with her?"

"Yes, sir." Lipkin stood up and retrieved his phone from a back pocket. He swiped through a few screens. "Let's see. Purple jacket, the necklace, of course, a compass, a watch."

Fields grunted. "Of course they wouldn't have mentioned anything specific about socks."

"No, sir."

"So this might or might not be hers."

"I'll bet a hundred other hikers have passed through here," Hernandez muttered under his breath, frowning.

"What's the range on these wood rats?"

"Excuse me?"

"How far away from this spot could it have retrieved these items?"

Alex thought a minute. "Not too far, I don't think. But there might be other nests around. They tend to live in loosely extended colonies."

He scanned the area immediately around him. "And a raven?"

"That could be farther."

"So then what happened to the necklace?"

"It's possible the raven flew off with it. Or another pack rat might have claimed it."

Fields stared around at the trees. "So more of these nests might be lying around here?"

"It's possible."

"You heard her," Fields commanded his two men. "Help her look."

They all five branched out now, searching for both pack rat nests and the necklace, which might still be lying nearby if the raven dropped it.

As Alex searched, she couldn't help but smile at the thought of the crafty raven and its break in this case. Ravens could be very determined and curious. Extremely smart birds, they also had a complex language and could recognize individual human faces. In fact, one researcher who had been mist netting and banding ravens realized that not only were the ravens she'd banded avoiding her, but they'd spread the word among other ravens in the community. Those other birds, who had not yet been banded, avoided her, too, and had taken to cussing at her from the trees when she came around. She resorted to wearing glasses, a false beard, and a pillow under a big coat in order to make them think she was someone different. And it worked. She was able to mist net and band more birds after that.

Alex picked around the detritus of the mossy forest floor, careful not to disturb anything. Then, about twenty feet in front of her, she spotted something shiny. Her pace picked up as she reached it. As she bent down over the object, careful not to touch it, elation sparked within her. "Over here!" she cried.

The necklace, with its purple drusy stone set in a silver bear paw, gleamed up at her, droplets of rain covering the chain.

She pointed it out to Fields, who photographed it. Then with a gloved hand, he picked it up. "This is hers, all right." He held out his hand expectantly. "Bag."

Hernandez reached inside his jacket and pulled out an evidence bag. Fields bagged and labeled the necklace.

For another two hours they scoured the area, moving in wider and wider circles. They found a few more pack rat nests, but no evidence of Amelia, nor any sign that a human had passed through the area.

Alex had moved quite a distance from the others, and she heard Fields's voice bark out, "Okay. I'm calling it for the day." She rejoined them and glanced around at the sky. Late afternoon had set in, and the rain had finally stopped, but thick clouds still obscured the sun. "We'll get SAR out here first thing tomorrow. Can you organize that?" he asked Wainwright.

"Sure thing."

"Then let's pack it in, people," Fields called. "I'm in the mood for some grub and a warm place to eat it in."

"And some dry shoes," she heard Hernandez mutter as he walked past her. They all met on the far side of the necklace site and began the long hike back.

"Okay. So who would win in a fight," she heard Lipkin ask Hernandez. "The Terminator or the Michelin Man?"

"We talking Terminator One or Two?"

"One. The original Terminator."

"That's easy," Hernandez said. "The Terminator. He'd just fill him full of holes. Michelin Man would deflate. Be flat as a pancake."

"But what if he has a soul?"

"What? Who?"

"The Michelin Man. I mean, he seems like a pretty jovial guy. Bet he has a soul," Lipkin replied.

"What's that got to do with it?" Hernandez looked at Lipkin like he must be crazy.

"If you have a spirit, you can beat the Terminator no matter how outgunned you are," Lipkin explained. "You're resourceful. Michelin Man could hide in a junkyard, disguised in a stack of old tires. Then when the Terminator arrives, Michelin Man could get him in one of those car-smashing things. Cube him."

Hernandez put his hands on his hips. "You got a point."

"Are you two back on that again?" Fields snapped.

They shut up immediately, lagging back a bit, studying the forest floor. Then Alex heard Hernandez ask Lipkin in a whisper, "Okay. Who would win in a fight: the ghost of Jesse James or Dracula?"

She smiled, listening in as they ran through their reasonings. But despite the light banter and her warm layers, Alex shivered, wondering if Amelia Fairweather had truly taken off for parts tropical, or if her body lay somewhere out in the forest, waiting in the dark and the rain to be found.

BACK AT THE RANCH HOUSE, everyone departed. Still fighting off a feeling of unease, Alex sat for a long time at the kitchen table, just reflecting on the day, the missing hiker, and the lone caribou out there, trying to gain back some of the territory his kin had lost.

She was feeling so much loss today. Sometimes it was hard for her to keep her spirits up. She'd lost her mom when she was twelve and missed her desperately. But it was more than just personal loss. She labored in the trenches of what often felt like a hopeless cause. Habitat destruction, overdevelopment, greed, species extinction. It felt insurmountable at times. So many people just weren't tuned in to what was happening to the planet. Biodiversity was plummeting, pieces of the intricate web of life just vanishing, leaving holes, weakening the very structure of life on Earth. Soon it wouldn't be able to support even humans, let alone all the magnificent species that would also be lost along the way.

She put her head in her hands, feeling a wave of grief wash over her. She thought of being out on the ice, of Casey's comforting presence, of the fear out there, not just for her own life, but for the lives of the polar bears, dwindling under the weight of climate change.

Moments like this snuck up on her, gripped at her heart, her throat. But she had to soldier on, keep fighting. The solution to hopelessness was taking action.

So she booted up her laptop and went over the new caribou footage, fascinated to see him meandering through the forest, nipping off branches from shrubs, pulling down lichen from the trees. Yes, she would continue to fight. Always, she would continue to fight.

THE NEXT DAY, ALEX SET out to check several locations where the caribou had been and change out the batteries and memory cards from some of the remote cameras. She'd packed her tent, sleeping bag, Sterno stove, and Zippo, anticipating a night spent in the backcountry.

She reached the first camera and opened it to look at the footage. No caribou at first glance, but she swapped the memory card to examine it more closely back at the house. At one of the spots where the caribou had visited on the collar camera, she swept the area, searching for additional tracks, but didn't find any.

She felt discouraged and lamented that more effective steps hadn't been taken to save the caribou herd. It was crazy. Governments would go to the trouble of tranquilizing, capturing, and translocating caribou, of penning in herds where pregnant cows could give birth and have young, and even kill thousands of wolves in the attempt to reduce predation. But what they weren't willing to do was tackle the two biggest threats to the mountain caribou population: the destruction of old growth due to logging, and climate change, which was reducing snowpack.

The Endangered Species Act was a valuable piece of legislation, but Alex had come to believe that its approach might be outdated.

It dealt with species as if they were isolated problems to solve. In reality, things needed to be addressed in a more holistic way. *What we need is an Endangered Ecosystem Act,* she thought. Protection that addressed an entire ecosystem would benefit so many species at once: wolverines, mountain caribou, the American pika, and of course, even humans.

Alex was in such deep thought on her way to the next remote camera site that she didn't see the gleaming trip wire until she'd almost walked through it. It was in a completely different area from where she'd found the tunnel.

She brought her body abruptly to a halt, hesitating, her ankle just millimeters away from tripping the wire. Carefully she slid her boot out and stepped over the wire. But as she placed her right foot down on the far side, she cried out in surprise when the ground gave away beneath her. She tumbled down into a pit, hitting the dirt sides as she fell. Her foot snagged on the trip wire as she careened downward, setting off a series of bells that jangled loudly.

She hit the bottom hard, her hip landing on a sharp rock. The wind gushed out of her lungs and she lay for a moment on her side, dazed, trying to process what had just happened. She heard the snapping of wood above her and a slab of rock crashed down over the opening of the pit.

TWELVE

From above, Alex heard the muffled jangling of bells fade away into silence. Pitch black enveloped her.

She fished her headlamp out of her jacket pocket, coughing as dirt and dust settled around her. Switching it on, she got her bearings. Her hip hurt like crazy, and she reached down to it, finding her pants torn there, her skin warm and sticky. She coughed a few more times, expelling grime. The pit was narrow, a little under four feet wide. Her legs lay cramped up against one wall at an odd angle, her head jammed against another. Finally, groaning, she managed to sit up, adrenaline coursing through her body.

The alarm bells. The squatter. Clarity seared Alex's mind. She had to get out of there. If he was nearby, he surely would have heard them. He could be on his way now. And if he was the one responsible for Amelia's disappearance and the ranger's death . . .

Quickly she shrugged off her pack. Dust and dirt sifted down from above. A large gray slab of granite completely covered the top of the pit, which was roughly fifteen feet above her. The walls of the pit were comprised of smooth dirt, and she had the uneasy feeling that they could collapse at any moment. She stood up, her hip giving her grief, and shone the light around the walls. About twelve feet up yawned the narrow black entrance to a tunnel. She wondered over it for a few moments, then realized the squatter must have added it in case he ever fell into his own trap by accident.

She assessed the situation. She had to get up to that tunnel or get to the top of the pit and try to lift the rock. She rummaged around in her pack for her folding camp shovel. She dug a small hole about two feet up off the ground, then another one four feet up, then six. She stuck the toe of her boot into the lowest hole and her hand in the highest. She pulled herself up, then dug another hole eight feet up with the little shovel. Then the soil gave away under her bottom boot and she slid back down.

The soil was just too loose. She used the tip of her shovel to jab at the dirt in different places of the pit, finding one wall more solidly packed. Now she dug small holes again, just big enough for the tips of her fingers and the toes of her boots. The depressions felt more solid, so she dug them a little deeper. Now she tried climbing again, digging holes as she ascended. Her shoulders and back trembled from the effort of trying to keep herself pinned to the wall while digging.

When she'd climbed high enough, she glanced over her shoulder at the mouth of the tunnel. Sharp, gleaming concertina wire coiled within it.

Hauling herself up the remaining feet, she at last reached the rock. She slid her hand along the rough granite slab and gave a test push, realizing it was immensely heavy. She shoved on it as hard as she could, but succeeded only in applying so much pressure that her hand- and footholds crumbled. She crashed back down to the bottom of the pit. The rock was immovable, far too big. She stared up, coughing in the dusty hole.

She could try digging out from under the rock but didn't want to risk it crashing down on her and crushing her if she destabilized the ground holding the slab in place.

Once again, she gazed up at the tunnel. It was her only option.

From the floor, she again started digging foot- and handholds up the wall. The dirt scattered and sifted down, and she used some of the more tightly packed soil and crammed it into the holds to stabilize them.

Her heart ticked up its pace. How long ago had those bells rung? Could he be up there, even now, waiting to finish her off if she got out?

She tied a climbing rope around her backpack's shoulder straps and the other end around her waist, leaving enough slack that she wouldn't be climbing with its weight on her. Reaching into her jeans pocket, she pulled out her multitool and opened it to the wire cutter. Then she gripped it in her teeth.

Carefully she climbed until she reached the level of the tunnel.

She felt its surface gingerly, finding it firm. She reached up with one hand and tugged on the concertina wire. It held fast, snugged securely into the sides of the tunnel. She needed more leverage. She hoisted herself up to eye level with the opening and held on to its lip. Then she grabbed her multitool from between her teeth and snipped away at the concertina wire. She flung the loose pieces of wire down onto the pit floor, hoping she wasn't about to fall down on top of them.

Soon she'd cleared enough room to haul her torso into the cavity.

She clipped the wire farther in, sliding it past her body to cast it out of the tunnel. Finally a big enough space opened up for her to drag her legs into the tunnel. But it was too narrow for her to turn around.

Struggling up onto her hands and knees, her back pressed firmly against the dirt roof, she hauled the rope up under her stomach. Her pack had never felt so heavy. Her hands burned with the friction, and as hard as she tugged, the awkward angle meant that she could get the rope up only a few inches at a time. Her back and shoulders ached. Finally her backpack hit the lip of the tunnel and stuck there. She couldn't pull it up any farther. Peering down past her stomach, she saw one of the arm straps peeking above the floor of the tunnel. Snaking her foot back, she hooked her ankle through the strap and yanked with everything in her. The pack stubbornly resisted, then snapped up inside the tunnel.

Alex exhaled, taking just a moment to rest, all too aware of the ticking clock and wondering if the squatter knew she was down here.

Ahead of her gleamed a maze of sharp wire, its razor sections flashing back at her in the focused beam of her headlamp. She crawled forward, snipping more and more wire away. Each time she tossed a piece down to the bottom of the pit, she had to awkwardly press her body against one side of the tunnel, with barely enough room to move.

At last she reached the end of the wire and snipped then tossed out the remaining pieces. Ahead of her the tunnel stretched farther into darkness. She didn't see any wires or triggers and grew suspicious. Maybe he had just counted on the concertina wire to slow people down but not stop them.

Tentatively, she crawled forward, the scent of soil so intense that she coughed. On her hands and knees she moved inches at a time, feeling along the dirt for other traps.

As she placed her left hand ahead of her, she felt something click beneath it. The soil pressed down and immediately Alex snapped her hand back. Ahead of her in the tunnel, a bright blue flame clicked on. Her headlamp fell on a nozzle connected to an air hose that extended up into the roof. With a hiss, a yellowish-white powder erupted from the nozzle opening, hitting the flame.

And suddenly fire engulfed her.

The tunnel flooded with bright orange flame, the roar all around her. It shot through the tunnel with a loud *whump,* extending all the way to the pit. And then the nozzle stopped its hiss and just as quickly, the fire vanished. The little blue flame clicked off.

Panicked, Alex slapped at her hair, putting out flames, and checked over her clothes and pack. She wiped at her eyes with her sleeve, worrying that she'd just been hit with something corrosive. But it didn't burn.

A yellow-white dust covered her clothing and pack, and she

struggled to brush it off, trying not to breathe in any powder, though she knew she had. Her mind darted to a terrible thought: *Anthrax*. She could taste whatever it was in her mouth.

The way it had flashed when it dispersed made her think of grain elevator explosions setting fire to diffuse particles suspended in the air.

Who was this guy? Why use all these nonlethal measures? To delay his prey until he had a chance to catch them? Imprison them?

She wondered if Irma or Amelia had spent time in some dank place like this one, trapped.

Carefully she studied the way ahead. Just beyond the nozzle, her beam fell on a wooden door, made up of several rough planks nailed together. She gazed down. How many more pressure plates lay beneath her, and how could she avoid them?

Gingerly she crawled to the door, hoping with every movement that she wouldn't set off another trap. When she reached the door, she pushed on it tentatively with one hand. It didn't budge. The air felt tight. Suffocating. She pushed harder on the door. Nothing.

She pulled out the little saw on her multitool and slipped it between two of the boards and went to work. Soon a sliver broke off. She made the opening wider, moving a little at a time, until a gap appeared wide enough for her to peer through. She pressed her headlamp against the crack and stared inside. Beyond lay another room similar to the one she'd seen before. A cot, some canned food. She didn't see anyone inside, and the place rested in darkness.

She needed more leverage. She had to kick the door. Flattening herself against one wall, she managed to turn around in the tunnel through a series of contortionist moves her body would complain about later. Then she dug her elbows deep into the dirt and, bracing herself, kicked both feet out with all her strength. The wood splintered a little but she was wedged in too tightly. She struck again and again, each time shoving the door farther toward the room. Then with a final kick, she sent it clattering into the space.

She shimmied out of the tunnel, standing at last on the other side. A dank smell of rotten food, rodent urine, and stale air hung in the small space. Could Amelia have been kept here? Or Irma? She played her beam over the place, and realized instantly that the answer was no. No one had been here in a long time. Mouse and chipmunk droppings covered the small cot, and a pack rat had built a nest beneath it. Rust covered the canned food. She picked up one of the cans and read its expiration date: *9/15/2009.* How long had this squatter been living in this area?

She didn't see other signs of recent habitation. No Sterno stove. No paperback novels, no lantern. She dared another sniff, finding no hint of kerosene or burning candles.

She left the chamber and followed a smaller tunnel that slanted upward. It came to a wall of dirt. But Alex felt like she wasn't that far underground.

She hesitated, worrying about burying herself down here. Then, determined, she pulled out the folding shovel and started digging. Dirt collapsed in around her, and she started filling up one side of the tunnel with excavated soil. Then she hit a loose patch and welcome sunshine streamed into the tunnel. Alex almost whooped aloud with relief, and would have if she wasn't worried that the squatter could be nearby. She dug furiously now, eager to get out.

When she'd cleared a hole big enough to crawl through, she cautiously stuck her head out and gazed around.

She didn't see any sign of him. But as she stared upward out of the tunnel, she noticed that he had suspended a massive log from one of the trees with a rope and designed the trap so that unwitting victims would trigger it, sending the log swinging down to their location and taking them out. She was lucky she hadn't fallen prey to that one. Now she peered into the trees, looking for other traps, but didn't see any.

Finally she climbed out, tugging her backpack after her. She stood up, strapping it on, and began to explore the area with as much caution as possible. She searched for more tunnel entrances and trip wires, wondering if any of the women had ever been held here. But she couldn't fight the feeling that the squatter hadn't used this area in a long time. If he did have Amelia, he was holding her somewhere else.

Carefully Alex left the area after a thorough search, and then consulted her GPS unit. She'd intended to stay out tonight, but she felt disgusting with the weird powder all over her and wanted to go wash out her gear. She'd call Sheriff Taggert when she got back to the ranch house and report the location of the tunnel.

After dusting herself off as best she could, she pushed on, looking forward to a long, hot shower. The sun dipped behind the mountains and the temperature dropped. Soon darkness completely overtook the forest.

But as she passed by the location of Gaia, the gigantic tree, an angry voice made her halt.

It echoed from the dark cluster of trees in front of her. "This time I'm going to kill you!"

THIRTEEN

Alex heard a radio squawk not too far away from her and instantly snapped off her headlamp. She dug through her pack and pulled out her night-vision scope. Aiming its infrared beam in the voice's direction, she wondered if it was that of the squatter. But instead, she saw Trevor, the man who had sped away from the tree several days ago, leaving Agatha without her supplies.

"I can't do it!" she heard him whisper. "I know he's here somewhere!"

Then a booming voice sounded to her left. "You're damn right I'm here!" She snapped the scope in that direction, seeing the logger, Clyde, come roaring out of the trees in Trevor's direction. Trevor took off over a rise, kicking up dust as he went. Alex saw the basket tumble out of his hand, spilling supplies all over the forest floor.

"Goddamnit!" Agatha cursed from above. Alex heard the woman's radio squawk once more. "He's done it again. Left me. Only this time he didn't even leave the basket. He took it with him. Is anyone else there?"

Her radio only crackled in response.

The logger spoke up. "No, no one else is here, little lady. I'm tired of these tree-huggers bringing you supplies. If I have to camp out here all week, I'll see you starved out of that tree!"

Alex crept closer, wincing as the logger let loose a slew of invective.

"You bitches are all the same!" he cursed. "You're just like my ex-wife. You think you can get away with anything and that there'll be no consequences. You goddamn feminazis think you can order us around."

"Actually, there's no such thing as a 'feminazi,'" Agatha called down, her voice perfectly calm. "A lot of people don't even understand what feminism is. From the dictionary definition: 'the advocacy of women's equal rights.' So you see, Nazism is the antithesis of equal rights."

"You think I don't know what I'm talking about? My wife started going to one of those women support groups, and the next thing I know, they'd talked her into leaving me. Told her she didn't need me. I'll be damned if she didn't need me. I took care of her for ten years! Gave her the clothes on her back, paid for her car. Then she starts whining about wanting a job! Like any woman of mine is going to work outside the home! I've got a reputation. I'm a provider." He paused, and Alex could hear him breathing hard in his anger. "Okay, so I hit her sometimes. Big deal. She needed to understand."

"Sounds like she did understand and finally left you."

"Shut the fuck up! What do you know about it?"

"Only what you're telling me," Agatha responded.

"I'll bet you have some rich daddy who put you through college, where some feminazis put these ideas in your head."

Agatha's patience snapped. "You can rave down there all you want. My people will get supplies to me, just you watch."

"The hell they will!" Alex heard the roar of a chain saw as he pulled the starter cord and revved its engine. "I've half a mind to cut this tree down right now with you in it!"

"Do it, and that federal judge will be on you so fast you'll be fined out of your house and home."

"Fuck you!" he cried, his voice shrill with anger. Alex fixed the scope on him, seeing him circling the tree, outraged, waving the chain saw around like a maniac. "I'll see you dead before that happens! In fact . . ." His voice trailed off, and he shut down the chain saw. He placed it on the ground and dug furiously through a nearby pack. He pulled out tree-climbing spikes and buckled them to his boots. "I'm gonna come up there and pull you right out of this tree. Everyone will think you just fell."

"You've been yelling at me up here for so many days straight that there's no end of witnesses who will nail you," she retorted.

"I'll take my chances. I've had it with you, bitch. You're dead!" He placed a strap around the tree and started to climb the massive behemoth. Alex couldn't believe how fast he ascended. He'd obviously been climbing trees and logging for a long time.

"When I get up there, I'm gonna have so much satisfaction hearing your bones crack all the way down. I want to hear you scream, you fucking bitch!"

Alex had to do something. The guy had finally lost it.

Even if Agatha weren't up there, he still wouldn't be able to clear-cut this section of forest, not with the moratorium on it while the court heard the appeal. Somehow this woman had come to represent everything the man hated. He was already fifty feet up in the tree. She had to act.

"Hey!" Alex called up.

"Who's that?" Clyde shouted, pausing in his ascent.

"It's Alex Carter. The biologist from next door. I've just phoned the police and they're coming out. You have no right to try to get her out of that tree. She's not doing anything illegal, but you are, attempted assault or murder." Actually, Alex didn't know if Agatha was doing anything illegal or not. She'd have to look that up later. But for now, she just wanted to defuse the situation. "You'd better come down now if you want to save face," Alex told him. "They'll be here any minute."

"You can't fool me. There's no cell reception out here."

"I've got a sat phone," Alex lied. "You want to come down here and explain to Sheriff Taggert why you were trying to climb a tree to murder someone?"

Alex watched through the scope while he paused. She was getting to him.

"They should be here in about five minutes. Think you can climb all the way up to the top of that two-hundred-foot tree, murder her, climb all the way back down, and murder me, too, before they get here? You're pretty fast with those spikes, but I bet even you couldn't pull that off."

He stared out in her direction, though she was sure he couldn't see her in the dark. The rage on his face was evident. Could this guy have also been crazy enough to attack anyone walking through the woods? Like Amelia or Irma?

"Fuck!" he shouted, then started to climb down. Once again, he moved at an incredible speed down the trunk of the massive tree. When he reached the bottom, he threw his tree spikes into his backpack, enraged, then stormed straight in her direction. She snuck off, taking refuge behind another of the giant trees. He turned on a flashlight, the beam playing over the trunks, trying to spot her. "I know where you live," he shouted. "I'm not going to forget this."

This time Alex stayed quiet. He played the beam over the ground, searching for any sign of her. When his back was turned, she took the opportunity to sneak to another tree a little farther away.

Finally he cursed and marched off in the direction of the logging camp. She heard his ATV start up, and its headlights flashed over tree trunks as he sped away.

When Alex was sure he was gone, she called up into the darkness of the tree, "You okay up there?"

"I've never been so glad to hear someone's voice in my whole life," Agatha called down. "I think he was serious. I think he really wanted to kill me."

"You might be right. He was certainly mad enough to." She

thought of her own suspicions of the man and someone taking shots at her. "He's obviously got other things eating away at him."

"Yeah. His hatred of women." She laughed. The sound was a welcome noise amid the darkness. "I don't suppose Trevor is anywhere around down there?"

"Nope. He took off. Never seen someone run so fast. But I did see where he dropped your supplies. I'll go get them."

"You're a lifesaver!" Agatha called.

Alex flipped on her headlamp and moved to the fallen basket. Apples, pears, bananas, energy bars, and bottles of water spilled out all over the forest floor. Scattered among them was no-rinse shampoo, the kind astronauts used on the International Space Station, and hand sanitizer.

Alex gathered them all up into the basket and carried it back to the tree. "Okay. I'm ready."

"I'll lower the hook." Alex stared up as the familiar rope came into view. She grabbed the hook and fastened it to the basket's handle. Then Agatha pulled it up into her lofty domain.

"That was a close one, I won't lie. I'm still shaking. I really thought he was going to climb up here. I was petrified."

"Do you want me to let the sheriff know that you're being harassed?"

Agatha hesitated. "I don't know. Do you think she'd try to make me come down?"

"I'm not sure."

"I guess I would feel safer with her or her deputies checking on me."

"Why don't I surreptitiously get a feel for how she might react?"

"That would be great. She must know I'm up here, though. I'm sure Clyde must have told her. Or maybe told the national forest rangers."

"I'll find out what people know."

"Thank you." Alex could hear her unpacking the basket. "I hope they send Dennis next time. If Trevor botches one more delivery . . ."

"I hear you." Alex could just feel that powder all over her, sinking into her pores. She longed to get home and rinse off. "Good luck up there."

"Thanks. I'll need it."

As Alex retreated into the dark, she hoped the angry logger would stay away and that she wouldn't run into him again on her way back.

FOURTEEN

As soon as Alex got back to the ranch house, she dumped her pack off on the porch and tried to dust off as much of the remaining powder as she could. Then she overturned the pack onto a chair and emptied its contents. She uncoiled her sleeping pad and tent and turned the hose on them and her pack.

Inside, she descended to the laundry room in the basement. She opened the lid of the washing machine and stripped off all of her clothes, throwing them in. Her sleeping bag would go in next.

Then she climbed the stairs and luxuriated in a hot shower, washing all of the gunk out of her hair and off her skin. She toweled off, then blew her nose vigorously and rinsed her mouth repeatedly with mouthwash. She didn't think she'd ingested poison. At least, she felt okay.

In the bedroom, she changed into fresh clothes. The washing machine had finished, so she stuck her wet clothes in the dryer and stuffed her sleeping bag into the machine.

She glanced at her watch. It was still early enough to call the sheriff. She retrieved her GPS unit from the porch, where she'd dumped out her pack. In the kitchen, she picked up the receiver and dialed Taggert's number.

"Dr. Carter?" the sheriff said by way of greeting.

"Hi, Sheriff."

"How are things?"

"Interesting. You know that tunnel I found?"

"Yes."

"I found another one. More extensive and booby-trapped."

"What the hell? Who is this guy?"

"Exactly what I'm wondering. This tunnel didn't look like it had been occupied in a while. But I thought I'd let you know where it is. I searched around the area in case he might have held Irma or Amelia there, but I didn't see anything that led me to believe he did. Still, I wanted you to know about it in case you want to check it out."

"Thanks. What are the coordinates?"

Alex read them off her GPS unit. "There's something else. Are you aware of an activist camping out at the top of one of the old-growth trees?"

"Agatha. Yes. Why, is something wrong with her?"

"There's a logger in the area. He's been harassing her."

Taggert sighed. "Clyde Fergus. Yep. I'm aware of that. I've sent deputies out to talk to him, but he's a hothead. Keeps getting worked up. He calls every day to report her, and I keep telling him there's nothing we can do while the case is being considered."

"He seems a little unhinged. Dangerous. He threatened to kill her tonight."

"What?" She exhaled with irritation. "Okay. I'll go out tonight and have a talk with him with one of the law enforcement rangers. Goddamnit. Tomorrow I'll call the logging company and see about getting him replaced. He's supposed to be just keeping an eye on the equipment, not harassing her." The sheriff sounded tired. "Thanks for letting me know."

"Of course. He actually got caught in a booby trap in a different area, too, the other day. I got him down." She gave the sheriff those coordinates, too.

"I'll send someone to check out the areas. Let me know if you find anything else."

"I will."

After they hung up, Alex made a quick dinner of pasta in marinara sauce with a little garlic powder. She carried it over to the dining room table, where she powered on her laptop. While she ate, she scrolled through photos from the remote cameras. There was no sign of additional caribou on the memory cards. She did, however, find images of a pine marten with two babies, and to her great excitement, an uncommon flammulated owl.

She clicked through more of the photos, seeing a black bear, a mountain lion with a cub, several mule deer, and a small group of female elk.

Next she downloaded the latest videos from the collar camera. The caribou continued its solitary existence from what she could see. It grazed and ruminated, slept and wandered. She felt sad that its population had been wiped out from the U.S.

Canada had made efforts to save the caribou, listing their southern mountain caribou population as threatened under their Species at Risk Act (SARA) in 2003. Later, in 2011, Alex had read that the Committee on the Status of Endangered Wildlife in Canada (COSEWIC) recommended to SARA that the southern mountain caribou be considered a separate designatable unit and be granted endangered status, which it was in 2014.

Alex knew that at one time, over eight hundred mountain caribou roamed the mountainous national parks of the Canadian Rockies. But now those numbers were dangerously low.

Jasper National Park, which lay to the north of Banff National Park in Canada, had four mountain caribou herds until recently. Unfortunately, the Maligne herd was declared extirpated in 2018, and two of Jasper's other herds were deemed too small to recover. One, the Tonquin herd, had fewer than forty-five members, and the Brazeau herd fewer than fifteen. Neither herd had enough females to ensure their survival.

Alex needed to find new places to search on the preserve and possibly more places to hang remote cameras. She opened her geographic information systems software, ArcGIS, and imported satellite views of the sanctuary. On top of these, she added layers for type of land cover and vegetation. From the results, she picked out several stands of old-growth hemlock and red cedar that she wanted to check out tomorrow.

She wanted to hear her dad's warm voice, so she called him, smiling when he picked up.

"Pumpkin!"

"Hi, Dad."

"What's new?"

"Happily, more caribou footage. And . . ." She wondered if she should mention the woman's necklace and decided it would be good to hear his reassuring thoughts.

"And?"

Though she'd avoided it previously for fear of worrying him, she told him now about the missing hiker, then described how she'd spotted the raven and the hiker's necklace on the footage.

"Oh, wow. Is it a good lead? Is she still alive?"

"I don't know. I took the FBI out to the site yesterday. They bagged the necklace. Maybe it'll have some kind of forensic evidence on it. Provide a clue."

"Do you think she could have run off? Left the necklace there to make people think she was still in the forest?"

"If she did leave it there on purpose to be found, she was taking a hell of a chance someone would actually run across it out there. But I think that's the best-case scenario at this point."

"Chilling."

"I agree. So tell me something good. What have you been up to?"

He took a deep breath. Alex could tell he was worried about her, but he'd never been one to fuss or try to scare her by being overly cautious. "Let's see. I'm on the North Rim now. Hiked out to Widforss Point today and painted in the afternoon. The colors are so vivid here. All these reds and golds. A storm had moved into part of the canyon, and I was actually looking down on storm clouds flashing with lightning. It was pure magic."

"It sounds like it. Did you get a good painting out of it?"

"Boy, did I. I sat there all afternoon painting it over and over again."

"Widforss . . . isn't he that painter you love so much?"

"He sure is. Gunnar Widforss. He painted a lot of the U.S. national parks in the 1920s and '30s. He was from Sweden and became enchanted with the American West. Traveled all over. Yellowstone, Crater Lake, Yosemite, the Grand Canyon. His watercolors are stunning! But he never really gained the financial success or fame he deserved, largely because back then people considered watercolors to be more of a sketching technique than a bona fide art form you'd want to collect. So a lot of the time, he just drove around and exchanged paintings for room and board."

Alex thought back to a happy memory of being in Yosemite National Park with her mom and dad. She had probably been about ten. "I remember the first time I saw his work, hanging in the Ahwahnee Hotel in Yosemite."

"That's right! They have quite a few of his originals there in the lobby."

"I thought at first I was looking at a photograph, and when I got up close, I was blown away. Couldn't believe it was watercolor."

Her dad sighed. "Sure would have liked to hang out with him and exchange tips. Sometimes I can almost feel his presence here. He loved the canyon."

"That sounds haunting. In a good way."

He chuckled. "Guess all this grandeur is getting to me. So what's next for you?"

"Continuing to check the video footage. Going out to where the caribou is hanging out to see if any habitat can be improved or if any other caribou are with him."

"Good luck with everything."

"Thanks, Dad."

They hung up, and absolutely beat, she climbed the stairs, changed into her pj's, brushed her teeth, and flopped onto the bed.

THE NEXT DAY, HER GEAR thoroughly sprayed off and washed, Alex set out early in the morning. She intended to stay out over several nights, barring getting stuck in any more booby-trapped pits.

She made the rounds of two remote cameras on the preserve, swapping out the memory cards. She visited the old-growth stands that she'd selected the night before. She searched painstakingly among those immense trees for scat or tracks but didn't locate any. By two in the afternoon, her stomach started rumbling.

She stopped at a huge pile of lichen-covered boulders in a small clearing. Dark crevices opened in the rocks, and the cool air issuing from those spaces felt welcome on her tired body. She hauled herself up onto one of the tallest rocks and took out one of the sandwiches she'd made that morning: mustard, avocado, and peppered Tofurkey slices on honey wheat bread. She dug into it, relishing the taste. Food always tasted better when she'd been out hiking.

She listened to crickets chirping in the grass and the trickle of a nearby stream. A red squirrel trilled from a tree, then started barking, clearly irritated. She glanced around for the source of its agitation and spotted a red-tailed chipmunk on the ground casting around for seeds. It was probably too close to the red squirrel's stash. Finally, with a flick of its tail, the squirrel dashed down the tree and chased off the chipmunk. Then the squirrel went to work stripping a pine cone, casting aside the parts it didn't want. But it kept registering its irritation, chirping around a mouth full of food. Alex couldn't help but laugh at the comical sounds of the little guy.

Her sandwich finished, she moved to the next stand of old growth and spent the rest of the afternoon carefully walking transects there, hoping to find caribou spoor. She found no signs.

At last, as the sun began to dip down behind the mountains, she decided to find a good spot to camp.

The sound of whitewater drew her into a meadow. A tumbling teal and white river streamed through it, deep purple Davidson's penstemon, scarlet skyrocket, and vividly pink fireweed growing along its banks. When she stopped to enjoy the delicate flowers, she spotted a fairy slipper orchid growing in a patch of shade. Her gaze followed the river's trek upstream to a waterfall in the distance, cascading down from a glacier in a hanging valley of the mountains beyond.

That settled it. This spot was magical, and she'd sleep here for the night.

A lovely flat spot beckoned her on the far bank, so she found a place where rocks would allow her to hop across the river.

She pitched her tent, staking it into the soil, then attached its rainfly. She stuffed her sleeping bag and pad inside, then propped her pack up against a nearby boulder. After unpacking her backcountry stove and small pot, she cooked a package of freeze-dried lentils and butternut squash and downed it, hungry after her long hike. Then she leaned against her pack as the sun set.

The clouds along the western horizon dazzled, shifting from gold to orange to red to pink and finally to a dreamy purple. Jupiter gleamed near Saturn, the first celestial bodies she could see.

The Big Dipper appeared as the sky darkened, and she used its handle to "arc to Arcturus," a star-hopping trick she'd picked up in an undergrad astronomy class. Above Arcturus, she picked out one of her favorite summer constellations, the Corona Borealis, which gleamed like a crown of jewels above her. From Arcturus, she "spiked to Spica" in Virgo.

Soon she could make out Scorpius, high enough that even its long, curled tail hung above the mountains. And behind it she spotted the asterism the Great Teapot in Sagittarius. Steam rose out of the Teapot's spout, the center of the galaxy itself, in clouds of brilliant white and gold. She continued to star hop like this until so many stars filled the sky that it grew difficult to pick out individual constellations in the dazzling array of lights. Her eyes traced the dark nebulosity weaving through the Milky Way, trails of dust clouds obscuring the stars beyond them.

Mosquitoes had found her by now, buzzing in her ears and at the back of her neck. Soon it would be too chilly for them. She donned her thick fleece coat, keeping some of them at bay while she continued to gaze up.

Finally her eyes started to droop, and she packed away her dinner things. She pulled her pack in under the shelter of the rainfly, stuck her boots next to it, and crawled into bed.

As she nestled into her sleeping bag, Alex relaxed gratefully after her long hike. She switched off her headlamp in the darkness and stared up at the tent ceiling.

She remembered seeing the eerie green glow of the northern lights from her tent out on the ice of Hudson Bay. Was it really so recently she was there? It felt like another lifetime ago. She closed her eyes, breathing in the familiar scent of her backcountry tent. A flammulated owl called out with a long series of low hoots. She listened in the ensuing silence for an answer, and a minute later, another owl called back from a different part of the forest. Several coyotes yipped and called from a nearby mountain. She smiled.

This, she thought, *this is where I'm most at home. In the backcountry, in the wilderness.* Here there was no traffic, no car exhaust, no one yelling, no angry motorists, no factories belching out black smoke. Just the peaceful sound of the wind sighing through the trees, owls calling from the darkness, coyotes serenading the velvety night.

She didn't feel alone out here. She felt at peace, part of something much bigger than herself, just another animal out in the forest. It struck her that she didn't exactly fit in with society. She often experienced a disconnect with people that made her feel far more alone than she did when she was actually by herself.

She could be with a group of people at a restaurant, all chatting away, and then someone would mention some pop culture reference that everyone but her would chime in on, and she'd realize how very different she truly was. This longing to help wildlife, to protect it in its natural habitat, pulled her more powerfully than anything else. She'd never married, while many of her childhood friends had. She'd never had a nine-to-five office job or cared about having the latest technology.

But out here—getting water from a river, sitting out on a sun-warmed boulder watching the wind ripple through the grass, deer passing close to her—this was her home.

She again smiled to herself, nestling farther down into the comforting embrace of her mummy bag. It was going to be cold tonight. She could feel it. But for now, the ground still radiated the heat of the afternoon, and she let her muscles release all the tension of the day.

The owls called out again and she listened to their conversation. Then she thought she heard a different owl, coming from another direction. An eerie, high-pitched almost-scream, like a long-eared owl's alarm call, maybe? But its call had cut off in the middle. She waited for it to sing again, curious. Then she heard it, a creepy wail, followed by a soft call of "Who." The flammulated owls stopped singing. Then the other owl called again, and she realized it wasn't an owl, but a very soft human voice. And this time it didn't sound like *who*. It sounded like *help*.

FIFTEEN

Alex sat up, listening in the darkness. She strained her ears so hard that all she could hear was the blood rushing through them. Then she heard it again, faint: "Help." A woman's voice. Alex quickly threw on her pile pants and thermal shirt, then unzipped the tent door. Grabbing her boots from under the rainfly, she slipped her feet in and picked up her GPS unit.

She couldn't tell if the voice was very weak or very far away. She snatched up her multitool and headlamp. The moon was so bright, she didn't really need the light, so she left the lamp off for now. If the woman was in trouble, no need to advertise her own location if someone dangerous was out there.

Her mind instantly went to the missing hiker. But this area was way off from where she'd vanished. And there was no way she could still be alive out here, after all this time, could she? Had she set out to live in the wild, like Chris McCandless, the hiker who journeyed into the Alaskan wilderness, never to return? But if so, why abandon her tent and supplies? Maybe it was someone different, an injured or disoriented hiker.

Alex waited for the call to come again to pinpoint the location. She stood there in the moonlight for so long that she thought the woman had given up and wasn't going to call out again.

But then she heard it, very faint, off to her right.

Alex headed in that direction, following the weak cries. She descended a ridge, finally needing to switch on her headlamp to navigate the steep, rocky terrain. But the woman seemed to be moving off. The more Alex homed in on her location, the more the position seemed to shift. The person was on the move, whoever she was. That meant she was mobile, though she could still be injured with a broken arm or a concussion, or even suffering from dehydration.

Alex reached the bottom of the ridge and entered a dense copse of hemlock. She sucked in a breath when she came upon a lichen-covered boulder with a thick, ropy string of blood dribbled across it. It showed bright red and fresh in her beam.

She paused, listening again. She heard the quiet voice asking, "Anyone? Is anyone here?"

She listened, too, for a third person, but didn't hear anything. Her gut told her the woman was alone and had heard Alex moving in the darkness, seen her light. "Hey," Alex called softly.

"Hello?" she heard the woman respond.

"Do you need help?" Alex asked in the general direction of the woman's voice.

"Yes!" she cried, and Alex heard her burst into tears.

"I'm coming," Alex assured her. "Just stay where you are. Call out so I can find you."

"Okay," came the weak reply.

Alex judged that she was about a hundred yards away, on the far side of the dense cluster of trees.

She was halfway there when a loud throbbing sound, like repeated, cacophonous peals of thunder, suddenly erupted in the trees above her. A blinding light flashed on, shining down on Alex, making her stumble over a fallen log in the dazzling brilliance.

"What the hell?" Alex cursed, catching her balance. She looked up at the intense light streaming down.

The woman screamed on the other side of the trees. "Run! Or you'll wake up *there*!" Then she sped away into the darkened forest.

The blinding light shifted, shining right into Alex's eyes. She flung her arm up, trying to shield herself from the glare. The low, terrifying blast of noise continued to emanate from the thing, the clamor deafening. Alex clapped her hands to her ears and ran in the direction she thought the woman had gone, but she couldn't see anything in front of her, her retinas too splotchy and burned. She tripped on a rock and went sprawling into the dirt. The thing zipped down, almost right on top of her, and she felt something cold and metallic brush her shoulder. She shoved it off and scrambled to her feet.

Then she took off into the forest, the glare now thankfully behind her instead of blinding her. She shut off her headlamp to mask her location. Weaving between trees, she used the thing's light to spot fallen logs or rocks she could trip over. But its pinpointing beam also meant it knew exactly where she was.

It hummed above her, zigzagging between tree trunks, zeroing in on her. Again that deafening blast went out and Alex clasped her hands to her ears. Then the tone pitched upward, becoming a piercing metallic shriek that made her teeth vibrate. She leapt over rocks and reached the river she'd camped next to. Splashing across a shallow part, she hit the opposite bank at a sprint, running up the steep embankment. Ahead she found a tightly gathered cluster of trees and raced for it, hoping the thing wouldn't be able to navigate it as quickly as she could.

She'd guessed right and it zipped upward, moving above the canopy. She could see its light flashing over the treetops, heading in the same direction as she was. So she whipped around, doing a one-eighty, and headed back down the bank toward the river. Instantly it reversed, too, tracking her movements. She didn't see how it could follow her like that, not through the dense tree cover.

She whipped around again, trying to orient herself, thinking where safety might lie. Miles to the southeast lay the ranch house and her car. To the west stood steep, jagged mountains. To the east lay the boundary of the national forest and eventually Kathleen's tower.

And to the southwest lay her tent and the river.

She wondered where the woman had gone. Maybe she had given this thing the slip while it hunted Alex. Or maybe it thought Alex *was* her and had mixed up its prey.

She wondered if she could somehow bring it down from the sky. A gap in the tree canopy lent her a sudden view of it, a blinding light far above the treetops. She couldn't judge how big the thing was, and there was no way she could throw something up there to knock it out of the air anyway. Its loud thrumming noise drilled into her brain, reverberating. She could feel the vibration in her breastbone. What the hell was it?

One thing was for damn sure. Alex wouldn't let the thing catch her and make her *wake up there,* wherever *there* was.

Ahead of Alex stretched a vast meadow. She knew she'd never lose the thing there. She needed cover. Denser, taller trees. She thought of the cluster of old growth to the east of her. When she'd walked through it earlier, daylight had barely reached the forest floor. She skirted the side of the meadow, keeping to the tree line, forcing the thing to skim far above her. Soon it would have to fly even higher when she made it to the older trees. She reached the edge of the grove and plunged into it, having to slow down now that the moonlight was obscured. She could hear the thing above her still, and she kept to the thick growth. She couldn't see it now, just its beam flashing in the upper canopy.

Alex paused, expecting it to continue on in the direction she was moving, but it didn't. It hovered above her location.

She stayed still, catching her breath. Still it floated directly over her. She decided to wait here, see what would happen. Maybe it would run out of fuel or give up the chase.

It moved slowly above her, its searching beam gleaming through branches. It reached a wider gap between the treetops and descended, then raised up again upon discovering the branches were still too thick there.

It flew off, and for a moment, relief swept over Alex. But then its beam pierced through the trees again, spotlighting the forest floor twenty feet in front of her. It shifted directly above that spot and started to descend. It was searching for a hole to pass through. It still knew exactly where she was.

SIXTEEN

Alex took off through the trees, keeping to the tightest clusters. The thing skimmed along above her, though again she couldn't see how it could possibly be spotting her through the thick branches. She ran on, trying to think of a place to hide or some way to force the thing to crash. Cliffs lay some distance ahead. Could she somehow trick it into smashing itself against the rock face?

A stitch formed in her side, and her mouth was so dry that it hurt to swallow. Sweat ran down her back and beaded on her scalp. A grove of old growth she'd visited earlier in the day stood some quarter mile away, and then she'd be that much closer to the cliffs. She headed that way, dodging between tree trunks. She didn't have to strain to know if the thing was following her. Its dazzling beam painted the upper branches, its terrifying low hum reverberating through the forest.

She didn't know what it was—only that it looked way too big to be a quadcopter of some sort. And the strange noises it made were like nothing she'd ever heard. She thought of old Bill in the town park, going on about aliens, and her blood froze.

Then it flew off. Darkness and silence overtook the forest again.

Had it given up? Or switched its pursuit back to the woman?

Alex paused, waiting. Minutes ticked by. She didn't dare head back for her tent. The thing could be waiting there. She didn't want to stay in the same place where it had last seen her, either. Her best bet was to hole up for the night in the patch of old growth she'd been heading for. She could rest, catch her breath.

She pushed on for the grove. She reached it and sank down at the base of a massive tree trunk. It took her five minutes to get her breath under control and her heart to slow. She ached for a drink of water.

The quiet solace of the forest descended upon her, and she closed her burning eyes. She wondered where the woman was, if she'd eluded the thing and gotten to safety.

Her body was just starting to relax when she heard the thing on the wind. A low hum. Getting louder. The thing was heading this way, probably searching for both of them. She looked up, scanning the branches for a flash of light. And then she saw it, a white beam skimming along the treetops. The hum grew louder and louder until it was that same rumbling vibration.

Her mind flashed illogically on a memory of being a little kid at a small-town parade with her mother and father. Local politicians drove by, waving, and then the local Harley-Davidson riding group thundered past, and she remembered their engine noise vibrating her little breastbone. The thing did this now. Its beam pierced through the trees directly above her. It knew where she was. Again. Even though she had moved.

Indecision seized Alex. How did it keep finding her? Did she have some kind of tracking device in her clothing? But all she had on were a pair of pile pants, her underwear, her boots, and a thermal shirt. She whipped off her shoes, feeling along the insides for any telltale lump or device. But they were the same faithful boots she'd had for years. And there certainly wasn't anything in her minimal amount of clothing.

She didn't know how it was tracking her, but it was. And her only choice now was to run.

Alex sped on, trying to remember what lay in front of her. Sweat trickled down her back. Then it hit her. Body heat. The thing must be equipped with forward-looking infrared, or FLIR. She would be a bright white Alex-shaped outline on a FLIR readout. She had to somehow mask her body heat.

Her mind raced for solutions. She recalled the large pile of jumbled boulders where she'd stopped for lunch. Wide spaces opened at the base of it. If she could somehow lose the thing and then make it to those boulders, she could hide beneath them. They'd been soaking up the sun's heat all day, and their residual warmth might cover her own.

She ran, heading for the boulder field. She reached it but ran past it, as if she were planning to continue on. The thing followed above. Then it shot ahead, searching for a place to descend. She took the chance and abruptly spun around, racing back for the boulder pile. A large, dark crevice yawned open in front of her.

She dove into it just as she heard the thing circle back. Then she was safely inside, pressing herself farther and farther into the cool dark slot. She felt the rocks above her. They were still warm from the sun's heat.

Above, she could hear the thing searching, flying back and forth. It moved off a considerable distance, its roar fading, and hope bloomed inside her. But then she heard it come back, doing sweeps above her.

She held her breath. Had she fooled it? Without emerging, she craned her neck to see out of the hole, saw the beam shining through the trees, spotlighting portions of the forest floor, ferns illuminated suddenly by the dazzling light, the glare shining over fallen, moss-covered trees.

And then, to her horror, the beam got brighter and more focused, the circle growing smaller, the roar growing louder. The thing had found an open space to descend.

It came into view and Alex fought the urge to bolt in sheer panic. The lights on it were so bright, she couldn't make out the shape of it, but she guessed it was at least ten feet wide. Lights pulsed in a rhythm across its front and suddenly it let out a blast of deafening noise, like the lumbering tripods in *War of the Worlds*.

Alex gripped the stone around her, panic seizing her. The confines of the rock blocked some of the lights and she was able to make out a few details on the craft. The thing rotated and a single, searching eye swiveled into view, a lens staring right at her. From its belly, another, smaller light flicked on and shone into the crevice, pinpointing her location.

Then it moved closer, and she saw a gleaming metal tube. From it extended a long tranquilizer dart, its needle dripping with some kind of liquid.

The craft rotated so that the needle pointed straight into the crevice.

Alex got down on her back and thrust out with her boot, kicking the needle aside.

She bolted out of the hole, striking the metal tube with her boot, trying to knock the dart loose. But it wouldn't come out.

The craft backed up abruptly, the needle still dripping, still installed in the tube.

The thing shot upward, well out of her reach, and Alex took off running. She needed someplace better to hide. Someplace where her body heat would not be seen. And then it hit her. The river. If she could make it to the river, even with this thing on her heels, and plunge into that icy-cold water, she could swim underwater for a considerable distance, up- or downstream, and possibly lose it. It would be a lengthy area to search, and hopefully by then the thing would run out of whatever fuel or battery it ran on.

Alex sped in that direction, her body firing on pure adrenaline. The craft screamed behind her, letting out deafening blast after blast, skimming along below the canopy, trying to navigate the tree trunks. She heard a metallic clang as it collided with something and she glanced back. It stopped moving, then very slowly maneuvered between a few trunks to a hole in the canopy and shot up through that.

It was just the head start she needed. She raced through the thick old growth, plunged into the next grove of giant trees, ran down the steep embankment to the river, and dove in.

The freezing water shocked her system, stealing all the breath from her lungs. Alex blinked in disbelief at the astonishing cold, her body momentarily frozen. Then she snapped out of it, managed a deep breath as she continued hurtling down the river. The current bore her along swiftly, tumbling whitewater dashing her against the rocks. She had to get her bearings, knew she should be going feet-first to protect her head from submerged rocks and trees.

She managed to spin around and in doing so got the briefest glimpse of the open sky above her, the thing some distance down-stream from where she'd jumped in. She held her breath and went under, and her feet jammed up against a cluster of rocks. She bent her knees, moving forward underwater until she gripped the rough stone surfaces with her hands. She pushed herself down deeper until her feet touched the bottom. She hugged herself to the rocks, desperate for a breath. She stared up through the current but didn't see any light infiltrating the turbulent water.

Her body now felt numb from the cold. The tremendous pressure of water pushed at her back, and she could feel small pieces of debris striking her, sticks and dirt clumps and pebbles.

She closed her eyes, concentrating on a single thing: holding her breath as long as she could. Her lungs burned and still she held it. Behind her closed eyes, stars popped and twinkled. Then, when she couldn't stand it anymore and thought she might involuntarily suck in water, she dared to surface.

Slowly she brought her head up beside the rocks. She lifted her face to be parallel with the water's surface and gently peeked through to the air, gasping in a fresh breath. At the same time, she stared around for the craft. She didn't see it up- or downstream, and finally dared a look around the rocks. She saw it then, hovering some two hundred feet downstream, the beam playing over the water. It continued downstream and she breathed gratefully. She started to shiver against the cold of the rock, the continuous push of icy water pressing in on her back.

Then to her horror, the craft turned and started back upstream, beam searching. She had to go under again. She hyperventilated, saturating her lungs, and then plunged back down. Gripping the rocks, she pulled herself to the bottom of the river. This time she kept her eyes open, watching for the light.

It hit her section of water moments later. But so much rock flour had been carried down from a glacier that the water was cloudy and the beam diffuse. She didn't think the craft would be able to make out anything in the river other than a vague mass of swirling white. The beam moved upstream, the light fading. Still she waited. She needed a breath. The cold now suffused her entire being, seeped into her core. She shivered violently, and that made it harder to hold her breath.

Then she had a terrible thought—if she didn't surface now and chance a breath, the craft could come back downstream when she could no longer hold her breath and it would pinpoint her then. She had to take a chance now. She surfaced, again letting only her face peek out. She sucked in a grateful breath, and spotted the craft some distance upstream, still searching. She breathed, waiting to see its next move. Then slowly, just as she had dreaded, it turned around, moving its search downstream once again.

Goddamnit! She plunged back underwater. At the river's bottom, she waited while the light filled the water and continued on. Then slowly she surfaced, watching the craft continue downstream. She gripped the rock, her body so cold now that her muscles were freezing up. She couldn't feel her lips or her fingers or feet. They were like blocks of wood resting against the rocks. From there she watched while the craft moved off into the trees, searching the left bank. But she didn't dare climb out. Not yet. It could come back.

And it did, crossing the river and searching the trees on that side.

Alex's violent shivering began to slow and then stopped. She knew what that meant. Hypothermia had set in.

Still she clung to the rocks as the thing searched both sides of the river methodically and slowly. She willed it away, cursed it, cursed whoever was operating it. And then to her immense relief, it shifted off into a deeper section of the forest and disappeared. Alex pushed off from her rock and swam at an angle to the shore.

When she reached the soft soil of the bank, she dragged herself out, panting. She was so cold now she couldn't feel her body at all. She slumped onto the chilly riverbank, unable to move. She tried to lift herself up with her arms, but they wouldn't obey her commands. Her legs and arms felt like useless spaghetti noodles.

With fear, she scanned the area, but no searching light met her gaze. She breathed a sigh of relief. Slowly she managed to drag herself away from the river and into the shelter of the trees, but she still couldn't make her body stand up.

At last, after lying for several long minutes just panting and aching, she managed to get her arms under her and push herself up into a sitting position. Her soaked boots felt like she carried twenty-pound weights on her feet. Gripping a tree trunk, she managed to haul herself up. Then she just stood there, dripping, feeling colder than she ever had in her life, even colder than she had felt in the Canadian Arctic.

Then slowly a warmth began to suffuse her body. It flooded her system, warming her from her core, then out to her extremities. She actually began to feel hot.

That wasn't so bad, she thought, *diving into that river. I'm already warm.*

She rose to her feet and, smiling, started walking through the trees, feeling so hot now that she was tempted to strip off her shirt and just hike in her bra. The shirt was uncomfortably hot and wet anyway. She shucked off the sodden, clinging garment and walked on. But her legs were too warm. She should take off her pile pants, too. She was suffocating in them.

She trudged on, then stopped to kick off her boots so she could ditch the pants. But then it struck her—*No. Wait. Hypothermia.* From some clouded part of her mind, she knew she probably wasn't hot at all, but was in actuality freezing to death. Hypothermic victims felt a rush of heat so intense that they often stripped off all their clothes in their delirium, hastening their own deaths from the cold. She paused, then forced herself to don her boots and shirt again. At least the shirt wasn't cotton, nor were her pile pants.

Cotton kills, she heard an outdoor leader from one of her childhood summer camps say. *If you get cotton wet, it only makes you colder.*

So she had that going for her. But where the hell had she been walking to just now? She'd just set off without a thought to her destination, and now her situation was precarious.

Fear seized her that she could completely slip into delirium and die out here. She had to force her mind to focus. What were her options? She couldn't hear the craft now. It had moved far away. She had to get into some warm, dry clothes and shelter. Her tent. Her sleeping bag. Where were they? She couldn't focus on her location. Were they upstream from here? She knew she'd camped near the river.

She had to keep moving. Try to stay warm. She chose upstream and kept to the trees, stumbling.

She could barely walk, and her mind flashed to strange memories, like she was trudging through a dream.

Suddenly she couldn't remember where she was.

Camping with my parents?

No. You're on a preserve. Some preserve somewhere.

Did I do all my grading? As a TA I have to finish grading that class with six hundred students. That pile of blue books is waiting back at my desk. So why am I wandering across campus?

You don't have to grade. You're thirty-one years old. You finished your PhD. You're not on campus. You're on a preserve. You're in . . . Washington. Yes.

In D.C.? With Ben?

No, the other Washington. Just walk. Walk, Alex.

She tripped on a log and came down hard onto a bed of needles and ferns.

I'll just stay here. Too tired.

She shut her eyes. The moss was soft. She curled up on her side. *I'll sleep here for a few minutes, and then press on.*

Her eyes snapped open. *No! You'll die. Get up! Get up, damn it!*

She forced herself to her feet, using another tree trunk to right herself.

Was I supposed to go bowling with Zoe? She's going to wonder why I'm late.

No. Just keep walking.

I wonder if she got us nachos already. I like the nachos at the snack bar there.

I'm sure she has. Just keep walking and you can have the nachos.

Why is the bowling alley outside? I won't be able to bowl through all these trees.

Yes, that is weird. Maybe the bowling alley is in a different direction.

Alex stumbled off back toward the river, but as soon as she got into the open along the bank, she froze. *No. Wait. That thing.* A thing had been chasing her. She had to stay in cover. *That's right.* Her tent. She was trying to reach her tent.

She stumbled on.

And then she saw it, in a small clearing up ahead. Her tent. Warmth. Clothes. Her sleeping bag. She stumbled to it, collapsing at the door.

But something in the back of her mind pulled at her. *No. Not here. It knows where this is. Probably spotted the tent.* She hefted the tent up, loosening it from its stakes, and then grabbed the corner of the material.

She dragged the tent into the trees and kept dragging it.

She fell. Over and over again she fell, her mind now completely clouded. She couldn't remember what she was doing. Why did she want to get warm when she was already overheating? The thought of getting into a hot tent and a suffocating sleeping bag was unbearable. Why was she doing this?

She stopped dragging the tent.

The river. She could cool off in the river.

She stopped herself. The sudden thought of being out on the ice in the Arctic flashed through her mind. *Hypothermia. Yes.* She had to get warm. But not here.

She dragged the tent.

Kept dragging it and dragging it until she didn't know how far away she was from her original campsite, but it felt a world away. A world of gauzy uncertainty and confusion. She pulled the tent into a circle of trees, onto a soft bed of moss, and climbed in. She started to get into the sleeping bag wet, then stopped herself. She stripped off all her clothes and then crawled inside the mummy bag, zipping it up over her head. And then an abyss rushed up and swallowed her whole.

SEVENTEEN

Kathleen Macklay awoke with a start, struck by the sensation that she was not alone in her room. She sat up on one elbow, her heart suddenly hammering, bleary eyes scanning the darkness. Her green Forest Service jacket lay draped over one chair, the curtains showing the dim glow of predawn light. She listened intently, hearing only the ticking of her Timex on the bedside table and a few birds beginning the dawn chorus.

Her heart slowed. *Must have been a dream,* she thought. She had to get up soon anyway, so she threw off the covers and stepped into her slippers. She shuffled into the kitchen, where she filled a big pot with water from the tap and put it on to boil and sterilize. Knowing it would take a long time, she also filled up a small teakettle. She loved to have her morning coffee while watching the sun emerge from beyond the peaks.

She showered and dressed while the water heated.

Grabbing some milk out of the small propane-powered fridge, she made a bowl of cereal. After pouring some of the kettle water for coffee, she carried her breakfast outside to the porch to welcome the new day.

Staring up at the fire tower, which loomed over the small Forest Service cabin, she couldn't help but smile. She loved working here. It was the best job she had ever had, and a welcome respite from the drama that came through the sheriff's department in Bitterroot.

She relished these summers when she could just sit up in the tower and drink in the vista of old-growth forests and snowcapped peaks. This was her favorite time of the year. She lived for it.

In past summers, she'd seen grizzlies, foxes, wolves, and even a wolverine powering across a mountain slope once.

She heard the high-pitched *swee swee swee zee* song of a Townsend's warbler ring out from the trees, followed by the rapid-fire drumming of a pileated woodpecker.

The forest woke up with her, and she felt part of it, alive and grateful.

Reluctantly, she turned to go inside, figuring that the water she'd put on the stove to sterilize might be getting hot enough now to boil. It had to boil for at least four solid minutes. She ducked inside her bedroom and donned her trusty Timex, with its handsome red dial and white Roman numerals. She'd had the watch since the 1960s and cherished it; it had been a present from her mother.

As she strapped it on, the feeling that she was not alone stole over her again.

Suddenly a shadow passed over the bedroom wall. She spun, her face slamming into a meaty hand that clamped dirty, gloved fingers over her mouth. She screamed, the sound muted, and a powerful arm wrapped around her middle, crushing her rib cage. Her vision swam, then tunneled.

She brought her fist back into the man's groin. With a guttural exhale, he released her. She ran from the bedroom, the man clambering close behind. Out in the kitchen, she grabbed the pot of boiling water and flung it back at him. He leapt to one side and she saw him fully now, a tall man wearing a thick balaclava and a helmet, dressed entirely in black combat gear. He wore body armor, dozens of Velcro straps with stowed weapons. He managed to dodge most of the boiling water, with the bulk of the wave hitting him on one leg. With his thick clothes, she doubted he felt it much.

Kathleen turned and ran, catching a glimpse of the butt of a gun on his hip, and a nasty-looking combat knife strapped to his thigh.

She raced toward her handheld radio, which sat on the kitchen table, grabbed it, and continued to thread her way through the cabin. She ran over her options. Her car keys were on the living room table. She could snatch them up, try to get to her truck.

Or she could dash outside and race up the stairs to the fire tower, slamming the hatch at the top. But he could outrun her on those stairs. Her best bet was to get to her car while radioing for help.

She heard the man crash out of the kitchen, roaring with anger. As she reached the living room, he circled around to another door that led to where she was. But it was okay. The front door lay behind her. She dove for her keys and snatched them off the table, then pivoted and raced for the front door.

He was fast behind her. She reached the door and flung it open, hitting him in the face in the process. She lifted the radio to her mouth. "This is Kathleen Macklay at Cascade Tower—"

Before she could finish, a forceful hand clamped down on her shoulder, but she twisted away from him. Then he was grabbing at the radio in her hand, pounding her forearm with his meaty fist. Her nerves screamed at the pain, but she clung to the radio. Then he swung in front of her, twisting her arm viciously and forcing her to drop it.

A pile of firewood stood beside her, and she grabbed a log and brought it up, connecting with his ear. But with the helmet and the thick padding of his balaclava, he only winced and held on to her wrist.

The sledgehammer fist came down again, and as it connected with her face, Kathleen tasted blood as her head snapped violently to the side. She caught a glimpse of her truck, so close, yet still too distant. She swung again at him with the log, but this time he deflected the blow with his forearm and came in with another powerful punch to the face that left her reeling. He held fast to her forearm as she crumpled to her knees, her head swimming, her vision tunneling. Then he wrenched the log out of her grip and brought it down on the back of her skull. She felt the rough bark bite into her scalp as a blinding pain erupted in her head.

She collapsed face-first into the dirt, breathing out a plume of dust as pebbles dug into her skin. She felt him pick her up, start crushing her again, her rib cage constricted, her lungs bursting for air, and then blackness took her.

EIGHTEEN

Alex awoke, groggy, and for a second didn't know where she was. She unzipped the mummy bag, surprised to find that she'd ended up in thermal underwear, a pair of hiking pants, her rain gear, and on top, two layers of polypropylene, a sweater, a fleece jacket and her Marmot rain parka, complete with wool hat and Turtle Fur. She frowned. Somehow she'd put on every single piece of clothing she had except . . . her gaze moved to the corner of the tent, where a crumpled pile of wet clothes lay, condensation collected on the tent wall above them.

The whole tent smelled musty. Then she remembered. The thing chasing her. The river. The freezing-cold water. Dragging the tent in a state of delirium. With a thump of her heart, she realized how close she'd come to wandering off, feverish, perhaps succumbing to the cold.

Now she sweated inside all the layers, the hot sun, high in the sky, beating down on the tent. She stripped out of almost everything, leaving on only her hiking pants and a thin wicking shirt.

She fumbled for her watch in the small tent pocket sewn into the wall. It was 11:36 A.M. She crawled out of the tent, blinking in the bright sunlight, seeing nothing familiar around her. The tent wasn't pegged down, and it sat at a tilt on a moss-covered rock. Her boots lay on their sides outside the tent door, and she felt them. Still wet. But better than no shoes at all. She pulled them on, then stood up and tried to get her bearings. She could barely hear the distant sound of water, perhaps the river she'd originally camped beside.

She pulled the GPS unit from her pack and waited while it fixed on satellites. It hesitated, locking onto only two, the tree canopy too thick for it to get a decent signal. She spotted a clearing some fifty feet away and walked to it, holding the unit aloft.

Soon it got a fix. She was a mile and a quarter from where she'd been camping and couldn't believe she'd dragged the tent that far.

It was a long hike back to the ranch house. She returned to her pack and pulled out her cell phone, not surprised to see that she had no signal. But she was so close to where she'd encountered the woman that she was tempted to return to the area now that it was daylight and see if she could pick up some clue. The woman could be injured, and a lengthy hike back toward the ranch house, where Alex knew she could get a signal, could mean life or death for the woman.

Quickly she rolled up her sleeping bag and pad, then strapped them onto the outside of her pack along with the dismantled tent. The sight of energy bars in her pack almost made her want to throw up. She didn't know how much river water she'd swallowed the night before, but she felt sick and had no appetite.

Slinging on her pack, she set off in her squishy boots for her previous campsite, nervously checking the sky as she went.

She navigated to the area using the waypoint stored in her GPS unit, and found the four tent stakes where she'd pulled the tent up in her delirium. She gathered these and stored them in the tent bag, then continued on to where she'd seen the woman.

She jumped at each caw of a raven, and once the buzz of a hummingbird almost made her dive for cover. Whatever that thing was, it had been close to getting her. She paused at the last place she'd seen the woman, alongside the river. She studied the ground for tracks but found none. The area quickly led to steep, rocky terrain.

Limestone strata, millions of years old, proliferated in this area.

She walked along the edge of a bluff. Over the years, rocks had eroded out of the steep incline, piled now at the base of the cliff. Trees grew from the crevices, emerald-green moss covering the gray rocks.

Then she heard something high-pitched and turned to see if a marmot sat out on one of the rocks. She didn't spot one. Then she heard it again, only it was wrong for a marmot. Too long to be one of their alarm whistles. She squinted into the sun, staring up at the bluff. It formed a steep cliff to her left, stretching up into a searing azure sky with a few brilliantly white cumulus clouds drifting above it.

The cry came again, a sharp, panicked sound, repeating itself. She followed the call, moving along the edge of the rocks, and as she rounded them, a cold breeze billowed out from a yawning black opening—a cave.

A mournful wail issued from deep inside the darkness. Alex paused at the entrance, listening intently.

"Can't," she heard on the breeze. "Can't." A woman's voice, followed by crying.

She pulled out her headlamp and held it in one hand, shielding the beam, and stepped into the darkness.

NINETEEN

Alex followed the sound, the air growing cooler and cooler. Soon it leveled out around sixty degrees Fahrenheit. A stream trickled across the floor, water dripping from somewhere deeper inside the cave, echoing in the darkness.

She stepped carefully across the subterranean creek, pointing her beam straight down.

"Can't," the woman pleaded, sniffing, then breaking into soft sobs.

Alex crept closer, worried someone might be with the woman, might be trying to force her to do something. But she didn't hear anyone else.

The cave veered around to her right and she followed it, carefully stepping over loose rocks and trying to make as little noise as possible. Then the sobbing grew louder, and she knew she was drawing close.

The narrow tunnel opened into a vast room. Stalactites hung from the ceiling, water cascading off their ends and splashing into shimmering pools on the floor. In the shielded, dim glow of her headlamp, a huddled figure came into view. Alex crept closer, seeing a woman shivering against one wall, naked arms hugging her bare legs, dressed in only a T-shirt and dirty, mud-covered shorts. A long gash, the blood now clotted, ran from her wrist to her elbow. Mud caked her from mid-calf down to the soles of her boots.

Shoulder-length silver hair draped over her arms, her head bent down, face unseen.

Alex's foot crunched on a rock, and the woman snapped her gaze up, wild eyes fixing on Alex. Alex knelt down in front of her.

"Can't!" the woman screamed.

Alex's breath caught in her throat. She definitely recognized her from the photo the sheriff had given her. It was Amelia Fairweather. Alex reached out her free hand in a placating manner. "It's okay. I'm not here to hurt you."

"Can't!" the woman screamed, crawling backward in terror, shielding her face.

"Amelia?"

At this the woman's eyes narrowed, confusion on her face. She fell silent.

"I'm Alex Carter. We've been looking for you."

She stared at Alex, brow furrowed, chin trembling.

Alex was staggered. Amelia had been alive this long, surviving out here for more than a year? Alex knew she had to get her to safety but wasn't sure the best way to proceed. With no way to reach the FBI, she'd either have to convince the woman to hike out with her, or leave her here while she got help, and that would take the better part of the day before she'd reach the ranch house.

"Do you think you can walk out of here with me? Get to safety?"

Amelia plastered herself against the wall, shaking her head vehemently. "Can't. Can't."

"I can go get help, then, but it might be a few hours before anyone can get back here. Will you stay here, where it's safe?"

Amelia shook her head, biting her lip, her eyes filled with terror.

Alex started to stand up, and Amelia's hand lashed out and clamped onto her wrist with so much force that Alex felt the bones press together.

"I have to go," Alex told her. "I've got to get help." She studied the woman's scared face. "Do you want to come with me?"

Amelia looked down, biting her lip. Then, not letting go of Alex's arm, she stood up.

"Okay. Let's go," Alex said gently, and gestured toward the entrance of the cave. "Let's get back before night falls."

Tentatively the woman walked out beside Alex, weak and tripping over rocks. She held on to Alex's arm with cold, trembling hands. Alex offered her an energy bar, but she wouldn't take it, so Alex forced herself to down part of it, the concoction tasting dry and bland in her mouth. It would be no good if both of them were weak from lack of food.

They walked into the sunlight, welcome warmth streaming down on Alex's skin. Amelia clung to her arm, so tightly Alex thought she might lose circulation if the woman kept it up. Alex double-checked their location on her GPS, and then headed for the ranch house, figuring out a route that would entail the least amount of hills and climbing.

Amelia trudged along beside her like an automaton, not saying anything, her eyes glassy, jumping at every little sound: a red squirrel trilling from a tree, a deer startling and leaping into the cover of bushes, the distant sound of a jet droning overhead.

Progress was agonizingly slow, and more than a few times Alex wondered if Amelia would have been better off waiting in the cave. But the woman was so incoherent, Alex couldn't be sure she would have stayed there.

And if that strange craft was searching for her and somehow figured out where she'd hid, it would all be over.

So they trudged on, one step at a time. Alex found herself staring down at her boots, lifting one, then the other, maintaining a robotic pace alongside Amelia. Exhaustion swept over her from her flight the night before, then almost freezing to death, and now carrying her heavy pack. But she didn't want to leave it. If they ended up having to spend the night out here, it could save their lives. So she kept up with her progress, sometimes counting her steps, sometimes singing a slow song in time with their footfalls. First it was "I'm Getting Sentimental Over You" and later "Stardust." Her dad loved swing music, and she found herself humming Tommy Dorsey and Glenn Miller tunes in her head.

Her dad.

How she missed him! Right now she could be hanging out with him in his guest cabin at the Grand Canyon, listening to music, talking over their day, sharing news stories they'd read.

The sun arced across the sky and dipped behind the steep mountains, and soon its warmth was lost to her. Amelia started to shiver, so Alex layered her up in polypropylene and fleece. They crossed meadows and navigated densely treed sections of forest. She kept checking her phone, hoping that some miraculous signal would appear, but it didn't. If she kept taking these gigs, she'd have to invest in a satellite phone, despite the expense.

They plodded on, crossing streams and stopping frequently to rest. Amelia still refused food. The gloaming set in, that enchanted time of day, and it gave her hope.

Then true darkness set in, and Alex pulled out her headlamp. They were only a quarter mile from the ranch house, and she nervously scanned the sky for the craft and listened for its singular hum.

Then the ranch house came into view and Alex wanted to sprint for its porch and erupt in a triumphant shout, but not wanting to startle Amelia, she kept silent and ushered the woman through the back door.

Alex bolted it behind them.

She guided Amelia over to a kitchen chair and then grabbed a blanket off the sofa in the next room. She draped it over the woman's shaking shoulders, then brought her a drink of water and convinced her to take a few sips. Amelia hadn't said anything since they left the cave.

Then Alex reached for the landline.

The sheriff picked up on the third ring. "Taggert." Once again, she sounded tired.

"Sheriff, this is Alex Carter. I found her."

"What? You mean Amelia?" She was instantly alert. "Her remains?"

"No. She's alive. She's here at the ranch house with me."

"Alive?" The sheriff went silent, obviously staggered by the news. Then finally: "Is she injured?"

"A little. We just hiked here together, so I don't think it's anything life-threatening. But she's definitely in shock."

"She's been gone for more than a *year*. A *year*. I can't believe she's still alive. Did she say where she's been?"

"Not on a beach in Rio, I can tell you that much. I don't know what's happened to her, Sheriff, but she's traumatized. She isn't speaking."

"This is terrible. I can leave right now to come get her."

"Actually, Sheriff, maybe I should drive her down there. It would save time, and I think she should get medical attention ASAP. Can you have EMTs waiting?"

"Sure thing. I'll call 'em now."

"We're on our way." Alex hung up.

She coaxed Amelia to take a few more sips of water, and then changed into a dry pair of shoes. She bundled Amelia into her car. As she pulled out of the driveway, she turned on the heat full blast. The woman shivered in the passenger seat, still not saying anything. They'd know what to do for her in town. She drove carefully, all too aware of the fragile state of her passenger, not wanting to jostle or bounce her too much on the pitted road.

Then they finally hit the paved section and Alex picked up a little speed. The town came into view, and Amelia jerked her head up, staring at the buildings, shrinking more and more into her seat.

"You okay?" Alex asked.

Amelia didn't look at her, just kept staring in horror at the buildings, whipping her head around nervously at everyone they passed on the street. At the end of the main drag, Alex spotted the sheriff's station and pulled into the parking lot. An ambulance waited there, two EMTs leaning against the hood, talking to the sheriff.

As she pulled in, they made their way toward her car.

The EMTs approached first, a man and a woman in their forties. The woman opened the passenger side and began assessing Amelia's condition, shining a small penlight in her eyes, taking her pulse. Amelia didn't move. She just stared down at the car floor. The male EMT pulled a gurney out of the ambulance and wheeled it over.

Gently they coaxed her onto it. The sheriff walked to the woman's side. "Amelia Fairweather?"

Amelia stared straight up at the sky, as if she didn't see the sheriff.

"Are you in any pain?" one EMT asked. Amelia didn't acknowledge her.

"Can you tell us what happened to you?" Taggert asked. Amelia continued to gaze vacantly at the stars.

"We'll take her to Cascade Mountain Hospital in Metaline Falls," the male EMT told her. "They're better equipped than the local health center."

Taggert took off her hat and ran a hand over her braided hair. "Okay."

They bundled Amelia into the ambulance.

Taggert's gaze, tired and full of sadness, shifted to Alex. "Too bad she wasn't talking. I'll have to make a trip down to the hospital tomorrow. Maybe she'll be talking by that time."

As the ambulance pulled out of the parking lot, Bill, the man with the long white hair Alex had seen in the park when she first arrived, raced up to them. She could smell alcohol wafting off him.

"Is that her?" he shouted. "They brought her back?"

"Who?" Taggert asked.

"Her abductors! Sometimes they don't bring you back, you

know. Sometimes you die while they're experimenting on you. Other times they bring you back, but you're all dazed, like she is. That's how they found Travis Walton."

"Travis Walton? What are you talking about?" Taggert asked.

"Travis Walton!" he shouted, as if the sheriff were completely stupid. "Abducted out of the White Mountains in Arizona."

Irritated, Taggert waved her hat at the man. "Are you on about aliens again?"

"It's no joke, Sheriff. Was she staring vacantly? Couldn't talk?" he demanded.

"Yeah," the sheriff barked, annoyed. "That's how most people are when they're in shock."

"But shock from *what*?" Bill cried triumphantly, as if he'd just made his point. "I've seen those lights out in the forest, Sheriff."

"That's a load of hogwash and you know it, Bill. Why don't you go home and sleep it off?"

Alex swallowed. She'd seen the lights, too. "Ummm . . . actually, Sheriff," Alex cut in.

"Yes?"

"There *are* lights out there," she told her.

"Oh no. Not you, too?"

"But I don't think it's aliens."

"And that's your mistake right there!" Bill shouted at Alex. "You think it's all normal and explicable, like swamp gas or some shit, and that's when they get you."

The sheriff sighed wearily and put her hat back on. She gestured at Alex. "You better come inside and make a statement. Tell me everything you know."

Alex nodded. As they walked toward the station door, Bill fell in behind them.

"Not you, Bill!" the sheriff reprimanded him. "You go home and drink some coffee, for god's sake."

"But, Sheriff—"

"But nothing! Go!" Her forceful bark made Bill flinch and he turned reluctantly on his heels and headed back out to the street, glancing forlornly over his shoulder.

Inside, Taggert gestured down the hall. "Let's go into the interrogation room. I can record your statement in there. It'll save time." She led Alex back to a door marked INTERROGATION ROOM 1. Alex didn't see an "Interrogation Room 2" and suspected that the small sheriff's station just had the one. Taggert opened the door and gestured to a table with a chair on each side. "Have a seat. Before we start, let me go call Special Agent Fields. He'll want to hear this. You want some coffee?"

Alex nodded appreciatively. "Yes, please."

"Be right back. Make yourself comfortable."

The chair squeaked on the floor as Alex pulled it out. Its cold metal sent a chill through her as she sat down. The intense events of last night and today had taken their toll, and for the first time, Alex felt her body relax. She was safe. Amelia was safe.

Taggert appeared moments later, two mugs of steaming coffee in her hands. She passed one over to Alex and took a seat.

"Is Fields coming?" Alex asked.

"No, it went straight through to voicemail. Called one of his colleagues, Hernandez. They're both out on a call and will check in later."

A digital recorder sat on the table, and Taggert switched it on. She identified herself, gave the date and time, and asked Alex to state her name, too.

"So can you tell me how you found Amelia Fairweather?" Taggert began.

Alex exhaled and then related the whole story. How she'd heard Amelia calling for help, the craft that pursued her through the forest, her realizing it could track body heat, then her plunge into the glacial river. She described searching for Amelia the next day, finding her in the cave.

The sheriff leaned forward in her chair, asking for details and clarification along the way. When she had caught Taggert up to the moment she and Amelia pulled into the parking lot of the sheriff's station, Alex paused. "There are a couple more things. I don't know if they're related."

"Go ahead."

"That logger who's been harassing the tree sitter?"

"Yes. I had one of my deputies speak to him."

"I just feel uneasy about him. He's really angry. Definitely hates women."

"Yeah, I've experienced that firsthand. He acted like my authority wasn't worth a hill of beans. Somehow I think if I were a two-hundred-and-fifty-pound balding man with a Coors beer gut, he would have taken me a lot more seriously." Taggert shifted in her chair. "And the other thing?"

"The squatter and his tunnels. I still think he could keep someone down there. Anyway, I don't know if either man is related to the strange craft or Amelia's disappearance, but it might be worth checking out."

"I certainly will." She jotted down a few notes. "Anything else?"

Alex finished her coffee and leaned back in her chair. Her whole body ached. "No, that's it."

Taggert ended the recording. "Let's go wait for Fields in my office. It's warmer in there."

Alex scooted out of her chair and followed Taggert to a large room with a picture window on the west side of the building. It was liberally decorated with various macramé hangings: an owl, a draping design with triangular patterns, several plant hangers.

Taggert followed her gaze. "I went through a serious macramé phase in the seventies."

Now Alex got a better glimpse of the woman's personality. She spied the pair of Birkenstocks stashed under her desk, some colorful socks that looked hand-knitted tucked into them. A ukulele waited on a small stand in one corner, and an array of snacks in green biodegradable bags lay scattered on her desk. Taggert picked one up and dug into it. Then she held it out to Alex. "Muesli?"

"No, thanks. I'm too tired to eat."

She offered Alex a comfortable chair on the opposite side of her desk. Alex sank gratefully into the cushioned surface. Her eyes burned with exhaustion. Taggert sank into her own chair and started unlacing her boots, presumably to put on the sandals.

Special Agent Harvey Fields appeared at the open door and rapped a knuckle on the frame.

"Come on in," Taggert called.

Fields stuck his head in, his expression grim. "You heard the news?"

Taggert blanched. "What?"

"Another woman's gone missing."

Taggert stood up. "What? Where?"

"From a fire tower in the national forest."

Alarm sprang up inside Alex. "It's not Kathleen Macklay, is it?"

Fields's eyes narrowed on her. "You know her?"

Fear punched Alex in the stomach. "Yes."

Taggert came around to the front of her desk. "What happened?"

"Rangers told me she radios in every morning at seven-thirty A.M. like clockwork. Then she checks in three more times during the day. Only, today she radioed just once, and it was cut off. By the time she'd missed her third report in the late afternoon, they drove out there for a welfare check. Found the door standing open. Her Forest Service truck in the driveway, her keys lying on the ground next to it."

"Could she just have gone for a hike?" Taggert didn't sound too convinced of her own reasoning.

Fields considered this. "There was also an overturned pot on the floor. Water everywhere. And it seems odd to drop your keys like that. Leave the door open. And why not radio in?"

Now Alex stood up, apprehension firmly taking root. The murdered ranger. Now Kathleen. She didn't want to utter what she was thinking out loud. It would make it real. Her mouth opened. "But Kathleen," she heard herself say. "She's the same age, the same physical type as Irma and Amelia." She didn't finish the rest of her thought aloud: *Serial killer.*

Fields pursed his lips. "We're worried about the similarities, too." And then he uttered what she hadn't dared. "We could be dealing with a serial killer."

Alex didn't want to believe it. "But the situation is different," Alex went on. "Kathleen wasn't abducted from the backcountry. She was taken from the fire tower. Why change his usual method?"

"The fire tower is still remote, so he's not running a huge risk of witnesses," Fields suggested.

Taggert sat down on the edge of her desk. "But it's still riskier than the middle of nowhere."

Fields conceded her point. "True. Maybe it was an abduction of opportunity. Maybe he was out on the Forest Service road, saw her, and just grabbed her on a whim. She does fit his type—early seventies, fit, outdoorsy."

Taggert shook her head. "If only Amelia was talking." She turned to Fields and filled him in on how Alex had found the missing hiker.

"That's incredible," Fields breathed. "She's still alive? After all this time?"

Taggert nodded. Then she added, "Have you gotten anything from the postmortem on Irma Jackson?"

"The lab's still working on it. We should have a report in the next day or so. I put a rush on it."

Panic rose in Alex's throat. She imagined her friend, so full of life, then pictured her scared and threatened. She had to do something.

Taggert stood with a hand on her hip. "Well, the good thing is that whoever has done this kept Amelia alive for over a year. So your friend could have some time."

"But what about Irma? She disappeared seven months ago, but for how much of that time was she already dead?" Alex asked.

Fields looked down at the carpet.

Alex's legs went weak and suddenly she found herself sitting back down in the chair. Nothing felt real. Could this really be happening? She'd just seen Kathleen. She was so excited to be starting her season in the fire tower. Maybe she had gone for a hike. Maybe she'd had a bad experience with a tourist or something, or some bureaucrat with the Forest Service, and had walked off to clear her head. Maybe she'd accidentally overturned boiling water on herself and called someone to drive her to the hospital. Maybe in her pain and haste, she didn't realize she'd dropped her keys. And as for the front door being open, it wasn't like the forest was abounding with thieves or anything. Maybe she just didn't think it was necessary to shut it.

But even as she thought those things, Alex knew she was wrong. Even if Kathleen didn't fear thieves, she knew not to leave the door open in bear country. They'd had more than one conversation about being bear safe. Kathleen was a staunch believer in always securing her trash. She didn't want a bear to eat her garbage, become habituated, and then be killed by rangers or state wildlife officials. She'd told Alex once that the very thought of it made her sick. She and Kathleen had that in common. She knew Kathleen had been responsible for getting bear-safe trash canisters installed around the town of Bitterroot, where she lived.

"Listen, Fields," Taggert put in. "Dr. Carter here might have a few leads."

Fields turned his gaze to the sheriff. "Oh, yes?"

"There's a logger who's been tasked with guarding equipment at the logging camp," the sheriff explained. "We've got a tree sitter who's been out there for some time. She was part of the activist group responsible for getting the judge to put a temporary moratorium on the logging there."

"Tree sitter?" Fields wrinkled his brow in confusion.

"She's sitting in the top of a two-hundred-foot tree," Alex said. "She's got a platform up there. Fellow activists bring her food and supplies. This guy is really angry she's there. And he definitely hates women."

"You know his name?"

Taggert shuffled around on her desk and picked up a paper. "Here's all his info." She handed it to Fields.

The agent made some notes in a small black notebook. "Got it."

"He might also have taken a few shots at me the other night," Alex told him. "I'm not sure." Alex related the story of the logs and her flat tire.

Taggert turned to Fields. "We determined it was a .308, probably from a hunting rifle, but that's all we know."

Fields scribbled. "Keep me posted if you learn anything else." He looked up expectantly. "What are the other leads?"

Taggert chimed in. "The squatter. He might be the guy who's been digging those tunnels."

Fields checked his notebook. "Facial recognition came up empty when we ran that photo of him through the system."

Taggert turned to her. "I forwarded him that photo you took of him."

Fields continued. "And we went out to that other tunnel site Carter reported. Didn't find any evidence linking either tunnel to Irma or Amelia."

Alex frowned. "Maybe we just haven't found the right tunnel yet."

Fields narrowed his eyes. "That's a dark thought. Anything else?"

Alex spoke up. "I think whoever is abducting these women is using a drone of some kind to track them. It can home in on body heat, and is armed with some kind of dart. Probably a tranquilizer dart."

Fields's mouth came open. "What the hell?" He jotted down a few more notes. "We can see if anyone in the area has purchased a drone or tranq drugs. This is good." He slid his notebook back into his jacket pocket. "We'll consider all of this. Thank you."

"What are you going to do for now?" Alex asked both of them.

Fields regarded her, considering. Finally he turned to the sheriff. "I think the next step is to call Cody Wainwright. We need SAR combing that area around the fire tower. If she did wander off, we'll find her."

"And if she didn't?" Alex asked.

Fields didn't answer. He just averted his gaze again to the carpet.

While the sheriff got on her desk phone, Alex turned to Fields. "I want to volunteer for the search."

"Of course. We'll need all the help we can get, especially someone who knows their way around this area." He appraised her. "You had any sleep?"

"Some. Last night."

"Go home and get some sleep. We'll start searching at first light." He reached for his wallet and pulled out a business card. "Call me if you think of anything else."

She nodded and took it. "Should I meet you at the fire tower?"

"Yes. That'll be our gathering point."

Alex stood up. "I'll be there."

She waved goodbye to Sheriff Taggert, who was filling Wainwright in on the specifics.

The sheriff nodded to her and mouthed, *Thank you.*

"See you tomorrow," Alex told Fields, then left the station. A sick feeling had taken up residence in her gut. Whether Kathleen had been abducted or had somehow gotten injured outside her fire tower, Alex knew something was seriously wrong. Kathleen was in trouble.

TWENTY

The drive back to the ranch house felt interminable. Alex's mind churned over Kathleen's disappearance, finding Amelia, what kind of person could have done this to them. Her body ached with exhaustion. But when she pulled into the driveway, she was suddenly wired.

Though she knew it was a long shot, she downloaded the caribou's collar camera footage in the hopes of seeing some glimpse of Kathleen. She studied all the ten-second video clips. In them, the caribou rested, ruminated, slept, walked, grazed. But there was no sign of Kathleen.

Finally she climbed the stairs and, feeling restless, packed up her backpack with everything she'd need to join the search party tomorrow. She wanted to leave before dawn so that she could be there at first light.

Then she lay down, her mind a tangle of thoughts, her heart in her mouth.

THE NEXT MORNING, ALEX DROVE the roads to the fire tower in the predawn light. Venus and Mercury hung bright in the eastern sky, the clouds there turning pink, then gold, then white as the sun crept up. She pulled onto the fire tower road just as the sun peeked above the mountains. The road wound up its series of steep switchbacks, first through ponderosa and then hemlock and red cedar.

Alex sipped hot tea from her thermos as she made her way up. A person definitely had to *want* to come up this road. It wasn't something you'd happen across by chance. And the fire tower seemed like a strange target for a robbery. She couldn't shake the feeling that someone had targeted Kathleen, or at the very least, if not her specifically, they knew the fire tower worker would be out here alone. The thought made her shiver. And it wasn't like Kathleen didn't know how to take care of herself. She'd worked in the sheriff's office in Bitterroot for years, and Alex knew that the sheriff there ensured that everyone working in the office knew self-defense, just in case all hell broke loose at the station.

Someone had driven up this lonely, steep, pitted road, overpowered Kathleen, and taken her. Unless Taggert's initial suggestion had been right and somehow Kathleen had walked off and gotten lost. Or maybe injured, unable to make her way back.

When Alex reached the top of the road, the fire tower came into view. A thin haze hung in the west, the mountains there fading away into lighter and lighter shades of blue.

By the small house at the tower's base, she spotted Sheriff Taggert and Cody Wainwright talking in front of the door. They waved as she pulled up and parked.

She approached them, crossing her arms against the cold of the morning. Standing next to Cody was Bill, the man from the town square who had been shouting at the sheriff about aliens.

"Do you know Bill Davis?" Cody asked. "He's very adamant about joining us today."

Alex extended her hand. "We haven't met officially."

He shook her hand, his skin calloused and dry. "I just hope we find your friend. Don't want to even *think* about what might have happened to her."

Alex wondered if he was going to suggest aliens might be at work, but he fell silent. She turned to the sheriff. "First ones here?"

Taggert hooked her thumbs into her utility belt. "Yep. Fields and two of his team are on the way. But we had a helicopter out here last night, searching with FLIR. Unfortunately, they didn't find anything."

Wainwright spoke up. "As of late last night, fifty-two people have volunteered to come out today and search."

Alex exhaled. "That's fantastic!"

The morning mist swirled around the base of the tower, the cold air clinging to her. But she knew that she'd be hot inside her polypropylene and fleece layers once she started moving around.

Soon cars began arriving, quickly filling up the small parking lot by the tower and then fanning all the way down the fire road, parallel parking on the shoulder.

Three SAR workers with trained dogs pulled up, their hounds eager to get to work, prancing in place as their humans gathered supplies out of their cars.

A few minutes later, Fields arrived with Lipkin and Hernandez. As they joined her by the house, Fields fell into conversation with Taggert. Alex moved closer to Lipkin and Hernandez and ended up inadvertently eavesdropping on them.

Lipkin stamped his feet, trying to keep warm in the early morning chill. Lipkin turned to Hernandez. "So who would win in a fight: a fruit bat or a banana?"

"You mean those gigantic fruit bats that fly around during the day in, like, American Samoa and Australia?" Hernandez asked.

"The very same."

"Well, if it were fighting a banana, I'd say the bat."

"What if the banana had nunchucks?" Lipkin added.

Hernandez looked incredulous. "How would a banana hold nunchucks?"

"What if it was a sentient peeled banana, and used its peel as sort of makeshift arms that could wield the nunchucks?"

Fields turned, eyes blazing. "Will you two knock it off? What is wrong with you?"

"Sorry, chief," Hernandez mumbled.

"And what's with this 'chief' stuff?" Fields demanded.

Hernandez looked stricken. "It's a sign of respect."

Fields shook his head and turned back to Taggert.

But Alex watched Hernandez turn to Lipkin and ask in an even quieter voice: "Okay. Who would win in a fight: a haunted ventriloquist dummy or Sir Arthur Conan Doyle?"

Fields spun on them and lost his patience. "Look, I don't care if your grandma had to fight a Dilophosaur chewing bubblegum and playing a cigar box banjo. You two need to knock it off!"

Lipkin stifled a snicker at Fields's words and Hernandez looked away, his jaw clenched, all seriousness now.

When everyone had gathered, Wainwright gave a shrill whistle with two fingers to his mouth and got their attention. "Okay, people. We're looking for a woman, white, seventy-two, probably dressed in a Forest Service uniform. It's possible she went for a hike and got injured, but it's more likely she was abducted. So what we're looking for here today is anything out of the ordinary. Articles of clothing, blood, signs of a struggle, boot prints. I want you all to break into groups of twelve, walk in a straight line, evenly spaced twenty feet from each other." He held up a notebook. "I've got a search grid here so we can fan out in different directions from the tower. Take your time. Study the ground in front of you. You see anything strange at all, don't touch it. Just blow one of these." He brought out a Tupperware box full of metal whistles and started handing them out. "Stay exactly where you are, and I or one of the deputies or FBI agents will come to you to examine your find. Are there any questions?"

No one spoke up, so Wainwright continued. "Okay. We want to thank all of you who came out today. Let's get started."

As Alex scanned the crowd, she wondered if the abductor could be one of these supposedly well-meaning citizens, offering help not because he cared, but because he wanted to keep a close eye on the investigation. It would give him a chance to go over the terrain with a large group of people, possibly removing evidence in all the hub-bub. She scanned their faces, wondering if she'd be able to tell at a glance if someone had done these evil deeds.

As Wainwright organized everyone into teams, Alex walked over to Taggert, who was deep in conversation with Fields. "Have there been any updates about Amelia?" Alex asked.

Fields shook his head. "She's still not talking. At first she wouldn't even let the doctors touch her. But now she seems to un-derstand they don't mean harm. If only we knew where she'd been for the last year!"

Disappointment took root in Alex's stomach. "Can I look around inside Kathleen's house?"

Fields shook his head. "It's an active crime scene."

She sighed. "Okay. I understand." Then she went around to where Wainwright was giving out assignments.

She became a cog in an even line with eleven other people and they set off into the forest, moving slowly, calling Kathleen's name, studying the ground for any hint of her. She could hear the other teams through the forest, shouting out. Wind rustled in the pines. She stared intently at the ground as she walked, hoping to find a clue—a piece of Kathleen's clothing, some sign of a struggle, her watch, anything.

Wainwright moved between different volunteer groups, giving them pointers as they moved along, checking on their progress. But by midday, none of the teams had turned up anything.

Wainwright called a break for lunch, and everyone broke off into smaller groups to eat sandwiches they'd brought along. Alex had only an energy bar, and she ate it in silence, not feeling like talking to anyone. A sick feeling had taken up residence in her core, and the thought of Kathleen facing off with her abductor right now, while Alex stood around with a bunch of people eating sandwiches, made her ill. She knew they had to eat, had to keep their energy up, but she struggled with a feeling of urgency.

Wainwright resumed the search, and this time he joined Alex's group. He walked beside her. "How are you doing? I heard you're friends with the missing person."

Alex bit her lip. "Not well. It makes me sick to think of her out there right now, probably scared or injured. Do you think it's foul play?"

He furrowed his brow. "I hate to say it, but from what the sheriff said about the state of her house, it sounds like it."

Alex continued to stare down at the ground. "I'd like to think she just went out for a hike, maybe after dark. The moon is so bright right now. A lot of people go for moonlit hikes. Maybe she fell, broke her leg, and we're going to find her today."

"I like that thought a lot better than that someone took her." Then a thoughtful expression stole over Wainwright's face. "It's possible the two things are unrelated."

"What do you mean?"

"Maybe Kathleen did go out for a night hike and fell, and she's waiting for rescue, and someone came up to the fire tower, saw the empty house, and broke in to steal things. They could have found her car keys, considered stealing her car, and thought the better of it, dumping the keys."

"Keep talking. You're making me feel better."

"If they were thieves, they wouldn't exactly be considerate enough to close the door after themselves. Could be why it was standing open."

Alex liked this idea, and hoped he was right. Still, it didn't exactly seem like the most lucrative place in the world to pull off a burglary. Why not a gas station or convenience or liquor store? They would have way more cash on hand than a Forest Service volunteer.

But maybe these perps weren't exactly thinking straight. Could be on drugs, desperate for any money at all.

"Did the sheriff say whether they found her purse?" Alex asked.

Wainwright nodded. "They did. It was on the kitchen table. No cash inside."

She perked up. "So maybe it was an unrelated robbery that happened separately from her vanishing, like you said. She wouldn't bring her purse on a hike."

Wainwright gave a weak smile. "We can hope." He looked tired.

"You done many of these searches over the years?" she asked him.

"Too many to count."

She dreaded the answer to the question but found herself asking, "Had many successes?"

He nodded. "Almost all of them. Only had a few that were totally elusive."

"What happened in those cases?"

He thought back. "One was a guy who had crashed his Cessna in the national forest. He'd radioed for help on his way down. We found the plane, but no pilot. But footprints leading away from the wreck told us he hadn't bailed out in a parachute. We found a makeshift campsite on the third day where he'd started a fire to keep warm. But we never found him. Never found any remains or any other trace that he'd ever been there."

"Wow."

"Then there was a father-son pair who went backcountry camping. An unexpected snowstorm moved into the area, and we learned from their family that they hadn't packed properly for cold weather. We found some of their clothes, scattered over a square mile of forest, as if they'd gone hypothermic and shucked everything off. But we never found them. Searched for almost two weeks before it turned into a corpse recovery rather than a rescue. But we still never found their bodies. That was about fifteen years ago."

These tales were not making her feel better.

Wainwright seemed to pick up on this. "But we've had some great successes, too. A family of four, parents and their two kids, got their rental car stuck in a snowdrift. After two days, the dad decided to hike off on his own to try and get help. The next day we found the family's car, with the mother and two kids in it, all bundled up and safe, though dehydrated. Took us another week to find the dad, but eventually we did. He'd collapsed from exhaustion and hunger but found a creek to drink from. If he'd just stayed by the car, we'd have found him a lot sooner. It's much easier to spot a car on a road, even a remote backcountry one, than a human walking through a dense forest."

"Tell me about another success," she asked him as they plodded along, staring intently at every inch of ground they passed over.

Cody smiled. "There was this guy who wanted to try living way in the backcountry. You know, get away from civilization. He had a pilot buddy of his fly him over the Colville and he parachuted out carrying only a water filter, some clothes, and a twenty-pound bag of rice. He was supposed to come back in three weeks, but after a month still hadn't emerged. His buddy told the rangers where he'd dropped him, and we searched that whole area. Found a broken homemade crutch next to the empty sack of rice. A little while later, we found a pair of his jeans, one leg stiff with dried blood. We kept searching. A week later we found him. He'd hit a tree on the way down and broken his leg in two places. Been staggering around the forest, trying to get to a road. But he hadn't brought a topo map with him, just a general large-scale map of the state of Washington. Crazy. But we carried him out on a litter and got him to a hospital where they set his leg."

Alex allowed a little hope to seep into her. So maybe she was just injured. It seemed weird to hope for a broken limb, but it was better than thinking she'd been abducted.

Wainwright eventually moved on to another group to supervise their progress. He was all bark when giving orders, no-nonsense, but she'd found his company comforting when he walked next to her, regaling her with tales of search and rescue. She allowed herself to think positively.

After six more hours of searching, none of the teams had uncovered anything. Soon twilight would set in. Wainwright blew his whistle and called everyone into a single group. "I'm calling the search for the day. We'd appreciate anyone who is willing to come out again tomorrow to search farther afield. Do I have any volunteers?"

Alex couldn't help but smile when she saw almost everyone raise their hands. She fought back a sudden choking feeling in her throat at the kindness of these strangers. It wasn't something she was used to seeing in her line of work—humans pulling together to do good—and she was grateful.

As the crowd broke up, all walking back to their cars, Alex remained behind in the darkening forest. In the distance, she could hear car doors slamming and engines starting up.

Wainwright approached her in the gloaming. "You coming?"

She nodded. "Yeah, in a minute. I just want to stand out here and think for a bit."

He gazed at her thoughtfully for a long moment, and then said, "Okay. Good night."

He moved off toward the fire tower, and Alex stood in the sudden silence of the forest. All day it had been filled with human voices, people shouting for Kathleen. Now the gentle, comforting quiet enclosed her. A flammulated owl sang a low hoot, a call often described as ventriloquial because it could be difficult for humans to locate the bird from the sound. Several crickets began to sing. To calm herself, she used an old trick to determine the temperature. She counted how many chirps they made in fifteen seconds, then added thirty-seven. It was seventy-two degrees outside.

She breathed in the scent of sun-warmed pine, gazing out as the blue shadows crept through the forest. A tremendous golden moon rose in the east. She stared at it for a long time, seeing the rabbit in the moon, and thoughts of *Watership Down*, which she'd read as a child, drifted into her head.

A bat flitted by her, its black wings silhouetted against the velvety violet of the darkening sky.

"Kathleen?" she said to the darkness. "Kathleen?"

Only the wind met her query, a sigh through the branches above her. Finally, reluctantly, she turned and walked back to the fire tower. She'd barely slept the night before, and her eyes stung. As she approached the back of the house, snippets of conversation floated to her on the wind. Taggert and Fields, discussing Irma's preliminary autopsy and forensic reports, which they'd received that morning. She stopped on the far side of the house, eavesdropping.

She picked up bits of phrases. "Strangled," "mummified," "stored somewhere," and "spores from some plant called *Diphasiastrum digitatum*." Alex crept a tiny bit closer to hear better, and listened while Fields said, "She didn't have any spores in her lungs, but her body was covered with them. But the weird thing is, that kind of plant isn't even native to this area."

The conversation wrapped up, with Fields mentioning he was going to grab a bite to eat, then go over the forensic report again. Taggert thanked him for his help.

Exhausted, Alex moved to the parking lot and climbed into her car, staring up at the huge moon, which, now that it was a little higher, bathed the terrain around her in silver.

She began the long, twisting drive back to the ranch house.

TWENTY-ONE

Feeling in low spirits, Alex had no appetite for dinner when she got back to the house. She paced aimlessly in the kitchen, running over her food options, and ultimately just slumped down in one of the kitchen chairs. She eyed the landline and decided to call Zoe. It would be good to hear her friend's voice.

She dialed the number, feeling a chill that wasn't entirely due to the temperature.

When Zoe picked up, Alex's spirits instantly lifted. "How are things?" she asked her friend.

"You want to hear the latest about disturbances on the set?"

"Definitely." Alex wanted to tell her about Kathleen, the search, finding the lost hiker, but in the moment just wanted to think about something else, something not so grim.

"I've found my sabotage suspect."

"Who is it? The actor? The suspicious cookbook-reading janitor? The producer's son?"

"None of them. I decided to do some research into the history of this movie in my off-hours. See if there were some disgruntled estate owners or something who maybe wanted to shut down the project because they didn't like how it was going."

"Estate owners?"

"Yeah. You see, this film is based on a series of pulp novels written in the thirties. It was a very popular series back then. The rights have passed down through the author's descendants, and they've been very resistant about allowing anyone to make films out of them."

"Why would they be? Wouldn't they get money from that?"

"Yes. But apparently, in the fifties, back when the author was still alive, this then-famous director approached him about making a movie for the first book in the series, intending to shoot the rest of the books if the movie did well. The author was ecstatic and agreed. Well, a studio threw all this money at the project, and it ended up being a total flop, with aliens made of papier-mâché hanging from easily spotted wires and all that. It bombed at the box office, and it's apparently so bad that it's become something of a cult film that people watch while riffing off it. The alien in it is considered one of the most ridiculous-looking monsters in film history. And the acting was so bad that it won numerous Razzie-type awards. The studio lost a ton of money and wouldn't let the director make another picture for them at all. Like, he was completely fired.

"He became a laughingstock, because people only associated him with this terrible movie. He couldn't find work. He ended up drinking too much, cursing Hollywood, and eventually vanishing. No one knows what happened to him. His family had him declared legally dead.

"In the years that followed, after the author passed away, and his heirs inherited his literary estate, they refused to let anyone make movies from the books, because they're still getting a handsome income from book sales, and they're worried that another bad movie might impact those sales. But through a series of weird loopholes and copyright issues, they ended up losing the film rights, so now the movie is being made."

"So you think whoever's sabotaging the movie is one of those heirs?"

"No. I've ruled them out. It's the director of the original film, Alex."

"What? Wouldn't he be, like, a hundred years old by now?"

"Maybe. If he's still out there somewhere. But I think it's more likely that he's haunting the set."

"Excuse me?"

"It makes sense. The weird electrical problems, the cold spots. The terrible smells."

Alex went quiet. "I guess it's possible . . ."

"Of course it's possible! I'm going to have to investigate more. Maybe get a Ouija board."

"Just don't do it by yourself. That way leads to *The Exorcist*."

"I won't be alone. I'll get some other people to help."

"You going to tell them your theory?"

She bit her lip. "Not just yet. I don't want to color their judgment. I'll just say I want to do it for fun. Everyone's talking about how spooky this soundstage is. Thing's been in use since 1929. I bet the director's not the only thing haunting it."

"Let me know how it turns out."

"I will. So what's new with you?"

Alex frowned and told her about Kathleen. Zoe listened, deeply concerned. Alex then told her about finding the missing hiker, the terrifying light in the sky, and then about the booby-trapped tunnel, and the panicked, claustrophobic feeling she'd experienced.

"Flame just exploded around you and then was gone?" Zoe asked. "And it was a yellowish-white powder?" She sounded like she was onto something.

"Yeah. That familiar to you?"

"It is. We use something called Dragon's Breath on the set. It's this powder. If you sprinkle some on a table and try to light it on fire, nothing happens. But if you have an open flame and then disperse the powder in the air, it catches immediately. It can make these really impressive-looking bursts of flame, but they go out really quickly."

"That sounds exactly like what happened."

"Weird. I don't know, Alex . . ."

"What?"

"I worry about you out there. What if you're next? This creep who's been abducting women?"

"I'm not his type."

"That's not very reassuring. I'm sure he'd still kill someone for seeing too much or figuring out who he is."

"You're right. That's not very reassuring."

"Don't you want to come down here to L.A. for a bit? Wait for these things to blow over? When the cops find Kathleen and catch this guy, you could go back then."

Alex bit her lip. As much as she'd like to see Zoe, she couldn't just leave while Kathleen was missing. "I've got to find her. I can't abandon her."

"You're a good friend."

"You should know." Alex laughed, wanting to lighten the mood. "You're pretty much my only one."

Zoe chuckled back. "That's not true at all! You've got . . . umm . . ."

"Yes?"

"Your dad."

Alex grinned. "True."

"And then there's that Ben guy with the land trust," she pointed out.

"Whom I don't really know." Alex shook her head, even though Zoe couldn't see her. "My job isn't exactly conducive to a social life."

"That's why you should come here! We could go dancing, go to some pubs. Meet new people. Talk to them. Go out. Remember what that's like? Going out?"

"Barely. How about I come see you when I'm done here?"

"Perfect!" Zoe exclaimed. "This movie will be wrapped up by then."

"Provided the ghost of the director doesn't succeed in completely tanking it."

"Ain't that the truth."

They talked a little longer about the film, the caribou, and how Alex's dad was doing. Then they hung up, Alex promising to be careful.

When she got off the phone, Alex looked up the Dragon's Breath powder used to create flashes of fire. She hoped there wouldn't be any ill effects from breathing the stuff in and getting it in her mouth. But she froze when she saw the two most common substances used in such powders. *Lycopodium clavatum,* or wolf's-foot clubmoss, and *Diphasiastrum digitatum,* or common ground cedar. *Diphasiastrum digitatum.* The latter was the spore found on Irma's body.

Immediately she looked up the geographical distribution of it. It grew only in eastern North America. She leaned back in her chair, a revelation hitting her. Fields was right. It wasn't naturally occurring out here. So either the ranger's body had been weirdly stored in the eastern U.S. and transported back here, or maybe the woman had been a victim of one of the squatter's booby traps while still alive. But, since none of the spores had been inhaled by her, it was more likely that she was already dead and had been *stored* in one of the tunnels.

She thought back to the tunnel, the fire, the yellowish-white powder cascading over her. She'd brushed most of it off, but surely there was still some on her pack. She jumped up and moved to where she'd propped it up against the couch. Most of the powder was gone, but under a flap that protected one seldom-used zippered pocket, she found some.

She dug through the box Ben had left and removed a microscope and a blank slide.

Pulling out her multitool, she went to work. She scraped some of the powder off onto a slide, then suspended it in a drop of water. She put a small glass cover on the slide and brought it back to the table under the light. She plugged in the microscope, switched on its light, and gently placed the slide on the stage.

Eagerly she gazed through the eyepieces, comparing the images she looked at with ones she found on a New York state university's botany page. It was definitely the same spore: *Diphasiastrum digitatum*. They were tiny and round with little sporangia standing out like bristles on all sides.

Alex jumped up and unrolled her topo map onto the dining room table. With a pencil she marked the two tunnel locations she'd found, the ones the FBI had already searched and found nothing in.

So did this guy have other tunnels? Ones no one knew about? And how could she locate them over such a vast area?

She paced back and forth in front of the map. What did those sites have in common? What appealed to him about them? Why had he picked them? She frowned, thinking. They'd been in sections of old growth. And both near a big boulder pile. And they'd been next to a creek, where he could get fresh water.

She bent over the map again, hands planted, scanning for similar locations. But it wasn't detailed enough. She had to load up ArcGIS.

She hurried back to her laptop and created a fresh file. On the map, she layered in locations of old growth. Then she put in a satellite image at a fine resolution. Next she added a hydrology layer with all the streams in the area, then told the program to select areas where streams and old-growth groves connected. When it had done so, she zoomed into each section on the satellite layer, seeing if a large rock pile stood in the vicinity. She found four right off the bat. And there had to be more.

A flush of excitement coursed through her. She had something. She could *feel* it.

Hurriedly she dug out the business card Fields had given her and rushed to the landline to call him.

"Dr. Carter? What can I do for you?"

"I think I'm onto something."

"Oh, yes?"

He listened while she described the powder in the booby trap and the traces of it on her gear, how she'd compared them to images of *Diphasiastrum digitatum* online. "That's the same spore that was on Irma's body, wasn't it?"

"Do I want to know how you know that?" he demanded.

Suddenly feeling awkward, Alex cleared her throat. "I . . . uh . . . may have overheard you and Taggert talking after we searched at the fire tower."

"I see." Stern. Disapproving.

"But listen. The two tunnel sites I came across seem to have a few things in common. Both of them were near a stream, in an area of old growth, and by a big boulder pile. We need to check every area where these three components are present in the landscape. We'll find more tunnels. And maybe we'll find Kathleen."

His voice didn't get any less stern. "Hmmm. That's an intriguing idea. But it's going to take a while."

"I've already located several using GIS," she told him. "I can send you the coordinates."

He went silent for a few moments, and she suspected he had a problem with a civilian inserting herself into the investigation. But she had to do something. Then finally, he said, "This is a solid lead. Thank you. I'll let the sheriff and SAR know."

"I want to help search."

"Of course. We'll need to use volunteers again. I'll keep you updated."

Alex checked his business card for his email address and quickly sent the coordinates to him. Then she leaned back in her chair, feeling slightly relieved. A little bit of her appetite returned. She managed to choke down a heated bowl of black bean soup, but her stomach was too nervous for her to enjoy it.

She thought over her plan for the next few days. She wanted to make an extensive trip into the backcountry and swing by as many of the possible tunnel sites as she could, maybe spend a week out there. She decided to call her dad, as she didn't know when she'd have access to a phone again.

She rinsed out the soup bowl and spoon and dialed him on the landline.

"Pumpkin!" he answered.

"Glad I caught you, Dad." Once again, she just wanted to spend a few moments thinking about something less dire. "What grand adventures are you having?"

"You'd be proud of me, Alex. I've signed up to contribute to a community science project."

Alex perked up. "What is it?"

"There's an endangered butterfly here, the Kaibab swallowtail. It only lives on the North Rim of the canyon. It's been vanishing due to habitat loss and pesticide use. So I've been spending part of every day documenting any sight of it, as well as locations of its favorite flowering plants."

"That's great! Have you seen it yet?"

"No, not in the adult stage, but I did find two of its caterpillars. I photographed them and uploaded the pics to this citizen science app they have here."

"That's great, Dad." Alex loved invertebrates, and they seldom received the attention that they needed or deserved. She had been a member of the Xerces Society for Invertebrate Conservation for years, and loved the work they did helping pollinators, fireflies, freshwater mussels, and more. Monarch butterflies were the one invertebrate that had caught the public's attention, which was wonderful, and had people planting native milkweed in their gardens. But so many other insects needed help.

In fact, Alex had been reading that the earth was currently experiencing an insect apocalypse that was going largely unreported. Insects had declined by 75 percent in the last fifty years, due to loss of habitat, pesticide use, and climate change. And insects were vastly important to ecosystems and human life, because they pollinated crops, controlled pests, provided food for other animals, kept the soil healthy, and contributed a multitude of other benefits. Not to mention the sheer joy of a summer evening when fireflies dazzled in meadows filled with the song of cicadas and katydids.

"I'm glad you're doing that," she told him. "That's important."

"And how are things with you? You don't quite sound yourself. Is everything okay?" He'd always been intuitive with her.

"No." She told him about Kathleen going missing, finding the lost hiker, and her intention to spend the next week or so visiting as many potential places where Kathleen could be.

"That sounds dangerous."

"I'll be out there with the sheriff's department, the FBI, and Search and Rescue," she assured him.

"I still don't like it."

"I can't sit around here and do nothing. I've got to help. Lots of volunteers are. We already searched the area around her fire tower today."

"Find anything?"

"Nothing," she told him, feeling the disappointment all over again.

"I don't blame you for wanting to find your friend, pumpkin, but please be careful out there."

"I will, Dad."

As they hung up, a pit of fear settled into Alex's stomach. Kathleen was out there, right now, maybe fighting for her life.

Dawn could not come soon enough.

TWENTY-TWO

The next day, Alex once again rendezvoused with the FBI agents, Cody, Bill, and the sheriff at the fire tower. As she pulled up in the predawn light, she was buoyed to see a number of volunteers already arriving. As before, cars had filled up the small parking lot and had now started parking along the fire road. Several Forest Service rangers had come in from neighboring districts to help, and she spotted their Jeeps parked among the volunteers' vehicles.

The area bustled with activity—people donning backcountry packs and pulling out trekking poles. She put on her own pack and joined Cody by the small Forest Service cabin. There they compared notes on a topo map. She'd marked likely tunnel locations, and after she'd talked to Fields, he had identified several more possible areas himself.

To be expeditious, Cody decided that after taking up the search around the fire tower area where they'd left off the day before, they would start exploring the possible tunnel locations if they didn't find any promising leads. They then broke into teams with a mix of FBI agents and rangers joining each volunteer group.

The extended search of the fire tower area proved fruitless, so Cody gathered everyone together once more, as the morning waned.

As the group clustered around him, he stood up on a log and boomed out his instructions. They passed out new maps with marked search areas where tunnels might be present. With their new assignments, people shuffled off, rejoining their crews.

Alex found herself on Cody's team with Agent Hernandez and fifteen other volunteers. They hiked farther out, exploring two possible locations but finding no tunnels. After a brief lunch break, they moved on to other areas for the rest of the afternoon, but again found no tunnels.

It was a hot day, and the refreshing rain showers that had graced her earlier hikes were nowhere in sight. By the end of the afternoon, the volunteers in her group had begun to lag. They mopped at sweaty brows and fanned themselves with hats. Many stopped to filter water from streams along the way and refill their empty bottles.

Each time they had come upon a possible tunnel location, they had branched out, searching, and Alex's spirit would lift. But after more empty sites, the worry in her stomach grew more acidic.

She heard Cody checking in via radio with the other search teams. No one had found a single tunnel or any kind of clue at the other possible locations.

Had Alex guessed wrong? Her stomach flip-flopped at the thought of wasting valuable search time that could have been spent in a better way, a way that might have led to Kathleen. Where was she?

Finally, as the sun touched the top of the peaks to the west, Cody called over the radio for everyone to return to the fire tower. "It's time to wrap up for the day, folks. Let's go home. Get some rest. We've got five more places to search, and we'll do 'em tomorrow. We'll start at the fire tower, break into groups, and search those areas. They're farther afield, so be prepared to camp out for the night. Eat good. Sleep good. And thank you all for coming out." Then he made a circle above his head with his finger to her little group. "Let's head back."

Alex paused. She didn't want to go back with them. She couldn't.

She'd packed enough supplies for a week in the backcountry. She had her lightweight MacBook Air and a solar-charging power bank with her. Maybe she could find more places to search. Leave the known five to the search party tomorrow. Cover more ground that way.

As the others began heading back toward the fire tower, Cody noticed Alex pausing. He approached her. "What is it?"

"I was just thinking . . ."

"Yes?"

She didn't want him to insist she go back with the others. She'd feel useless returning to the ranch house tonight. And what would she do if she did go back? Break out her laptop and search more areas with GIS. Same as she could do from out here, as she didn't need the internet to do so. She could be close to another site even now. It would save precious time to already be in the backcountry tomorrow.

"We're pretty close to a couple of my remote cameras," she told him. "I think I'll stay out tonight, check them out in the morning." When he stared down at her, his brow furrowed, she added, "Maybe there will be a clue on them."

He bit his lip, sticking a hand on his hip. "I don't like you out here by yourself."

"I'm not the killer's type," she said for the second time in two days. "I've been fine so far." *Except for being chased by that light,* she thought grimly. She wondered if Taggert had told him about that.

"It's the 'so far' part of that sentence I don't like."

She slid off her pack. "I've got plenty of supplies. I'll be fine."

"Well, I can't force you to come back with us."

"I'll just check the two cameras and rendezvous with you all tomorrow at one of the search sites." She patted the folded topo map sticking out of her jacket pocket. Of course, if she found other places to search, she knew she'd do that first.

He exhaled. "Okay. But I'm not a huge fan of this plan."

"Neither am I, to be honest," she told him. "But I can't just go back and spin my wheels."

"I understand." He stared around at the forest. "Tomorrow will be the fourth day she's missing. Hopefully we'll have plenty of volunteers willing to spend the night out then. We can cover more ground that way if we're not walking all the way back to the fire tower at night." He held out his hand. "Give me your topo."

Alex pulled it out of her pack. Cody unfolded it, eyes scanning the lines. Then he pointed to one of the search areas outlined in red. "This is the one I'll be at tomorrow. Meet me here if you can." He handed back the map.

"Okay."

And with that, he straightened his pack on his shoulders and turned away. "You just be careful," he said over his shoulder.

"Always."

When everyone had gone, Alex began casting around for a suitable campsite. She found an amazing meadow strewn with wildflowers along a burbling creek. With the remaining sunlight, she propped up her portable solar power bank against a rock to get the maximum angle of light, then plugged her laptop into it to recharge.

Then she sat down cross-legged in the meadow. Her whole body ached. She didn't know exactly how many miles she'd covered in the last couple days, but moments of rest like this had been few.

She leaned her hands back and turned her face up to the sun, taking a moment just to breathe and steep in the forest. She'd been in such turmoil since hearing about Kathleen that she hadn't spent time just to sit and be. Now she took in everything. The wind in the pines, the drifting clouds in the deep azure sky, one of them looking like a penguin, another a baby bison.

A varied thrush called from the trees. Its song always sounded to her like a police whistle. Then she heard the almost surreal, variable notes of a Swainson's thrush, one of her favorites. The birdsong danced through the trees, echoing. She smiled.

A Clark's nutcracker gave a buzzy call, and a woodpecker drummed out a rhythm. Beside her, a butterfly landed on the delicate white petals of a patch of blossoming Sitka valerian and paused to collect nectar. A deep peace suffused her, and with it, a new determination to find Kathleen.

As the sun dipped below the horizon, a chill set in. She thought of the strange craft and its searching beam and didn't want to pitch her tent in an open site where she'd be easily spotted. So she gathered up her solar power bank and laptop and set up her tent inside the tree line.

She threw her sleeping pad and bag inside and then set up the rainfly, stashing her pack under it. She made a quick dinner, warming up some freeze-dried vegetable korma with her camp stove. Then she crawled inside her tent, kicking off her boots next to her pack. Firing up her laptop, she brought up ArcGIS and began layering data again. She pulled out the topo and donned her headlamp as true darkness set in.

All the places where the teams planned to search tomorrow were marked with red Sharpie. Maybe they'd missed something. It was too good of a lead not to have panned out; she could feel it. She brought up her original GIS map that she'd created last night. Then laboriously she reviewed all the sites where the significant landmark components were in play. She noticed three outlying ones that hadn't been searched yet, and weren't marked on the SAR topo map, either.

One wasn't that far away. She could check it out tomorrow, see what she found. The clock was ticking for Kathleen, and since Alex was already out here, she could do some recon. She didn't want to pull Cody and the others away from promising leads, especially since nothing had turned up at all the other sites where she'd hoped to find tunnels. Tomorrow those last five sites could also be busts. Maybe her theory was wrong. Maybe Fields would come up with a new idea tomorrow. Something more productive. And in the meantime, Alex would check out these last three.

She downloaded the coordinates into her GPS unit and marked them on the topo.

Then she shut down her laptop and stowed it beside her sleeping bag. She changed into a thermal shirt and leggings, donned a thick pair of warm socks and her wool hat, and shimmied into the sleeping bag. Already cold had set in, the mountain night not holding on to the heat of the day.

She shivered slightly, thinking of Kathleen, wondering where she was just now. Then she thought of the strange craft, its piercing beam and thundering noise, its pursuit of her through the forest.

Sleep would not come easily tonight.

TWENTY-THREE

The next day, Alex awoke to early morning sunshine warming one side of the tent. Condensation had collected on the fabric during the night. She sat up and unzipped the tent door, listening to the chorus of birdsong in the forest around her.

She breathed a sigh of relief that the mysterious light hadn't visited her in the night. She stripped off her thermal sleeping clothes and donned her hiking gear, then pulled on her boots. Outside, the meadow stretched green and inviting on the far side of the tree line. She breathed in the rich scent of sun-warmed pine and moss, and stretched. It seemed crazy that a day as glorious as this one could be fraught with what she now had to face: the search for her missing friend. The beauty of this natural setting felt like the antithesis to the ugliness that humans brought down upon each other. It didn't seem possible that such violence could exist in this place, dappled in golden sunshine and filled with the solace of the whispering brook.

She filtered water from the stream and quickly ate an energy bar. Then she packed up her tent and hefted her pack onto her shoulders, buckling it in place. Time to resume the search.

Using her GPS, she navigated toward the first possible location that she'd determined last night. Soon she spotted the large pile of boulders that had fallen in antiquity from a steep cliff. The stream she'd camped near trickled down from this area, and she entered the quiet darkness of a section of old growth. Lichen hung from the tall branches, and she slung off her pack at the base of a tree.

Now she searched painstakingly, looking for trip wires and bells, booby traps and footprints. Moving in ever-widening circles, she bent low, sometimes feeling with her hands in areas that looked like someone might have passed through. But all she found were a couple deer hoofprints and some moose droppings. No sign of a human.

She returned to her pack. Was she wrong? Was it just a coincidence that the tunnels she'd found were centered around these three things—stream, old growth, boulder field? She frowned. Was she wasting precious time?

She pulled out her GPS unit again and selected the next area from her waypoints. Two miles away. She had to at least check out the other two. She didn't know where else to search, and no one else had ideas, either.

Hefting her pack back onto her shoulders, she set off for the next point.

Dark clouds gathered overhead, and soon the air smelled of ozone and a light mist began to fall. Alex didn't pull out her rain gear, but simply fit a rain cover over her pack. She welcomed the cool moisture on her face and arms. In one dense copse of trees, she startled two feeding mule deer does, who lifted their heads in alarm and stared at her. She moved to the far side of the trees, not wanting to disturb them, and as she hiked away, they resumed their meal.

More than once a red squirrel erupted in a flurry of barking as she passed beneath a tree. She climbed up steep ridges and down the other sides, crossed little streams, and navigated around cliffs and rock formations.

She passed the foot of a glacier winding down between two massive peaks. It wasn't the typical white and blue, where ice crept by on the surface. Instead it was a rock glacier, a swath of stones covering the river of ice beneath it. A cold wind drifted down from it, and at its foot, a river of meltwater flowed from the base, chunks of ice floating in it.

Alex stopped to catch her breath and stare up at the awesome sight, then pressed on.

Finally she reached the second possible tunnel location, and the huge boulder pile came into view.

Carefully Alex approached it. Limestone rocks, covered in gray, yellow, and brilliant orange lichen, stacked to a height of thirty feet. She stepped into the cluster of giant trees, then moved into a clearing. As before, she watched the ground carefully. The last thing she wanted was to get swept up in a net trap or fall into another pit. She shucked off her pack and leaned it against a tree trunk. Then she picked up a long stick and prodded the ground with it as she proceeded.

As she felt along the soft bed of pine needles, a rusted wire came into view. Excitement seized her. She'd done it! She'd found another tunnel! So she hadn't been wrong all along.

Adrenaline coursing through her, she followed the wire's path, finding a bell dangling from a nearby tree. Dirt and pine needles clumped along the wire's length, and in some sections, soil completely covered it, caking it in place. The wire had been there a long time. She poked gently at the ground on the opposite side of the wire, finding it solid, and then stepped over. Now she worked her way around the clearing, searching for traps both on the ground and in the trees.

Then, against a long feeder log, she spotted part of a dark opening. Hesitantly she crept to it, finding it covered with severed branches, their needles long since fallen off and clustered brown around the ground. The limbs had been laid out a while ago. She moved them aside, watching for wires. Pulling her headlamp out of her pack, she switched it on, shining the beam around the tunnel entrance. It led straight down beneath the massive log.

Strapping on the lamp, she crawled on her hands and knees into the earthen hole. A dank, mildewy, sooty smell tickled her nose and she suppressed a sneeze.

The place felt deserted. Even before she'd crawled all the way in, she knew she wouldn't find Kathleen here. But maybe she could pick up clues.

The tunnel sloped down, stretching for ten feet before it opened into a small chamber. This one was smaller than the other two she'd been in, and of a rougher construction. Only a handful of branches shored up the dirt walls. One had collapsed partially, spilling rich, black soil into the center of the room.

A small shelf lined one wall, and on it she found two dust-covered mystery novels from the seventies, and two plastic bottles with nozzles, filled with a yellowish-white powder. *Diphasiastrum*. She grabbed both bottles.

She crept in farther, finding a collapsed tunnel on the opposite side of the chamber. Covering part of the wall and floor were spores of *Diphasiastrum*. It looked like a trap had gone off, similar to the one that had hit her in the tunnel, showering the section of the room with the powder.

As she drew closer, she cringed at a sudden stench of decay.

There, in the soil, was a perfect imprint of a human body, as if one had lain there for a long time.

Peeking out of the ground beside the depression, half buried in the loam, lay something metallic. Alex reached for it, carefully dusting the dirt away from its edges. She wasn't about to pick it up. It could be a trigger for a trap of some kind. But then she saw what it was: a Forest Service shield.

Irma.

Alex left it in situ.

She had to notify Fields and Taggert about this location. But she'd seen nothing to let her know that Kathleen had been here or had ever even been in the area.

She turned around, walking at a hunch under the low ceiling, and stopped suddenly when she saw something crumpled in the corner next to the shelf. Its bright purple, soft texture shone in the beam from her headlamp. Material of some kind. Fleece. Alex moved to it, unfolding it. National park patches from dozens of locations covered the fabric. Amelia Fairweather's jacket.

This sealed it. Not that Alex had doubted it, but the tunnels and the missing women were definitely connected, and whoever the squatter was, they needed to find him. Kathleen could be suffering right now, held against her will.

The fact that belongings of both women were here meant that Kathleen could be nearby. There was still another possible location close to this spot. Alex pulled out her phone and took a photo of both the jacket and the shield in situ. She had no cell reception, so she couldn't send them out.

Then she pressed on, feeling close now.

TWENTY-FOUR

Alex emerged from the tunnel, blinking in the bright sunlight. She replaced the branches in front of the opening and pulled out her GPS unit to navigate to the next spot.

Her heart weighed heavily as she stepped through the forest, worried about Kathleen, feeling a twinge of fear at the thought of a killer stalking these peaceful woods.

She descended to a small stream and took the opportunity to filter some fresh water into her bottle. Then she climbed a rise on the other side of the creek. She wasn't too far from the tunnel when she detected the scent of woodsmoke on the air.

She stopped, sniffing, then pulled out the topo to study the area around her. No campsites or national forest cabins for miles. It was possible some backcountry camper had made a fire, but there was a strict prohibition on backcountry fires right now due to the danger of starting a wildfire. Only small stoves were allowed.

If it was an illegal fire or something ignited by a lightning strike, she wanted to make sure it didn't spread. Smelling the air as she went, she followed the scent to a small clearing among a cluster of huge trees. In the center stood a ramshackle old building, built with a mix of mossy stones and sun-bleached logs. The roof, partially caved in, had been covered with an old canvas tarp. Mildew grew on it in big dark splotches.

Smoke issued from a half-collapsed chimney. The place looked like it hadn't been in good shape since maybe the 1930s, and with its stone architecture, she wondered if it had been an old backcountry cabin that had been used by rangers on their long patrols.

She pulled out her topo, not seeing it marked on the map. Whatever it had been, it had fallen into such disrepair that the U.S. Geological Survey no longer felt the need to mark it as a viable landmark.

She walked closer, keeping behind the massive trunks, using the obstructed line of sight to creep nearer.

She could hear the clattering of dishes inside, the clinking of glass and pots and pans. Suddenly a furious voice roared through an open window. Alex instinctively knelt down, gripping the rough bark of the tree in front of her.

"What the hell do you think you're doing, woman?"

If there was a response, Alex didn't hear it.

"I've told you a million goddamn times that I want my coffeepot rinsed out by lunchtime. I don't want to wait here while your lazy ass has to clean it out when I'm ready for my lunch!" She heard the crash of glass, something shattering.

This time Alex did hear a meek reply, a woman's voice, whimpering.

"Do I have to remind you about this?" She heard another smash and the woman let out a yelp of pain.

Alex shifted to a closer tree, then another, keeping out of sight. She shrugged off her pack and leaned it against the trunk.

"I'll teach you a lesson you'll never forget!" Now Alex was close enough that she heard furniture crash, and a lashing sound like a belt or a whip snapping and hitting something.

"Stop! Stop!" the woman screamed, her voice twisted with agony.

"I'll kill you this time!" the man bellowed, his voice cracking in livid rage and fury.

"Stop!" the woman screamed again, and suddenly Kathleen bolted out of the door into the small yard, but was jerked back violently, collapsing into the dirt.

Alex stood. A long chain stretched from the inside of the house, shackled to Kathleen's ankle.

The man roared out of the house, a belt raised above his head. He brought the buckle end down hard on Kathleen's back. She rolled, covering her head with her hands, curling into a fetal position.

The man's face twisted with perverse joy as he raised the belt again. He stood about six feet tall, lean and wiry, with an unkempt mane of white hair framing the pale, red-blotched face of an alcoholic. His ragged, dirty clothes hung off his shoulders. She guessed he was in his seventies.

Alex ran to the back of the house, using it for cover, and stared in through the window. The place was small, just two rooms, a main room and a bedroom. No one else was there. She raced around the front of the house just as the old man lifted the belt again.

Alex's Jeet Kune Do training flooded into her mind. She'd been studying the martial art since she was a kid, and muscle memory took over. As she reached the old man, she lashed out with a medium-range kick, striking him in the solar plexus. He grunted, staggering backward, and she used a leg sweep to knock him onto his back.

He reached up and grabbed her arm. She clamped her own hand over his and spun around 180 degrees, holding fast to his arm. This close to him, she could smell the vile odor of urine and a body that hadn't been washed in who knew how long. Her eyes teared in the stench. She drove the heel of her palm into his elbow, hearing a sickening crunch as it caved in, bending back the wrong way.

Then reaching to her side, she grabbed her bear spray out of its holster and blasted him in the face. He screamed, clawing at his eyes with his one good arm. She brought her heel down into his face, instantly stopping his scream. His nose erupted in an explosion of blood and his whole body went limp.

"Alex!" Kathleen croaked, tears streaming down her face. Alex knelt beside her friend, gathering her up in her arms.

Alex's gaze fell to the shackle. It was an ancient thing, worn and flecked with both dried and fresh blood. A rusty bolt held it closed. Alex whipped out her multitool, opened its wrench, and went to work loosening the closure. The man had cinched it down tight. Kathleen gripped Alex's arm as she worked, glancing nervously at her prone captor. Alex didn't know how long he'd be out. Finally the bolt turned a little with a powdery cascade of rust and Alex twisted the wrench quickly.

When it was loose enough, Alex gripped it with her fingers and rapidly unscrewed it by hand, clearing it from the shackle. The metal band fell to the ground, exposing Kathleen's swollen, bruised, and bloody ankle.

Kathleen's mouth opened in horror and she pointed. "Alex!"

Alex twisted, looking over her shoulder, a bolt of fear shooting through her. The man scrambled to his feet and raced into the house.

He emerged seconds later carrying a shotgun.

"C'mon!" Alex flung Kathleen's arm over her shoulder and lifted her to her feet. They hurried away as the man wiped at his red and swollen eyes.

"I'll kill you both!" he shouted, firing off a blast. But he couldn't see clearly, and the shot went wide.

Kathleen ran as best as she could on her injured ankle and they made it to the trees. Now they wove between the trunks as the old man cursed and fired off a second shot, again missing them by a considerable distance. Alex dared a look back, seeing him wiping his eyes furiously against his shoulders, his broken arm dangling at his side, the other holding the shotgun, waving it around like a madman. He fired off a third shot, and this one peppered a tree next to them. Alex snatched up her pack as they passed it.

They didn't stop. Kept running. Alex headed for the rise that led down to the stream.

She remembered seeing another dense cluster of rocks about an eighth of a mile past the tunnel. They could hide there if they needed to and crossing the creek would mask their movements.

They ran up over the rise, Alex bearing some of Kathleen's weight as she hobbled along. Alex kept checking their six, not seeing the man. They half slid, half jogged down the other side of the embankment and splashed into the freezing water. Kathleen lost her footing on the slippery rocks and almost fell, but Alex caught her in time. They forged through the icy stream as it gushed around their calves. When they'd gone about a hundred feet, Alex ushered Kathleen out of the water and onto the opposite bank, heading for the boulder pile.

At last they reached the cover of the rocks and took refuge on the far side of it. Kathleen slumped down, gasping for breath.

Slipping out of her backpack, Alex fished out her water bottle and gave it to Kathleen. She drank gratefully. "I can't believe you found me." She panted. "How long have I been gone?"

"Four days."

"God, that short?"

Alex nodded.

Kathleen took another sip. "Felt like forever." She reached tentative fingertips to her face. Multiple bruises had swollen her features, some marks older and yellow and green, some bright red and purple. A cut on her cheekbone oozed blood. A nasty lump had swollen on the back of her head.

"When we get to safety, I'll clean those wounds," she told Kathleen. "I don't think he'll be right on our tail. He'll have to flush his eyes out before he'll be able to see. And I'm pretty sure I broke his nose. His arm, too."

"Then you think we're safe for now?"

"Let's play it on the cautious side and keep moving."

Kathleen shivered and Alex pulled her warm parka out of her pack and gave it to her. Then she donned her own fleece jacket.

Alex checked her topo map, found their current location, then pulled out the search grid map. It showed where the different search teams would be exploring and camping for the night. Cody's location was the closest source of help from where they were, much closer than the other SAR locations, and faster than trying to make it all the way back to the ranch house.

She pointed to the location on the map. "Cody, the head search and rescue guy, who's been looking for you, is at a location about six miles away. He was planning to spend the night there, so he should still be there when we arrive. Think you can do that?"

Kathleen grimaced. "I'll have to."

She drank a little more, and then Alex took a swig.

When they'd caught their breath, Alex helped her up and they continued through the forest, heading for Cody's location.

"What happened?" Alex asked when they'd gained some distance.

Kathleen shook her head. "I don't know. I just woke up one morning at the fire tower, and this guy was there, inside the cabin. He had a mask on. We fought. He just . . ." She swallowed. "Crushed me until I couldn't breathe anymore. I think he drugged me when I was unconscious, because when I woke up, I was already in the cabin, shackled. That guy was crazy. It's like he wanted a slave. Someone to cook and clean. To obey his every word."

"Do you know who he is?"

Kathleen shook her head. "Only that he said his name was Otis. I'd never seen him before." She touched the bruises on her face. "Others had been there before me. I don't know what happened to them. But when he put that shackle on . . . it already had someone else's blood on it."

Alex told her about finding the two women's belongings stashed in one of his tunnels, and how she'd found Amelia, alive but in shock.

Kathleen squeezed her eyes shut, swallowing. "That makes sense now. He talked about other women who had been there. One of them had just left. Recently, too, was my impression. He was furious about it, kept beating me, saying if I tried anything like that, he'd kill me on the spot."

"Amelia must have been with him for over a year."

"God." Kathleen shook her head in amazement. "I can't even imagine that. A year! How is she?"

"Last time I checked, not saying anything. In shock."

"I can imagine. Amazing that she got away from him, though. If I had been there for a year with that kind of abuse . . . she must be incredibly strong." Kathleen's gaze grew far away. "I don't think other people were so lucky."

"What do you mean?"

"From his angry tirades, I gathered that he'd had a wife at one point. He always cursed about her. Said she'd run off, but I don't think she did, Alex." Kathleen turned to her, her brow creased, eyes wide.

Alex stepped over a log, then helped Kathleen maneuver it with her bum ankle. "What do you think happened?"

"There was this pile of rocks behind the house. He'd . . . he'd go back there and pee on it. A couple times a day. He'd laugh when he did. Once, in a fit of rage, he went out there and kicked the stones around. I think she was buried under there." Kathleen shuddered. "He had me get the firewood once. It was right next to the rock pile. The chain barely reached that far, so I couldn't really look around, but while I was out there, I think I saw . . ."

When her friend went quiet, Alex prompted gently, "Yes?"

"Part of a hand. Skeletal fingers. Peeking out from the rocks."

Alex regarded her with horror. She touched her friend tenderly on the shoulder. "What did he want with you?"

She nodded. "To do all the domestic chores." She grew thoughtful. "There was another guy out there, too. He came by the house a couple times. I got the feeling from the sound of his voice that he was younger. Otis gagged me and locked me in this root cellar both times before he came over, but I could hear them arguing."

"About what?"

"Everything. How to build a snare, what the best kind of am-

munition was, how to track animals. The other guy said he was going to hunt bighorn sheep by a rock glacier, but Otis told him going
that high was a waste of time, that the valleys had the best game.
He'd brag about all the animals he'd poached, some that he shot just
for fun. The younger guy admonished him for being wasteful, and
I heard Otis get up and belt him. But mostly, Otis just berated him.
Ran him down.

"The other guy, he was real submissive around him. Otis told
him how stupid he was, how he couldn't do anything right. Once
the guy wept, and I heard Otis hit him again. For a while, I thought
Otis had been the one who snatched me from the fire tower, but I
started to wonder if it was the younger guy. Like doing a favor for
Otis. Or under his orders. But then again, I'm not sure if the younger
guy even knew I was down there in that root cellar. I mean, if he did,
then why did Otis always force me down there and gag me?"

"You said the man who took you from the fire tower wore a
mask?" Alex asked.

"Yeah."

"Maybe Otis didn't want you to know what he looked like."

"That makes sense."

They passed by the foot of the rock glacier. Water streamed
from the base, forming a silty, iceberg-clustered stream before roaring off down the mountain as a tumbling whitewater river.

It drowned out all sounds around them, and Alex found herself
glancing backward more than usual, worried Otis might sneak up
on them.

Then she paused.

"What is it?" Kathleen asked, leaning on Alex's shoulder.

"Did you say that he never went up to the glacier?"

She nodded. "Yes. He groused that there was no good game up
here, and too little vegetation to use as cover for sneaking up on it."

Alex stared up at the vast glacier. Just as when she'd first seen it,
it didn't look like a traditional glacier. No stream of broken blue and

white ice snaking down in a U-shaped valley. Instead, it just looked like a rock field. Only when she'd gotten up close had she been able to see the jagged crevasses in the ice beneath all the rocks.

"Glaciers are melting at a record pace," Alex commented absently.

"I know."

"And that means they are constantly changing. New crevasses opening. Others closing."

"What are you getting at?"

She met Kathleen's gaze. "It means that the last time Otis was up here, the glacier could have been completely different. Maybe at one time he knew where the dangerous crevasses were, but he doesn't anymore."

"What are you thinking?"

"This guy's an expert tracker, right? We don't know how close he is behind us, and you're in no condition to run. We've got to slow him down."

Alex spotted a huge boulder deposited by the glacier years before when it was bigger. "Go hide behind that rock. I'll be right back."

Alex jogged along the foot of the glacier, stopping before she hit the cascade of water streaming off its base. Large crevasses opened at various places all the way to where the glacier disappeared over a rise. But those were too big for what she had in mind.

Then she saw it, about fifty feet up. A narrow crevasse, less than three feet wide. Now she just had to see how deep it went.

She started to climb, tentatively touching each rock and testing her weight before she stepped down on it. The last thing she wanted was to step on a rock that would tip upward, causing her to fall or break her leg in a crevice.

She scanned the area for Otis and then looked back to Kathleen, who had knelt down behind the rock and was watching her.

Alex gave her a reassuring wave and kept climbing. Some of the rocks teetered under her feet, but not enough to become dislodged.

Afraid she might suddenly break through and plunge down into icy darkness, Alex felt her heart hammer.

The wind streamed down the glacier's surface, strong enough to toss her off-balance a few times. At one point she windmilled and had to crouch down onto a rock. Then she kept climbing.

From the foot of the glacier, Kathleen watched her anxiously.

The cold wind bit into Alex's skin, and her ears stung from the gale. Carefully she stepped on rock after rock, well aware of the time it was taking, and hoping that it would be worth it.

And then she'd reached the crevasse. She lay down flat on a rock and carefully slunk forward, then peered over the edge. It yawned into a black abyss. "Hello!" she called down into it, her voice echoing and then fading away somewhere deep inside.

This would work.

She shimmied away from the opening and glanced around for some large, flat rocks. She spotted some and dragged them over to the crevasse. Then she heaved them over the opening, leaving them precariously balanced by just a tiny edge on one end.

With the crevasse opening sufficiently covered, she stood up. She could see Kathleen's anxious face peering out from behind the boulder. She stared out in the direction of the old cabin, but didn't see Otis. She flashed Kathleen the okay sign to let her know she was fine, and Kathleen nodded and gave her a wave.

Then she started back down and jogged to where they'd come out of the forest. She scanned the area with her binoculars. He couldn't be far behind. Sure enough, she could see the old man's struggling form coming over the rise they'd passed just twenty minutes before. He was still too far away to see them, and all of his focus was on the ground.

She ran back and put her arm around Kathleen to support her. "C'mon. We're going to backtrack a little way."

Fear filled Kathleen's face. "Are you sure?"

"Yes." She helped her hobble back to where they'd emerged

from the forest. Here a series of rocks stuck up from the earth, covered with lichen.

"Move from rock to rock," Alex told her. "Don't step on the soil."

Together they jumped from rock to rock. Kathleen winced with each leap but bit her lip and continued to move.

For a few minutes they did this, leaving no trace, until finally Alex felt like they'd covered enough ground. Then they slipped into the woods.

She set Kathleen down on a log, and she gratefully sighed and rubbed her ankle.

"I'll be right back. If the worst happens, just keep going."

Kathleen stared at her, agape. "What?"

She gripped Kathleen's shoulder. "Stay safe." Then she retraced their steps, jumping from rock to rock. When she reached the glacier, she backtracked all the way to the crevasse. Turning back toward the forest, she pulled out her binoculars again and watched Otis's slow progress.

She couldn't hear anything except the roar of whitewater and the wind.

Otis snuck cautiously out of the tree line, and Alex lined herself up with him so that the crevasse was in a direct line between them. She examined his weapon, guessing it was a twelve-gauge shotgun. That meant he'd have to be no more than fifty yards away from her to be certain of a kill shot, so she started to move that far from the crevasse. She hoped in his eagerness, he'd take a direct route to her.

He spotted her then. She pretended she was injured, limping and moving up and across the rocks.

He focused on her, his pace picking up. Just as she hoped, he didn't notice their tracks vanishing into the forest. She took another glance at him through the binoculars. He snuck forward, bringing his shotgun to bear with his one good arm. He'd bound his injured arm to his side tightly with an old belt, but still he winced as he walked, grimacing at every jarring step. A red rash clustered around his irritated eyes where she'd blasted him with the bear spray, and he rubbed at his face with his sleeve.

He walked in their tracks to the foot of the glacier and then stepped up onto the rocks. Carefully, he tested each step just as she had done. She'd hoped that maybe he'd forgotten this was a rock glacier, but he clearly remembered.

As he neared her, a huge grin spread across his face. She moved so that the crevasse lay directly between them. Her heart started to thump painfully. If she miscalculated this . . . When he was fifty yards away from her, almost on top of the trap, he brought up the gun. She braced herself for the blast and dove down. He fired off a deafening boom that echoed off the mountains around them. It went wide. Alex stood back up, continuing to limp over the rocks.

He drew closer, now almost on top of the crevasse. Alex held her breath. Taking careful aim this time, he took one more step forward, and reached the rocks she'd placed so meticulously over the crevasse, their far edges barely stable there. Eager to get a better shot, he hurried to step down onto one of the flat rocks, and his weight caused it to pitch violently. He screamed, his leg going down into the ice, his weight crashing into the other flat rock. It gave way beneath him and he slipped down into the crevasse. The shotgun went off as he shrieked, plummeting out of sight. His screams echoed down from the mountains and then faded away.

Alex watched, tensed, gripping a rock in front of her so tightly that her fingertips had gone white.

She waited, her ears still ringing from the shotgun. She forced her breathing to slow, her hands to stop trembling. She had to know if he was dead. Slowly she moved down the glacier and crept to the edge of the crevasse. She dared a look in.

She knew that at least this part was deep, a steep section angling away into darkness. There was no way for him to have somehow caught himself and been waiting there a few feet down to blow her head off.

She peered into the black. Cold air issued up from beneath her, ruffling through her hair. She listened. No cries for help. No blast of the shotgun.

Otis was long gone. If he hadn't died from the impact, he'd freeze to death down there.

Alex remained for a few more minutes just in case he was somehow managing to crawl out. When she still didn't hear anything, she descended the glacier, returning to Kathleen.

Kathleen stood up as Alex reached her, using the massive log she'd hidden behind for support. "He went in!" she said breathlessly.

"He sure did."

"Is he dead?"

"I think so. We can take our time now."

Kathleen exhaled, clearly relieved. For several long moments she was just silent. Alex was still shaking from the terror of acting as bait. Then Kathleen stared up at the sun. "How much light do we have left?"

Alex checked her watch. "Seven hours. Plenty of time." She held out her hand and Kathleen took it, groaning as she put weight on her ankle.

"Let me fashion you a walking stick," Alex offered, scanning the forest floor for a suitable candidate. She found one just the right height and retrieved it.

Kathleen tested the weight. "Perfect. Thanks."

Then they headed off for Cody's campsite. And though Alex knew Otis was either dead or dying, she couldn't help but steal a last look at the glacier, fear crawling over her back. And what of the man who had visited Otis? Had he been the one to take Kathleen, and was it the squatter?

Alex frowned. Whoever he was, he was still out there.

AFTERNOON LIGHT SLANTED THROUGH THE trees as they walked. Kathleen stumbled and fell once, banging her knee on a rock.

"Great. Just what I needed." She pulled up the cuff of her pants, finding a red bruise already forming there.

They stopped frequently to drink and eat energy bars. Kathleen reveled in a small bag of dried fruit Alex had packed. But eventually her friend's energy began to flag. Alex didn't like the thought of them out there in the forest tonight, not with Otis's buddy possibly nearby. She wondered again if he was the squatter. It would make sense. One of his tunnels had been used to store Irma's body and Amelia's fleece. And she didn't doubt he knew this forest intimately, a lot better than they did. He could be out there right now, watching them.

"I'm sorry. I don't know how much farther I can go without a long rest," Kathleen admitted.

Alex regarded her friend, saw her haggard expression, the weary eyes, the trembling chin. "You can do it, Kathleen." She checked her GPS unit. "We only have two more miles to go."

Kathleen's eyes lifted. "That's it?" The hope in her voice tugged at Alex.

"That's it." She wanted to get her friend's mind off the pain. She thought about what Kathleen had said in the café, about learning Polish. "So tell me about this fascination you have with languages."

Kathleen managed a slight smile. "I'm trying to learn helpful phrases in as many languages as I can. You know, like 'please,' 'thank you,' 'yes,' 'no,' 'you're welcome,' 'how are you,' et cetera? 'Where is the nearest bookstore?' Right now I'm learning them in Zulu, Polish, and Navajo."

"Navajo! That's fascinating."

Kathleen nodded. "I love the sound of it. So far I've learned more Polish than anything else. I know a little Russian, and they're similar in some ways, so that's helped. It's the figures of speech I find the most interesting from culture to culture." She winced as she stepped over a log.

Alex wanted to keep her distracted. "So tell me some Polish idioms."

At this, Kathleen actually grinned. "There are some great ones."

"Like what?" Alex asked, genuinely intrigued.

"There's *Nie wywołuj wilka z lasu*. Doesn't that sound pretty?"

It did. "What does it mean?"

"'Don't call the wolf from the forest.' As in 'Don't ask for trouble.'" Kathleen struggled along, and Alex admired her incredible strength. She imagined she'd had next to no sleep on top of being injured. And the way she'd torn into the dried fruit and energy bars made her think she'd had very little food, too.

"What are some others?" Alex prompted.

"*Myśleć o niebieskich migdałach*. 'Dreaming of blue almonds.'"

Alex chuckled. "What does *that* mean?"

"It's like drifting into a pleasant daydream," Kathleen explained.

"I like that one."

"One of my favorites is *Nie mój cyrk, nie moje małpy*. Basically, 'Not my circus, not my monkeys.'"

"Like, 'Not my problem'?"

Kathleen smiled at her. "Exactly. And if you ever want to tell someone off or get rid of them, you can say, *Wypchaj się sianem*. 'Go stuff yourself with hay.'"

"I'll remember that one. I can think of quite a few people I'd like to see stuff themselves with hay."

They continued chatting, Kathleen teaching her more phrases. Often they stopped to rest, just listening to the birdsong in the trees, watching the sun stream down onto the forest floor.

Alex's GPS unit beeped. They were nearing Cody's location. "We're here!" she said, feeling triumphant.

As they entered his camp, Alex's eyes fell on the welcome sight of Cody sitting on a stump, carefully placing his stove and food into his pack. The whole camp had emptied out. Cody's was the last tent remaining, and he was in the process of taking it down. He'd already folded up the rainfly.

"Cody!" Alex called out.

He turned, seeing them, and broke into a huge grin. "I don't believe it! Is this Kathleen?"

Alex nodded, catching her breath. "Are we ever glad to see you!"

He rushed to them solicitously. "Here," he said, putting an arm around Kathleen. "Come sit down over here."

Kathleen's eyes went wide as she stared up at him, then she went unsteady on her feet. He took hold of her arm before she fell. "You okay?"

She hobbled along beside him, leaning heavily on his arm. "Yes. My ankle's just killing me."

"Here," he said, helping her over to a large fallen log. He lowered her down onto it.

"Where is everyone?" Alex asked.

"Moving on to a different sector. Thought we'd spend the night here, but since we didn't find anything, we're using the rest of the day's light to move to a spot closer to the next site. Get an early start tomorrow. I was about to join them. I can't believe you found her!"

Alex broke into a smile. "Me neither! And we're lucky you were still here."

"This is great news! Everyone will be so relieved!"

"How's Amelia?" Alex asked.

"Still not speaking."

Kathleen rubbed at her bruised ankle. It looked infected. "Will you come look at this damn ankle again, Alex? I think it's getting worse."

"Sure." As she knelt down in front of Kathleen, Alex looked up at Cody. "Can we use your radio?"

"Of course. I'll go get it."

As he headed off toward his tent, Kathleen grabbed Alex's arm in a crushing grip. "It's him," she whispered to Alex.

"What?"

"The young guy, the one who visited Otis. I recognize his voice. It's him."

TWENTY-FIVE

Just then Cody emerged from the tent with his radio. For the briefest of instants, Alex allowed herself to hope that maybe he hadn't had anything to do with Kathleen's abduction, that maybe Otis had grabbed her from the fire tower and that Cody hadn't known Kathleen was being held prisoner there when he'd visited Otis.

Cody held the radio, staring down at it, a frown on his face. Maybe he'd give it to her. Let her radio for help. "It's weird," he said, turning the radio over in his hands. "This thing was working earlier. I radioed Bill. But now it's not working. I know I just put new batteries in it . . ."

Alex's gaze fell to the handgun strapped to his hip. "Do you have a sat phone?"

He shook his head. "Never got one. Too expensive." He flipped the radio over and opened up the back. "Maybe something went wrong in the circuitry. I might be able to fix it."

"Want me to take a look?" Alex offered.

"I think the thing's busted." He lifted his head then, meeting her gaze. His eyes shifted from Alex to Kathleen and back again. Kathleen kept her head lowered, still massaging her ankle as if nothing was wrong. He stared down at Kathleen. "So where were you all this time?"

She still didn't look up. "Held prisoner in a little cabin."

"By who?"

"I don't know who he was."

Cody's mouth pressed into a grim slash. "So what happened to him?"

Alex decided not to fill him in on the details, especially if Cody was in on the kidnapping. "He's still back there," she told him. "We just ran." Maybe that would urge Cody to go check on Otis, giving them more time.

"So what do you ladies want to do?"

Alex thought back to the map, to the red areas marked where search parties were active. With Cody's radio "broken," she imagined he'd suggest they rejoin the other searchers. Offer to "escort" them there and make sure they met with some kind of misfortune along the way.

If they could somehow extract themselves from his company, she could look at the map and figure out a plan.

Alex quickly thought of a lie. "We'll have to just head on to our rendezvous point," she told him. She tried not to stare at his gun, praying he left it in the holster.

"What rendezvous point?"

"I'm due to meet up with Fields in an hour. We picked out a spot between our two search areas," she lied.

"What about Kathleen's ankle?"

"Oh, she'll be fine. You should have seen her trucking along earlier."

"You can leave her here with me. Then Fields can call in a team with a litter."

Kathleen stood up. "I'm okay walking it. Can't stand waiting around now. Just want to get this over with. Put it all behind me."

"What are you going to do?" Alex asked him as nonchalantly as possible.

He glanced behind him at the tent, then at his pack leaning

against it. His gaze fell to the gun on his hip. "I'll just continue on, meet up with Bill and the others, tell them we can call off the search."

"Okay. See you back in town," Alex told him.

"I feel like I should go with you," Cody pressed.

She waved him off. "That's kind, but not necessary."

"But what if that guy finds you again?"

"We'll be okay. There are two of us now."

"I feel bad just letting you limp off into the forest."

"Fields will be along shortly. Don't worry. We've made it this far," Alex assured him.

He screwed up his mouth, his brow creased. "Okay. If you're sure."

"Besides, like you said, with your radio broken, you have to go tell Bill and the others that the search can be called off."

He bit his lip. "That's true." He didn't move. "Okay. See you."

Kathleen placed her arm around Alex's shoulder and they set off from Cody's camp. Alex fought the urge to break into a run, knew she couldn't with Kathleen, anyway. But the impulse to bolt surged up inside her nonetheless.

As they moved off into the trees, Kathleen whispered, "Is he following us?"

Alex didn't dare look back, but she turned her head to the side as they walked, listening. "I don't hear anything." They reached a little creek and walked along the bank where they had to step over fewer obstacles. Alex considered stopping to refill her water bottle, giving her time to surreptitiously look back, but if they had actually fooled him just now, she wanted to gain as much ground as possible.

Finally she looked back, using mainly her peripheral vision to spy in the direction of Cody's camp. No movement met her eye. Then she stared back in earnest as they kept moving.

She didn't see him at first, then spotted him between the trees, taking down his tent. So maybe they had fooled him. Or maybe he hadn't known that Otis had held Kathleen. Maybe his radio really was broken. *And maybe dogs can fly*, she thought.

A creeping sensation crawled up her back.

Kathleen's ankle had already swollen up two times the size it had been when Alex released it from the shackle. "I'm beginning to suspect your ankle is fractured."

Kathleen sucked in a breath. "I didn't want to say anything, but I think you might be right. Or I might have a torn ligament or something. I can walk on it. Really. I just want to get out of here."

"Let's rest awhile. If you want, I can find a safe place to stash you, go and get help, and come back."

She squeezed Alex's arm. "Please don't leave me. If Cody is head of SAR, we know he's got amazing tracking skills."

Alex grimaced. "He certainly showed his stuff at the fire tower on the first day of the search for you."

"He'd find me."

"Okay. We won't split up. But we need to find a place for you to rest."

They walked down the bed of the stream for a quarter of a mile. "This cold water feels so good on my ankle," Kathleen breathed.

Alex laughed softly.

"What is it?"

"You reminded me of my dad just now. He's a total optimist. That sounded like something he'd say. We're being chased by a possible kidnapper and murderer, but you're happy that the cold water feels good on your ankle."

Kathleen smiled.

"I remember once," Alex reflected, "I was on a camping trip with my parents. We were driving up this steep mountain in Wyoming. A sudden mountain squall kicked up. Thunder, the sky almost black, and this shower of hail hit us. Huge golf-ball-sized hail. My mom was driving and cursing. The windshield wipers couldn't keep up with these ice balls. I remember rain gushing down the dirt road, becoming little rivers. 'Don't worry,' my dad said. 'The hail will be smaller on the east side of the mountain.' My mom burst out laughing. My dad's eternal optimism. After that, it became a joke with our family. 'Don't worry,' we'd tell each other when bad things happened, 'the hail will be smaller on the east side of the mountain.'"

Alex felt a pang of missing both of her parents, especially her mom. In some ways, those memories of her felt like a dream, a dream of a better life, when her mom was still alive, and Alex knew true joy without the painful twinge of loss mixed in.

When they'd trekked along the creek for another quarter mile, they peeled off into a dense pile of boulders. Vivid orange and gold lichen communities grew on the rough gray granite. Large dark, cool spaces opened between the rocks. She pointed to the biggest one. "We can crawl in there. Rest awhile."

"Sounds heavenly."

Alex tucked Kathleen into the small cave, then wriggled back out. She found a fallen pine bough and used it to brush over their tracks all the way to the creek and back. Maybe Cody wasn't following them, but she didn't want to take any chances.

She made a pillow for Kathleen out of her pack and draped her extra clothing and jacket over her friend. Kathleen fidgeted, nervous, breathing shallowly, and then started to relax. Alex kept constant vigil.

She pulled out her topo maps. Now that they suspected Kathleen's ankle was fractured, the nearest area where searchers would be was likely out of their reach. It lay some seven and a half miles away. The ranch house was too far away, too, and they didn't have a lot of light left.

But where could they go? Where would there be a radio?

A radio. It hit her.

The tree sitter.

She pulled out her GPS unit and brought up the coordinates for the tree, hoping Agatha was still in it, and hadn't been chased off by the logger. It was a little over four miles, as the crow flies. She frowned, looking down at Kathleen's exhausted form. She murmured in her sleep.

She studied the topo. From here, they'd have to cross a river called the Rubicon. Alex hadn't seen it before and wondered if it would be crossable. With all the rain they'd been having, and the few hot days that would have caused extra snowmelt from the mountains, she worried it might be a torrent. But it was their best bet.

Her mind made up, Alex felt a little better. They had a plan. They'd make it. She folded up the maps and left out her GPS unit. She checked outside again, staying in the cover of the rocks. She scanned the terrain with her binoculars. And then she saw what she was dreading: Cody cresting the ridge in the distance. He was following them after all.

She gently shook Kathleen, who, exhausted, had somehow managed to doze. "I'm sorry to get you up. But Cody's out there. We need to move."

TWENTY-SIX

Kathleen got to her feet and they slunk out of the rock pile, keeping it between them and Cody so he wouldn't spot them. They moved into the dense cover of the trees beyond, stooped low, moving from trunk to trunk.

As they entered the trees, Alex spotted another huge jumble of rocks off to their left. They could use it for cover.

Kathleen tripped on something and fell forward, catching herself on a trunk. A bell jangled in a nearby tree. Alex froze. *The squatter.* They'd stumbled on another of his hideouts.

"Wait a minute!" Alex grabbed her shoulder. "Don't move."

"What is it?"

"Traps."

Staying where she was, Alex scanned the area, worried that a net might snap them up, or a tree trunk swing down from the branches and strike them. Maybe it had just been a perimeter alarm.

She searched the ground visually, finding the wire that Kathleen had tripped on, following it up the trunk of a nearby tree to the small bell. Then she crept from one tree to another, finding similar wires strung along between trunks.

"We're definitely on his turf."

"Whose turf?"

"That squatter I told you about. The one who makes the tunnels. I don't know who he is. But either he's involved in your abduction, or Otis happened on one of his old hideouts and used it to store Irma's body."

"And he lays traps in the forest?"

Alex lifted her gaze to the trees, searching for snares. "I think he lives out here. From the looks of him, he has for some time."

Carefully, signaling for Kathleen to stay put, Alex made her way across the grove. She passed a massive fallen log covered with moss. A spider had woven a delicate web between two ferns that sprouted up from a section of mossy soil, and dew gathered on the silvery strands, reflecting the sunlight.

Next to it, several large pieces of bark leaned against the horizontal trunk. She lifted one aside, finding the dark entrance to a tunnel beyond.

For a brief moment, she entertained the notion of stashing Kathleen here and running for help. But the guy could come back. Or he could even know Otis and be part of it. She replaced the bark and continued through the grove, watching her every step and pausing frequently to stare up into the trees.

And then she saw it. A swinging log trap.

He'd hoisted a hefty log up into one tree and attached it to a rope that draped over a neighboring tree's branch, identical to the trap she'd seen at one of his other sites. All someone had to do was trip on the rope buried underneath a bed of pine needles, and it would release the log, swinging it down straight into the person.

Alex backtracked the way she came, wondering how much progress Cody had made, if he drew close behind.

She returned to Kathleen and signaled for her to crouch down. They crept to another gigantic nurse log, climbed over it, and hunkered down on the far side. It provided excellent cover from the direction they'd come.

Kathleen rubbed her ankle, wincing at the pain. "What are we doing?"

"I've got an idea."

Kathleen lifted her eyebrows.

"A trap of our own."

Now they could hear Cody moving through the brush behind them at a fast clip. Alex hoped he would be in too much of a hurry to look carefully at the ground.

She peered above the top of the mossy log, seeing him hike into view. She crawled over the trunk, Kathleen grabbing at her arm. "Where are you going?" her friend whispered.

"I'll be right back," Alex told her.

She skirted around from where Kathleen sat hidden and crept from tree to tree. Cody looked down, evidently following their tracks. The ground was so wet, the soft bed of moss and lichen so spongy, that keeping track of them when they'd just passed through wouldn't be too hard for him.

As he arrived at the edge of the grove, Alex stomped down hard on a fallen stick. It cracked.

He snapped his head up, instantly spotting her. She took off, leaping over fallen logs and rocks, heading in the opposite direction from where Kathleen hid. Cody rushed forward, his boots thudding on the ground behind her. Her heart hammered in her chest, feeling like it would burst through.

She could hear his ragged, labored breathing, sense his proximity. Then he was too close. He grabbed at her hair, the back of her shirt, but she sprinted on, tearing loose.

He cursed, boots plowing through pine cones and sticks, the crack and snap of the forest beneath his heavy footfalls.

And then she veered for the log trap. Knew exactly where the rope lay buried. Deftly she jumped over it, squeezing her eyes shut for one terrifying moment as Cody closed in behind her. She heard him stumble, then the rope snapping tight, the crack of the log tearing free. The rush of air as it swung down. Alex threw herself to the ground, pine needles stabbing at her face as she spat out dirt. She looked back just in time to see the log strike Cody in the side, lift him clear off his feet, and throw him ten yards away like a limp doll.

He landed hard, crying out, sprawled on the forest floor in a heap of limbs. But he stayed down only a moment. Grunting, he dragged himself into a sitting position, giving a sharp cry of pain.

Alex scrambled to her feet just as he forced himself upright. He grabbed his side, his face pinched with pain, and stuck a hand out to balance against the trunk of a tree.

Alex didn't wait for him to catch his breath. While he was still looking down, she signaled for Kathleen to stay put and pressed a finger to her lips. Then she ran forward, shouting, "Kathleen! Wait!" as if she were pursuing her. She wanted to draw him away.

Alex dared a look back, seeing Cody stumble. He pitched forward, tumbling onto the forest floor, then managed to struggle to his feet again. While his gaze was diverted, as he tried to get his feet steady beneath him, Alex gestured for Kathleen to meet her at a large tree on the far side of the grove.

Alex paused, wondering if she should fight Cody now, break his arm or his knee. Injure him to the extent that he couldn't pursue them. But then his hand reached down to his side and he pulled out his gun, aiming it at her hesitating figure.

Alex ducked just as Cody pulled off the safety. She ran at a stoop toward the tree where she'd meet Kathleen. The bullet struck a trunk just to her left.

Cody let out an angry slurry of curses and fired one more round at her back. She darted between trees, obstructing his line of sight. She heard another deafening shot but didn't see where it landed.

Then she was at the tree, Kathleen rushing to her side. "Are you okay?" she asked Alex.

"Yes. He didn't hit me."

They peeled away from the tree, running through the forest, getting as much distance between them as possible. Kathleen grimaced but kept up a fast pace, and Alex was more impressed with her than ever.

"How close is he?" her friend asked, panting.

Alex glanced back. "I don't see him. That log hit him in the side. I imagine he's got at least bruised ribs if not broken ones. It'll slow him down."

They pressed on, gaining a quarter mile of distance, the going tough. Moving through a thick forest without a trail, stepping over undergrowth, and laboring through dense sections of shrubbery was hard work. But soon they heard the roar of the Rubicon River.

"We're getting close!" Kathleen cried, hope in her voice.

Alex grinned, relief flooding through her at the sound of the tumbling water. "We just need to cross and then it's not far to the tree sitter and her radio!"

They picked up their pace, buoyed by the sound of the river. Thick clusters of willows crowded along its bank, and they had to move parallel to the water for a time before finding an opening big enough to squeeze through. Here moose, elk, and black bear tracks pressed into the mud. They'd found a game trail to the water's edge.

But when they reached it, they found a raging river so swollen with the recent rains that it was impassable.

Alex and Kathleen halted at the river's edge, gazing in horror at the roaring water. There was no way they could cross it, and Cody was fast behind them.

TWENTY-SEVEN

"We'll never be able to cross that!" Kathleen yelled above the roar of the water.

"There's got to be another place," Alex told her. "Let's move downstream."

Kathleen nodded.

But as they turned to retreat back down the game path, Alex in the lead, she came face-to-face with the squatter.

Alex's mouth went dry. She immediately went into her Jeet Kune Do fighting stance.

But the squatter held up his hands in a placating manner, palms toward her. "I'm not going to hurt you," he told her. He gestured them forward. "C'mon. I know a place where you can cross."

Alex stayed put, not sure what to do. Kathleen gripped her arm. "Who is that?"

"The squatter I was telling you about."

The man turned, seeing that Alex hadn't followed.

"C'mon! You don't have much time. He's not far behind."

"I say we go with him," Kathleen urged her.

Alex moved forward cautiously, keeping her distance from the man. When he saw that they were behind him, he took off at a sprint downriver. The going was rough, river-smoothed stones like bowling balls beneath their feet, wet and slick in some places. Alex dared a look behind, not seeing Cody yet. But she knew he was close.

They navigated the uneven bank, finally reaching a smooth sandy section where they were able to move at a faster pace. Kathleen pressed on behind Alex, Alex's wary eyes on the squatter.

He stopped abruptly ahead of them and disappeared into a dense section of willows. She stopped in the same place, peering down another game trail leading to the water, seeing him standing at the river's edge. He pointed up. Alex ducked down the trail. When she emerged from the dense willows, she saw a U.S. Forest Service crossing basket. A cable extended across the swollen river. Her heart sank when she saw that the basket waited on the far side of the river. They'd have to pull it across first.

"Here!" the man shouted above the din of the water. "I'll keep him occupied."

Alex wanted to ask who he was, why he was helping them. But they had no time.

Metal towers stood on opposite ends of the river, with short ladders leading up to small platforms. Alex jumped up onto the metal landing and started pulling the cable. The whole setup was rusted and stubborn, and after a screech of metal, the cable wrenched free and the basket began its slow trek across the river. Kathleen climbed up beside her and helped her pull.

But just then, Alex heard the snapping of branches, saw chaotic movement in the willows, and Cody appeared below them, gun drawn.

The squatter stepped out in front of him and placed a hand on his chest. "Cody, this has to stop."

"Get out of my way, Jacob."

"Haven't we suffered enough because of him?"

Cody narrowed his eyes. "He's our *father*."

"Yes, who murdered our mother and god knows how many other women."

Alex continued to pull on the cable. They shouted with such anger that she could hear them even above the rush of water.

"He's old now. He needs our help!" Cody insisted.

"Needs our help for what?" the squatter, Jacob, countered. "To abduct more victims for him? You have to let him go. He's twisted you into something monstrous."

"Who are you to talk?" Cody fumed. "You abandoned him! Abandoned *me* to him! You left home, got to see the world."

"In the military! You think I didn't see my share of hardship over there? You think I don't still have nightmares?"

"When you came back home, I thought you would help me deal with him."

Jacob looked down, biting his lip. "I wanted to help you. But I didn't know how." Then he returned his gaze to Cody. "Don't you remember all the cruel things he did to us? That he still does to you? He doesn't care about anyone but himself."

"But we're the only family he has."

"And he doesn't deserve us."

Alex's hands burned on the cable, Kathleen breathing hard as she helped tug at it. The basket was halfway across.

Hatred burned in Cody's eyes. "I know it was you who moved that ranger's body to the town square."

"I had to do something. People were dying!"

"They could tie it straight back to him."

"That's what I was hoping for."

"What kind of son are you?" Cody demanded.

Jacob shook his head. "I don't want to be his son. But I can still be your brother."

"Then get out of my way! If they make it to a radio, we're screwed!"

Jacob frowned. "Let them. It's time for this to end."

"No!" Cody rushed forward, raining a fury of blows down on his brother. Jacob reeled backward under the power of his brother's rage, flinging up his arms to protect his face. He stumbled and fell backward, Cody advancing, wincing and gripping his rib cage.

Jacob held up a placating hand. "I don't want to fight you!"

"Then stand aside!"

Jacob stood up defiantly. "I can't. Let them go."

Alex pulled with everything in her, drawing the basket closer to their side of the river. It was three-fourths of the way across now, moving slowly above the tumbling water.

Cody raised his sidearm.

"Alex!" Kathleen's voice trembled with fear. "Get down!"

But before the shot could go off, the squatter collided with Cody, knocking him to the ground. Jacob pummeled his brother, straddling his body. He grabbed Cody's gun and tossed it into the willows.

At last the basket arrived on their side of the bank. Kathleen climbed inside, struggling with her injured ankle. Alex followed suit.

They grabbed on to the cable and began pulling themselves across, but sudden resistance made Alex glance back. Cody stood up on the platform, feet planted on the crossing supports, the cable seized in his fists. Blood streamed from his nose and a cut on his cheek. He started pulling them backward.

But he was no match for Kathleen and Alex's combined strength, and they still gained ground across the river.

Cody wouldn't give up. He planted his feet on the support, lifting himself off the platform, and pulled with everything in him. Then Jacob climbed up onto the platform and pulled at Cody's leg, forcing him to tumble back down to the ground.

Alex watched the two brothers clashing. Cody managed to knock Jacob down and then hunted around for the gun in the willows. He seized it and took a classic firing stance.

"Get down!" Alex yelled over the roar of the river. She and Kathleen hunkered in the basket, forced to let go of the cable.

A shot pinged off the metalwork, and Alex felt something sharp sting her face.

"What are we going to do? Should we jump?" Kathleen yelled, staring down into the churning icy water.

Alex peered out through the metal grating. They were only halfway across. Jacob lay unmoving on the ground. Cody was about to take another shot, and they were suspended helplessly over the water. If she stood up to move them, she'd be an easy target.

But if they jumped in the water here, they'd quickly be swept away. She stared downriver, seeing water spewing out over jagged boulders, whirlpools and eddies frothing in a fervor.

Cody pulled the trigger again, but Alex didn't hear a shot. She winced, covering her face, then looked up to see him checking the chamber, then angrily rummaging through his pockets for another magazine. She sprang up and started pulling them across, feeling every muscle in her arms and shoulders straining to work faster. Kathleen popped up and helped her, and they made it two-thirds of the way across the river before Alex saw Cody slam home more rounds. He extended his arms, but suddenly Jacob rolled over and lurched to his feet. He seized Cody's firing arm.

Alex didn't stop pulling on the cable, didn't pause for a moment as she watched the fight unfold. Cold water splashed up, spraying her legs.

Jacob clashed with his brother, driving his gun arm skyward. A shot blasted over the roar of the river.

Three-quarters of the way across.

Another shot fired off. Jacob landed a powerful punch to Cody's face. He staggered backward, tumbling down on his back on the riverbank. Jacob fell on top of him, fighting for the gun.

"We're almost there!" Kathleen called. Alex snapped her gaze back to the far side of the shore. Just a few more feet and they could leap out, start running again.

On the opposite bank, Jacob sat on top of his brother, his feverish blows pounding Cody's face. But Cody bucked his hips upward, throwing off his brother, still maintaining his control over the gun.

With a bump and screech of rusted metal, the basket clinked home on the far side of the river. Kathleen scrambled out of the basket, followed closely by Alex.

Cody struggled to his feet and his brother tackled him again, driving him down onto the sandy shore. She saw the gun go flying again into a patch of willows.

"Let's go!" she heard Kathleen yell. She glanced back to see her friend a good fifty feet away, limping into the tree line.

"He could just ride the basket across after us. We've got to stop him," Alex called back.

"There isn't time!"

"We've got to just hope his brother can keep him fighting long enough. Run into the trees. Keep going. I'll catch up to you."

As Kathleen took off, Alex pulled her multitool out of her pants pocket and climbed up onto the platform.

Quickly she began unscrewing the bolts holding the basket's wheels in place. She got four of them loose, her heart hammering as she worked them, continually staring back across the tumbling whitewater at the fight unfolding on the opposite bank.

Cody had managed to stand up, but his brother tackled him to the ground again. Cody broke free, kicking his brother in the chest, and then scrambled into the willows, groping hands searching for the gun.

Alex got another bolt out. Most of them were rusted tight and she couldn't budge them. She wouldn't be able to detach the basket. But she could weaken its hold on the cable.

The crack of a shot made her wince, and she lost her balance, falling backward onto the riverbank.

"Alex!" Kathleen cried from the trees.

"I'm okay. Keep going!"

Alex scrambled to her feet, seeing Cody on the far side of the bank, gun recovered and pointed right at her. Jacob was sprawled in a heap at his feet. She ran in a zigzag pattern away from the water, her feet sliding in the sand and slipping on round, river-smoothed stones. She crashed down hard on one knee, then made it to the tree line.

Kathleen waited a hundred feet in, and Alex quickly joined her friend.

She glanced back, seeing Cody pulling the basket back to his side of the water.

"We have to keep going," Alex panted.

"How far to the tree sitter?"

Alex mentally went over the preserve's map. "Less than a mile, I think. I'll look if we get a moment to rest."

She glanced back at the river. The basket was almost on Cody's side now. They struggled up a rise, time passing at an agonizing pace. Kathleen was moving far more slowly than she had before. Alex looked back, seeing Cody now in the basket, pulling himself across. He'd holstered his gun. Kathleen gripped Alex's arm as they slid in dirt and rocks on the steep incline. Alex hit a loose patch of soil and slipped, sliding several feet down on her stomach. She scrambled to her feet and reached Kathleen. Her friend's breathing had become ragged.

Behind them, Cody had made it halfway across the river. Then with a snap and a groan of metal, the basket came crashing down into the water, torn metal shrieking as it plummeted into the icy churning beneath. She heard Cody scream in surprise, then saw the basket sinking, Cody's fingers laced through the metalwork as his head plunged underwater.

She stared. Maybe he'd drown. The basket sank out of view.

Then she saw Cody's blond head pop up a few dozen feet downstream, bobbing along in the fierce current. He collided with a sharp rock and then another, his arms flailing as he tried to swim to shore. But the current was too strong. It swept him into the V of the rapids, and she saw his head pop up two more times before he vanished completely around a bend.

"He's down!" she said, clawing to the top of the precipitous incline with Kathleen in tow. And then she saw why her friend was moving so much more slowly. Blood streamed down her leg.

She'd been shot.

TWENTY-EIGHT

Kathleen tumbled down at the base of a tree. "I don't know what's wrong with me. I can't seem to focus."

Alex rushed to her, finding her friend's eyes glassy and dazed. "You've been shot."

Kathleen stared at her. "I have?"

"Yes."

"I don't think so. I'm just cold all of a sudden. Can't run as fast."

Shock, Alex thought.

Gently Alex reached down to Kathleen's thigh. The bullet had torn through her pants, the fabric completely soaked in crimson. "I need to see how bad it is."

"Oh my god," Kathleen breathed. "I *was* shot!"

Alex pulled out her multitool and cut the hole in Kathleen's pants wider. When she separated the fabric, she saw a deep wound weeping blood. She bent down to examine the other side of her pants. No exit hole. "I think the bullet's still in there."

"That's bad, right?" Her friend started to shake. "I'm freezing."

Alex pulled her warmest fleece out of her pack and wrapped it around her. "We need to stop the bleeding."

She rummaged through her pack, finding her emergency medical kit. Pulling out gauze and tape and alcohol wipes, she mentally pored over the steps to cleaning a wound. Her breath came too fast, and she struggled to remember, her own hands shaking now.

Her combat pilot mother had gone over this with her. But that had been years ago. She forced her breathing to slow, her mind to still. For now, she could only stanch the bleeding. Luckily the bullet had missed Kathleen's leg bone and her femoral artery. She put pressure on the wound, applying thick gauze and fixing it in place. Then she took off her belt, used her multitool to punch a new hole in it, and fashioned a tourniquet, cinching it down tight.

Kathleen breathed in through her clenched teeth at the pain.

The bleeding slowed, soaking into the dressing.

Alex pulled out a map, trying to judge the distance to the tree sitter. "Do you think you can walk? It's about three-quarters of a mile to the tree sitter."

"You should just leave me here. Get to safety. I can hide, and you can double back for me."

"No way am I leaving you." She stared back in the direction of the river. A blood trail led straight to their location. If Cody had managed to crawl out of the river, it wouldn't take him long to run beside the bank and pick up their trail.

"We've got to move. At least a little. Find a better hiding place. He'll find you here."

Kathleen grimaced and grabbed on to a tree trunk to pull herself up. Alex helped her. "Well, at least it's the same leg as my bum ankle. Still got one good leg." She managed a smile.

Alex smiled back, once again in awe of her friend's strength. On the forest floor, Alex found a fallen branch just the right height and fashioned a crutch for Kathleen. Then she stared around, wondering where she could stash Kathleen while she made a dash for the tree sitter and her radio.

But she didn't see a rock pile or dense cluster of bushes. This part of the forest had been cleared recently, by the look of it. The USFS had come through and gathered up dead wood, stacking it into conical piles for fire mitigation.

A group of ravens gathered in a tree, conversing about their day, clacking their beaks, gurgling, cawing. She'd always loved the varied range of their vocalizations and felt a little piece of calm rise up in her at the sound of them. As they cawed, more ravens flew in from different parts of the tree to join the others, until a large group of seventeen clustered on the branches.

She was just considering leaving Kathleen for a moment to scout farther afield when the flock of ravens erupted in a flurry of wings. Alex snapped her gaze upward, seeing them take off in a classic "plow," a sure sign that an animal had disturbed their rest. She knew that plows usually veered off in the opposite direction of the disturbance.

They wouldn't have startled like that for a deer or a black bear. This was another kind of animal. A human. She pulled out her binoculars and studied the base of the tree in which the ravens had been. A Steller's jay cawed and took off from farther away, flying toward them. Alex hoped the disturbance was being caused by Jacob, but the pit in her stomach told her they wouldn't be that lucky.

"We need to move. I think Cody's coming."

"That guy's like the Terminator," Kathleen breathed. She put her arm around Alex's shoulders and they moved deeper into the trees, Alex searching for a hiding place. They covered ten feet without a blood trail, then twenty. Kathleen sucked in sharp breaths with each step, and Alex saw that already she was close to soaking through the gauze.

Alex bent down. "I'm going to fireman carry you."

"You can't! I'll slow you down too much!"

"I'm not taking no for an answer." She lowered her shoulder to Kathleen's midriff and then lifted her friend off the forest floor. She moved quickly now, Kathleen jostling at her back, holding on to Alex's arms and the straps on Alex's pack. They covered fifty feet, a hundred. Alex kept moving until her entire body ached and her legs trembled with muscle exhaustion. She spotted a huge fallen tree covered with moss and ferns.

She headed for it, fear gripping her at the thought of Cody spotting their retreating forms. But when she stared back behind her, he still hadn't come into view. Maybe the disturbance hadn't come from him at all. Maybe it *was* a deer. She gently placed Kathleen down by the log and together they lay on the far side of it, the soft bed of moss yielding beneath their bodies.

Alex strained to listen for the sound of approaching footsteps but could hear only the complaining of a Steller's jay in a nearby tree, followed by the trill of an annoyed red squirrel. Then everything went silent except for a light wind whispering through the boughs.

She tensed, listening. Then she heard it. The crack of a branch, then labored breathing. But with the way sound traveled in a forest, she guessed that whoever it was, was still some distance away, not right on top of them. She held her breath as the crunch and cracking of footsteps passed by the huge tree where they lay hidden. Alex and Kathleen both pressed into the ground, shielded by the massive log. The person was laboring for air, as if their ribs were cracked or bruised.

Cody.

He stopped, and Alex squeezed her eyes shut. Kathleen's fingers found hers and they clasped hands tightly. Alex clenched her teeth, her jaw muscles aching with the stress.

He shifted farther away from them and paused again. Then he backtracked, his breathing ragged. She could hear him poking around in the vegetation. He'd lost the blood trail. She hoped he wouldn't see their boot impressions on the forest floor.

Then he started in their direction again, but stopped. She could hear him cursing under his breath. He'd definitely lost track of them.

She heard him backtrack again, then move farther away.

To her immense relief, his footsteps receded until she couldn't hear them anymore.

Kathleen let out a long, quiet exhale. "Oh my god. I thought my heart was going to pound right out of my chest," she whispered.

"Ditto. My teeth hurt from clenching."

Finally Alex dared a look above the log, barely peeking her head up. She saw no sign of Cody. But still they lay there, listening, worried he might return, backtrack to where the blood trail ended and try again.

When twenty minutes elapsed with no sign of him, Alex finally dared to rise to her feet. She checked her GPS unit. "We're only a half mile to the tree sitter."

"What if he knows about her? Figures we might head that way?"

"We have to take the chance. She has the closest radio."

"What about the logging camp? Do you think that logger is still there? The one who was harassing her?"

Alex shook her head. "I can't be sure. Last time I talked to the sheriff, she was going to see if she could get him kicked off the site. I think the tree sitter is our best bet. The logging camp is a lot farther away."

Kathleen struggled to her feet. "Okay."

Alex took another look at her leg. She changed out the soaked gauze, glad to see that the bleeding had slowed. But the wound was bad, and the quicker they could get Kathleen to a hospital, the better.

Together, they set off for Agatha.

TWENTY-NINE

As they stepped through the forest, the last golden light of the day reaching patches of the emerald-green mossy ground, Kathleen struggled.

"We just have a little farther to go," Alex reassured her.

"Is the hail going to be smaller on the east side of the mountain?"

Alex laughed. "Yes. Yes, it is."

"Then I'm game."

Alex smiled at her friend.

The sun dipped behind the mountains, and instantly the air grew colder. Kathleen shivered and Alex pulled out her rain gear, took off her own jacket, and made Kathleen pull them on. The cold wasn't going to help Kathleen's condition, but the darkness would provide them with extra cover.

She checked her GPS unit again, turning on the compass feature to navigate. Just 932 meters to the tree, Gaia. They crept quietly through the forest, Kathleen leaning heavily on Alex's shoulder.

When they drew within a hundred yards of Agatha, Alex signaled for Kathleen to take refuge behind a massive tree. Gently she lowered her friend down to the forest floor, and relief spread across Kathleen's face.

"I'm going to check the area ahead. It's possible Cody knows about the tree sitter and might be waiting for us there."

The dim light of dusk gathered around her. A flammulated owl called out. Alex crept forward. Even the angry logger would be a welcome sight now. He'd likely have a radio or sat phone, something to report in to his logging company with.

She got near the base of the tree and crouched down among some huckleberry bushes, listening. At first she didn't hear anything. Then she detected faint stirrings up in the tree. She hoped it was Agatha moving around and not Cody, lying in wait.

Alex had to take a chance. "Agatha?" she called quietly. She knew how well sound carried in the woods, and she didn't have to speak very loud for Agatha to hear her up on her platform.

"Is that Alex down there?" came the reply.

"Yes. And I need help."

"What's wrong?"

"I need a medevac helicopter and the police."

"Seriously? What happened?"

"My friend's been shot. And the guy is still out here."

She heard Agatha shifting around. "God, I hate to tell you this, but they sent Trevor again and he forgot the batteries for my radio. I've been without communication for two days."

Alex sank into true despair. Her mind just wouldn't believe it. They'd come this far for nothing.

She stared around the dark forest floor. "Any chance he just left the basket down here? Or spilled the batteries out in a panic?"

"You're welcome to look, but I don't think so. He attached the basket. I think he just forgot to add batteries to it. He also forgot to put in drinking water. Nice, eh? If it hadn't been raining on and off, I don't know what I would have done."

Alex placed a hand on the ancient tree, her mind reeling. This was just one setback after another. And Kathleen didn't have a lot of time. She'd lost a significant amount of blood, and as night set in, it was going to get even colder.

"What can I do?" Agatha called down.

Alex thought a minute. Sooner or later, Cody would think to check this area. A wild part of her hoped that maybe he knew he was busted, worried that Alex and Kathleen might have already reached help. Maybe he'd taken off, far away from here. Gone on the run. Especially now that he knew his brother wasn't willing to keep the family secret.

One thing was for certain: Kathleen couldn't keep going like she had been. But Alex didn't feel safe leaving her where she was. She stared up into the dark branches of the massive tree.

"Do you have a climbing harness up there?"

"Sure."

"Can we lift my friend up into the tree with you?"

"I . . . I don't see why not. You think . . . you think that guy is going to come looking for her?" Her voice sounded scared and far away.

"He might. I'm not sure. But she'd be much safer up in the tree with you than down here in the open." She stared in the direction of the logging camp. "The logging camp is what, two miles from here?"

"Something like that."

"Do you know if that logger has a radio?"

"He does. I've heard him on it, complaining about me."

"Okay. Then this is the new plan. I'm going to get my friend. Can you lower the harness and we'll lift her up?"

"Sure thing."

"Now this time you're the lifesaver," Alex told her.

She took off at a run, in the last hints of the gloaming, which provided enough light for her to make her way to the tree where she'd left Kathleen.

When she found her, Kathleen lay slumped awkwardly against the trunk, eyes closed, arms drooping at her sides, mouth slack, and for a second Alex's heart crawled up into her throat.

She knelt beside her. "Kathleen?"

Her friend stirred, groggy eyes opening, unfocused.

"I've got good news and bad news," Alex told her.

"I don't think I can take any more bad news."

Alex forced a smile. "Then I'll just tell you the good news. You get to lounge in a tree while I sprint to the logging camp."

"She doesn't have a radio?" Kathleen's words slurred.

"No. But it's okay. I'm going to use a different radio and get you medevaced out of here. C'mon."

She hooked her hands under Kathleen's arms and boosted her up. Kathleen sucked in a sharp breath when she put weight on her leg. Alex scooped her up again in a fireman's carry and hefted her over to the base of the tree.

The harness dangled down from climbing ropes. She buckled Kathleen into it, not an easy feat, as Kathleen had to lift her injured leg and winced with every movement. But then she was strapped in.

"Ready!" she called up. She felt the rope go tight, and then together, using the harness's pulley system, Alex and Agatha began lifting Kathleen up into the tree.

As Alex pulled, backing away from the tree, she realized with staggering clarity just how high Agatha was in Gaia's branches. She estimated more than two hundred feet of rope passed between her hands before she felt it jerk to a stop.

"She's here," Agatha called down. "I've got her on the platform."

"You okay up there?" Alex asked them.

"I'm good," came Kathleen's weak reply.

Then Agatha pulled the rope back up into the tree, out of sight.

"All right. I'm off," Alex called up. She didn't want to carry extra weight, but wanted to be prepared, so she moved to a thick log and stripped unnecessary items out of her pack: her sleeping bag and pad, her tent. She covered them with fallen branches. Then, with the pack much lighter, she slung it on and departed.

True darkness had now set in. The moon hadn't risen yet, and it was so inky black that she couldn't see her way at all. She hated the thought of pulling out her headlamp but saw no alternative if she was going to make it to the logging camp in any decent amount of time.

She took a long drink of water, then switched on her headlamp and took off at a sprint.

THIRTY

Alex had covered only a quarter mile from the tree when a low humming noise filled the air above her. She snapped her gaze up, seeing a piercing beam of light flashing through the canopy.

The craft.

Panic rose inside her. She pressed against the side of a tree, even though she knew with the craft's heat-seeking ability that it was futile. The thing dipped beneath the treetops, its bright spotlight swiveling straight for her. She knew there was no way to hide from it under these conditions.

And if it could find her warmth amid the tree trunks, it would soon find Agatha and Kathleen.

She had to lead it away, think of some tactic to take it down from the sky.

She dashed from the tree as the thing spotlighted her in a dazzling beam. It blasted the loud throbbing noise that had terrified her when it was some unknown thing chasing her through the darkness.

She glanced over her shoulder at it, throwing up an arm to shield her eyes. She didn't know what it was—some kind of homemade craft?

She couldn't let it get a clear shot at her, so she wound between tree trunks. It let out a deafening blast, forcing Alex to slap her hands over her ears. Its penetrating beam didn't leave her for a moment as she ran. But she knew it had to get close if it was going to try to fire a dart at her. If only she could somehow lure it down to her level, hit it with something, force it out of the sky.

She paused at a huge tree and ran to the far side of its trunk. On the ground lay a long branch. She grabbed it, clenching it in her fists. She'd have to move quickly, not give the craft the chance to fire. It let out another blast of deafening noise and her heart hammered in response. Whatever the hell it was, it was effective in scaring the hell out of a person.

Alex gripped the rough bark, waiting for the thing to circle the tree and spotlight her again. And she'd be waiting. But she had only one chance. She had to hit it just right.

The beam crept around the side of the tree and Alex circled, buying time, steadying her breathing, making sure she'd picked a spot where the craft had room to descend. It lowered until it was at her height on the opposite side of the trunk.

Then she leapt around and faced it, pinpointing where the dart would come out. The craft was way too close to get a good view of her and it started to wheel backward. Alex couldn't make out anything on its frame in the glare from the lights, but she knew that frequently, drones had cameras on their undersides, supported on a gimbal.

She swung the branch laterally, bringing it to bear on the underbelly of the craft. It connected and caught on what she suspected was the camera, and the craft jerked violently to the side from the force of the blow. It was lighter than she had expected. She leapt forward and rained another blow down on it, this time on top, driving it farther toward the ground.

The dazzling lights blinded her, and all she could see were green and red spots in front of her eyes. But the loud thrumming of the machine shifted to the side and she struck again and again, driving it into the dirt and pine needles. Now her eyes stung and teared from the searing light, and she came down with the branch with everything in her.

She heard a plastic crunching sound and something flew off the machine and hit a nearby tree. She didn't want to accidentally make contact with the dart in her blindness, so she kept striking the craft with the end of the branch, like a jackhammer driving into its fuselage.

More pieces flew off it, scattering on the forest floor. Then she smashed at the lights, cracking LED bars. But still they burned. She needed to remove its power source. The housing split beneath the force of her attack, and she felt something big come loose. It thumped into the soil, and instantly the lights went out and the motor died.

Sudden silence descended over her, but all she could see were bright bursts of color on her burned retinas. She closed her eyes, still gripping the branch so tightly that the bark bit into her skin.

Slowly the bright spots faded and at last Alex could see. She switched on her headlamp and took in the damage.

Before her lay the wreckage of a large quadcopter. The craft was smaller than she'd imagined, but had long, extended LED light bars coming off it on two crossbars, and a light ring around the edge. Speakers protruded from its underbelly. And on the right-hand side she saw the metal tube with the tip of a tranquilizer dart sticking out of it. A large battery lay on the forest floor, and she could see now that the things that had pinged off the craft and struck the trees around her were propeller blades. She stared down at the mess. The thing was not going to fly again.

She took a moment to catch her breath, then finally, with shaking hands, she put down the branch. Bark had cut her right hand along the web between her thumb and index finger, and a large splinter stuck out of the palm of her left hand. She tugged it out.

Angrily, she grabbed the tranquilizer dart out of its housing and stashed it in an outside pocket on her pack. Then she stormed away, resuming her trek to the logging camp.

As she ran, Alex became aware of a light illuminating part of the forest, brilliance streaming through the trunks up ahead. As she drew closer, she heard a dull thrumming sound, like an idling motorcycle. She drew to a halt, fear seizing her again. She stared toward the light, catching her breath. Another drone? No, she realized, the light was stationary.

She jogged ahead, feeling a stitch forming in her side, and soon a large clearing full of stumps and machinery came into view. The logging camp. A small generator hammered away in the center, powering three tall work lights that cast sharp shadows around the equipment: bulldozers, skidders, de-limbers.

No sign of the activists or their banners or tents remained. Alex guessed they'd been ordered to clear out.

A camping trailer stood at the edge of the clearing, a light on in the curtained window, the shadow of a man inside bent over a dinette. She ran for it, but before she got there, the shadow moved, and the door to the trailer banged open.

"Who the hell's out there?" boomed Clyde, framed in the doorway. He flashed a Maglite around.

Alex stopped, trying to catch her breath.

"Don't bother being quiet. I see you on the security monitors."

The beam of his flashlight fell on her, and she approached, holding her hands up in a peaceful gesture. She stopped before him, desperate for a breath, leaning over with her hands on her knees. She took off her pack, leaning it against the bulldozer. The fresh air felt good on her sweaty back.

"You're that biologist," he said gruffly.

"Yes. I need to use your radio," she managed to gasp out.

He put his hands on his hips and she saw his radio there, clipped to his belt. "What for? This is official Diamond Logging Company equipment. For use only on company business."

She stood up, the stitch in her side giving her grief. "Please. I need to call the sheriff or the FBI. It's an emergency. My friend's been shot."

He screwed up his face in confusion. "What? Like in a hunting accident? I didn't think your type hunted."

"It wasn't an accident. A man is after us. The same man who murdered that ranger in town."

The logger looked around in the blinding glare of the site's lights. "And he's around here?"

"Yes!" Alex's patience had run out. "Please. Your radio."

"I guess I could call *for* you," he finally offered. "Who do you want to call again?"

"Just call the sheriff. Now, please! Tell them the killer is Cody Wainwright."

"Cody Wainwright!" Disbelief passed over Clyde's face. "Now, I find that hard to believe. I've had beer with that old boy on quite a few occasions. He's as solid as they come." He regarded her with suspicion.

"I'm telling you the truth!" Anger flared up inside Alex. She would take the radio by force if she had to.

Just then the crunch of boots on pine needles snapped her attention to the far side of the logging camp. Cody Wainwright strode into view. "I'm the one who needs your radio," he said in a low voice, moving forward. "I've been attacked. They tried to kill me. My radio went into the river."

Clyde looked from Alex to Cody, uncertainty creasing his forehead. "What happened, now?" he asked Cody.

"I said I need your radio," Cody growled. He struggled forward, clearly banged up. His brother had left him with a black eye and a bloody gash on his cheek. Blood crusted around his nose. He clutched at his ribs with one arm. The other rested on his sidearm. She was disappointed to see he hadn't lost that along with his radio. It must have been securely snapped into his holster. She noticed that now the holster was open.

"I think I'd better just call the sheriff," Clyde stammered, clearly sensing something was wrong.

In a flash, Cody pulled out his gun. "I'm sorry to hear that."

The crack of the gun rent the night air, Alex's ears ringing. She dove down, seeing the bullet strike Clyde in the head. He crumpled to the ground as she sped away into the shadows.

But Cody was close behind. He clicked on a headlamp, pinpointing her in the beam, and leveled the gun on her. She rolled, then raced for thicker tree cover. He aimed at her receding form, firing once, then twice, both times striking tree trunks as she dodged and weaved. He gave chase, cursing, shooting at her twice more, but between the motion of his running, the darkness, and the densely clustered trees, he missed both times. He drew closer. Too close.

"Goddamnit!" he cursed and shoved the gun into his holster. Then he ran at her with a rage that made her heart thump in fear. She sprinted farther into the darkness but saw the beam of Cody's headlamp bouncing along right behind her. He was lunging, hands grabbing, and then a streak of movement as he dove forward, snaring her legs. Cody's arms snaked around her, tackling her with an astonishing force that knocked the wind out of her. She crashed hard to the ground, Cody's crushing weight falling on top of her. Her chin hit the dirt and she bit down hard on her tongue, tasting blood. He began to crawl up her torso. When he reached her waist, she drove an elbow back into his nose. He grunted in pain, and his grip on her loosened as his hand instinctively flew to his face.

She twisted, bringing one leg up, and drove the heel of her boot into his side. He curled up, trying to protect his middle, and she rolled free, turning over on her back. She kicked hard, landing a blow to his already injured nose. If only she had her pack, she could have jabbed the tranquilizer dart into his arm.

She scrambled to her feet and turned to face him, throwing her hands up in the defensive Jeet Kune Do stance. Her best chance now was to disable him, exactly what she'd been trained to do. She kept moving, her training kicking in. *Don't freeze up. Don't let your feet turn to cement or your mind go numb with shock. Keep moving. Analyze how your opponent is approaching.*

He straightened up, wiping away blood, and faced off with her. He held his hands up like a brawler, someone without training, but full of rage and something else. *Desperation,* she realized. After all this time, after everything she'd overheard, after the way Kathleen had described Otis belittling him, running him down, even physically abusing him, he was still trying to protect his father.

"You don't have to do this," she told him. "Your father isn't worth it." She debated telling him that it was no use protecting his father anymore, that he was gone, down a deep crevasse in a glacier. But the rage over losing him might make Cody all the more dangerous and reckless.

Now he went for his gun, knowing he wouldn't miss at this close range. As he brought it up, she stepped into his space, using a sweeping, circular motion with her hand to knock it out of his grip. It went flying, landing in a cluster of dark bushes.

As they struggled, his headlamp blinded her, shining into her eyes, making it difficult to see his movements. Still inside his space, she headbutted him under the chin, and as his head snapped back, she reached up and drove her thumbs into his eyes, sliding between the eyeballs and the tissue of his eye sockets. It wouldn't blind him, but it would hurt like hell.

He screamed and she brought a knee up into his groin. In the next instant, she snatched the headlamp off his forehead.

Gasping, he went down on his knees and then dove for the bushes where the gun had vanished. He rooted around, blinking his eyes in pain and struggling in the darkness without his headlamp.

It would take him some time to find the gun, and Alex had only moments. She raced away from him, heading back for the cover of the heavy machinery in the camp.

She reached the logging equipment and stared around for something to use, anything. She was unarmed, by herself, and he could well recover his weapon from the bushes. She saw the skidder, a large machine on massive tires with a huge claw in front for grasping and transporting logs. She gazed back—still no sign of Cody.

She crept between the equipment and headed toward the trailer, reaching Clyde's body. She groped around on his belt, and her hands closed around the radio, finding it sticky with blood.

She wanted to be as quiet as possible, so she climbed into the trailer and shut the door to muffle any noise. When she heard the welcome squeal of the radio, her body flooded with relief. She tuned into the frequency Fields had been using for the search and rescue operation.

"Agent Fields, this is Alex Carter, over."

A momentary wait, then another squeal, and Fields's voice came over the radio. "Carter? Where are you?"

"I'm at the logging camp. Listen, I've found Kathleen, but she's been shot. It's Cody Wainwright. He's behind this. He's armed and not far behind me. I need help out here."

"I copy," Fields said. "Can you take cover until we get there?"

"When's your ETA?"

"At least half an hour. But we've got a helo. Can you make it till then?"

Alex's heart sank. "I'll have to," she told him. "I better go silent now."

"Understood."

She turned the radio off, and the heavy feeling of silence was overpowering in the wake of the welcome sound of Fields's voice.

She knew she didn't have half an hour. Cody was only a few minutes behind her, maybe more if he didn't realize she'd headed back to the camp. But he'd realize it soon enough, knowing she was desperate to reach a radio. She had to make a stand now. Especially if he'd found the gun again. And she couldn't risk him doubling back to find Kathleen. She moved through the trailer, searching in vain for a gun. She did find a half-empty box of .308 ammo, though, the same kind that had shot out her tire. On the table she found that Clyde had been filling out an insurance claim for the logging company for a whole load of logs that had been lost during a rainstorm. She glanced at the date. It was the same day those unburned logs had tumbled down the mountain and struck her car. So it had been Clyde in that truck, and probably Clyde who had taken the two shots at her, trying to scare her off. He'd likely gotten rid of the rifle afterward.

Alex kept searching, but the only weapon in the place was a butter knife lying sticky with jam on the dinette.

She had to think. Had to find a way to slow Cody down. Incapacitate him. She thought of the *Diphasiastrum* powder in her pack.

She hurried outside and knelt down again by Clyde. Her fingers found a ring of keys attached to an extending reel on his belt. She unhooked them, despairing to see the sheer number of keys.

She grabbed her pack, then unbuckled the top of it and reached inside. She felt for the cold, smooth metal of her Zippo lighter. She found it and pulled it out, along with both plastic bottles she'd found filled with *Diphasiastrum* powder.

Stashing her pack under the skidder, Alex stood up, gazing around. She didn't hear any sign of Cody and wondered if he'd found the gun and picked up her trail again. She crept forward, finding a bulldozer sitting in front of a de-limber, a machine with an enclosed cab on treads, and topped with an extending arm that shucked the limbs off tree trunks.

Now she gazed down at the massive ring of keys. She could start the camp's machines, but she still needed a way to deliver the *Diphasiastrum* powder. It was already in plastic bottles. She just had to remove the tips of the nozzles and she'd be good to go. She stared up above the de-limber, seeing a low overhanging branch from one of the massive trees that had so far survived the clear-cutting onslaught.

She returned to her pack and removed the coiled climbing rope strapped to the outside. Then she felt along the ground for a good-sized rock and found one next to the bulldozer.

Returning to the tree, she let out enough rope to reach the low-hanging branch and tossed up one end of the cord. On the first try, it fell short, so she let out more rope. Then she whipped the end around, gaining momentum, and let it fly skyward again. It looped over the branch and the other end fell back toward her. She grabbed it. Then, using a tight knot, she fastened that end to the rock and tied the other end of the rope to the frame of the bulldozer. She climbed inside the dozer and quickly familiarized herself with its controls.

Now Alex returned to the de-limber and set the two *Diphasiastrum* bottles on their sides at the end of its arm, nozzles pointed toward the front blade of the bulldozer. She took up the slack on the rope so that the heavy rock suspended directly above the two bottles. Carefully, she unscrewed the small tips on the nozzles.

Then she crept up into the operator's seat of the de-limber. Sweat broke out on her back, trickling down between her shoulder blades. Her heart thudded and her hands shook as she sorted through the mass of keys. She tried a few and found the right one half a minute later.

It was the moment of truth. As soon as she turned the key, the machine would roar to life. She had to be ready. Be quick. It would bring Cody, and he might have the gun by now.

Alex squeezed her eyes shut and took a deep breath. Then she started it up and leapt down from the de-limber.

She raced to the bulldozer, climbed up into its cab, and sorted through possible keys, finally jamming the right one home. The engine coughed and sputtered, easing into a smooth idle. She flipped on its lights, and the brilliant beams pierced the dark at the edges of the camp. She raised the bulldozer's front blade as high as it would go.

Now she leapt down and ran back to the de-limber. There she crouched, Zippo ready to go in her hand, waiting for Cody to come.

THIRTY-ONE

With the two engines roaring, their lights blazing, Cody had to know where she was. But she couldn't hear his approach over the noise. She just had to hope she'd spot him before he saw her. She waited, crouched down by the de-limber.

Five minutes went by, then ten. She began to think maybe he'd given up—couldn't find her and figured he'd have to make a run for it. Or maybe he'd left to go find his dad, not realizing he was already gone.

But then a figure came staggering into the logging camp. She saw immediately that he held the gun in front of him, aiming it at the bulldozer's bright lights. It went off with a cacophonous bang and she clamped her hands to her ears as the shot pinged off the side of the cab.

She had to act now. She flicked on the Zippo and placed it in front of the *Diphasiastrum* bottles, then slunk back to the bulldozer. The glare of the dozer's overhead lights was so bright that she didn't think he'd see her climbing up into the cab in the deep shadow behind them.

Carefully she unwound the rope from the frame and gripped the end tightly, holding the weight of the rock suspended above the *Diphasiastrum* bottles.

Cody came closer, his gun hand wavering. The chase had taken its toll on him. As he lumbered into the ring of light, she could see his haggard, bloody face, the broken nose.

He threw up his free hand, trying to shield his eyes from the glare and locate her.

She lay down in the cab of the bulldozer, barely peeking out from the floor to watch his approach. With one hand holding the rope and the other gripping the blade control, she waited.

He took another shot at the bulldozer, and she heard it ricochet off the treads. A third shot blasted dirt up from the ground, spraying over her. She held her position, fighting the fear of a bullet tearing through her skull. But she guessed he couldn't see her yet and was just trying to flush her out. Her whole body shivered but she didn't give ground.

He came closer to the de-limber, seeing the flickering light from the Zippo sitting out in the open.

He walked toward it, gun pointed, ready to fire, and as soon as he crossed in front of the *Diphasiastrum* bottles, Alex let loose the climbing rope.

The rock careened down, smashing the bottles, and letting forth a billowing cascade of yellow-white powder. Instantly it ignited in the flame, releasing a blast of fire right at Cody. He staggered back, caught in the blaze, slapping at his clothes and stumbling right under the bulldozer's blade. Alex clenched her fist on the control and let the blade drop, smashing down on top of him.

She heard him scream and stopped the blade's descent when he was hopelessly pinned beneath. She didn't want to kill him. But she had to stop him.

She jumped out of the cab, finding him thrashing in the dirt, his gun hand stuck out, and she kicked the weapon out of his grasp, then grabbed it.

With the weapon pointed at his head, she warned, "Just stay there, Cody."

She walked backward to her Zippo, never taking her eyes or the gun off Cody, and snapped the lighter closed.

Cody squirmed, trying to dig in the dirt to free himself, but the soil was too packed. If he did start to get out, she'd jab him with the tranquilizer dart. She pulled it out of her pack, ready. But then he just went limp. "I did it for him, you know," he told her, spitting out dust. "I didn't *want* to hurt anyone."

Exhausted, Alex slumped down and sat cross-legged a few feet away, still pointing the gun at him, her other hand gripping the dart. She didn't respond, just watched his tired, defeated face in the glow from the machinery.

Twenty minutes later, she heard the welcome beating of helicopter rotors. Then the blinking lights of the helo came into view and a wind kicked up as it landed in the clearing. The pilot cut the motor and Fields jumped out, followed closely by Lipkin and Hernandez.

She rose to her feet, holding out the gun handle-first to Fields, who took it. Then she climbed into the bulldozer and lifted the blade off Cody.

"Damn," Hernandez said, taking in the scene. "How the hell did you pull this off?"

Fields bent down, snapping the cuffs onto Cody's wrists. When he hefted him to his feet, Fields turned to Alex. "Where's Kathleen?"

"With the tree sitter. I can direct you there."

He barked at Lipkin and Hernandez, "Watch this creep until we come back with the helo." He hooked a thumb at Alex. "Going to evacuate the gunshot victim first." Then to Alex: "C'mon."

They piled into the helicopter and put on headsets. She directed the pilot toward the tree location. "There's a meadow not far from there where you can land," she told him.

They arrived and with joy, Alex rushed to the base of the tree and called up to Kathleen. "It's over. You're going home."

"Hallelujah," her friend called down from the tree.

With Agatha's help, they lowered Kathleen down from the branches and the medevac team secured her on a litter. In moments they lifted off for the hospital.

Fields turned in the front seat and regarded Alex in the back. "So how the hell did you figure out it was Cody?"

She told him about finding his father's cabin and her escape with Kathleen. Then their trap out on the rock glacier, and hiking to Cody's camp, only for Kathleen to realize they were in danger from him. She mentioned how the squatter had helped them.

Fields grunted and turned back around. Then he said into the headset, "Hey, Carter. Who would win in a fight? You or a family of kidnapping murderers?"

Despite everything, she couldn't help but laugh. "Me."

"You're damn straight," he said, turning to her and honoring her with his first smile. "You."

Alex held Kathleen's hand the whole way to the hospital.

AFTER LANDING ON THE ROOF, the medevac team quickly rushed Kathleen into the hospital. Alex stood with Fields out on the helipad. He hooked his thumb back to the chopper. "I've got to return to the logging camp. Get that creep airlifted out to a holding cell. You want a ride?"

Alex obviously didn't have her car with her, and with the hospital more than a hundred miles from Bellamy Falls, she decided to fly back with him so she could retrieve her Jeep and come back to check on Kathleen.

With Alex and Fields aboard, the helicopter returned to the logging camp. Alex stared down as the helo spotlighted Lipkin and Hernandez, waiting with a handcuffed Cody. They set down and Alex climbed out as they loaded Cody in. A tangle of worry and thoughts clouded her mind.

"We can give you a lift back to town," Fields offered.

"My car's at the ranch house," she told him.

"I can drive you back there after I secure this guy," he added.

"That's kind of you. But it's not a far hike from here, and to be honest, I could use the quiet time."

"Hiking through a forest in the pitch black is your idea of quiet time?" Fields asked, raising his eyebrows.

She smiled. "It is."

He shook his head. "Okay. But for the record, you're crazy."

His words reminded her of Zoe's. "So I keep hearing."

Fields made arrangements over the radio to get a crime scene unit up to attend to Clyde's body, ordering Lipkin to wait for them. Then, with Cody loaded in, the others lifted off. Alex said her good-byes to Lipkin, then retrieved her backpack and walked into the forest. A quarter mile away, she stopped in the quiet dark. She took a deep breath. Stared up at the stars. Waited for a meteor to streak by, and made a wish upon it. Then she set off for the ranch house.

THIRTY-TWO

Interrogation Room, Bellamy Falls Sheriff's Station
Two days later

Special Agent Fields and Sheriff Taggert sat in the small interrogation room across from Cody. A doctor had treated his wounds, and Cody hadn't requested a lawyer. Fields leaned forward in his chair, fixing Wainwright with a stare. All the fight had gone out of the man, and Fields gazed across at someone defeated. Just before entering the room, Taggert had informed Cody of the death of his father. A ranger had rappelled down the crevasse in the rock glacier and found Otis's body, battered and bloody. He'd broken his neck on impact.

Now Cody sat solemnly, his eyes red and swollen from crying.

Fields opened the questioning. "You want to tell us how you got wrapped up in all this?"

Cody bit his lip and took a shuddering breath. He crossed his arms. "It was our dad."

When he went silent again, Fields wondered if the guy was going to clam up. "We're listening."

Cody shifted uncomfortably in his seat. "When we were growing up, our mom was still with us. But our dad kept moving us around to a bunch of squatter camps all over Washington, Idaho, and Montana." He sniffed and went silent.

"And then what happened?" Fields prompted.

"When I was about seven and Jacob twelve, our mom just vanished one day. She said she was going off to fish, but she never came
back. Our dad told us she'd run off, that she didn't love us anymore."
He wiped his nose on the back of his hand. "He got real weird after
that. Kept going on about how it was a woman's job to tend to the
kitchen and take care of children and how she'd failed. It was like he
was obsessed with the idea, got angrier and angrier."

Fields put his elbows on the table, waiting for Cody to continue.
The guy had obviously suffered some kind of emotional or physical
abuse.

Finally he resumed. "About three months after she disappeared,
Dad brought home the first woman. She wept the whole time and
kept trying to leave." He shook his head. "I didn't understand why
she'd come to take care of us in the first place if it made her so unhappy." He darted a glance up at Fields, then at Taggert. His gaze
strayed to the door and he crossed his arms tightly across his chest.
"I didn't know, okay? I was so young. I didn't understand that he'd
abducted her. And then she disappeared a few months later, too."

"Do you know what happened to her?" Taggert asked.

Cody shook his head. "He told us she'd run off like our mom.
Blamed us. Said we were too much trouble. And then . . ." His voice
trailed off.

Fields studied his face. "Yes?"

"And then he brought home another woman. She cried the
whole time, too. But this time he got this shackle and chain to make
sure she wouldn't leave. He said it was so she wouldn't wander out
into the forest and get lost." He stared up at them. "I *believed* him,"
he said defensively. "I was just a kid. But Dad said she didn't do
things the right way. He was always going on about how lazy she
was, that she was no good. And then one day he took her out to
the stream to do some laundry, and when he came back home, she
wasn't with him."

Taggert shook her head. "What about *her*? Do you know where she is now?"

Cody shrugged. "He moved us around even more after that, living off-grid in different states. I'm not even sure where we were when she vanished. But he kept bringing us back to the cabin we'd lived in when we were real little, when our mom was still with us."

"Where is this place?" Fields asked.

Cody stared up at him as if Fields had missed something obvious. "It's where he was keeping Irma and Amelia. Where you found that fire tower worker." He smiled softly then, his gaze growing distant. "I liked it when we'd go back there. It was familiar. I felt closer to my mom there."

"What a fuzzy, warm, familial picture," Taggert muttered, but Cody didn't seem to hear her. He just went on with his story, his thoughts wrapped up in the past.

"Then one day Dad went out to get firewood, and he didn't come back. I was about seventeen then. At first Jacob and I thought he'd left us, too. I begged Jacob to go search for him. Jacob didn't want to. He's older than me. He thought we should just take off. Said Dad was bad news. But I wouldn't believe him. I begged him and begged him and practically dragged him out of the cabin. We found Dad, pinned down under this fire-weakened tree. It had fallen on his leg and broken it." Cody laced his fingers, gripping so tightly his knuckles went white.

"So what did you do?" Fields asked.

"He wouldn't go to a doctor. Said they only made things worse. We set his leg as best we could. But then he told us we had to find a woman to take care of him. He'd seen this one woman in town and liked her. Said she wouldn't mind taking care of us, we just had to persuade her. He said that me being practically a kid without a mom would pull on her heartstrings. Even if we had to initially take her by force, he swore she'd grow to love us.

"Jacob refused. But I did as Dad asked. I grabbed her from

town." Here Cody paused, blinking tears out of his eyes. He looked up plaintively at Fields. "You got to understand that I *believed* what my dad told us. I didn't know any different. I didn't realize that none of those women wanted to be around us, that we had stolen them from their lives." He sniffed. "At least, not until this one.

"When I got her back to the cabin, Dad put on the shackle." He shifted his gaze to Taggert. "That was the day Jacob just took off. He joined the military, becoming an Army Ranger. He was gone for years. And even I stopped coming around so much to Dad's. It was hard to see that woman there, to know I'd put her there, but I didn't know what else to do. And then Dad got rid of her. So I had to take another woman. Dad was getting old and weak by then, you know? And I couldn't just abandon him. Couldn't betray my own dad." He met Fields's stern look with pleading eyes. "You understand, right? I mean, my own dad?"

Fields pursed his lips. Of course he didn't understand. His own childhood had been no cakewalk, but he'd turned to helping people in need as a result, not committing crimes.

Cody shook his head, clasping his hands together. "That's when everything fell apart. I . . . accidentally killed the next woman when I got her back to the cabin. She just kept fighting, you know? She fell backward on the corner of the stove. Hit her head. I couldn't believe it. I just went numb. Dad helped me bury the body. Told me to go out and get someone else. But I didn't want to do it anymore. I had a life in town. A career. I was sick at the thought of what I'd done. But he threatened me. Said he'd turn me in for killing her. He just held it over me."

He stared up at them, chin jutted out. "I didn't have a choice! And I was really careful with the next woman. But I felt so trapped. And I couldn't believe it when I saw Jacob in the woods. He'd come back, determined to stop us. We felt so betrayed when he retrieved Irma's body from where we'd stashed it and strung it up in the town square. It wasn't the first time he'd done something like that, either.

And then he put booby traps in places he knew we used for gathering wood or hunting." Cody peered up at them, suddenly looking hopeful. "Did you find him? Jacob?"

Fields wasn't about to volunteer any information to this creep. His agents and the sheriff's department had searched for Jacob after Kathleen's rescue, but so far had found only abandoned tunnels and no sign of him.

"You didn't, did you?" Cody said, wiping at the mucus beneath his nose. "He's gone. He left me. Again." Fields watched Cody's face crumple and he started to sob. "Believe me, I felt bad each time I had to take a new woman. I really did! But Dad said he couldn't survive out there on his own."

Fields frowned, thinking of how Otis had pursued Kathleen and Alex through the forest, despite having a broken arm and supposedly being old and weak. He had no doubt that Otis had played up any infirmities to keep Cody roped in.

Cody went on. "And he wouldn't come live in town. He was really stubborn. You don't know what it was like," Cody told them earnestly. "He was mean. So mean. No matter what I did, he'd berate me, belittle me, even beat me sometimes. I kept thinking if I could just find the perfect woman for him, he'd forgive me. But instead I just let him down over and over again." He wiped at his eyes. "I wasn't a good enough son."

Fucking hell, Fields thought. *Not a good enough son? What kind of number did the monster do on this guy?* Cody didn't even seem to grasp the vile enormity of what he'd done.

"So what did you do then?" Taggert asked.

"I was ashamed. Ashamed I kept letting him down. So, like Jacob, I withdrew. Took to building a life for myself in town, stayed away for longer periods of time. But I couldn't completely leave him. When he needed someone new to take care of him, I'd try to find women in the forest. Modified a drone to make hunting easier. That's how I found Amelia out there. But after she left, Dad wanted someone new. He'd seen Kathleen one day when he was hunting near the fire tower and wanted her. So I got her for him."

What the hell, Fields thought. *He talks about it like he picked up some groceries for his old man.*

Fields and Taggert listened to more of Cody's story. He gave them information on eleven missing-person cases in Montana, Washington, and Idaho, going back three decades.

When at last Cody was done, Fields leaned back in his chair and sighed. At least this one case was going to bring closure to a lot of families, even though the news would be heartbreaking.

EPILOGUE

The evening Kathleen was airlifted to the hospital, Alex had returned and spent most of the night with her. They'd removed the bullet and she was resting comfortably when Alex had left to go home, shower, and get some sleep.

The next few days Alex slept in, visited Kathleen a few times in the afternoons. This morning she rose after noon, feeling rested at last. She ate a leisurely breakfast, drank two cups of strong, hot tea, and sat at the kitchen table, going through the footage of the caribou that had come in over the last few days.

As she studied the videos, she continued to make detailed notes and a picture began to form. So far the caribou spent about 40 percent of his time eating, 23 percent ruminating, 11 percent traveling, 12 percent just gazing out while sitting or standing, 7 percent napping, and a small percentage of time drinking or licking the soil for nutrients. It was all valuable data that would inform the land trust of how they could improve habitat further.

The phone rang.

Alex picked it up, happy to hear Zoe's voice on the other end. She filled her in on the latest news, Zoe listening intently, only interrupting with gasps.

"Are you okay?" she asked Alex after she was caught up.

"I think so."

"And they're sure they got all the guys? There's not, like, a third deranged brother out there, hanging out in the forest, waiting for another unsuspecting hiker?"

"God, I hope not."

"Crazy."

"Tell me about it."

"You really need to get a less dangerous job," Zoe admonished her. "Like fishing in shark-infested waters wearing a suit made out of chum."

Alex laughed. "I'll keep that in mind. On the good side of things, I submitted evidence of the caribou using this land to the judge who's considering the logging moratorium."

"So that old growth might be saved?"

"I hope so," Alex told her. "So what about your own mystery?"

Zoe chuckled. "Oh, after all that, it turned out to be raccoons."

"What?"

"Yep. They'd been living in the walls of the old soundstage. Chewing wires, leaving half-eaten food, and pooping. Found a whole wall stuffed full of raccoon excrement."

"Yuck."

"But it explains the lights and air-conditioning being on the fritz, and all those bad smells. Apparently some of the poop had caught on fire in there due to a shorted-out wire, but there wasn't enough oxygen for it to spread."

Alex smiled. "So it was just raccoons. Not a ghost or a vengeful actor."

"Nope."

Alex thought a moment. "But wait—I get how raccoons could be responsible for making the alien go haywire that time you were up on wires in front of the green screen, but how could raccoons have caused it to walk over to your trailer? I mean, shorted-out wires wouldn't have allowed the alien to walk in such a calculated, direct manner, would they?"

On the other end of the line, Zoe was quiet.

"Zoe?"

"I hadn't thought of that. How *could* the alien have come to life like that?"

"I don't know. A ghost, maybe?"

"Goddamnit, Alex, just when I was feeling better about everything."

"Just keep the Ouija board handy."

"Damn it. This is just like one of those TV shows from the eighties where the episode is about ghosts or vampires or something, and everyone blows it off at the end because of some logical explanation, but then the camera cuts to a candle moving by itself in a window, or the characters discover an ancient portrait of the very guy they suspected was a vampire, and *boom*—there he is, centuries old and probably really was a vampire the whole time."

"Have you been watching episodes of *Murder, She Wrote* again in your downtime on the set?"

"Maybe." Zoe sighed. "Well, the good thing is that we wrap tomorrow. So if there is a ghost in the old soundstage, it only has one more day to haunt us."

They talked for a few more minutes and then a klaxon on Zoe's end called her back to set. "Gotta go. You take care out there."

"I will."

They hung up and the phone rang again almost immediately. It was Sheriff Taggert.

"Sheriff. How are you?" Alex asked.

"Good. You recovered okay from your ordeal?"

"Getting there." A breeze wafted through the open window, bringing with it the scent of sun-warmed pine.

"So Cody made a full confession. Guy is seriously messed up. The FBI just started excavating the rock pile and land behind Otis's old cabin and so far have found the remains of not just Cody's mother, but two other women, one stashed in an old tunnel of Jacob's. Otis was using the tunnels to hide evidence."

"Gruesome," Alex breathed.

"Cody said he wasn't sure where his father had buried bodies in the other states, but at least no other women will be taken."

"At least that part is good news."

"And I've got some more. That federal judge who was deciding on the logging moratorium? He just ruled that the loophole exploited by that congressman was unlawful, especially after receiving your information that a mountain caribou had returned to the area. The moratorium on logging the old growth just became permanent."

Alex stood up. "That's fantastic!"

"Amelia's finally talking, though she's not saying much yet. But she perked up considerably when her daughters flew out to see her."

"I'm so glad to hear it."

"And Agatha is coming out of the tree today," Taggert added.

"Oh, wow. This day gets better and better."

"From what I gather, quite a crowd is there to welcome her down if you want to head over."

Outside a Swainson's thrush sang its lyrical phrase of notes. The woods called to her. "I think I will."

After they hung up, Alex finished sipping her tea. She thought of Jacob returning to the area to expose his brother and father. She suspected that he had erased those images on her remote cameras because he didn't want anyone to know he'd returned, or to track places where he was hiding out.

She gazed out the window at the green forest beyond. After the chaos of the last few days, she longed for the peace that the woods brought her.

She geared up, filling her daypack with a couple energy bars, her water bottle and filter, and her camera and GPS unit. Then she headed out into the brilliant afternoon.

She aimed first for Agatha's tree. As she drew closer to it, she could hear cheering coming from the forest. She came over a rise, seeing a group of activists gathered at the base of Gaia, hugging one another. A man played a joyful melody on a concertina, and two other people joined in on hand drums. People danced. She saw Dennis, the first activist she'd met, among them. He spotted her as she approached.

"Dr. Carter!"

"Hi. Heard Agatha's coming down."

"Yep. She's just gathering her things now."

Alex cast around for the skittish Trevor, but didn't see him amid the throng. She wondered if he'd gone home, embarrassed at his flub-ups.

A climbing rope dropped down out of the tree, its end flopping in the soft bed of soil and pine needles below. Alex gazed up to see Agatha descending in a climbing harness, the same one she'd used to haul Kathleen up into the tree several nights before.

Agatha plopped down, and before she could even detach from the rope, her comrades closed in, hugging and high-fiving her. Alex waited for them to finish embracing their friend and shouting their cheers and then approached Agatha as she climbed out of her harness.

She held her hand out. "I'm Alex Carter."

Agatha grinned and drew Alex into a bear hug. "Nice to finally meet you." Agatha was a skinny wisp of a person, with a mass of fiery red dreadlocks and a freckled pink face.

"Thanks again for what you did for my friend," Alex told her.

"And thank you for the times you scared off that logger." She frowned. "I heard what happened to him."

Alex looked down. "Yeah. It was pretty brutal."

People still pressed in close, shouting and cheering. More started dancing as the drums and concertina picked up in pace.

"Congratulations on saving this grove," Alex told her.

Agatha gazed up into the dense branches that had been her home for the last seven months. "It was entirely my pleasure."

Agatha hugged her again, and then Alex left the group to its celebration, entering the preserve and climbing a small rise. Soon the sound of the music faded away, replaced by birdsong and the trickling of a nearby creek. She hiked on, breathing in the restful scent of the forest, the sun warm on her back.

As she entered an area of old growth, she suddenly heard a branch break to her left. She snapped her head in that direction, and there, standing in a patch of sunlight and pulling lichen down from a low branch, stood the caribou.

Alex grinned.

She watched him munch lazily on the green witch's hair, then take a few steps forward to browse on the leathery green leaves of a western teaberry shrub. She could hear the distinctive clicking sound of his feet as his tendons stretched over the foot bones. All caribou made this sound when they walked; she imagined hearing a vast herd of caribou moving along, clicking as they went.

The bull spotted Alex but didn't run, instead merely eyeing her warily, ready to bolt if she made a sudden move. So Alex stood as still as possible, listening to the droplets of a recent rain drip off the branches onto the soft bed of moss below. The forest smelled wet and fragrant, the rich scent of earth and moss.

The caribou continued to graze, then stood ruminating, his jaw working in a circular motion, his large brown watery eyes fixed on some distant point on the horizon. She took in his short little tail, much shorter than other deer tails, which helped him avoid frostbite in the long winters. Patches of sunlight fell on his velvety antlers. Soon the blood-rich velvet would dry and start to fall off. Those antlers, once shed, would become an important calcium-rich food source for all manner of wildlife, including rodents, weasels, foxes, and even other deer.

But before that, in the fall, if he found mates to compete for, this bull's antlers would be a handsome asset.

Alex sat down on a lichen-covered boulder and watched as the caribou slowly went on his way, eating as he moved through the forest.

Then she continued on her rounds, checking two of the remote cameras, swapping out memory cards as she went.

Finally, as the sun sank below the mountains, Alex turned reluctantly back toward the ranch house, torn between staying out there in the wild and wanting to phone the hospital to check on Kathleen.

She was almost home when a shadow moved in the trees, some fifty feet in front of her. Alex paused, waiting, then went down to a crouch beside a tree. The shadow withdrew out of sight. But it had been a man. She was sure of it. The squatter? Some party involved with Cody she wasn't aware of?

She listened, her hand gripping the tree, its rough bark sharp against her palm. She waited, not seeing anything further. Maybe it had been a trick of the light. Quietly she straightened up, but remained where she was.

Then the slightest noise jerked her attention to the right. Something almost imperceptible shifted among the trees there. She froze. The shadow moved, straightening up as she had done, one hand resting on a tree. She could see the whole figure now, silhouetted black against the spaces between the tree trunks. A man, his arms at his sides, the silver gleam of moonlight flashing off the long barrel of a rifle strapped to his back.

He came forward then, more boldly, stepping out into the open. Alex half turned to run, then snapped her eyes back to him. Shoulder-length black hair framed a familiar face, the pale skin washed in silver moonlight. Casey. He locked eyes with her. She gripped the trunk harder.

A wave of emotion swept over her, an overwhelming torrent of mixed feelings. Part of her, bonded to him by their experience out on the Arctic ice, wanted to rush over to him, hug him fiercely. The other part of her, the part that kept her rooted against the tree, was torn by her trepidation that something was seriously wrong with the man. He'd killed people. But then, she had, too. And the people he'd killed were violent, hateful, and despicable. But she'd only ever killed in self-defense when she had no other choice. She knew that wasn't the case with him. He'd sought people out. Hunted them.

"Alex." His voice came to her so softly that for a second she wasn't sure if she'd actually heard it.

Her feet wouldn't move. As unstable as he might be, she knew deep down he wouldn't hurt her.

He didn't come closer, just stood there in the shadows. "I wasn't going to come," he spoke again, even softer this time. "But I heard about all the trouble, the violence. The abductions. Just wanted to check on you." The sound of his familiar voice, its lilting Scottish accent, brought forth a flood of memories and emotions. He shifted his weight. "I'm just . . . I'm just sorry about everything."

He stared at her for a long moment, his face searching hers, a haunted look in his blue eyes. Then he leaned forward as if he were going to close the distance but stopped. "Okay," he whispered. With a final look he turned, moving off into the shadows of the trees.

When he was fifty feet away, she finally shifted her feet and stepped out from the trees. "Casey."

He turned.

She took another step, and another, then she was moving toward him with purpose. In a moment they stood face-to-face and Alex took in his familiar features, remembered how he'd had her back more than once. Something haunted lived inside him, something that compelled him to take justice into his own hands. But he wasn't evil. She knew that. And she knew he cared. She remembered with a thump in her chest that she cared, too, that she'd fought for his life as hard as he'd fought for hers.

"Casey," she whispered. She reached out. She was just going

to touch his hand, but the next moment he'd opened his arms and she was inside them, pressing her face against his neck, feeling the warmth of his skin.

"I wondered if I'd see you again," she whispered into the collar of his warm coat. His scent filled her senses, a hint of spices and warm skin.

He looked down at her, his intense eyes meeting hers. "You didn't tell them about me. Back in Churchill. You didn't mention Boston."

She pulled away. "I wasn't even sure if Casey MacCrae was your real name or where they'd be able to find you."

"And that's why you didn't tell them?"

She held his gaze, her stomach suddenly deciding to do an acrobatic routine. After a long moment of silence in which she could hear the blood thrumming in her ears, she whispered, "No. That wasn't why."

She suddenly became all too aware of their proximity. She could smell his breath and its faintest hint of something sweet. One lock of his black hair was hanging across his forehead, framing his blue eyes. He radiated warmth. She stepped back.

"Did you find the missing women?" he asked.

"Yes, I did."

"I knew you would."

"Can you stay?"

He shook his head. "Something bad is brewing. Something I have to address."

"What?"

"The less you know, the better."

"What is this, plausible deniability?"

"Something like that. Wish me luck." And then, smiling, he gripped her arm and turned, disappearing once again into the night.

For a long time Alex stood in the darkness, wondering if he'd return. But he didn't. She felt strange, her heart aching slightly. At last she turned back toward the ranch house, thinking over the day and all its triumphs.

She thought of the caribou, making its way through the forest, returned to its former habitat. And now that the old growth would remain intact, it had an even better chance of survival.

Perhaps, Alex hoped, the mere thought of it making her heart swell, perhaps the gray ghost of the forest would survive after all.

AFTERWORD

I've been delighted over the last few years to volunteer to review footage for two collar camera projects for barren-ground caribou herds that move between Yukon, the Northwest Territories, and Alaska. Like Alex Carter's joy in seeing the footage of the caribou moving about in his habitat, so have I absolutely loved seeing glimpses inside the lives of caribou as they've roamed with their herd, raised their babies, and foraged in breathtaking landscapes.

But all is not well. As I mention in this novel, the southern mountain caribou population is in dire straits. The old-growth boreal forests they rely on are being clear-cut at an alarming rate. A warming climate means that snowpack has been reduced, so even where lichen still grows, the snowpack often can't attain the necessary heights for caribou to reach the food high in the trees. The change in forest composition brought on by logging means younger forests, which attract moose, deer, and elk, and with them come the wolves, which then predate on the mountain caribou, an extra stressor that normally mountain caribou wouldn't experience. Legal protections for the caribou, including moratoriums on logging old growth, are not strong enough.

Mountain caribou live in much smaller groups than their barren-ground counterparts, often numbering only around fifty members in a herd. With the increasing threats from climate change, logging, and unprecedented predation, these herds have grown even smaller. This means that a single incident can wipe out an entire herd in one go. In Banff National Park, the mountain caribou herd there diminished to a handful of animals. And on one dark day in 2009, an avalanche swept down a mountainside north of Lake Louise and killed all of them in one swoop. The Banff mountain caribou population was officially gone.

And in the contiguous U.S., they are also now gone. So how did the mountain caribou, despite being listed on the Endangered Species Act (ESA) in the U.S. in 1984, come to be extirpated in the lower forty-eight?

Getting effective protection for a species through the ESA is a far longer, more complicated, and often politically charged process than many people realize. To even be considered for it, a species has to be in a severe decline already. Then the U.S. Fish and Wildlife Service (USFWS) can take years to review the case before a decision is made to list. But even once a species is listed as endangered under the ESA, action must be taken. The USFWS must develop a recovery plan and designate critical habitat. This can take many, many more years, and the government often overshoots these deadlines and is then sued by conservation organizations to come up with a plan. By the time all these pieces come together, the animal, as with the mountain caribou in the lower forty-eight, could already be gone.

We live in an unprecedented time, when humanity's activities have altered the earth in innumerable and often dangerous ways. We've fragmented and destroyed habitat, changed the composition of the atmosphere, and driven many species to extinction.

We hear a lot of the "doom and gloom" narrative in our news. Each report issued by the Intergovernmental Panel on Climate Change (IPCC) warns us that because of our inaction, it is now too late to avoid some of the effects of climate change. We're already seeing disastrous wildfires, sea level rise, catastrophic storms, flooding, and drought. It is easy to feel hopeless after hearing such news, to feel like it's too late to take meaningful action.

But it's not too late. As the IPCC reports say, if we act now, we can still stave off the *worst* effects of climate change.

Instead of succumbing to inaction out of hopelessness, let's all work together.

On the spectrum of doing nothing to being a 24/7 dedicated activist, there are a lot of steps we can take, such as writing letters to representatives and board members and CEOs of fossil fuel companies, engaging in community science, doing beach and river cleanups, cutting down on meat intake, engaging in demonstrations, and more.

Right now many governments are considering climate change legislation, but are slow to enact anything that would make a truly meaningful difference. We need to make our voices heard, not just by these governments but by the corporations who donate to our representatives.

We have to keep fighting, because if everyone just gives up, if everyone feels hopeless to the point of inaction or apathy, then truly nothing will ever get better, only worse and worse.

Instead of thinking of climate change as something we must make sacrifices for in order to address, let's reframe it and think of all the wonderful things we have to gain. Imagine what a bright future we'll have together with cleaner air, cleaner water, healthier bodies, and a thriving planet full of delightful biodiversity that we can all enjoy. Everything is connected, and a healthy environment benefits all species, including us. Together we can make a difference.

TO LEARN MORE ABOUT MOUNTAIN CARIBOU

Book

Moskowitz, David. *Caribou Rainforest: From Heartbreak to Hope.* Seattle:
Braided River, 2018.

Documentaries

The Last Mountain Caribou. Produced by Bryce Comer. 2018. Film.
http://thelastmountaincariboufilm.com/the-film.html.

Last Stand: The Vanishing Caribou Rainforest. Dir. Colin Arisman.
Produced by David Moskowitz. Caribou Rainforest, 2017. Film.
https://caribourainforest.org/film.

Podcast

"Saving the Mountain Caribou." Produced by Matt Martin and Chris
Morgan. Written by Chris Morgan. *The Wild,* April 20, 2021. NPR.
Podcast, 28:00. https://www.kuow.org/stories/saving-the-mountain
-caribou.

*To Learn More About Using Collar Cameras on Caribou, Including Video
Examples of Footage*

"Fortymile Caribou Herd: Video Footage from Caribou Collars." Alaska NPS,
May 8, 2021. Educational video, 01:45. https://www.youtube.com
/watch?v=2IRiXDoP-vA.

Ehlers, Libby, et al. "Critical Summer Foraging Tradeoffs in a Subarctic Ungulate." *Ecology and Evolution* 11, no. 24 (December 2021): 17835–17872. https://onlinelibrary.wiley.com/doi/10.1002/ece3.8349.

Volunteer Opportunities

1. If you'd like to collect lichen to aid in the supplemental feeding of mountain caribou, you can do so through the Selkirk Conservation Alliance. Learn more here: https://scawild.org/come-collect-lichens-with-us/.
2. You can also collect lichen through the Arrow Lakes Caribou Society: https://arrowlakescaribousociety.com/lichen-collection-for-southern-mountain-central-selkirk-caribou/.
3. To discover all kinds of wonderful community science projects you can contribute to, involving a number of different species, visit these two websites: https://www.zooniverse.org and https://scistarter.org.
4. If the community science project that Alex's dad was involved in intrigued you, the Xerces Society has some amazing opportunities where you can help bees, butterflies, and other invertebrates: https://xerces.org.

Organizations That Support Caribou Recovery

Arrow Lakes Caribou Society: https://arrowlakescaribousociety.com.

Caribou Rainforest: https://caribourainforest.org.

Conservation Northwest: https://www.conservationnw.org/our-work/wildlife/mountain-caribou.

Selkirk Conservation Alliance: https://scawild.org/south-selkirk-mountain-caribou.

Yellowstone to Yukon Conservation Initiative (Y2Y): https://y2y.net/caribou.

Wildsight: https://wildsight.ca/programs/mountaincaribou.

To Learn More About the Inland Temperate Rainforest

Use this link to travel virtually to the stunning inland rainforest: https://y2y.net/ucfilms.

Yellowstone to Yukon Conservation Initiative (Y2Y) has a very informative website for old-growth information: https://y2y.net /oldgrowth.

Social Media Group Dedicated to the Mountain Caribou

Mountain Caribou Initiative: https://www.facebook.com /mountaincaribou.

ACKNOWLEDGMENTS

Many thanks to the absolute best agent *ever,* Alexander Slater, for all that you do. Thank you for believing in this series. I'm very grateful to my wonderful editor, Lyssa Keusch, for her invaluable feedback. Sincere thanks to Nancy Singer for once again doing an incredible job with the interior design.

Thank you to Jeff Wells, Martin Kienzler, Gabrielle Coulombe, Libby Ehlers, and Mark Hebblewhite for answering my technical caribou capture and collar camera questions.

Many thanks to Detective Corporal (Ret.) St. Charles County Sheriff's Department Scott Stricker for advising me on police procedures.

Hearing from readers is always a delight, so thank you to all who have reached out to me to say that you enjoyed the previous books in the Alex Carter series. Special thanks to Dawn, Jen, Jon, Tina, Gordon, and Sarah.

Many thanks to my lifelong friend Becky. And as always, my heartfelt thanks to Jason, fellow wildlife researcher and activist, my kindred spirit, for believing in me and encouraging me.

ABOUT THE AUTHOR

In addition to being a writer, Alice Henderson is a wildlife researcher, geographic information systems specialist, and bioacoustician. She documents wildlife on specialized recording equipment, checks remote cameras, creates maps, and undertakes surveys to determine what species are present on preserves, while ensuring there are no signs of poaching. She's surveyed for the presence of grizzlies, wolves, wolverines, jaguars, endangered bats, and more. These experiences in remote corners of wilderness inspired her to create the Alex Carter mystery series. Please visit her at www.alicehenderson.com, where you can also sign up for her newsletter.